THOUGHT CATALOG BOOKS

The Worst Kind of
Monsters

The Worst Kind of Monsters

ELIAS WITHEROW

Thought Catalog Books

Brooklyn, NY

THOUGHT CATALOG BOOKS

Copyright © 2016 by Elias Witherow

All rights reserved. Published by Thought Catalog Books, a division of The Thought & Expression Co., Williamsburg, Brooklyn. Founded in 2010, Thought Catalog is a website and imprint dedicated to your ideas and stories. We publish fiction and non-fiction from emerging and established writers across all genres. For general information and submissions: manuscripts@thoughtcatalog.com.

First edition, 2016

ISBN 978-1945796098

10 9 8 7 6 5 4 3 2 1

Cover photography by © DasWortgewand

This one is for my parents. I love you both very much. And I hope you never, ever read this book.
Also for Dave. You're a damn good pal.

Contents

1

The Tall Dog

We always expect life to be easier than it actually is. Why is that? Why do we assume we are owed happiness? Why do we act so surprised when things go wrong? Is it the society we live in? Is it the false advertising that surrounds us at all times? Is it because of the things we watch or the books we read? Why is tragedy always so shocking?

Life is a slog of disappointment and misery. Sometimes we are graced with pockets of joy, a brief respite from all the hardship. In these moments, we feel like we have figured out what the purpose of our existence truly is: love, family, culture, travel, natural beauty.

But it's all bullshit.

Those fleeting hours of contentment are nothing more than a quick breath between beatings. It's a ray of hope that gets stuck inside our minds like a cancer. We hold onto it, we beg for it, we scream for it. During times of unbearable mental agony, having something to hope for is worse than if there was no hope at all. Hope is a lie. It's a disease that tricks our minds into thinking this painful reality is going to evaporate like a puff of breath on a cold wind.

And let me assure you, reality is a brutal, bloody corpse.

Now, you might be reading this and thinking: I'm not like

this. I have a good life, a healthy family, and I'm financially secure.

Let me tell you, I hope you enjoy your quick breath of clean air because there's a bomb falling over your head. You might not see it yet, but it's descending at a tremendous speed. When you least expect it, it'll land and devastate your entire existence. It will destroy everything you love and it will leave you broken and weeping in the fucking gutter.

Why am I telling you this?

Why should you listen to me?

Because the bomb has already dropped on me. Because the fallout is unbearable and I can't seem to find a gasp of clean air in this toxic wasteland of life. My throat burns, my eyes water, and I can't speak for fear of tearing my silenced throat.

My wife is dead.

She died a year ago and left me alone to raise our little girl, Heather. Heather is all I have left. She's the gas mask I struggle to hold onto. She's the choked cries of desperation I emit from between bloody teeth.

Heather is five now. We did our best to recover from the pain of my wife's death, a loss of a companion, a removal of a mother. I shudder to think my daughter has to face the bloody blade of life at such a young age. She needs to be sheltered from it; she needs protection.

And for a while, I thought I was providing that.

But that was before...that was before the nightmares started.

That was before the Tall Dog.

I scrubbed sleep from my eyes, rolling in the darkness to check the clock. Three AM. I groaned and pulled myself from the warmth of my sheets. Heather was crying from her room, calling my name. She must have had a bad dream.

In a daze, blinking sleepily, I shuffled out of my room and down to hers. The house was silent and my feet scuffed over the cool hardwood floors. *Heather never has bad dreams*, I thought, yawning. *Did I let her watch something scary before bed?*

I entered her room, the space illuminated by a pink ballerina nightlight, and went to my daughter's side. She was curled up in a ball with her hands over her face. She was sniffling and her pillow felt damp with tears.

Cooing, I scooped her up and told her everything was OK. After she calmed down some, I asked her if she'd had a nightmare. She looked up at me with big teary eyes and nodded. She hugged me and asked if she could sleep in my bed. I told her of course.

"It won't come in your room?" Heather asked me as I picked us both up off the bed.

I paused.

"Sweetie, what are you talking about?"

She wrapped herself tight around me and whispered, "the Tall Dog."

I didn't know what to make of her nonsense phrase, and so I told her there were no dogs coming into the house and that we were safe. I felt her relax against me as I walked us back into my bedroom. I laid her down in my bed and stroked her hair until I heard the soft snores of sleep. I laid down next to her and exhaled heavily. Sleep returned to me in a rush of heavy fatigue.

The next day, life resumed its predictable repetition. I got Heather ready for school and then rushed to prepare myself for work. I left her downstairs in front of the TV, happily munching on some toast as I scurried to shower and shave. It was like this every morning, but I was used to the frantic pace.

As I threw my sports jacket on and bustled into the hallway to go downstairs, I paused. I bent down and wet my thumb with my tongue. I scrubbed it along the hardwood floor, wiping away a streak of dirt that ran toward Heather's room. I gritted my teeth and reminded myself it wasn't a big deal. She was five years old and couldn't be expected to remember to take off her shoes all the time.

Standing, I hurried down the stairs and collected my daughter to begin our day. I switched off the TV and grabbed Heather's pink Barbie backpack, asking her if she had to go to the bathroom before school. When she said she didn't, I snatched the car keys off the kitchen counter and ushered her to the front door.

As I followed Heather out, I hesitated, my hand freezing before I closed the door all the way. I stuck my head back inside and listened. I could have sworn I had heard something from upstairs. After a second, I shrugged and closed the door, locking it tight.

The day passed like so many before it. The hands on the clock pushed forward triumphantly and finally announced the end of the workday. Not long after the trumpets of freedom were blown, I found myself at home once again. I ordered pizza for us, a rare delicacy to my daughter, and spent the evening watching children's shows on Netflix. I barely saw the images on the screen, the fatigue from the day washing over me in heavy waves. A stomach full of pizza didn't help, either.

Heather shifted and snuggled into me, resting her head against my chest. I smiled and kissed her shoulder, telling her that after this episode it was time for bed. She put up her usual resistance, but I battled it valiantly. That was something I'd had to learn how to do. My wife had always been the one to say no and knew when to say enough was enough. I was always the softie, allowing Heather to get away with a multitude of activities. It was hard to say no to her big, cute brown eyes brimming with innocent pleas. My dad-heart melted every time and I would eventually cave, begging her not to tell her mother.

But after the brain tumor took my wife away from us, I had to learn how to balance my daughter's requests with fatherly affection and parental standards. I thought I had found a reasonable balance. With each passing day I would discover another piece of the puzzle and take another step closer to becoming a functional single parent.

When the show ended, I told Heather to go upstairs and brush her teeth and get ready for bed. Groaning, she obeyed and I began to pick up the kitchen. I placed our plates in the dishwasher and threw out the empty pizza box. I checked my watch and saw that it was almost eleven. I sighed, not realizing how late it had gotten. I should have put Heather to bed two hours ago. I exhaled. It wasn't the end of the world.

After the kitchen was clean, I turned off all the lights and made sure the front door was locked.

Satisfied, I climbed the stairs and went to check on Heather's progress. To my delight, I found her already in bed and asleep. I went to her and gently kissed the top of her head, smiling to myself. She really was a good girl.

I turned on her nightlight and closed her door behind me. I went to my own room and prepared myself for bed. As I slid into the cool sheets, I decided that tomorrow after school I would take Heather to the park so she could ride her bike along the community bike trail. Content with my plans, I closed my eyes and drifted off to sleep.

Darkness. Haze. Groggy. I slowly peeled my eyes open in the black, my head spinning. Why was I awake? What time was it? I rolled over and looked at the clock. Three AM. I blinked and closed my eyes, deep drowsiness filling my body like hard liquor.

Heather was crying. I forced my eyes open again. That's why I was awake. I pulled myself into a sitting position and scrubbed my face with the palms of my hands. Why was she crying? Another nightmare?

As I stood, I prayed that this wasn't going to turn into a regular thing. I stumbled around in the darkness and pulled my door open. I stepped out into the hall and paused, cocking my head toward the stairs.

I…thought I heard something moving downstairs.

Another wave of cries from Heather's room forced me back into motion and I shuffled down the hall and opened her door. The room was bathed in soft pink light, the tiny ballerina illuminating the walls with her glowing body. I went to my daughter and knelt by her bed, whispering softly that Daddy was here and everything was OK.

She wrapped her arms around my neck and hugged me tight, soft sniffles escaping her bubbling nose. I stroked her hair and asked her if she'd had another nightmare.

She pulled away and looked up at me, her eyes brimming with tears. "Yes, Daddy, it was awful!" she cried. "And…and when I woke up…" she trailed off, struggling to get herself under control.

My eyes melted, "What is it, sweetie?"

"When I woke up and the Tall Dog was whispering in my ear!" she sobbed, collapsing against me.

I felt my stomach churn slightly. Prickles of unease rose along my arms like tiny mountains of fleshy fear. This was the second night in a row she had mentioned this Tall Dog. I didn't know what the hell she was talking about or what it was, but it was clearly bothering her. I wondered if someone at school had told her something or she had seen something scary on TV about a dog. Whatever it was, it was giving my daughter nightmares and I needed to find a way to make it stop.

Suddenly, Heather squeezed my neck and I heard her gasp. Before I could react, she buried her face against me and started sobbing even harder, her whole body shaking. Confused, I pulled her off me and cupped her face in my hands.

"What is it? What's wrong?" I asked urgently.

Heather pointed behind me toward the open door. "It just peeked around the corner and was looking at you!"

I spun around, my heart thundering. There was nothing

there. Of course there was nothing there. Why would there be? Putting a hand over my chest, I forced myself to settle down.

"There's nothing there, honey," I said. "It's just shadows. It's late; do you want to sleep in my bed again?"

Her eyes remained locked on the open door as she slowly nodded. I picked her up and rubbed her back as I walked us out of her room. There was nothing to be afraid of. She'd just had a bad dream. As I walked down the hallway, I paused in the darkness. I looked to my right, down the stairs, down into the gaping maw of black.

Did I hear something moving down there?

Heather squeezed me tight and whispered into my ear, "It's going into the basement."

I shifted her weight in my arms, her words sending a shiver of unease down my spine. I told Heather there was nothing down there. I brought her into my room and tucked her into bed. I sat beside her and rubbed her head until she drifted off to sleep. It took longer than it had the previous night, but once she was breathing easy, I went to my bedroom door and stepped out into the hall.

In the dead of night, when surrounded by heavy darkness, fear has a way of making monsters out of the shadows. I forced myself to remain calm, reminded myself that I was an adult, and stood at the top of the stairs. I looked down, the enclosed staircase revealing nothing but the square black mouth at the bottom. I listened, holding my breath.

Silence. I shook my head, telling myself that I was being ridiculous, and went back to my room. I closed the door and lay down next to Heather. I stared at the ceiling, mind alert and awake. I knew I wasn't going to be falling asleep anytime soon.

I pulled my phone off the nightstand and brought up the Internet browser. After taking a moment to think, I searched the term "Tall Dog." I scrolled through some dog-show sites that popped up and finally found a link to a message board. I clicked it.

My heart skipped a beat as I read the question at the top: **My son keeps having nightmares and complains about something called "The Tall Dog"…does anyone know what the hell this is? It's happened three nights in a row! It's driving me crazy! Help!**

The top answer sent a chill rocketing through my body.

It read: **Your son is telling the truth! GET HELP! The Tall Dog is real and it will keep coming back! It's attracted to deep sadness and it won't leave your son alone until it gets what it wants! IT IS VERY DANGEROUS! I know this sounds insane but I'm telling you the truth! I've come across others who have encountered this thing! IT IS VERY REAL AND VERY DANGEROUS!**

I put my phone down and stared into the darkness. My heart was racing. This couldn't be true, could it?

Every part of me wanted to write it off as a bizarre coincidence, but it was so…specific that I couldn't. *What am I supposed to do with this information?* I thought. *This is crazy; stuff like this doesn't happen, doesn't exist.*

And yet here I was, staring at a warning on my phone while my terrified daughter lay curled up next to me. It was unnerving. I turned on my side and stared at the closed bedroom door. Just outside the door were the stairs leading to the ground level. As I closed my eyes, I pictured something long and lanky pulling itself up them, its snout dragging along the wood. I shivered and forced the image out of my head.

There was nothing out there.

The next day, Heather didn't mention anything about the nightmares and I didn't ask her. I wanted this to go away and bringing it up in the daylight didn't seem like it would help my cause. I prepared her for school and then got myself ready for work.

As we left the house, I realized just how tired I was. The lack of sleep last night was taking its toll on me, and I made a mental note to stop and get more coffee after I dropped Heather off.

While I drove, my mind wandered back to the message board warning. In the daylight, it seemed a little silly. I pushed the fear back into the corner of my mind and scolded myself internally for being so irrational. I reminded myself again that I was an adult and didn't believe in monsters and things that go bump in the night.

After I dropped Heather off, I went and got another cup of coffee and then drove to work. My brain accepted the caffeine gratefully and as I sipped on the steaming liquid I pondered what my wife would make of the whole thing. She'd probably say I was being stupid and to man up. The thought made me grin and I suddenly missed her.

Eventually, I pulled into the office parking lot and began my day. It was Friday, and I was hoping I could leave a little early. The crisp morning air was a prelude to a possibly beautiful day. I still planned on taking Heather to the park. I had hopes that the fresh air and sunshine would erase her nightmares, burning them away in a blaze of brilliance.

Well…things didn't go as planned.

Halfway through the day, I got a call from Heather's school. I sat, dumbfounded, as the principal told me I needed to come pick my daughter up. When I asked why, he informed me that Heather had started biting her classmates and wouldn't stop until a teacher forcefully pulled her off someone.

I closed my open mouth, shock erupting across my face. There had to be some kind of mistake; my daughter didn't do things like that! The principal assured me that he was just as surprised as I was but that she needed to be taken home for the day. The other kids were scared of her and the parents were being notified.

Great, I thought, *I'll be the single dad with the violent child.* As soon as the thought popped into my mind I got angry with myself. *Who cares what they think? I need to go see if my daughter is all right!*

I informed my boss of the phone call and he nodded me out the door. I thanked him and told him I'd make it up on Monday before bolting for my car.

As I drove, I tried to make sense as to the possible reasons why Heather would act out like this. She wouldn't just *do* it! One of the kids must have been picking on her. One of them must have provoked her. She wouldn't just start biting kids.

I sat at a red light, anxiously drumming my fingers against the steering wheel. Something was going on with my daughter and I needed to get to the bottom of it. First the nightmares and now this. Clearly, Heather was going through something and as a responsible parent, I needed to find out what it was.

I gritted my teeth as the light turned green and I gunned the engine. I wondered if it had something to do with my wife. I wondered if this was Heather's way of coming to terms with her death a year later. I felt my eyes suddenly well up and my knuckles turned white.

It wasn't fair that she had been taken away from us. What had we done to deserve such sadness? What was going through Heather's young mind in the absence of her mother? What could I do to fill that sorrow?

And then I started to panic, the creeping thoughts of Heather's upcoming teenage years. What if this was the end of our good relationship? What if she started blaming me for her mom's death? I knew she was only five, but time has a way of preserving deep hurt and forming scars that never heal. I realized just how much I needed to be there for my daughter in these early years, these crucial developmental times. How I acted could make or break the way she viewed…everything.

As these thoughts scrambled my mind, I pulled into the school parking lot and was slammed with a realization that chilled me to the bone.

I remembered the message board warning: The Tall Dog is attracted to deep sadness.

I shook my head. *No, don't start going down that road. That's insane and there's no such thing. She's forming waking night-mares in order to deal with what she's going through.*

Steeling myself, I ran into the school.

Before I knew it, I was sitting in the principal's office listening to him apologize for making such a big deal out of this and that it was more for the other kids than for Heather. I barely heard him, nodding as his words washed over me in waves of numb noise.

Finally, a teacher led Heather into the room and I scooped her up in a big hug. I kissed her on the cheek and saw that she had been crying. I told her I loved her and that we were going to go home. She nodded silently at me, her big brown eyes filling with tears.

I told the teacher and principal that I was sorry for the incident and assured them it wouldn't happen again. They both smiled and thanked me, but I saw something else behind their masks of public decency. Judgment. They saw me as a single father with no idea how to raise a little girl. They saw a struggling man with no answers. They saw someone who had lost his wife and was still finding a way to live without her.

I suddenly got angry, a spike of adrenaline coursing through my veins, but I kept my mouth shut. I turned and left, hugging my daughter to me as I stormed out of the school. I didn't know if it was righteous anger or embarrassment, and I didn't care. They had no idea what I had gone through, what I was dealing with. Who were they to judge me?

I put Heather in the car and drove us home in silence. I fought to get myself under control. I reminded myself that this wasn't about me, it was about my daughter. She was the one who needed help; she was the one who needed loving support.

We eventually arrived home and I checked my watch. It was almost four. I abandoned the idea of going to the park and instead sat Heather down on the couch. I placed myself next to her and told her I needed to talk to her about what had happened at school.

"Sweetie, are you doing OK?" I asked gently, gauging her mental state.

She looked at her hands and nodded.

I cleared my throat. I was always so bad at this.

"Is it true you bit those kids today?"

I saw her lip quiver and she slowly nodded without looking up at me.

I sighed, "Honey, you can't bite, you know that, right? Why did you bite those kids?"

She shrugged again and I saw a tear roll down her cheek.

Be brave, I told myself, *you can't back out now.*

"Were you mad at them? Did someone say something mean to you?"

She put one hand in her pocket and slowly shook her head, eyes still downcast.

"Heather, can you look at me?" I asked softly.

She turned her eyes to mine and I saw she was crying openly now. She kept fidgeting in her pocket.

"Can you promise me you won't do it again?" I asked.

More tears ran down her cheeks and she cried, "I'm sorry, Daddy! I'm really sorry!"

I leaned down and kissed her on the head, "It's OK, honey, I know you're a good girl. Daddy loves you. Just please don't bite anyone again, OK?"

She sniffled back another outburst of tears and her hand kept twisting in her pocket.

I finally noticed and patted her leg. "What's in your pocket, Heather? You have something you want to show me?"

She suddenly looked embarrassed and shook her head, but

I prodded her and after some coaching she finally pulled out a handful of brown nuggets.

I blinked, wondering why my daughter was carrying around a pocketful of dirt and then my heart slammed so hard against my ribcage I thought it would break.

"Sweetie," I said, trying to keep my voice under control, "is…is that dog food?"

She balled her fist up and hugged the nuggets to her chest, staring at her feet that dangled from the edge of the couch.

"Where did you get that?" I asked, feeling a deep disturbance roll over me.

"I found them," she answered quietly.

"And…and what are you doing with them in your pocket?" I asked, a flurry of nerves fluttering in my chest.

Heather looked up at me. "They taste good."

I forced myself to breathe and held out my hand. "Why don't you let me hang on to those and I'll make us an early dinner, OK?"

Reluctantly, she handed over the nuggets and I plastered a smile to my face. I asked her if she wanted to watch some TV while I made dinner. She offered me a small grin and nodded sheepishly.

As I turned on her shows, I fought with the voice screaming in my head. Something was going on here. Something really, really awful was happening to my daughter. I didn't know what exactly, but the past couple days seemed to mark a turning point in her behavior.

I stated preparing dinner, begging myself to stop overreacting, but I couldn't shut it out. The nightmares, the Tall Dog nonsense, the biting, and now she was eating dog food?

I didn't know what to do, didn't know what to say to her. I wanted to ask her about her mom, ask her if she had been thinking about her recently, but I was afraid to. I didn't want to open up a wound I couldn't close. What if she started asking questions I couldn't answer? What if her behavior got worse?

I began to wonder if I needed to take her to see a therapist. As the thought entered my mind, I violently slammed the door on it. There was nothing wrong with my daughter, she was just a vibrant little girl who had a few nightmares and bit a couple kids! So what? When I was her age, I'm sure I did things much worse and I turned out fine!

Yes but…what is the Tall Dog? What does that mean?

I shouted internally at myself to stop thinking about it. There was no such thing and I needed to face the problems I could handle.

I finished making dinner in mental agony and prepared two plates. I went to the couch and sat with Heather, both of us eating in silence as cartoon images danced on the screen.

When I woke up the Tall Dog was whispering in my ear…

I gritted my teeth around my food. I wasn't thinking about this bullshit anymore.

I crawled into bed, mentally exhausted. It had taken me forever to get Heather to sleep. She had begged to sleep in my bed, but I told her no and I'd keep my door open in case she woke up scared. I didn't want her to start forming bad habits.

I rested my head against my pillow and stared out into the dark hallway from the crack in my door. I shut my eyes and said a silent prayer that Heather would sleep through the night. Maybe then all this would be over and she would go back to being the little angel I knew she was. I didn't want to continue down this road of parental speculation and assuming that every little bad action was a foretelling of a bleak future for her.

I let out a long breath and waited for the gentle arms of sleep to rock me into the world of dreams. It didn't take long.

My eyes snapped open, bloodshot and wide. I was soaked in sweat, the horrific nightmare still clinging to my brain with razor-sharp claws. I rolled onto my back and wiped sweat from my face. I swallowed hard and waited for reality to clear away the cobwebs of slumber. My heart was racing and I put a hand over my bare chest, willing it to slow.

My wife. I had been dreaming about my wife. She had been in a hospital bed, screaming my name and clutching her head. I had been beside her, crying, begging her to tell me what was wrong, but she just kept screaming. I began to scream for a doctor and that's when I realized all the lights in the hospital were off and no one was in the halls. I kept screaming for help, pleading with my wife, until I finally heard a noise.

From the blackness of the hall, a doctor in a bloody lab coat came crawling into the room on all fours. His eyes were wild and he started barking at me, his mouth foaming. I backed away from him, shock and terror rising in me like a dark mountain.

The doctor lunged at me, teeth bared, and that's when I woke up.

I pulled my hands across my face, forcing the images from my head. What a horrible nightmare. I realized my stressed mind was probably mixing all my current worries into a terrifying nighttime cocktail, sneaking up on me and pouring it down my throat while I slept.

I looked over at the clock. Three AM. I snorted, eyes wide, grateful that at least it was me instead of Heather who had woken up tonight. If I could take her fears from her, I gladly would. I just needed to be careful I didn't end up burning myself out.

As I rolled on my side to face my door, I heard something from downstairs.

Immediately, my mind exploded into alertness, the nightmare fear still fresh on my breath. I lay in silence, ear cocked and listening, my heart racing.

There.

It sounded like something was…walking around.

Get up, you have to get up, I thought, fear tingling my stomach. *It's probably nothing, it's probably the house settling. Maybe Heather got up for some reason or is sleepwalking.*

I pulled the covers off me and swung my feet over the side of the bed. I jumped as I heard more movement.

What is going on…?

Tense and terrifyingly nervous, I crept to the door. I paused, staring out into the empty hallway. I didn't hear anything.

I slowly opened the door and went out into the hallway.

Something was making noise at the bottom of the stairs. I balled my sweaty hands into fists and steeled myself. The house was impossibly dark, every corner filled with grinning black. The floor underneath my feet creaked as I slowly edged myself over to the top of the stairs.

I looked down.

And something was looking back up at me.

I stifled a scream, terror clenching my throat like an iron grip. My eyes bulged and my breath rushed from my lungs in a wave of cold fear.

It was long and slender, its hairless body a sickly gray color. It looked like a dog, but it was greater in length and bone-thin. Its snout pointed up at me from the foot of the stairs, easily two feet in length. Its eyes were completely white and swollen in their sockets like bloated marshmallows. It was on all fours, its front two legs resting on the first two steps.

As it gazed up at me, it began to pull itself upright. My knees turned to liquid and I watched in absolute horror as it rose to stand on two legs, its head towering toward the ceiling. Its neck was long—too long for a dog—and it snarled at me, its mouth full of black, needle-like teeth.

It started slowly walking up the stairs toward me.

I backed away in frantic desperation, unable to comprehend what I was looking at. I tripped over my own feet and fell, not able to tear my eyes away from the advancing monstrosity. As it neared the top of the stairs, it crouched back down on all fours and I saw its swollen white eyes pulsing with excitement.

I tried to scream but found that I didn't have the breath. It was the most terrifying thing I had ever seen and every alarm in my head was blaring with furious urgency. I scooted backward with my hands into the safety of my room and stood, grabbing the door and slamming it shut in one violent gesture.

I stood with my back against the wood, sucking in hungry lungfuls of air. What the hell was that thing?! What was it doing in my house?! Where had it come from!?

Heather.

Oh, no…

I pressed my ear to the door and heard footsteps pad down the hallway toward Heather's room. I scrambled in the dark for some kind of weapon. I grabbed my discarded work pants that were lying in a pile on the floor and slid the belt from the loops. I wrapped it around my knuckles, turning the buckle outwards.

I went to the closed door and took a deep breath. I couldn't let that thing hurt my daughter. I opened the door and stepped out into the dark hall. My eyes scanned my surroundings but I didn't see it. I knew it had to be in Heather's room.

I cautiously crept down the hall, ears trained to pick up any sound of the creature. Heather's door was wide open and faint pink light drifted out from the inside.

I entered her room and froze. The monster, the Tall Dog, was on all fours by Heather's bed. Its snout was inches from her ear and its mouth moved rapidly, but I couldn't hear any noise. It was like it was speaking directly into her dreams. Heather's eyes were shut but she had begun to stir, soft cries escaping her lips as the Tall Dog silently filled her mind.

Suddenly, it realized I was in the room and whipped its head around. Its eyes seemed to vibrate in their sockets, thick white pus leaking from the gelatinous, milky scleras. It silently bared its teeth at me, its mouth filling with sharp, ebony darkness.

I took a step back, feeling my throat tighten, and gripped the belt harder in my hand. I needed to get it away from Heather. My heart was seizing in my chest and my back was coated in a cold layer of sweat. I forced my knees to lock and I licked my dry lips.

The Tall Dog turned away from the bed and rose up up on two legs, towering over me. Despite its appearance, it didn't move like an animal. Its balance was perfect and its legs and muscles twisted and flowed with the confidence of a human.

"What do you *want*?!" I whispered, holding my ground as a trickle of sweat slid down my face.

It leaped at me.

I screamed, raising my hands to protect my face as its long body crashed into mine. I fell to the floor, its sinewy flesh pressing mine to the wood. Its breath was hot on my face and stars exploded across my vision, my head bouncing on the ground. With the energy battered out of me, I blinked back darkness and scrambled desperately, trying to get it off of me.

It pinned me where I lay, its powerful legs digging into my sides. I looked up into its hideous face and the white ooze pouring from its eyes dripped into my hair.

It leaned down and opened its mouth, its jaws parting to reveal rows and rows of black teeth. I watched in horror as its throat began to open, folds of dark flesh parting like oil and water.

And then I heard my daughter screaming from deep down inside.

"Daddy, help me, please! Don't let it take me! Daddy *please*!!!"

Heather's voice was shrill with panic and it sent waves of chilling terror through my body. No, this wasn't happening, that wasn't my daughter, it couldn't be! Please, God, NO!

The Tall Dog snapped its jaws shut and I shoved it off of me, a surge of energy igniting my muscles. It skittered on all fours toward the open door and I scrambled to stand, breathing heavily.

"What did you do to her!?" I screamed, shaking in fear and fury. "What have you done to my daughter!?"

The Tall Dog crouched and eyed me, sniffing the air. I waited for it to strike, waited for it to move. This creature was going to kill me, I knew that, but I was ready. I stood my ground in the dim light, trembling, accepting whatever happened next.

Instead of charging me, though, it turned away and sprinted down the hall. In shock, I listened to it crash down the stairs and onto the ground floor. More footsteps followed then faded and I realized that it was gone, leaving me shaking in horror.

I turned to Heather who lay motionless on the bed. I threw the belt onto the floor and went to her side, prayers flowing from my lips. Tears leaked down my cheeks as I grabbed Heather and lifted her head to rest on my lap. Her eyes were closed and her body was still.

"Please, God, I'm begging you, no, no, no!" I cried, my mind collapsing. "Heather, baby, my angel, wake up, Daddy's here, please, sweetie, wake up!"

I shook her, pleading, drool and mucus bubbling from my face as reality tore my exhausted brain in two.

Suddenly, her eyes flickered and then she opened them. She stared up at me, blinking rapidly as if she wasn't sure where she was. I let out a cry of raw relief and hugged her tight against me, more tears pouring from eyes. I sobbed, rocking back and forth on the bed, clutching her to my chest. I thought I had lost her, I thought she had been taken away from me.

And then Heather began to bark.

My bloodshot eyes widened and I pulled her away to look at her face. Her eyes roamed around the room curiously and her tongue lolled from the side of her mouth. Drool leaked from her lips as she sat on my lap, panting. She finally looked up at me and let out a series of yaps, all signs of humanity draining from her eyes.

"Heather, stop it, stop that!" I cried, shaking her. "Don't do that! It's OK, it's gone, it's gone, sweetie!"

But she didn't stop.

She jumped from my arms and began to run in circles as if she were chasing an imaginary tail. She stopped and cocked her head at me, shouting a sharp bark as if she wanted me to play with her.

I sat on the bed, watching her, and gripped my face with sweaty hands.

I began to scream.

Heather will never be the same. That night, I rushed her to the hospital and begged the doctors for help. After examining her and bringing in a multitude of specialists, they informed me that she wasn't in control of her mind any longer. They told me she would never regain it. Something had been taken from her that couldn't be replaced or repaired.

I don't know how long they ran tests on her as I desperately expended all my options, desperate to try anything. I couldn't imagine a life without her. I wept and prayed until I had nothing left to offer. Nothing changed, nothing helped, and I wondered if anyone even noticed.

You see...life is an unflinching monster. It doesn't care about you, it doesn't take your side; it simply is. It took my wife away and opened up a wound in my daughter's mind. A wound I didn't even have the courage to ask my daughter if it even existed.

Something horrible had caught scent of that gaping wound; something had grown hungry for it. It had entered our life and slipped into the gory cracks of my daughter's hidden, suppressed sadness. It had replaced her mind with its own and had devoured the fractured remains of a confused and hurt psyche. And I knew I had lost Heather forever to it.

So now I stand here, in the darkness, over my daughter's bed.

I grip the pillow with shaking hands. ? Tears roll down my face and I beg God to forgive me.

But whatever is laying in this bed...I know it's not my daughter.

2

The House In The Field

It all started when I was seven. That was twenty years ago now. I was a curious kid, always out exploring our family's land, taking the trek out to the woods across the grassy fields. I would collect rocks, watch animals, and splash around in the streams I discovered, most of the time by myself. I didn't need company. I never felt lonely. Or maybe that was just because I was used to being alone.

My parents owned a farm, a vast sprawling plot of land that stretched for miles in every direction. It was beautiful country and the golden sun accented the acres of mint-green cornstalks that lined our back yard. My father worked hard, spending his days tending the crop with the help of a few farmhands. My mother took care of the house and the occasional trip into town, stocking up on the essentials. They were a good team and they loved each other very much. They loved the life they shared and depended on one another.

During the school year my mother or my neighbor would take Trevor and me into town for lessons, alternating days. Trevor was my age and my only friend. During the summers I didn't see him much, his own duties grounding him at his parents' farm eight miles down the dirt road. Occasionally our parents would get together and share a big country dinner while Trevor and I wolfed down our food and went out to play.

I was a happy kid, content with my life. I don't remember ever feeling isolated or lasting unhappiness. My parents were good to me and the expansive surrounding land consistently kept my explorer tendencies busy.

As I stated, we lived off a single-lane dirt road, miles from town, miles from everything. Behind our ranch-style house were the cornfields, rows and rows of stalks that reached out and touched the horizon. At least that's how I remember it. I often worried about getting lost in the green labyrinth whenever I had to go fetch Dad for supper, the tight stalks towering over my head.

In front of the house was a wide stretch of flat open grassland that expanded for a couple dozen acres before reaching the tree line where the woods grew dense. I loved to explore those woods, most of my summers spent venturing deeper and deeper inside their sap-crusted guts.

But this isn't about the woods. This isn't about the cornfields.

This is about the house that suddenly appeared in the field across the street.

I was seven when it suddenly appeared. I remember going to bed on a hot June night, sleep slowed by the heavy heat. When sleep finally came, it didn't last long. I woke up sometime in the night, my throat parched from the thick air. I went to get a glass of water and as I passed my bedroom window, I saw it for the first time.

The first thing that struck me was how tall it was. Three stories, its roof reaching for the star-filled sky. It was the biggest house I had ever seen up until that point. My little hands gripped the windowsill and my nose pressed against the glass as my eyes took in this new wonder.

It sat directly across the dirt road from our house, only a couple hundred feet from our front porch. It was painted dark green, or so I'd see in the morning, and it looked well-kept. The dark windows were framed by hideous yellow shutters, looking like mold in the silent moonlight. It had no porch, just a single ugly door the same color as the shutters.

I stared at it, my young mind growing excited at this new mystery, the following day already filling with thoughts of exploring it. But of course I couldn't. That was someone's house. Someone was living there. As these thoughts destroyed my enthusiasm, I remember how badly I wanted to run and wake my parents and share with them what I was seeing. At the time, the concept of a house suddenly appearing across from ours was fascinating. I didn't think it scary or even odd. It was just something that happened and my young seven-year-old mind just accepted it.

Eventually, I went and got a glass of water and went back to bed, my mind buzzing with possibilities.

The next morning I bounded out of bed, the sun only barely warming the sky with splashes of deep purple and puddles of soft pink. I raced to my window to make sure I hadn't been dreaming. The house still stood, dark and motionless.

I thundered into the kitchen, almost knocking over my dad, anxious to show my parents. I felt like it was my own personal discovery, like somehow I was responsible for it being there. After my dad scolded me, probably irritated by my burst of early morning energy, I asked him if he had seen the house.

He didn't seem to know what I was talking about as I hurriedly pulled him to the front door, my mouth running like a dirt bike. I flung the door open and pointed to the house, my feet padding down the steps of our porch.

My father stopped in the doorway, eyes scanning the field, a look of confusion on his face. He looked down at me with a worried look and then back at the field. He scratched his chin and motioned for me to come inside, telling me to stop being ridiculous, that if I had this much energy I could help him out in the fields today.

He couldn't see the house.

At that age, my mind couldn't wrap itself around that fact because…well…it was right there! I continued to point and tell him, but it didn't do any good. He was blind to it.

This left me frustrated and confused. I didn't know why he couldn't see it. I wanted desperately for him to acknowledge what I had found in the middle of the night, but no matter how much I talked and argued, it was of no use.

I spent the day helping my dad in the cornfields. Shortly after breakfast, three of the usual farmhands arrived and we went out back for our day's labors. If they could see the house, they showed no sign of it. I even asked Louie, the guy who had been helping my dad the longest, if he noticed anything on his way in. He ruffled my hair and said that seeing me up this early was the only thing he witnessed. I shook him off, getting angry as to why no one saw it.

As I went about my chores, I couldn't stop thinking about the house. The looming, quiet way it sat in the long grass, its three levels begging for investigation. I wanted to tell Trevor but knew I wouldn't be able to today. He would believe me. He would be able to see it, I just knew he would. Trevor shared my sense of adventure and I knew that the next time we played together, our time would be spent discussing and maybe even snooping around the house. There was such an air of mystery about it that I felt myself almost physically pulled toward it. I couldn't see it from my place amidst the corn, but I could tell you exactly where it was from any point that I stood.

The sun tugged itself across the sky, one labored hour after another, and finally my dad announced it was time to call it quits. I walked back to our house next to my dad, listening to him talk to the three workers about what needed to be done tomorrow and what time to come back in the morning.

They plodded up the back porch and were met by my mother, who offered them all cold beers which they took with big smiles. Feeling tired and slightly annoyed still, I walked around the side of our house, wanting another look at the green house with yellow shutters.

I turned the corner and stopped dead in my tracks.

The house was gone.

I rubbed my eyes, convinced my mind was playing tricks on me. As I opened them again, the field still stood empty, the grass rustling like running water as a warm breeze passed through it. I turned completely around, eyes searching in all directions, thinking that maybe I had misplaced the location it was in. Nothing but grass was in front of me and corn behind me. I squinted and scanned the distant tree line at the far end of the field in front of my house, but nothing stood out.

Feeling angry, I kicked at the dry dirt, knowing now that Trevor would never believe me. I had wanted to show him so badly, desperate for anyone to acknowledge this inexplicable phenomenon. I remember cursing for the first time then. After I did it, I nervously looked around to make sure my mother hadn't heard me. Her voice floated in the warm air toward me and I felt relief wash over me as I realized she was still on the back porch. So I cursed again, kind of liking the way it made me feel tough.

Sighing, I dejectedly shoved my hands in my pockets and rolled my head back to stare at the evening sky. The darkness of a storm was creeping in from the west, down the road where Trevor and his parents lived. I watched as the billowing black clouds piled over one another and felt the air wince as distant thunder shook it.

Later that night the storm reached us. Rain shook the walls and lightning split the sky, the blinding white veins followed closely by cannon-blast thunder. I sat in my bed, feeling a little afraid, contemplating whether to go into my parents' room or not. My dad was probably snoring through the whole thing, but my mom might be awake. I didn't want them to know I was scared, though, because after all, I was seven now.

As another bone-shaking blast of thunder fell from the sky, I slid out of bed and went to my window, forcing myself to go and watch the thing that was scaring me. My dad always told me that brave men only get brave when they stand up to the thing that makes them want to run away. And so I planted my feet firmly in front of the window and watched as nature crashed down around me.

The wind was howling, causing the house to tremble, and I listened to the rain slam onto the roof like a thousand galloping hooves. Another bolt of lightning illuminated the land, its sparking suddenness causing me to blink.

And then I saw it again.

The house was back.

I frantically cupped my face against the glass, trying to see through the rain-streaked pane. I could make out its shape, a dark square hole cut into the night, and I waited for more lightning. My heart was racing, excitement bubbling up inside of me. It was back; I knew I hadn't imagined it! I wanted to go and tell my parents, loudly exclaim that I wasn't wrong, that there was a house across from us. The thought of waking my father in the middle of the night kept me in my room.

After a few bated minutes, another flash lit the world and I focused on the house in the brief second it was illuminated.

The front door was wide open.

Now, I don't know why, but I remember seeing that and feeling terror slowly begin to creep its way into my mind. I knew that something was wrong, that people don't open their front doors in the middle of a storm. But there it was, completely open, rain and wind pushing through toward the blackness inside.

Unease wormed its way through my stomach and I swallowed hard, suddenly aware of every shadow in my room. I gripped the windowsill and waited for more lightning. A few moments later, it came, bringing with it another glimpse of the house across the street.

Something was standing in the doorway staring directly at me.

It was blurred by the storm, but I could tell it was big and looked like a twist of colors in human form.

I dove for my bed, illusions of bravery shattered in an instant, and dug myself deep into the covers. I lay there shak-

ing and feeling like I had just seen something I wasn't supposed to.

The next day the house was gone again. Part of me was
a little glad because it gave my young mind time to wrap
itself around what it had seen. I kept replaying it over and
over again, my imagination giving the human-shaped blur
details and features. But whatever images I conjured were
soon erased by the reality of my memory. And that reality was:
I had no clue what I had seen.

I ate my breakfast in the kitchen, listening to my parents
talk about the day's plans. My ears perked up when my mom
told me we were having the Harveys over for supper. I would
finally be able to tell Trevor about everything! Excitement
pushed away my cautious fears of the previous night, and I
gobbled up the rest of my pancakes in a couple bites.

My father said he didn't need my help today and so after
I helped Mom with the dishes, I sprinted out the front door
toward the woods. With the house gone, it felt like just
another wonderful summer day bursting with early morning
possibilities. Should I go swimming? Should I build a fort?
Maybe once Trevor got here we could play Lewis and Clark!

Whooping and hollering, my feet took me across the grassy
field toward the tree line. As I passed the spot where the mysterious green house had sat, I wondered what would happen
if it suddenly appeared with me running over its spot. Would
I magically be inside of it all of a sudden? Or would I be flung
high into the sky as it came rocketing out of the ground?
Feeling suddenly nervous, I put on an extra bit of speed and
passed over where it had rested.

The day passed in a blur of imagination and summer heat. I spent most of it splashing around one of the streams, collecting rocks and pretending I was fighting Indians. It was one of those days that shaped how I look back on my childhood, where everything seemed just right, a day of make-believe and adventure.

As I lost myself in whatever fiction I was enacting, the thoughts of the house faded further and further from my mind, burned away in the growing heat. The sun climbed to a blistering climax, then began the slow descent, dipping toward the horizon and fanning out in pool of color that mixed in the sky like melting popsicles.

Not realizing how late it had gotten and also how hungry I was, I threw the last of the pebbles I had picked up into the stream and began to make my way back to our house.

I wondered if Trevor and his parents had shown up yet. I looked up into the sky, trying to gauge what time it was. From the way my stomach was rumbling, it had better be time to eat.

I broke through the tree line and was about to sprint the rest of the way when I stopped.

The house was back. Except something was different.

The house was facing me.

I felt unease creep across the ground and climb up my legs. This wasn't right. It was supposed to be facing my house. Why was it like this now? I swallowed hard, my own house now blocked from sight. I watched the windows, dark and empty, looking for signs of life, looking for signs of the thing in the storm.

It was motionless. I began to make my way around it in a

wide circle, keeping my eyes on the front door as I walked. I kept expecting it to burst open and some creature to come charging at me. But it didn't. Nothing moved. Getting halfway around it, I made a break for my front porch. My legs kicked through the knee-high grass, shoes digging into the soft earth as I ripped my eyes away and focused on my destination.

Panting, I clambered up the steps, sucking in lungfuls of evening air. I turned around and almost fell over.

The house was back facing mine.

I stared for a moment, sucking air, and waited for something to happen. In my mind, the house was alive, some kind of living beast that watched me. I didn't know what it wanted or what its purpose was, but I was beginning to feel like it was dangerous.

Turning away, I went inside. I was greeted with a savory aroma, a gentle heat filling the air with mouth-watering smells. I heard commotion in the kitchen along with the rolling laughter of conversation.

I walked into the dining room and was greeted from the stove by my mother, who informed me I had kept Trevor waiting. I said my muttered hellos to Trevor's parents, who smiled and returned my greeting before returning to the conversation with my parents I had interrupted.

I went to the bathroom to wash up, followed by Trevor who was excitedly telling me about a fort he had been building in the woods by his house. I shared with him my adventures of the day and together we began to make plans to sleep over at each other's homes with hopes that tonight would be one of those nights.

As I dried my hands, I asked him if he noticed anything on

his way to my house. He looked confused, and so I led him down the hall to the front door. I opened it and pointed to the green house with the yellow shutters. Hesitantly, I asked him if he could see it.

He chuckled and slapped me on the back, saying of course he could.

Relief washed over me and, closing the door behind us and stepping out onto the porch, I began to share with him my strange experiences with the house in the field. His eyes grew wide and a smile split his face in half. The longer I talked, the more I saw his eyes light up.

He asked me if I had explored it yet or poked around the outside to see if I could get inside. I shook my head violently, expressing the feeling of fear it emitted. I told him it wasn't safe, that something was wrong with the house. I told him my parents couldn't see it and that something had been watching me in the storm. This only egged him on, sparking his enthusiasm to explore it.

As I tried to talk him out of it, I heard my father call me to set the table. Groaning, I complied and the conversation ended there. Trevor helped me fill the water glasses and soon we were sitting around a table filled with steaming food.

I didn't care about the banquet in front of me. It was just an obstacle to playtime. Disregarding the hard work that went into the preparation, I dug in with a vengeance after my father said grace. My mother shot me a look or two as I proceeded to stuff my face, pounding the food down with mouthfuls of water.

When my plate was clear, I looked across the table and saw Trevor was of the same mindset. I waited the appropriate amount of time and then asked if we could be excused. My father waved us away, commenting on my poor table manners, but I barely heard him as Trevor and I shot for the front door.

The sky was an expanse of brilliant deep purples and blues as the sun departed for the day. Stars twinkled above us like tiny candles, their light pulsing as the sound of night critters filled the air and sang up to them.

Trevor and I sat on the front steps, giving ourselves a moment to let the food settle. We stared across at the dark house, waiting to see some flicker of life. The moon glowed in the deepening darkness, lighting the field and joined in its efforts by a sea of blinking fireflies.

Trevor was anxious to go look in the windows, expressing these desires in statements of bravery and courage. I shook my head, knowing that some mysterious malevolence shrouded the looming house. It was a gut feeling, a twisting in my stomach whenever I thought about the thing in the storm.

After fruitlessly arguing with me, Trevor stood and announced he was going to go by himself and have a look. I snapped my eyes to lock with his and hurriedly voiced my opposition to the idea. No matter how much I pleaded, there was no changing his mind. He called me a big chicken and pranced around the porch clucking and waving his arms. This did nothing to change my mind and I continued to shake my head in disagreement.

Sighing, Trevor ceased his antics and trotted down the steps to the grass. He gave me a wink and a thumbs-up, telling me I was being a baby. I watched him walk toward the house, my heart beginning to beat faster.

I felt like I should stop him, that I should tell my parents, but what would they do? They would see him walking toward an empty field and my dad would probably slap the back of my head.

He was thirty feet from the house, his outline in the dying light nothing more than a black smudge of movement. I could hear him calling to me, but his words were muffled by the night.

Twenty feet now, his pace was slowing. My mouth was dry and panic was rising in my throat. This was a bad idea, this was such a bad idea. I balled my hands into tiny fists, feeling the sweat coating my palms.

Ten feet from the door now. All was silent, the house an unmoving giant, its yellow shutters now looking like dirty teeth, the greasy yellow popping in the darkness. Trevor was almost there, his footsteps cautiously taking him to the right of the front door, his target a first-floor window.

That's when I saw something in the third-floor window on the far left of the house.

It looked like a candle, a soft glow popping through the dense darkness. It wavered there in the middle of the window and then began to move. I watched as the light passed from window to window, then disappeared. Frantically, I called out to Trevor to come back, running down the stairs and toward the field.

He was about to look in the window when he heard me, turning and taking a few steps toward me. I crossed the road and kicked into the long grass, slowing and waving my arms for him to return.

The light was on the second floor now, its glow smoothly hovering past the windows. It was getting closer.

Terrified to go any further, I danced from foot to foot, heart thundering in my chest, my face contorted into frantic terror. Trevor was calling out to me, asking what was wrong. I screamed at him to come back, that something was coming, that he was in danger. And then I cursed at him. It was the only thing I could think of to get his complete attention.

Hearing me swear, he finally began to trot back to me, throwing a look over his shoulder. The light was gone, but as he made his way toward me, I saw it reappear on the first floor, shining in the window Trevor had been about to look into moments before.

It stayed there, just floating in the darkness, and I felt something looking at me from the black. Trevor reached me spewing questions, and I grabbed his shoulders, spinning him to look at the light.

As soon as he saw it, the house went dark.

We stood there, breathing heavily, unsure of what had just happened. I asked him if he had seen it and he nodded slowly. We knew now that something was definitely in there. That something had seen us. I felt exposed, the plump moon working as a spotlight, making me feel like I was on a stage that was watched by whatever was in the house.

We turned and ran back to my house, both of us sharing silent guilt that we had done something we shouldn't. The fear of being found out, the anxiety of getting in trouble flooded us as we scampered up the porch and pushed our way back inside.

I should have told my parents something at that point. Even

if they didn't see the house, I feel like if I had tried to explain it to them, maybe a shred of my honestly would shine through and give them a sliver of belief. But I didn't. Neither of us did. We knew snooping was wrong and we'd get in trouble if they did, in fact, believe us.

As we took our places at the table, now filled with hot pie, Trevor and I exchanged a look that vowed complete silence. Our parents asked us why we were back so soon, Trevor's mother joking that the smell of dessert was the cause.

I didn't feel like eating, my stomach a mess of knotted emotions, but I dutifully shoveled steaming cherry pie into my mouth, barely tasting it. I was afraid they would find out, that whoever was in the green house would suddenly knock on the door and tell our parents what we had done. It was the illogical fears of a child, the haunting giant that loomed over every kid's life: Getting In Trouble.

After we finished eating, I asked my parents if Trevor could spend the night. After some discussion between the adults, they agreed, extending the stay to two nights. Apparently Trevor's dad needed to borrow our tractor, but we needed it for just a few more days. So, when the tractor was available, my dad would drive it down to them along with Trevor.

My fear subsided a little, the excitement of two whole nights together causing the unease to fade.

We whooped for joy and jumped around the house, cut short by a bark from my father to settle down. We scurried up to my bedroom and began to make plans for the stay. With so much time available, we decided that tomorrow we would begin construction on a tree fort in the woods. Crude sketches were made in crayon, both of us lying on our stomachs on the floor, heads knocking together as we crammed around the piece of paper we were drawing on. Story lines were spun as to who we were and why we needed to build a fort, our vast imaginations manufacturing motives and villains. It was exciting, our conversation fueled by sweet pie, and I felt like I could burst for joy. Looking back, it's one of those feelings that you only get as a kid, where everything is perfect and it's just you and your buddy with the whole world to play with.

Eventually we heard his parents call him to say goodbye, making him promise to behave and listen to my mom and dad. As I waited for him to come back, I glanced out my bedroom window.

The house was gone again.

It was midnight. Trevor lay snoring in the sleeping bag my mother had taken out for him. He was curled up, his head barely poking out of the opening.

I didn't know why I had awoken. The house lay silent, my parents long asleep. Even with Trevor there, I remember feeling scared, like something was in the room besides us. I looked toward the corners, the closet, my cracked bedroom door. Shadows formed monsters, then dispersed as my eyes focused.

I thought about waking Trevor but didn't want to be called a chicken again. I felt exposed, like something was watching me. Like something at the window was watching me.

I chanced a glance at it, but the moonlight was the only thing that trickled through. No eyes, no faces pressed to the glass…no candle hovering in the darkness.

As soon as the thought crossed my mind, I felt a shiver run

down my back. I didn't want to be thinking about that when it was this dark and everything was so silent. Something was drawing me to the window, though. I could almost feel a physical pull toward it, goading me to go to it.

I resisted at first but knew I wasn't going to be able to fall back asleep until I had gone to the window. Quietly, I slipped out of bed, being careful not to step on Trevor's head. I tiptoed toward my window and felt dread begin to rise like bile. With every step my mind repeatedly begged me to go back to my covers. Over and over, the thought rippled through my mind: *Don't look, don't look, don't look!*

I reached the window…and looked out.

My eyes went wide and I felt a scream rising in my throat as I slammed my hands over my mouth. My heart was a wild drumbeat in my chest and I felt myself grow sick with gut-slamming fear.

To this day, thinking about what I saw that night fills me with horror.

The house was back, standing where it always stood, dark and silent.

But something massive was peeking at me over its rooftop.

Its head was enormous, spanning almost the entire width of the house, its almost human eyes terribly wide with sick excitement. Two colossal hands gripped the roof, making the whole thing look almost like how a child would peek over a table.

It made the night look white, the darkness that colored its mass almost burned to look at. Two white eyes punctured through its black, human-shaped head, shining like two full moons. Its irises were the sharpest crimson, almost neon in the way they glowed.

Just visible over the peak of the roof was its mouth. It was grinning, its massive square teeth practically exploding out of the shadows of its coal-black face. They radiated like its eyes did, their bleached white starkness accenting just how inky black the rest of its head and hands were.

I was frozen in place, the whole world melting away like burning wax. My eyes locked with...whatever it was, and its smile widened. It never blinked, those two perfectly round gleaming eyes reaching into my brain and ripping up every fear I ever had.

I waited for something to happen, feeling like at any second I would scream or pass out. It just watched me, smiling, its mouth stretched to immense proportions. Its long ebony fingers shifted on the roof every few seconds like it, too, was waiting.

And then something said my name from the crack in my bedroom door.

I spun, a scream already halfway up my throat. From the partially open door, I saw an impossibly large eye and half a mouth smiling at me, one midnight-black hand reaching inside to grip the wood.

I dove toward my bed, digging myself deep into the covers, shaking and crying. I heard my door open and Trevor stirring on the floor. I peeked out from my safe haven and saw it.

It stood in the doorway, a tall, human-shaped figure. Its skin was a constant swirl of dark colors, looking like paint being gently mixed in real time, its face the same liquid texture with one giant eye popping in and out from the surface.

The mouth faded in the same manner, a constant, twisted grin emerging from its hideous face.

And then it spoke. Its voice was one and many at the same time, sounding like a collection of vocal cords being filtered through running water.

"Come with us."

I shrunk down into my sheets, every ounce of my being trying to scream, but the sound was caught in my throat, choked back from fear.

I heard movement and then a thump followed by a silky dragging sound. I shifted in my cotton force field, sweating and trembling, wanting, needing to cry out for my parents. I chanced another look to see if it was gone.

My room was empty.

And Trevor was gone, along with his sleeping bag.

As I ripped myself free from my bed, heart thundering, I heard my friend from the hallway begin to wake. I couldn't make out what he was saying, but it was muffled and confused. Then his tone shifted and I began to hear him panic.

I begged my parents to wake, shutting my eyes and willing it to happen. I heard heavy footsteps and the dragging sound retreating down the hall, Trevor becoming more and more vocal. I heard him begin to cry, his voice soft and muted.

The front door crashed open, causing me to jump and emit a tiny squeal. *Thump, thump, thump.* I heard the sound of the monster and Trevor receding. I ran to my window, feeling tears begin to form around my eyes.

The monster had Trevor trapped in his sleeping bag and was dragging him down the porch and across the field toward the house.

The death-black giant looked down at them, his teeth shining in the moonlight, crimson eyes ever wide with excitement. The monster who had Trevor didn't look back as it continued its march across the field. I watched as the front door opened on its own, the darkness inside seeming to ink out into the night.

Finally, I screamed. I screamed until I couldn't scream anymore, my voice cracking in high-pitched horror.

I heard my parents wake from their room in the back of our house as the monster entered the green house.

As my dad came charging into my room, I watched Trevor squirming frantically in his sleeping bag, then disappear as the door was shut behind him. He was in there, in that horrible house, with that thing.

My dad grabbed me by the shoulders, shaking me, asking me what was wrong, what happened. Tears running down my face, I took one last look at the house in the field.

It vanished.

That was twenty years ago. That night, my parents called Trevor's parents and then the police. I explained over and over again what I had seen, but no one believed me. It was chalked up to a kidnapping, and over the next couple months a thorough investigation was initiated. Trevor's parents never spoke to mine again.

The house never reappeared and neither did Trevor.

That is, until two days ago.

I got a phone call at work from the police, telling me they had found someone. A child. They said the child knew me and kept asking for me from his hospital bed. They said that my name was the only word he would speak.

I hadn't thought about the house in the field or Trevor in years, but as soon as the policeman finished, I knew who the mysterious child was.

Trevor.

I rushed to the hospital, my heart a disjointed mess of frantic thunder. I was questioned by the police on my arrival, asking me for my full name, date of birth, and where I worked. When they seemed satisfied, they told me I could see the child under police supervision. Something was off, though. They all seemed…quiet, shaken.

As I was about to enter the room Trevor was in, the officer escorting me placed a hand on my shoulder. He told me to prepare myself, that what I was about to see might be upsetting. Confused and a little unsure, I pushed into the room.

My breath was robbed from my lungs as I saw what lay in the bed.

A child lay above the sheets, his small body rising and falling with labored breath. His size was the only way I could discern his approximate age.

His entire form, from head to toe, was covered in a pure white glaze. His eyes, his mouth, his shining hairless head, everything. He looked like a mannequin made from snow-white yogurt but hardened and sleek.

Its head turned to me and then it said my name. I recognized the voice instantly, memories of my childhood collapsing like an avalanche of nostalgia. It was Trevor.

I went to his bedside, pulling up a chair, hands shaking as they reached out to touch his. My voice cracked as I said his name, my mouth suddenly dry.

I asked him what happened.

This is what he said:

Trevor: "How long has it been?"

Me : "T-twenty years."

Pause. Trevor: "It can't be." *Another pause.* "It will happen soon."

Me: "What will happen?"

Trevor: "They're coming."

Me: "Who?"

Trevor: "The Grins. They took my youth away…they will come as children."

Me: "A-are you talking about…what happened all those years ago? About…the monsters we saw?"

Trevor: "They will come as children. They will come from between the colors. From between the colors. They will come as children."

Me: "Trevor, please, help me understand, where did you go? What happened in that house?"

Trevor, voice shaking: "They took me between the colors. Took my years away from me. Took all those children's years away from them. All of them. So many houses; so many children. They are ready. They will come now as children."

Me: "Who is coming?"

Trevor: "The Grins."

Me: "What does that mean? What are The Grins? D-do you mean…that thing we saw in the house? Please, help me understand."

Trevor, growing frantic: "They will walk among us, waiting until they have grown, waiting to reveal themselves. The darkness, red eyes, oh, such red eyes. They will come as children and we will see them smile. We will watch them grow. The Grins, they will eat everything! They will eat the world out of existence!"

At this point Trevor went into a fit, his body convulsing and sputtering. I was hurriedly shoved out of the room as the nurses went to work, trying their best to calm him. The police told me I would need to leave for the day but that someone would be by to question me.

Trevor died later that night.

I don't know what happened that night my friend disappeared into that house. I don't know where he was taken, what was done to him. I'll never know. But what I do know is that it was real. I can't explain it, I can't make sense of it, but that coal-black giant with the red eyes, that thing that came into my room…those were real.

Trevor's final words stuck with me. They made me afraid. There was such conviction in them, such sureness.

They are ready. They will come now as children.

As I drove home, I pulled out my phone and dialed my wife. I needed to know what my son was doing.

3

Empire Snuff

I love to write. I love to write horror in particular. There's something about the creative freedom it allows, the flexible walls of reality you're allowed to bend. It's a place where you can put down your darkest thoughts or wildest ideas. It's a space you enter with no light, no sound, and there's already blood on the walls. Horror is a sticky, upsetting ordeal where you engage in a contract with the author that gives him or her permission to get inside your mind and rip out your insecurities by the gory handfuls.

As scary as it can be to experience these things as a reader, it's worse for the author. Imagine taking your most demented thoughts, examining them, asking why they're in your mind, and then placing them on a platform for the world to see. You present it under the white light of a blank page and then bleed its twisted, black blood into words. You craft monsters and motives with the sickest intentions, you breathe life into characters you plan on tearing apart. You give these people families and loved ones you intend to destroy. You become a fictional god of death, a puppet master with knives for fingers, slicing them over your keyboard in brutal strokes of cruelty.

I don't write this to promote what I do. I don't do this for some kind of warped respect. There is no honor in becoming a psychopath for the duration of a story. There is no glory in holding out the broken remains of your characters for the reader to see. Horror is a disturbing business, a cold and lonely road with no happy ending.

When you finish writing a story you sit back and exhale, relieved that these things are finally out of your mind. You're relieved that you survived the journey and that you could make sense out of the darkness that has been screaming to be released.

I'm sure there are those out there that turn their nose down at horror. And why not? It's developed a bad reputation over the years. Recycled ideas, cheap scares, girls with black eyes and cryptic messages. We're all familiar with the clichés. We've all seen the steady decline of fresh content. We've all groaned as the big reveal unfolded and it turned out they were dead the whole time (gasp!).

Now, I have no misconceptions.

I'm not going to change the horror world. I'm not going to think of an idea that is so revolutionary it will flip the way we think about horror on its head. I'm not going to come up with a plot so incredible that publishers are going to throw piles of money at me.

No…I'm here to tell you that I've found the end of that long dark road. I've found where it leads, tracked my steps with an anxious mind, and come out the other side.

I've seen where horror can take you.

And I'm here to tell you just how far you can go.

I stared at my computer screen with numb eyes. I cursed the blinking slice of black on the blank page. I willed it to move, begged it to take the first steps of my new story. If I could just get a paragraph down I knew I'd be able to slip into the comfortable flow of a moving narrative.

I racked my brain, scrambling for the words to start my dark tale. I needed to write, but my mind stubbornly refused to communicate ideas to my fingers. The space between my ears soared into the demented realm of terror, desperately clawing at possible entries into this new endeavor. I didn't know what was wrong with me; I had written SO many of these things. Never had I suffered such crippling writer's block and the mountain of immovable clichés threatened to suffocate me with the mundane.

I had already tried the usual brain stimulation: long car rides with loud music, sitting in the dark while chain-smoking, watching my favorite horror movies. Nothing seemed to tickle that muscle in my head that sparked my supply of spooks and scares.

I sat up in my chair and ashed my cig in an empty beer bottle. I took one last drag and then shoved the butt down the neck of the bottle, listening to it sizzle in the dregs. I pulled another one from my pack and lit it, begging the nicotine to ignite my mind into action.

Smoke rose from my lips in waves of indifference and I rubbed my face in frustration. I wanted to do something big, something that no one had done before. I wanted to create a name for myself in the world of horror, a legacy that remained long after I did.

I just wanted to write! I had done fairly well for myself in my recent literary excursions, building a small following in some online communities. Most of the feedback was positive, which in turn fueled my desire to do something bigger and better, really give my readers something that would WOW them. It's the dream every young author goes through when they first start out.

But then the ideas begin to fizzle and you burn through all your good material, much like an aging comedian, but you know...with more gore and severed heads.

I took another drag from my cigarette and drummed my fingers on my desk. Maybe I had nothing left? Maybe I had exhausted all my ideas and now was left with nothing but "fresh" takes on old ideas. It was discouraging, frightening. What if the inspiration I had so passionately begun this journey with was now diminishing into the frayed remains of worn-out tropes?

No. No, I couldn't accept that. I had so much more to offer, so much more to give. There was a black fire in me that I hadn't revealed yet. There was a hunger buried in me I hadn't yet explored. I had lived with it my whole life, shielded myself from it, denied it.

But it was there and it burned hotter with each day. The more I immersed and dedicated myself to all things horror, the more I wanted to push the limits. With each successful story, I was fueled to take the reader to darker and darker places.

And in doing so, I felt my hunger expand and rise, its gaping jaws begging for forbidden flavor. I knew where I was headed. I knew what I wanted to do. I wanted to experience things that were not talked about. I wanted to live stories that should be left in warped imaginations. I wanted to extend my parched tongue and drink the drops of unspilled blood.

"Goddamn it," I muttered, stubbing out my cigarette and pulling up my web browser. I needed to do something about this intolerable writer's block, to find some way to get the wheels turning.

I browsed a couple of my favorite horror sites, flicking through the images and articles with eyes that weren't really paying attention. I had done this in the past and I felt like I had squeezed all the juice of possibility from these pages.

Today I needed to delve deeper.

I had played around on the deep web before, the hidden Internet behind the Internet. Today, I was going to really emerge myself in it, really soak my mind its twisted machinations.

It didn't take long to find some hidden sites. I had been here before; I knew the channels I had to take to reveal the shadow the surface web cast.

I sat up in my chair and scrolled through a site that portrayed animals being crushed in clear plastic bags. My mouse hovered over one video titled "Fat bitch crushes little bitch." The thumbnail showed an image of an obese woman standing over a small dog. I rolled my eyes. No thanks. I wasn't on here to observe weird fetishes.

It didn't look like I was going to find anything that interested my dark desires and so I jumped over to another site. This one seemed to be a black-market Craigslist. As I scanned the page, I saw an assortment of items on sale, ranging from hardcore drugs to murder. This tickled my interest and I clicked on an ad that boasted: Hitman for Hire! I quickly read the summary of the services offered and chuckled to myself.

This couldn't be real, could it? Apparently this guy would kill anyone you wanted for ten thousand euros.

Like I said earlier, I had been on the deep web before, but not like this. I had merely dipped my toe into the cesspool, a curious peek beneath the curtain. Back then, when I had first started writing, darker issues scared me. Not personally of course, but professionally. I was worried about the content I was confessing. I didn't want to allow my readers to wander too deeply inside my mind.

But now I felt like maybe I could. I felt like I had gained enough confidence in my craft to shine a little honesty on my stories. I wanted to illuminate the black corners of my thoughts and create stories I had only fantasized about before. I wanted to shock them, throw them down the dark hole of my mind, and see if they could survive.

I idled on the page a while longer, my interest dwindling. After exhausting my patience, I decided to check out a site one of my friends had talked about a few months ago. Apparently it was a snuff site, a place where you could watch real people being killed.

I stared at the ceiling, trying to remember what he had said it was called. I pulled out my phone and sent my friend a quick text. As I waited for his response, I mentally prepared myself for what I was hopefully going to see.

I had never actually seen anyone murdered before. What better way to stimulate the mind? I didn't know why I hadn't thought of it earlier. It excited me, a nervous anticipation for the horror I was about to experience. How would I react? Would I be disgusted by it? Would I be able to handle it? How far could I push myself?

My phone chirped and I smiled to myself as I read the message. My fingers raced to the keyboard and soon I was staring at a red and black website. In bloody font were the titles of literally *hundreds* of snuff films. I sat there with my mouse hovering over the top video link.

I paused. Did I really want to go down this road?

You've known for months this is where you were headed...

I smiled and clicked the video.

The screen faded to black and then showed two middle-aged men on their knees. Their hands were bound behind their backs and one of the men was wearing a straw hat. It looked like there was a barn behind them, its red wall a foretelling of the violence to come. For some reason, I was surprised to see it was being shot in the daylight. I leaned in closer to my screen, licking my lips, eyes lighting up.

From the corner of the screen, another man walked into the shot. He was holding a knife and he went and stood behind the man with the hat.

Without a word, he grabbed the man by the hair and began slicing into his throat. My heart jumped into my mouth and I audibly gasped, gripping the sides of my chair.

I couldn't *believe* how much blood there was.

To my shock, the victim wasn't screaming. He curled his chin down to his chest in an attempt to escape the blade, his mouth opening and closing in silent agony. The other bound man turned his head away, his mouth forming a thin grim line. He didn't want to see what awaited him.

The man holding the knife stopped cutting and tilted the victim's head the other way. He placed the bloody blade on the untouched side of his neck and began to saw inward toward the throat from the opposite side. I watched in fascination as streams of thick blood gushed from the wounds, splashing to the earth.

After a few seconds, the executioner hit bone and I could see his muscles bulge with effort as he struggled to sever the head. With a tearing sound, he finally managed to rip it from the body. He held it up for the camera to see and then tossed it to the side.

And then he started on the other man.

My heart was racing in my chest as I watched a repeat of what had just happened. My tongue slid between my lips as I concentrated on every detail, drinking it in. I realized that very few people had ever seen what I was now seeing. As the thought rippled across my mind, I shivered with excitement.

Once the video was over, I grabbed a cigarette and lit it with trembling fingers. I gasped down the smoke and couldn't help but smile, my eyes alight with wonderment. This was incredible. I had just seen someone die. I had just watched a human being *executed*.

I hastily clinked on other video.

And then another.

And another.

And another.

I couldn't stop watching them. The morbid stage before me was an untapped vein of shock and brutality that I had never experienced before. It was like having sex for the first time, the surprise of euphoric pleasure blocking out everything else. I wanted more of it, wanted to repeat the experience over and over again, each time bringing with it new and undiscovered ways of enjoyment.

Hours rolled by, my state of consciousness completely enveloped by this new pastime. I continued to chain-smoke, eyes held captive by the vicious images displayed on the screen. I indulged my mind with video after video, a starving glutton for the raw violence. I could feel my mind digesting it all in voluminous chunks, a carnivore for carnage.

Before I knew it, the sun had set and was rising again, the magnificent beauty of its spanning color a contrast to the depraved, pernicious images.

I stared out the window, blinking as the light crept over the horizon. My mind was fatigued, enervated by the monstrosities I had witnessed. I rubbed my hands over my eyes, pulling sleep from them like cobwebs.

"Jesus Christ," I muttered to no one.

My life began to develop a predictable pattern after that night. I would go to work, come home, and watch hours and hours of snuff. I would close the curtains, smack a cigarette from my pack, and dive back into the deep web. It was all I wanted to do and I found myself going to bed later and later, the nighttime darkness adding to the savage nature of what I was devouring.

After a couple weeks, it was all I could think about. I floated through my days, working my day job in a dreamlike state, and then rushing in hopes to repeat the cycle. The more videos I watched, the more my hunger grew. I felt something emerging from inside of me, that deep darkness I had kept hidden for so long. It crept out from its lair and began to fill me, its long tendrils coiling around my mind in an obsessive grip.

After a couple months, I began to seek out more graphic material, tearing the Internet apart for the highest quality videos. I wanted to find the bottom of the well, the absolute peak of human cruelty. I ignored the moral warnings that occasionally shot from my subconscious, pushing away the fragile arguments that bubbled to the surface.

And just when I thought I had reached the end of the road, just when I began to wonder if I had seen everything there was to see, I found them.

I found Red Rooms.

It was almost an accident, my finding them. I was chasing a link down an endless rabbit hole when I found myself on a site I had only dreamed existed. After a few minutes of excited exploration, I realized that what I was looking at was a live stream.

A couple feet from the camera was a man bound to a chair. He was weeping and seemed to have given up any hope of escape. On the sidebar there was a list of items with price tags next to them. Hammer: $500; Crowbar: $300; Blowtorch: $600; Hacksaw: $900; Needle Nose Pliers: $200; and the list went on and on.

I couldn't believe it. I could buy instruments to torture this man? Is that was I was looking at? Just the thought sent a shiver of raw excitement down my spine. Who was watching this right now? How many people were sitting at their computers pondering this man's suffering?

There was a timer at the top of the screen that read 3:17 and was counting down. Below the clock was a list of items that had already been purchased by the unseen viewers. My eyes ate up the instruments of agony and I felt a smile slowly stretch my face. I was going to see this man crawl to his death, ripped apart piece by piece in a grand showing of live snuff theater.

I pulled my feet up on my chair and lit a cigarette, watching as the clock gradually counted down to zero. When it did, the numbers faded and a graphic of a round green light lit up next to the video feed.

Two men entered the screen wearing ski masks.

And then they began to torture the bound man, working their way down the list of purchased tools.

And *I couldn't get enough of it.*

This marked another turning point in my life. From then on, I became infatuated with Red Rooms. I found out when they were being streamed (usually every three weeks or so) and managed to save enough money to purchase an instrument of torture at every live event. The first time I did it was...*breathtaking*. I spent $200 for a pint of bleach and watched, absorbed in the sick display, as they slowly dripped it into the man's open eyes. The thrill of knowing I was responsible for his screams excited me in ways I had only dreamed possible. I felt an energy rush through my body as a diadem of darkness settled over my mind. I wanted to do more, spend more, stretch the limits of pain into realms unreached.

Weeks rolled into months, my money squandered away and saved until the next live stream. It was all I thought about, all I wanted. What little social life I had slowly faded to nothing. I didn't talk to anyone outside of work, didn't go out, didn't seek out company or companions. Death and snuff were all I wanted, all I thought about. It was the only thing that stimulated me, the only thing that got my heart racing.

Now, I didn't worship death, didn't think the world needed to be eradicated. I didn't hold a grudge against humanity, I wasn't angry at society. I just found live murder absolutely enthralling. The unflinching act of what I watched, the splash of human blood, the screams of a person in agony…it was all so real. It was unfiltered human suffering, boiled down to its most basic form. It was a forbidden wickedness, a proscribed evil.

All thoughts of writing were gone. I tried once but gave up after half a page. How was it possible to write about such savage acts? How could I translate the howls of pain into black and white? How could I describe the way a person's body slumps when they finally die? Trying to describe it on paper felt cheap, like I was robbing the act of its shocking brutality.

I realized it wasn't possible to write in color.

But I wasn't disappointed, I wasn't heartbroken. I didn't think it had anything to do with my skill as a writer. I began to understand that some things could not be appreciated unless seen. No matter how bad an author might want you to experience what they envision, what they see, sometimes it is simply impossible. It's like trying to write down how music sounds. You can describe the instruments, explain the beat and rhythm, the ups and downs, but at the end of the day…at the end of the day you simply *cannot hear the music.*

A year passed.

I continued in my ways, scraping by, saving, waiting, and then finally purchasing machines of death as a new victim was procured. Looking back, I have a hard time forming concrete memories of that year. Everything was so similar, every day so robotic. During the weekends I would hole up in my apartment and watch and rewatch snuff films, filling my mind until the next live stream. I was a slave to the violence. It remained fresh and new each time I witnessed it. My mind never numbed to it, the blade of its cruelty never dulled.

And then the opportunity of a lifetime emerged from the depths of the deep web. Right around the one-year mark of my new obsession, I was contacted by the hosts of the live snuff channel. They sent a direct message to my account and when I saw it, my heart began to race.

They said they had noticed my loyalty to their work. They said they appreciated all the money I had donated to their bloody productions. They said I was an inspiration to the art of snuff, a true patriot to the darker side of life.

And they asked if I wanted to participate in a live event.

I had to re-read the message four times before I was convinced I wasn't dreaming. Could...could this actually be real? Were they really inviting me to go and partake in their live shoot? It was too good to be true, the thrill of possibility overwhelming me. I sat back in my chair, staring at the message on my screen. After a moment, I slid a cigarette between my teeth and smoked the entire thing while in a trance-like state.

Finally, I placed my trembling hands on the keyboard and replied. I told them I would be honored to be a part of their work and asked for the details and date. I asked what I needed to bring or do to prepare. I asked what they wanted of me.

It wasn't long before I had a new message. Licking my lips, I opened it. My breath left my body in a rush of adrenaline.

They were offering the spot of executioner...to me.

Three weeks went by in a rush of excited impatience. I couldn't stop role-playing the eventual scene in my mind. I was going to kill someone. I was going to star in a snuff. I would finally be able to enact these dark fantasies that had been dominating my thoughts for the past year. Time and time again I pictured myself sliding a knife between someone's ribs or strangling them with my bare hands. I didn't hold any malice in my heart; it was just an overwhelming sense of curiosity. I would be the one who would feel their life leave their body. I would be their end.

The more I thought about it, the more I knew I could do it. There was no question there. Not once did I pause and ponder my ability to kill. This is what had been growing inside of me since my humble beginnings. I had always known it was there, this morbid hunger.

I did wonder what would happen afterward. Obviously, these were dangerous people I was dealing with. Obviously, they were professionals in their craft. I could tell just by the quality of their shoots: the lighting, the set, the clean design of the website. Everything pointed to a small-time organization that had a very good system running and somehow they had kept it all under the radar. As I pondered these things, ideas began to grow in my mind.

One of these ideas was a need to protect myself in case anything went sideways. I decided that I would slip a small knife inside my shoe in case I found myself in a less-than-desirable situation.

But the way I was imagining things, everything would go off without a hitch.

I was told to meet them outside of town by an abandoned warehouse around eleven at night. They would transport me to the spot of the shoot and from there we'd begin filming. When it was done, they would drive me back to my car and I'd be on my way. They obviously didn't worry about me telling anyone because of my involvement on their site and I clearly wasn't going to run to the police. That and the fact they were setting the table for me to murder someone.

Now, I'm not stupid. I played around with the possibility that I was being set up as the victim. That maybe this was their way of reaching out to their viewers and getting new meat for their chopping block. Hence, the knife I would stash in my shoe.

I knew it was extremely dangerous and a huge risk to my personal safety, but it was such a rare opportunity I decided it was worth the risk. I was at the point in my obsession where I needed to take that last step, I needed to extend beyond just viewing murder. I needed to partake in it. I needed to feel it.

I needed to hear the music.

I needed to see the color.

That's how I found myself in a van three weeks later with a bag over my head. I was nervous, feeling the road bounce beneath me. The knife in my shoe felt hard under my foot, a solid reminder of my insurance in case this went wrong.

I had driven to the instructed location and waited half an hour for the black van to arrive. I was a mess of nerves and emotion, unable to believe that the time had finally come. I had spent so much time imagining this moment, I couldn't fathom that it was actually happening.

Only one man had been sent to retrieve me, someone my age in his early twenties. He seemed incredibly casual about the whole thing, shaking my hand upon arrival and apologizing for the bag over my head. I told him I understood as the rough cloth was pulled over my face. It's not like he tied my hands or anything; he just asked that I keep the bag on until we arrived.

As we drove, I told him I was surprised they had reached out to me. I heard him chuckle and say that sometimes as an incentive to keep watching the live streams they'd allow dedicated viewers to perform the executions. He said I probably hadn't noticed in the past, as each person was required to wear a black jacket and a ski mask they provided.

He said they would have contacted me sooner, but they hadn't traveled out my way in some time. Obviously, they moved around a lot and when they reached my neck of the country, they decided it was time to extend a hand. I told him I greatly appreciated the opportunity and silently felt a little uneasy that they knew where I lived.

After about an hour, we came to a stop and I was allowed to remove my mask. I blinked and scrubbed my eyes, letting them settle on my surroundings. We had stopped at another abandoned warehouse, this one much larger than the one I had been picked up at. It was surrounded by swaying trees that danced in the dark moonlight, a gentle breeze filling the air.

The man who drove me got out of the van and motioned for me to do the same. Gravel crunched under my feet as I followed him toward the looming superstructure. It was a mess of broken brick and jutting steel beams, a relic long forgotten by time and man. I felt the wind rustle through my hair and I breathed in the quiet night. I could tell by the inky sky just how far we were from any kind of civilization.

We passed a few parked cars and then entered the silent ribcage of broken construction. It was dark, the way lit only by the glowing moon. The man leading me seemed to know where we were going and told me over his shoulder that we were shooting in the basement. I stumbled over loose rubble and stayed close to my guide, feeling the pull of excitement tug at me.

I followed him down some wide stairs, being careful not to trip, and saw lights at the bottom. We reached the basement and I was overcome with a sense of awe.

Sitting in the middle of the vast open basement was a man bound and gagged to a chair. His head slumped to his chest and I could tell he was unconscious. Surrounding him were stage lights, set up and connected to a running generator. They were spaced out to light the scene, but far enough away they wouldn't make it into the live stream.

Two men were set up ten feet from the bound man, an array of wires and boom mikes entangling their space. One man had an expensive-looking camera set up on a tripod and was testing its functionality and frames while the other man placed multiple mikes around the lights. Both men barely looked up at me, their scruffy faces indifferent to my arrival.

The last man, though, turned to me and came to meet us at the bottom of the stairs, a big smile on his face. He was about thirty years old and had a hollow look around his eyes. His face was gaunt and pale, but not sickly. He looked like someone who had seen hell and decided to make the most of it.

He shook my hand and dismissed the driver to go back to the van and wait for me to come back up when the deed was done. I watched him go, a sense of wonder filling me. This was actually going to happen. I was really going to do this.

"You nervous?" The man asked, still smiling and gripping my hand.

I shook my head. "I just can't believe you're letting me actually do this. I can't help but wonder what the catch is."

The man snorted. "No catch, man. Just a way of saying thank you for all the money you've put into our little illegal operation. And no one cares who's doing the actual killing, just so long as the viewers get to see their tools used. Why not give back to the community you know? Let someone live out a fantasy."

I looked at him. "Is that what this is to you? A fantasy?"

I saw his eyes grow distant and his tone shifted slightly. "It used to be. I had a partner who enjoyed this more than me, but…well…things didn't end up working out. I see this as a…a sickness I live with. I can't make it go away, can't stop my need to…to kill people. At one point in my life I almost killed myself over it, but eventually I learned to live with it…and then I learned how to make a profit from it. Work with the gifts God gave you, am I right?"

I nodded, feeling things cement in my mind.

He pointed to a workbench at the far end of the basement. "Over there are the tools you'll use as they come up on the laptop. I'll be standing offscreen to instruct you which ones the viewers have purchased and in what order to use them. Now it's essential to not kill this man until we have reached the end of the shoot, OK? I know this is exciting and all, but I'm going to be seriously pissed off if he dies before we're done with the list."

I felt a hunger seize my stomach, ideas exploding in my mind like fireworks. "I understand. You don't have anything to worry about. I was born for this."

He slapped my back. "Glad to hear it. I've seen men change their mind once they're actually here, but you…I can tell you're here to see this to the end. I can see the lust in your eyes. I've seen it before. I can tell you're a killer."

I could feel a cold darkness swallow me up. "I won't let you down."

"You ready to get started?"

I smiled. "I think this is going to mark the beginning of a whole new life for me."

The man turned to the two techs and shouted instructions for them to get set. They seemed bored by the whole thing, a familiar irritation I had seen in others. I got the feeling they didn't like their boss very much. Good.

I joined the director by the workbench and watched as the sound guy went to the bound man and slapped him awake. He groaned around his gag and then his eyes lit up with fear as he realized where he was. He began to scream, the sound muted by the dirty cloth in his mouth. I wondered who he was, where they had scooped him up. I knew they must be incredibly careful with whom they chose, scoping out potential victims and tracking them for weeks. The infrastructure of such an operation was impressive.

The director opened a laptop on the workbench and pulled up the familiar website. As he got the list of torture devices in order, I ran my hands over the array of tools splayed out before me. My fingers brushed over the cold steel, the possibilities of each one luring me to its grip. I smiled, my mind set. There was only one way this was going to go. There was no turning back now.

"OK," the director said, glancing at the screen. "Wow, looks like the first one on the list is…a chainsaw!" He turned to me. "Now be careful with this one, don't get carried away. Maybe cut up his legs a little bit, hack off an ear…nothing fatal or too bloody. This is a tricky one to start with; we have a lot more to go, OK?"

I spotted the massive weapon on the floor by my feet and picked it up, gripping it with sure hands, "This is a fantastic choice," I said, smiling.

"Good. Now here, put these on," he said, pulling out from beneath the workbench a black jacket and ski mask. I bent and scooped them up, my wardrobe for the performance. I pulled the ski mask over my face and was pleasantly surprised at the freshly washed aroma. The jacket was a little big, but I dutifully buttoned it up and tested the stiffness, flexing my range. Satisfied, I nodded at the director.

The director cupped his hands to his mouth, "OK, you two—ready?" They gave him a thumbs-up. My heart thundered in my chest and I felt a mass of energy fill me, a pulsing excitement. I stared at the man in the chair, my eyes meeting his and I saw helpless fear reflect back at me. He was crying, struggling against his restraints, desperately trying to free himself from the waking nightmare.

"Go live!" The director yelled, bringing his hand down in a chopping motion.

I hefted the chainsaw in my hands, its still blade begging

to be brought to life. My eyes never left the man in the chair as I approached the circle of stage lights. From the darkness I came, bringing with me tools of death. How appropriate, how fitting, that the light would expose just how stained I had become.

I stood just outside the circle of light and put the chainsaw down to rev it. I glanced at the two techs and they seemed bored, one of them with his eye to the camera and the other hovering over a laptop that was plugged into some kind of circuit board. I gripped the pulley and yanked it, giving the viewers an unseen preview of what was coming. The small engine growled from the black and then sputtered back to sleep. I pulled the string a couple more times, but the engine always faltered back into silence. The cameraman looked up at me and twirled his fingers at me, annoyed.

Hurry up.

I glanced over my shoulder and saw the director coming to help me. He seemed irritated. He shoved me to the side, flicked a switch, and gripped the cord. He yanked it once and the chainsaw screamed to life. The man in the chair was weeping, shaking profusely, his bloodshot eyes full of unimaginable horror.

"Thanks," I said, grinning. "It's been a pleasure working with you."

Time to do this.

I suddenly grabbed the director and shoved him toward the man in the chair. Surprised and caught off guard, he tumbled forward into the view of the camera. He tripped into the bound man but caught himself as the chair rocked from the collision. The two techs looked up from their work, confused as to what was happening.

As the director turned to face me, his eyes shining with confused anger, I stepped into the halo of light, grinning like a madman.

In one swift motion, I drove the chainsaw into the director's stomach, muscles straining as I lifted his body up into the screaming blade. Blood and flesh exploded onto my mask in waves of grisly carnage, the warm fluid coating the fabric with streaks of gore.

The director's mouth was open in a silent howl, blood running down his chin as the chainsaw chewed up his insides. He made the mistake of grabbing the churning blade, desperate to remove the source of agony. His fingers were shred in a splash of blood and bone and one of his thumbs whizzed off into the darkness.

I gave the chainsaw some more juice and tilted the blade down, letting my victim slide to the ground in a pool of his own innards. He looked up at me, confusion painting his face as he screamed, unable to believe what I had done.

I didn't hesitate.

I brought the chainsaw down and severed his head.

And fuck, did it feel *good*.

Blood gushed onto the dirty floor, spouts of thick red pooling around the dead body. I bent down and picked up the head by the hair, the snarling chainsaw in my other hand. I stepped toward the camera and shoved the mutilated face into the lens.

"You see this? You see what I did to this man?!" I yelled into the camera. The two techs were frozen with disbelief, unmoving as shock held them still.

I lowered the head and looked directly into the lens. "This man was the mind behind the...the *show* you all enjoy so much. He constructed this bloody theater, built a foundation of entertainment around his own violent tastes."

I suddenly smiled into the camera. "But I'm in charge now. From now on, I call the shots. I understand your need for this." I splayed my hands out at the bloody floor. "I understand your desire to partake in this gory display of death. I used to be like you, sitting behind my computer, paying for tools of torture...I'm not here to change that. In fact, I'm going to make it easier. I'm going to lower the price on the site, I'm going to host more events, and I'm going to raise the quality of what you're paying for. I want to give you the performance you deserve."

I took a step back and raised my arms. "As a sign of good will, I will refund all of your money for today's little hiccup. I understand that this wasn't what you expected to see today...I apologize for that...and I'll be in touch with all of you very soon."

I looked up from the camera at the two tech guys. "Shut it down." They didn't move.

I revved the chainsaw I was still holding. "I said shut it the *fuck* down." The cameraman scrambled in a panic and the red light on the camera went off. Neither of them moved, just stared at me, waiting for me to make a move or say something. They seemed terrified, the disruption of their practiced routine rattling their senses into shock.

"How much did he pay you?" I asked, throwing a thumb over my shoulder at the headless body.

The sound guy licked his lips and fought to get himself under control. I found his fear almost comical when examining his line of work.

"Two thousand a shoot," he finally managed to mumble.

I looked at the cameraman. "Same for you?"

He nodded.

I shut off the chainsaw and tossed it to the side, "I'll double that if you stay and work for me. All I ask is that you show me the ropes of this business. Get me up to speed on running the site, who the contacts are, how you guys scope out the victims. If you do that, I'll give you four grand a shoot. Each. I know you're probably shocked I just cut your boss' head off, but I promise you don't have to worry about me...acting out again. That was a necessary action I needed to make in order to get my foot in the door. So what do you say? Are you ready to help me build the most successful snuff site on the deep web?"

They two men looked at each other and I saw a silent conversation pass between their eyes. After a second, they turned back to me.

"We're in."

I smiled. "Fantastic."

I turned around and walked to the man in the chair. He had been silent throughout the whole ordeal, but now that my attention was on him, he began to whimper, unsure of what I had in store for him. I squatted down in front of him and looked up into his eyes. He was probably thirty-five, a good-looking guy with short brown hair. I reached up and placed my hand over his chest, causing him to cry out and squirm away from my touch.

"Your heart is beating so fast," I said softly. I reached up and pulled the gag from his mouth. The man gasped in lungfuls of air and ran his tongue over his teeth, grateful to be free of the cloth.

"Please, I'll do whatever you want, please don't kill me," he bumbled, fresh tears pouring from his eyes.

I pinched his cheek and smiled. "Don't worry, buddy, it's your lucky day. You're old product, a relic from previous management. I have no use for you."

I paused, "Unless..." I cocked my head. "Unless you want to come work for me?"

His eyes grew wide and I could tell he was struggling to find an answer that wouldn't end in bloodshed.

I shook my head, "Ah, forget it. Don't worry about it. You're not cut out for this kind of life. Go home, you're free to leave." I reached into my shoe and retrieved the knife from under my foot. I cut the man's ropes and pulled him from the chair.

I dug into my pocket and fished out my wallet. I handed the man two hundred dollars in twenties and told him to give it to the driver who was waiting upstairs.

"Tell him to take you home. Tell him it's The Boss' orders."

The man looked at me like he couldn't believe it. I couldn't blame the poor bastard.

"Can I trust you'll keep this between us?" I said, leaning toward the man. "You're not going to go to the police about this little misunderstanding, are you?"

He shook his head violently.

"Good, now get out of here," I said, pushing him toward the stairs. As I watched him go, I felt a calm settle over me.

This is where I was supposed to be. This is what I was supposed to be doing. I felt that familiar darkness stir inside of me and flow down my body and out my fingertips, finally free after years of suppression. I was finally whole. I was finally being honest with myself and it felt incredible. I felt like I could finally breathe after years of suffocation.

I had a lot to learn, a dangerous and haunting road ahead of me. I had taken a huge risk doing what I did, but a necessary one. Before I came to this place, I had made up my mind that I was going to try to take over this business. My hunger of late had grown to a point of uncontrollable lust and I knew this was the only way I could live with it. I knew I could create something truly vicious given the opportunity. I was nervous, yes, but I was ready for it, excited to take the first steps in my new life. I was determined to build the most successful snuff site the Internet had ever seen. I was going to revolutionize the word "torture." I was going to bring new meaning to murder. I was going to build a kingdom around me, a kingdom I would rule.

I was going to build an empire of death.

4

The Goat Room

My phone buzzed in my pocket. I reached for it, only half-listening to the sales meeting I was in. My boss was rattling on, stressing about how we needed to push numbers, increase our revenue, the usual slog. The other eight salesmen around the table looked as bored as I did, staring with half-lidded eyes, mouths slightly ajar. We heard the same pitch every year and honestly we were tired of it. If someone was dead-set against buying, there was literally nothing we could do about it.

I loosened my tie and checked my phone under the table. The number was blocked. My heart skipped a beat. Could this be?

It was a text. It read: *Congratulations, you've been accepted.*

I wanted to jump up and pump my fist into the air, excitement rising in my chest like lava from a volcano. I couldn't believe it. After all this time, I had finally done it. After all my hard work and dedication, all those times I went the extra mile and thought no one noticed, it felt good to know it was all worth something. It felt great. The possibilities this would open up, the life it could lead to…it was everything I had ever wanted.

I shot a glance at my boss at the head of the room (still rambling and pointing to a pie chart on the projector) and quickly sent a message back:

When do I start?

I placed the phone on my leg, drumming the tabletop as I waited for an answer. I forced myself to breathe. I felt like I could burst for joy. I was tempted to give my coworkers the finger and walk out of the meeting, but I resisted. I could stay professional about this. I wanted to call my wife and tell her the good news. She would be so proud of me. And the kids!? Wait until they heard what a hotshot their old man was about to become!

I was so proud of myself. I was setting such a good example for my family. I was really doing this. And to think they picked ME?! I couldn't help but smile thinking about it. I always knew that I would make something of myself some day. And my time had come.

My phone buzzed again and I quickly checked the reply text:

We start tonight. Meet at Quincy Office at 8 PM for orientation. Feel free to bring your family. And well done!

I felt like I could die with excitement. Tonight!? My guts bubbled and I shifted in my seat. There was so much to think about, so much to prepare. I thought about what lie ahead of me and worms worked their way into my stomach. Starting something new was always nerve-wracking, but I had wanted this for so long!

I pulled up my wife's number and sent her a quick text, not able to help myself:

They chose me!!!!! Orientation is tonight at 8! U and the kids can come! SO EXCITED!!!

The finality of it hit me then. Something about sharing the

news with my wife made it real. This was really happening. I was really going to do this. Our lives were about to change forever. I was about to lead my family into the next tier of class. People would respect us, look up to us even, and say, "Wow, good for you, you really stuck with it and it paid off."

I stood up suddenly, pocketing my phone. My boss and fellow salesmen looked up at me, eyebrows cocked. I looked around at their washed-out faces, almost feeling sympathy. How many of these poor saps would die at this job? How many of them had already settled into the monotony of what their lives had become? That's what separated myself from them. I strove to do great things, I pushed myself and walked that extra mile. I had passions, fire in my chest.

"Do…you want to say something, Thomas?"

I blinked at my boss, staring down the long table at his expectant face. I almost started laughing. I couldn't help it. Suddenly this job seemed hilarious. Suddenly being in this room and listening to my boss give me a pep talk was *comical*. This guy really thought what he was saying was important! HA! As if, right?! The urgency of which he stressed bumping our numbers, the way he shook his finger at us…why, it was a real gut-buster!

"Thomas?" he called to me, finger hovering over the all-important pie chart.

I looked around at everyone, a small smile planted on my lips, "Uh…" I snorted, shaking my head, "Uh, I think I'm done here, guys. It's been a real pleasure, but, uh," I started laughing, not able to hold it in any longer, "but I got better things lined up! Take care now, you hear?" And with that, I marched myself out the door, followed by shocked stares.

When I got home, my wife met me at the door with a big hug and a sparkling smile. She told me she had left work as soon as she got my message. She was beaming, ushering me inside and taking my coat, compliments bubbling from her lips. She told me she was just *so proud* of me and all the hard work I had put into this. She told me I was special, that she had always known I was, and finally other people had noticed.

I asked her where the kids were, smiling myself, the excitement and rush still fueling my emotions. She told me they were at school, but she had called the principal and notified her that she needed to pull them early. They would be excited, too; I just knew they would. I asked her when she was going to pick them up, and she said soon.

"What should I wear tonight? Are we going to be there for the whole orientation? Will they let us stay?" she asked, running into the bedroom and pulling out dresses from the closet.

I shrugged, grinning like an idiot. "I don't know, hun. I guess we'll find out."

She spun around, a small blue dress pressed to her frame. "How's this? Is this good? Oh, Thomas, I'm just so happy I could burst!" She ran over to me giggling and kissed me, her arms around my neck. She looked up into my eyes, admiration shining from her own.

"Can I tell everyone?"

I laughed. "They'll all be at orientation! You can tell them then before we start! You know how these things go; we've been to enough of them, right?"

She smiled, a picture of beauty from ear to ear. "I know, I know, it's just so wonderful!"

I smiled back at her. "Good things are happening to us, baby; stick with me and you'll go places."

She kissed me again and then looked up at me, her face serious. "Are you nervous? Are you going to be OK?"

I was nervous. I was really nervous. But it was the good kind, the churning anticipation of just wanting to *get to it.*

"I'm fine, honey," I said reassuringly. "I've waited a long time for this. It's what I've always wanted. It's what I want for our family. I want our kids to look back and say, 'My dad really made something of himself.' I want a better life for you, for us." I hugged her tight and kissed the top of her head. "It's going to be a good night."

We picked up the kids together, my two boys, from their middle school. They climbed into the back seat, positively *beaming* that they had gotten a half-day. I wanted to take them out, have some fun, celebrate.

As my wife pulled the car out of the school parking lot, I leaned over my seat, grinning, and looked at my children.

"I bet you guys are wondering why you got to leave school early." I couldn't help but feel a little smug. They weren't going to believe this.

They both shook their heads.

"Well," I said, folding my hands, "Your ol' dad is going to ORIENTATION tonight! I've been accepted! Isn't that great, kids?"

Both my son's mouths dropped in unison, followed shortly by whoops of excitement. I laughed and clapped my hands, enjoying their reaction to the news.

"Do we get to go?!" my eldest asked.

I nodded, "You sure do. All of you get to go."

Well, that did it. They screamed, the hype just too much. I laughed until tears rolled down my face, watching the delight ripple across their faces like shock waves. It's wonderful to have kids. Often times they say or react in the ways adults aren't allowed.

Finally, I raised my hands and told them to settle down, still wiping the tears from my eyes. I told them we were going to have a family day of fun to celebrate and then after that, I was taking them to dinner. More eruptions of joy followed (along with a few "this is the best day EVERs") and I chuckled again, asking them what they would like to do first.

After some discussion and negotiation among my family, we decided that we were going to go to the movies. After that, it was off to our favorite burger joint for dinner and milkshakes.

In truth, I was grateful to fill my day with activities. It'd take my mind off the hours between now and 8 PM. I felt like if I didn't do something to pass the time, I'd explode with anticipation. I just wanted it to be time already and start this amazing new phase of my life. I wanted to get to that moment where I could look at my family and say, "Guys, I did it."

We spent the afternoon in the movie theater, slurping down overpriced soda and munching on stale popcorn. It was awesome. During the movie I would catch my wife looking at me, her face lit by the large screen. I'd look back at her and wink, both of us sharing a loving smile. I could tell just how much this meant to her, how much she appreciated me in that moment.

After the movie, I wiped butter from my kids' fingers and ushered them back to the car. Despite having just consumed a barrel of popcorn, my sons moaned that they were *sta-a-a-arving!* Having not eaten but a few kernels myself, I was glad to hear it. I checked my watch and saw that we had two hours before we had to be at the Quincy office.

We drove across town, our ride filled with commentary about the movie we had just seen. (My sons loved it; my wife, not so much.) I argued with my oldest about some of the plot points, goading him a little bit just because I was in such a good mood. My wife shook her head, smiling to herself and enjoying the positive energy that sparked around us.

Thirty minutes later, I pulled into the restaurant and parked. Already shouting out what they wanted to eat, the boys bounded from the car. I opened my door and got out, telling them to settle down, that the burgers weren't going anywhere.

As I watched my wife follow our kids, it hit me like a shotgun blast.

You're going to the Goat Room tonight.

I bent over, suddenly in need of air, and sucked in the evening sky. I blinked a few times, clearing my head, the realization crippling my mind. I pulled in another couple breaths and chuckled. The gravity of the night before me was astounding.

At that moment, I felt like the luckiest guy in the world.

I looked up and saw my wife calling me, asking if I was OK. I straightened and gave her a thumbs-up and a big smile. I walked to them at the front of the restaurant, taking in my surroundings, letting the setting sun cast its warm rays across my face. *What a time to be alive.*

We got a booth and ordered our food (I got my usual Buffalo Burger), watching the day fade into night through the windows.

We chomped through the patties, my kids devouring theirs with alarming speed, and I ordered us all a round of milkshakes (as promised). I didn't think they needed any more sugar buzzing through their system, but what the heck; we were celebrating, weren't we?

As I watched my youngest slurp down the last of his frothy treat, I wiped his face with a napkin and checked my watch. My eyes met my wife's and I nodded to her.

"You ready?"

I paid the bill and herded my family back to the car. From the restaurant, it was only a ten-minute drive to the Quincy office. As the night blurred past the windows, I felt myself grow quiet. My wife seemed to notice and did her best to shush the kids. She knew I needed some serenity, the weight of the evening approaching fast. She squeezed my arm and offered me a smile. I returned it and focused on the road. I was grateful for her support, grateful for my wonderful family.

"You doing OK?" she asked quietly.

I nodded. "Better than ever. This is just a big step for us, you know? It's a lot to take in."

She squeezed my arm again. "You know how proud the kids and I are of you, right?"

I glanced in the mirror at my sons (now with their phones out), and peace came over me. One of the biggest fears of a father is to fail his family. I knew I would never have to worry about that again. I had done it. I had taken the final step to ensure a good life for them, a comfortable life. Knowing that, I gripped the steering wheel a little harder and grinned.

We pulled into the Quincy office, its many floors towering above the parking lot. I found us a spot and noticed a few familiar faces already entering the building. The kids took notice as well and began to unbuckle and call out to their friends. I let them go, turning the car off and smiling as they raced to their buddies.

The cool night air tickled my skin and I felt a kind of euphoric awe settle over me as I got out of the car. I walked around to my wife, taking her hand in mine. As we walked inside, we waved to the Parkers and Kleins, both of whom had just arrived.

The interior of the building was air-conditioned and I nodded my hello to the security guard at the front desk. My wife signed us in (she always insisted on being the one to sign us in) and we went to the elevator. There was already a small crowd gathered around them, all waiting to ascend. I spotted my kids excitedly talking to their friends and I guessed they were already spilling the news.

Troy saw me and made his way over to us. He shook my hand and exclaimed, "Thomas, I heard your kids talking, I heard YOU got the promotion! Is it true?"

My wife answered before I could, admiration lacing her words. "It sure is, Troy; I always knew he'd get it one day. He's such a dedicated man, how could he NOT get it?"

I blushed as Troy slapped me on the back and congratulated me. He called his own family over and told them the news, earning me another round of thumbs-up and courteous congrats. At that point, the news was spreading around the lobby and I was suddenly assaulted by a barrage of handshakes and hugs from all our friends and acquaintances. They all wished me luck and I detected notes of jealousy from more than one of them.

Finally, we piled into the elevators and pushed the button to take us to the top. The whole way up I got slaps on the back and smiles, an endless stream of affirmation. It was a good feeling, a great feeling. I looked at my kids and saw their eyes glowing with respect for their ol' dad. I reached out and ruffled their hair.

A *ding!* announced our arrival at the top and we poured out, the doors closing behind us to collect the next batch in the lobby. My shoes clicked on the marble floors and I saw Kent and Bradly (both rocking beautiful gray suits, I might add) already waiting for everyone.

They held up their hands, smiling and quieting everyone. White light illuminated the hallway, casting a glare off the floor that almost stung my eyes. I blinked and focused on what Kent was saying.

"All right everyone, settle down!" he announced with a grin. "I know it's a big night tonight, but we've all done this before. You know the drill, follow Bradly to the conference room and we'll get started in just a little bit."

He turned to me. "Except for you, Thomas! You come with me and I'll start prepping you for orientation. When you feel like you're ready, we'll join the others in the conference room."

I turned to my family and gave them all a big hug. I kissed my sons on the head and my wife on the lips. She beamed up at me and gave me one quick nod. *Go get 'em.*

The tide of people flowed down the hall, led by Bradly,

toward the conference room. I went the opposite way, led by Kent, who brought me to his office. A beautiful polished oak desk dominated the room, the walls lined with oil paintings nailed to dark wood. It was quite the contrast to the modern marble design of the hallway and as the door shut behind me, I felt like I was in a different building.

Kent waved for me to take a seat on the plump leather chair opposite the desk. With a contented sigh, he plopped himself down in front of his computer and leaned back, folding his hands on his chest. I took my seat across from him and licked my lips, feeling a little nervous.

"Are you nervous?" Kent asked, grinning.

I chuckled. "Yeah, I think so. But that's a good thing, I think. I'm excited."

Kent nodded approvingly. "Good, good. We had a lot of applicants this quarter, more than we ever had. That makes your selection all the more noteworthy. I want you to know you should be very proud of yourself."

I felt myself blush. "Thank you, sir; that means a lot. I feel very honored to have been chosen and I hope I won't let you down. I must say, I feel very confident in myself."

Kent tapped the top of the desk. "Excellent! Now let's get down to business. I know you're aware how the first part of this goes, correct? I'll take you to the conference room and swear you in. After that, you'll say a few words to everyone and assure them of your dedication. After that, Bradly and I will escort you...well...I think you know the rest."

I nodded. "Then I go to the Goat Room."

Kent grunted. "Yes, then we go to the Goat Room."

I leaned forward. "Can my family come with me?"

Kent eyed me and I could see gears turning behind his eyes. "Are you sure you want them to?"

I nodded enthusiastically. "Yes, if that's OK with you. It might be vain, but I want to show my kids what hard work will get you."

Kent shrugged. "Well, it's fine by me. It won't be the first time a new promotee has asked to have his family join him."

"Thank you, sir."

He waved my thanks away. "Think nothing of it. Now, do you have any questions for me? I'm assuming you know what happens after you're swore in and we move you? It's a silly question. I'm well aware you understand, but it's something I have to ask."

"I understand," I said. "And I have only one question…it's about my family…"

Kent cut me off with a curt slice of the hand. "Worry not, Thomas. You've ensured a better life for not just yourself, but for them as well. The very fact that you're sitting here has already sealed that."

"Again, thank you, sir."

He sat in silence for a moment, letting the words sink in. Then he stood up and ushered me to the door.

"You ready?"

"Yes, sir."

He led me out the door and down the hall, our footsteps echoing off the walls. I realized my palms were sweating and I wiped them on my pants. Everything I had worked so hard for was finally coming to fruition.

We entered a large room that was dimly lit. I looked to my left and saw the familiar stadium seating filled with shadowed faces, all excitedly watching me. Kent led me to a small table under a spotlight. As soon as we crossed the threshold of light, uproarious applause shook the room. I couldn't help but smile, staring out at the familiar faces. I felt like I was in a college classroom about to give some freshmen a lecture that would change their lives.

Bradly was waiting for us by the table, clapping along with the rest of them. I squinted and saw my wife and kids in the front row, beaming from ear to ear. I gave them a little wave and centered myself behind the table with Kent and Bradly standing at either shoulder.

They let the applause continue for a few moments before Kent raised his hands, quieting them. He walked around to the front of the table and began to speak.

"Good evening everyone and thank you for coming! Tonight marks the thirty-second promotion! Tonight we honor our devoted friend Thomas! Let's all give him a hearty congratulations for all his hard work and contributions!"

More applause spilled from the crowd and I began to feel like a celebrity. The room eventually settled and Kent turned to me, picking up a small black book from the table. He motioned for me to put my hand on it. I knew the drill. I had watched the thirty-one others before me go through the same ritual. I couldn't believe I was standing up here, no longer just an observer.

I placed my hand on the book, already knowing the words that came next.

"Do you, Thomas James Martin, swear to uphold your position to the best of your abilities?" Kent asked loudly, his voice echoing into the now-silent room.

"I do."

"Do you swear to give your life, if need be, in order to further our cause?"

"I do."

"Do you swear upon your faith and family that you will proceed with the purest intentions?"

"I do."

Kent then nodded, giving me a hidden wink, and passed the book over to Bradly, who took it and motioned for me to place my hand on the cover again.

"Lastly, do you swear your loyalty and motivations are in accordance with our guidelines and that you will see this through until you have completed your task?"

"I do."

He cleared his throat. "Thomas James Martin, I hereby congratulate you on your promotion, thank you for all you have done thus far, and pray for your continued dedication through all you endure."

"Thank you, sir," I responded.

Bradly glanced at Kent and they both nodded. The book was lowered and I was deafened by cheers and whistles. I smiled so hard I thought I'd rip my face in half. I winked at my wife and waved a hand to the crowd. Bradly and Kent both shook my hand and offered more congratulations. Bradly motioned me forward, offering the floor to me so that I could address everyone.

The room quieted as I licked my lips and prepared the words on my tongue.

"It is such an honor to be standing here tonight," I said, my voice strong and sure. "I owe so much of this success to the patience and guidance of these two men right here." I pointed to Kent and Bradly, who nodded their thanks to me.

"I also want to thank my family," I continued, "for their undying love. I want to thank you all for your kindness tonight. I promise not to let you down. I promise I will see this through to the very end if need be." I paused, scanning the room, slowly taking it all in, meeting everyone's eyes. "I love each and every one of you. I believe in what we do. I believe in you. I always have. And tonight I ask that you believe in me."

I quieted the applause before it could start, shaking my finger at them. "One more thing, one more very important thing before I depart."

They waited, hanging in suspense, excited faces in dim light.

I raised my hand into the air. "I swear to you I will be the one you've been waiting for!"

The crowd went wild.

Kent and Bradly motioned for me. It was time to go. I waved to the people and exited the room to cheers and whistles.

It was time.

It was time to go to the Goat Room.

I had a sack over my head, the fabric blocking my sight completely. Kent was silent as he drove the van out of the city. Bradly was driving another one that held my family. I remained quiet, unsure if it was appropriate to speak. I felt the road vibrating through the floor as we trekked through the night. This was it. No going back now. I swallowed and felt my heart skip a few beats.

I don't know how long we drove. This was part of the promotion ceremony that I had never been allowed to see. I knew what we were doing, but I was clueless as to how long it would take to get there. I wiped my hands over my knees, scrubbing more sweat from them. I summoned the faces of my family. They probably had to be blinded as well. I smiled inwardly, imagining my kids with black bags over their heads. They were probably complaining, giving Bradly a hard time.

Time stretched and the darkness inside the hood became my world. Thoughts about the coming hours filled the black. I was confident in myself. I had always been a strong person and tonight I was going to prove that. I reflected on all the smiling faces and applause I had received. They were counting on me. I wasn't going to let them down.

Finally, after what felt like a few hours, I felt the van jerk to a halt and my ears picked up the spray of gravel under the tires.

"We're here," Kent announced, breaking the long silence. "Give Bradly a moment. He's bringing your family inside now."

I sat in the darkness as the van idled. My stomach churned as nerves wormed their way through my intestines. I took a breath to steady myself. I was ready.

"Let's go," Kent finally said, pulling the cloth from my eyes.

I rubbed my face, letting my vision adjust. We were at the end of a gravel road in the middle of an open field. In the far distance I saw woods swaying in the night sky. A large single-story building stood before us, its plain concrete walls bare of windows. Despite its sprawling size, I only saw one entrance. I glanced at Kent and saw he was looking hard at me.

"You ready to do this?"

I nodded. "Of course."

We exited the van, the small rocks crunching beneath my feet. A yellow moon hung fat in the sky like an infected boil on dark skin. I followed Kent up to the entrance, noticing a few more cars parked in front of the building, along with the van my family had come in. They were already inside, waiting for me. I wiped a hand across my face. *Steady* now.

Kent pushed through the large black door, the entrance lit by hanging fluorescent lights. I didn't see anyone, the interior as bare as the concrete walls that lined it. The air was musky, some long-forgotten odor rising from the ground. I wrinkled my nose and followed Kent down a long hall, our feet echoing across the bare concrete floors. The ceiling was high over our heads, lights hanging from it like dead bodies, motionless in the still air.

"Where is everyone?" I asked.

"Waiting for you," Kent answered without turning.

We turned down another hallway and were stopped by two large double doors. They pulsed with red light and I could hear sound from the other side. Candles illuminated the space, stuck into the walls like knives, hot wax running down the cement like dried semen.

Kent turned to me. "Here we go. Ready?"

I nodded, pushing down my nerves.

Kent pushed the doors open and heat wafted across my face. The room before me was huge, circular in shape, its walls curving like a swollen stomach. A bright red light lit the space, shadowing everything beneath it in an eerie glow.

Seated along the far wall was The Word, his tall figure hidden by flowing red cloth that draped over his head and ran down to pool on the floor. He didn't move under his garment, giving him a strange, statue-like appearance. Seeing him sit upon his bone-white throne, I wondered what he looked like, the fabric revealing nothing but a gentle pull around the mouth when he breathed.

Sitting to the left of him was my family, somber, but I could see a muffled excitement underneath their watchful eyes. Spanning out past my family were the rest of the Executives. They sat in their perfectly pressed business suits, eyes trained on me as I stood in the door. It was the first time I had seen them, knew who they were, and a couple of the faces surprised me.

The floor was covered with red markings, circles and hard angles crisscrossing along the concrete. Candles littered the floor, rising from the ground like broken teeth. The air was heavy and thick, almost fog-like, the red light obscuring my vision slightly.

I felt something prod my back and I turned to see Kent motioning me forward. Hesitantly, I moved toward the middle of the room and stood before The Word. I wondered where everyone else was, the prior thirty-one who had been promoted. I didn't see them anywhere. Perhaps they'd come later? My eyes circled the room, meeting the gaze of the higher-ups. I wasn't going to let them down. They'd see.

"Hello, dear Thomas," The Word said, breaking the pregnant silence. His voice rolled across the space between us like a bulldozer.

I bowed my head slightly, a sign of respect. I couldn't believe he was actually speaking to me. It was hard to not pop with pride. My children would one day tell stories of this night, every detail of the tale spooling out in front of me in real time.

"Before we begin, I'd like to thank you for your unwavering loyalty. It has not gone unnoticed and tonight you will reap the rewards of your efforts and commitment to us." The Word shifted slightly, the cloth covering his head wrinkling in the haze. The lack of any eyeholes gave his appearance an almost eerie look, as if under that robe, something inhuman dwelt.

"Thank you, sir," I said, hoping it was OK to speak.

He dipped his head. "I'm happy to see your family here. They should witness what their father and husband is about to do. They should be very proud of you, as am I. Now, are you ready to begin? Are you prepared in both mind and body?"

"Yes," I said, steeling my voice.

He spread his arms, the red cloth swallowing his limbs. "Let us begin then."

A door opened to the right of me, one I hadn't noticed, and two huge men stepped into the room. They were stripped down to their waist, their faces covered with hoods, one white, the other black. Bulging muscles coiled across their shoulders as they carried in a large chest decorated with flakes of black and gold. They came and stood beside me, gently lowering the chest.

When it was set, they turned to The Word and waited for his signal. My legs felt weak and I forced my knees to stop clacking together. This was what I had been waiting for. This is what it all came down to. I had talked the talk and now I had to walk the walk.

The Word stood, the red gown rippling across his body like dripping gore, and spread his arms again. "Thomas, you were born a man and now must be reformed into the Image of our Lord. Kneel and be baptized with the blood of our God so that your blood may be one with his!"

The men with hoods pushed me to my knees and I felt sweat bead along my forehead. It was suddenly excruciatingly hot in the room, the red light warming the air like fire. The ground was hard under my knees, my joints popping as I took my place, head raised and ready.

The man with the white hood opened the chest and took something out. He came and stood behind me, cradling my head with his bicep as he placed something in my mouth.

I took the funnel into my throat, holding it steady with my teeth. He reached back into the chest and pulled out a clear jug that sloshed with fresh goat blood. I gripped the funnel harder with my teeth. The jug he held had to be at least two liters and it was filled to the brim.

The man in the white hood took his place behind me and wrapped a meaty arm around my neck, holding me in place. My heart danced in my chest like a wild drum. Sweat trickled down my spine in anticipation. I could feel my kids watching me.

The hooded man took the top off with his teeth and tipped the mouth of the jug into the funnel. Blood sloshed into my mouth, taking me by surprise. It was warmer than I had imagined. I closed my eyes as it streamed across my tongue, flowed down my throat, and filled my stomach. It tasted like burnt metal, the thick liquid coating my insides.

More...more....more...

I began to sputter, opening my eyes and realizing I still had over half the jug to drink. My stomach felt distended, a bloated bubble of sick nausea. I began to cramp and I had to fight my gag reflex as I ingested the blood, feeling it mix in my gut with bitter acid.

The man tightened his grip around my neck as he felt my body tense. I fought to keep the fluid down. I felt like I was drowning. I forced my eyes shut again, my stomach howling as it continued to fill. I hiccuped and burped, spraying red out the side of my mouth. It felt like the blood was rising back up in my throat, trying to escape.

Please, I begged myself, *don't throw up.*

Suddenly, my abdomen hitched and I felt the contents of my stomach hurtle up my throat toward my mouth. The man holding me felt it, too, because he tightened his grip, locking my mouth shut around the funnel. He shoved a finger to block the hole just as blood and half-digested buffalo burger rocketed into my mouth. With no exit, the bile and mixed blood exploded out of my nostrils like gory fireworks.

I choked and struggled to breathe, my nose burning with stomach acid. I squeezed my watering eyes shut and forced myself to swallow the vomit back down. My body screamed in protest and I let out another gooey burp, traces of stomach bile leaking from the corners of my mouth.

Suddenly, the funnel was removed and I fell forward onto my hands, gasping for air. I took a few steady breaths, testing my body and wiping my mouth with the back of my hand. Tears leaked down my face from the revolt my body had put up.

Well, I thought, *the easy part is over...*

I crawled back to my knees, still sucking in the hot air, feeling my stomach gurgle. The Word was sitting again, his figure motionless. Kent and Bradly were standing on his right, watching me with intensity. I looked toward my family and my wife offered me a secret smile. My youngest gave me a small thumbs-up, a grin plastered across his little face.

"The Blood of the Goat is now your own," The Word boomed from his throne, "for change starts on the inside, and from the inside, one can change anything he desires."

He motioned to the man in the black hood. "Thomas, you have ingested His blood, filling your mind and heart with His warmth. Now, reflect on these miracles as you transform into His image."

I gritted my teeth as the man in the white hood held me still again. Black Hood reached into the chest and I shut my eyes, preparing for the miracle. I felt my lips tremble and I bit down on them. I needed to be strong. My family was watching.

Black Hood grabbed my right arm and began sawing it off at the elbow.

I screamed, eyes bulging as pain exploded like thunder. My arm convulsed as the muscles were severed from bone, the hacksaw chewing through my skin and spraying blood across my face. The corners of my vision blackened as the saw screeched across bone, sending lightning bolts of pain charging across my body.

And then it was over. I fought to maintain consciousness, the agony unbearable. White Hood didn't release his grip. I watched through bloodshot eyes as Black Hood set the bloody hacksaw down and pulled a blowtorch from the chest. A blue tongue of flame poked from the spout as he brought it to my squirting stump and began to cauterize the open skin.

I screamed even louder, the pain beyond anything I thought possible. Seconds later, I blacked out.

When I came to, head pounding and vision blurry, Black Hood was cutting off my other arm. After he sliced the last strip of skin from my new stump, my mind went dark again.

The world swam, red color and hot air. I was on my back, White Hood staring down at me. He gently slapped my face, rousing me from the nightmare darkness. I blinked at him and tried to speak, but the words died in my throat.

White Hood looked up and told Black Hood to keep going, that I was OK. I wanted to see my wife's face, I wanted her to tell me the pain would end soon. I knew it was going to be bad, but this was excruciating, far worse than I ever imagined. I tried to block it out, telling myself that it was almost over, that this is what I wanted.

Black Hood began to saw my legs off, the blade spewing through my flesh, just above the knees.

I passed out in a torrent of misery and pain, my howls dying in the air.

I coughed up a mouthful of mucus and blood as I regained consciousness. My body was a furnace of agony. Something itchy was covering my face. My vision was limited. Heat. My limbs felt funny. Someone was talking, a voice muffled by my dreamlike state. I wanted to throw up. My head felt like it had been stuffed with burning coals.

I tried to climb to my hands and knees, blinking the darkness away, but something wasn't right and I fell back down. I shook my head and felt hands grip me and gently pull me up.

I shook my thundering head, the black pulling away from my vision like a spider web.

Metal hooves had been screwed into my elbows and knees, my body slumped and weak as I stood on all fours. The transformation was complete. I had done it. The itchy mask covering my face must be the skin of a goat, my eyes now seeing out of the empty eye sockets. I felt my head was bare and guessed they had already shaved it and implanted the horns in my skull with a hot knife.

I steadied myself on my new limbs, my hooves clacking against the cement floor. My body shook with effort, my muscles weak and exhausted. I ground my teeth and forced myself to stay upright. I could feel the goat horns digging into my skull. The skin pulled over my face smelled like rot and scraped against my cheeks like sandpaper.

The Word stood and I suddenly noticed there were more people in the room than before. Well...*people* was a stretch. To the right of The Word were the thirty-one who had come before me, the thirty-one who had gone through what I had and failed. They shuffled where they were, heads held low to the ground.

A herd of unworthy goats.

Their hooves shot echoes across the walls, an array of once-human-beings just like I had been. Men, women, all with goat faces pulled over their own, horns jutting from their bare heads, downcast with shame. Leashes were tied to collars around their throats, the ends of which were held by Kent and Bradly.

The Word leaned forward on his throne, assessing the state I was in. White Hood and Black Hood were planted on either side of me, arms crossed. I stared straight ahead, doing my best to stay upright.

"Well done, Thomas," The Word said finally. A smattering of claps rounded the room, the Execs in suits nodding their approval. My wife had tears running down her cheeks and a smile that shone like the sun. My kids were slapping their palms together in awe at my resolution.

The Word waited for the room to silence. When it calmed, his voice became deadly somber.

"The rest is up to you now. You know the words?"

I nodded, feeling the weight of my new horns pressing my chin to the floor. I worked my jaw so I could see properly out of the eyeholes of the goat skin. *Almost there,* I thought, *I've almost done it.*

The Word leaned back on his throne, scanning the room with unseen eyes, "This is it, my friends. Not a word will be spoken during this time. Thomas needs complete silence and total focus. I think we can afford him that, yes?" He turned his covered head to me. "When you're ready."

The two Hoods backed away against the far wall and the red light above us dimmed. I noticed now that the scarlet symbols beneath my hooves were glowing. Candles lined the edges to form a circle.

I took my place at the center of the pentagram.

I closed my eyes, concentrating. I pushed all thoughts from my brain, emptying my head. I focused on breathing, on the heat that swirled around me. I saw the red light filtering through my eyelids and let it dance behind my eyes. Sweat and blood dripped off my new face and fell to the floor. My limbs screamed in their new form, but I silenced the tormented flesh.

I drew in a long breath and then spoke, my voice strong and determined:

"Dear Father, Lord God of the Goat, I come before you, not as Thomas, but as one of your flock. I have cast aside my worldly form. I long to be one with you. I have consumed the holy blood, I have whittled my body to mirror your Holy Image. I am yours, my life, my love, my future, my suffering. I beg you to return to the earth and lead us into glorious paradise. We stand ready, humbled, and in awe of you. I have displayed my undying devotion to you and my desire to follow in your footsteps. I pray of you, please, return to us now and lead us into your kingdom!"

As the last of my plea left my mouth, the room shook slightly and a soft cry went up from the bystanders. Their eyes went wide and they looked around at one another, mouths agape.

My heart pounded in my chest as the pentagram flared and blood began to seep from the edges. I couldn't believe it. This has never happened before, not a single person had conjured any kind of reaction.

The herd of human goats looked up at me with shock and awe, their eyes bulging under their masks. The Word stood, his hands gripping the armrests of his throne as the floor quivered beneath us. The light flickered above and a few of the candles went out, a sudden wind stirring the air.

I shuffled my hooves on the floor, trying to keep upright as the quake continued, blood pooling from the symbols around me. Even through the pain, I felt a smile creep across my face.

I always knew I could do it. My wife had her arms around our boys, a look of utter amazement plastered to her face.

And then the commotion ceased.

The ground solidified beneath me and the red light stopped flickering, returning to its constant warm glow. The dust froze in the air and then gently wafted back to the ground, the wind leaving as quickly as it had come. I watched in horror as the pentagram sucked the blood back into its borders and the glow faded.

And we were left in silence.

"No, no we were so close!" The Word roared suddenly. "What did we do wrong!? What did we do?!"

The Execs cast their eyes to the ground, devastating disappointment leaking from every face. Kent and Bradly shook their heads at me, frowns pulling their mouths to the floor.

"WE WERE SO CLOSE!" The Word continued to scream. "WE THOUGHT THIS WAS THE ONE! WHAT DID WE DO WRONG!?"

Kent raised his hands defensively, "Sir, we followed the bloodline down to him. We were sure it was the right line. We've narrowed it down so much, it HAS to be him!"

The Word waved a hand at me from under his robe. "I'm disgusted by the sight of you. Someone get him out of my sight! Put him in the pens out back with the rest of them!"

"No!" I shouted suddenly, "No, let me try again! I can do this, I know I can! Please!"

Black Hood was grabbing me, dragging me back and away from The Word, growling at me to shut up. I felt something clasp around my throat and I was suddenly jerked forward.

I had been leashed.

No, NO!

"Please, just give me another chance! I'm the one! I know I'm the one! I CAN DO THIS!"

Black Hood kicked me into line along with the rest of the goats. They were streaming out the side door, pulled along by their own leashes as White Hood led them out of the Goat Room.

Just as I was about to be pushed through the door, The Word turned to me, an arm raised.

"Wait a moment. We weren't wrong…we had the right bloodline…"

He turned to my eldest son, "Just the wrong person."

I thrashed against my leash, screaming, "No, he's not ready for this! HE'S NOT READY FOR THIS! GET YOUR FUCKING HANDS OFF MY SON!"

5

There's Something Wrong With Dad

Fifteen years ago, something terrible happened to my family. It's taken a lot of therapy and drugs to help me cope with it. I still think about those days a lot. I can't seem to get some of the images out of my mind. They scare me, they keep me up at night. I want to forget, but I can't seem to.

My therapist told me I should write it all out. She said that it would help purge some of these memories. I'm not sure if I believe her, but I'm going to try. I have to. I need peace of mind. I can't keep living like this.

A couple things you need to know before I begin: 1) My family didn't believe in technology. We didn't have a TV, a computer, a phone, anything. My dad believed those things would rot your brain out and he was always happy to tell people just that. 2) My family didn't like to be bothered. Our house was out in the hills down a dirt road. We didn't have neighbors. We didn't have company. It was just us. My mom, my dad, and my brother Jay. My mom homeschooled us and my dad would take his truck into town to work at the bank.

I wouldn't say we were an unhappy family. My mom, Ann, was caring, kind, and had a passive way of dealing with things. She was a soft-spoken, submissive woman. My brother, Jay, was two years younger than me. I loved my brother. He was a troublemaker and I constantly had to cover for him, hiding some of his more mischievous actions from our parents.

And then there was my father, Henry. He was an old-fashioned kind of man. Strict, but honest. He believed in a moral code, believed in being an upstanding example, and was a hard-working provider for our small family.

That was before everything went bad.

That was before my father changed.

I was sitting at the breakfast table happily munching my toast. My six-year-old brother sat across from me, slurping down his milk. My father walked into the kitchen and asked Jay to stop being so rude before going to my mother and pecking her on the cheek, bidding her good morning.

My mother smiled and helped him with his tie, telling him his lunch was packed for the day and to come home safe. My dad threw on his sports jacket and grabbed his briefcase from the kitchen counter. He ruffled my hair and leaned down next to me.

"Are you going to be good for your mom today, champ?" He asked. This close, I could smell his cologne, his face freshly shaven. He was a good-looking man, tall and dark with broad shoulders. I had always looked up to him and admired his physicality.

"Yeah, dad, I'll be good," I answered.

Smiling, my dad went to my brother and asked him the same. My brother shrugged his shoulders, a goofy grin on his face. One of his front teeth was loose and it stuck out at an angle, the object of much fruitless wiggling.

"Maybe today that'll come out," my dad said, examining it.

He kissed Jay on the forehead and said a goodbye to my mother, blowing her a kiss, and was out the door. As I finished my toast, I heard him fire up the truck and back it down the gravel driveway.

My mother began cleaning up the breakfast dishes, telling Jay and I to finish up and fetch our schoolbooks. I hated school, as all children do. I thought it was boring and a waste of time. The woods and hills were more interesting to me than words and pencils.

Groaning, I brushed the crumbs from my shirt and motioned for Jay to come with me to our room to collect our school supplies.

The day passed like so many before it. Jay and I sat at the kitchen table, doing our schoolwork, listening to our mother, and trying not to die of boredom. At lunch my mother made us peanut-butter sandwiches and we were allowed to go outside for an hour. This was always my favorite part of the school day.

Jay and I bounded from our house and went to the woods. We climbed trees, threw rocks at each other, and then finally took turns rolling down the grassy hill we lived on. I remember how warm it was that day, the June heat foreshadowing an even hotter July.

We heard our mother calling us back in and we obeyed, steeling ourselves for the final stretch of schoolwork. Hours seemed like years in that kitchen, but three o'clock always came. When the hands on the old clock made a right angle, we were allowed to close our books for the day.

That evening, Jay and I decided to make paper airplanes on the living-room floor as my mother prepared supper. I remember the delicious smells wafting though the house as we folded newspaper into planes. Jay had just finished his first one, holding it up proudly, when dad came home.

From the second he walked into the door, I knew it was going to be a bad night. We all have those memories of our fathers, probably when his temper got the better of him and everyone was on eggshells. This was different, though. There was an aura of tension around him that I had never seen before.

He didn't say anything when he walked in, just tossed his coat over the back of a chair and put his briefcase down. My mother turned from the stove and smiled at him, welcoming him home and asking how his day was. Dad said nothing as he went to the sink and filled a glass of water. He drained it in one long gulp and set the glass down.

He turned to Jay and I, something hard and dark in his eyes.

"What are you doing?" he asked, his tone sharp.

"Look, dad, it's a B-52 bomber!" Jay said proudly, swooping his paper plane through the air.

My father took a step forward suddenly and snatched it from his hand, examining it. He lowered the plane and stared at us. "Is this the paper I was reading this morning?"

I swallowed. Yep, dad was in a bad mood.

"I told them they could use it; I thought you were finished reading it," my mother intervened.

My dad turned to her. "Well, maybe you should ask me next time. Do you think you can handle that?"

My mom blinked. "I'm sorry honey. I didn't think it was a big deal."

My dad said nothing, just pulled a kitchen chair out and sat down, watching us. I felt uncomfortable. I felt like he was looking for an excuse to be angry. He wasn't usually like this, but there had been a time or two his anger had gotten the better of him. For the most part, though, he wasn't a violent or even a loud person.

"Bad day at the bank, dear?" my mother asked, stirring a pot full of sauce she was preparing.

My dad turned to look at her. "I had the worst day I've ever had." He shook his head, "You can't even imagine. None of you can. The things I go through to put food on this table."

My mother turned and frowned. "Aw, I'm sorry to hear that. Can I get you a beer?"

Dad nodded.

My mom went to the fridge and pulled one out, handing it to him and putting a hand on my dad's shoulder reassuringly.

My dad went to twist the top off but pulled his hand away with a snarl. "Ow! Shit! Of course it's not a twist top, why would it be?" I could see a drop of blood on my dad's hand from where the cap had cut him. I began to look for an excuse to leave the room before dinner.

"Relax, dear, I'll get you a bottle opener," my mom said, trying to cool his rising temper.

My dad shook his head. "Oh, don't bother!" Raising his arm, he smashed the neck of the beer against the table and shattered it. He poured the beer from the fragmented neck into a glass before tossing the empty bottle toward the trash can. It missed and shattered on the floor.

"Henry!" my mom said, her voice a soft hiss.

My dad took a long pull and set the glass down hard on the table, "Maybe next time you should get the twist-off caps. Maybe you should think about *me* every once in a while."

Not wanting to fight, my mom quietly turned around and continued making dinner. My dad took another drink from the glass and looked at Jay and I. I quickly looked down at my half-made paper plane and mindlessly fiddled with it. I didn't want him to even know I existed.

"Tommy," my dad called me. My heart froze. I looked up at him, panicked.

"Were you good today?" he asked. "Was Tommy a good boy for mommy?" His voice was condescending and his eyes bore into mine.

I nodded.

He drained the rest of his beer, staring at me, before putting it down and muttering, "You better have been."

As my brother and I tried to melt into the floor, my dad stood and went to the bedroom to get changed out of his work clothes. I let out a sigh of relief and looked at Jay. He grimaced at me and shook his head, his loose tooth jutting from his upper lip.

"Be good tonight," I whispered urgently to him.

I picked up my plane and decided to stash it in my bedroom. I didn't want to give my dad any excuse to flip out tonight. Out of sight, out of mind.

As I walked down the hallway toward my bedroom, I passed my parents' room. I glanced inside and saw my dad.

He was standing by the bed, shirtless and facing the door. For a split second I froze, expecting him to bark at me for something. But then I saw he had his hands over his eyes, his elbows jutting away from his body. He didn't move a muscle, just stood like that silently, like he had been turned to stone.

I didn't know what to make of it, the odd display unnerving me. I didn't stick around to find out what he was doing and quickly scooted down the hall to my room. I deposited my plane on my dresser just as I heard my mom call everyone for supper.

Jay and I trotted to the table as my mom placed a steaming bowl of hot spaghetti on it, smelling of garlic and basil. Jay rubbed his stomach and swooned, expressing to mom how hungry he was. I took my place at the table next to him as my father entered the kitchen.

Wordlessly, he took a seat at the head of the table, opposite my mother who shot him a cautious glance.

He folded his hands and turned to me. "Why don't you say grace for us tonight, Tommy?"

I nodded and closed my eyes, locking my fingers together. "Dear Jesus, thank—"

I jumped as my dad slammed his hand down on the table. Jay let out a little squeak and my mom visibly flinched.

My dad leaned toward me. "Now Tommy, how do you expect Jesus to hear you when you talk so softly? Start over, but louder."

My heart was thundering in my chest and it took conscious effort to keep my voice from shaking. My father's outburst was so sudden and out of character for him that I didn't know how to respond.

I lowered my head and began again. "Dear Jesus, thank you for the food and thank you for mom who made it." After a pause I added, "And thank you for dad who goes to work for it. Amen."

My mom echoed my "amen" and told me that was a nice prayer. Jay was staring at my dad, unease blooming in his eyes.

Dad looked at the bowl of spaghetti and I saw his jaw clench. "This again. I guess it's not your fault, Ann, that you can't cook anything but noodles. It's not like your family had the money to send you to college to make something of yourself."

My mom looked up at him, shock rippling across her face. My dad met her stare, his face carved from stone. He was daring her to say something to him, anything. Wisely, my mom lowered her eyes and began spooning out the steaming spaghetti.

Jay immediately dug into his, twirling his fork around the sauced noodles and shoving them hungrily into his mouth. I winced as he slurped down a mouthful, causing the red gravy to squirt from his lips.

My dad turned to him, his eyes ice. "Jay. What have I told you about being rude at the table?"

Jay froze, fork halfway to his mouth, "Uh-uh..." he stuttered, mind blanking.

My dad curled a finger at him, "Come here. Now."

I felt my heart sink into my guts and turn to rot. I was breathing heavily, not wanting my brother to be in any kind of trouble. I watched as he slid from his chair, fear in his eyes.

"Bring me your plate," dad said in that same iron voice.

Jay turned and took his plate, slowly walking it over to stand in front of my dad. My father looked him over, shaking his head, his mouth twisting into a grimace.

"I didn't raise a pig," he said darkly, "but if you insist on being one, you're going to eat like one."

He suddenly grabbed Jay's plate and threw it on the floor, shattering it and spraying spaghetti everywhere. I jumped in my seat again, forcing my eyes away and praying I'd disappear. My mom gasped and her mouth fell open.

My dad pointed to the floor. "Go ahead son, if you're so desperate to be a barnyard animal, you can eat like one!"

Jay looked at my mom and I could tell he was on the brink of crying, unsure what to do, begging someone for help.

"Henry, don't you think you're overreacting a little bit?" my mom ventured timidly.

My dad slammed his hands down again, his voice rising. "Ann, if you don't raise these kids to be—*gggungrate*—hate it when the wind blows north!"

Everyone paused. I chanced a glance at my dad. *What?*

My mom said nothing, waiting for her husband to continue. Jay sniffled beside me and I reached out a hand and took his, squeezing it gently.

My dad blinked and one of his eyes rolled up into his head and then righted itself. It happened so fast I almost didn't see it. He cleared his throat and gave his head a quick shake.

My father blinked a few more times and then looked at me and Jay. He saw me holding his hand, Jay on the brink of tears.

"Tommy, let go of your brother's hand," he said, his eye twitching slightly.

I obeyed, our sweaty palms separating. I watched my father, food forgotten, my throat dry and mouth parched. I didn't understand why he was acting like this. I had never seen him this hostile toward us. I knew that sometimes when he had a bad day at work he came home frustrated…but never like this.

What had happened today?

My father looked at me in my seat, waving Jay to sit back down. "Tommy, your brother was being punished. Do you know why I punish you boys? It's so that you understand right from wrong. Now, I just saw you trying to comfort your brother." He leaned toward me, his breath hot. "That tells me that you're on his side. That tells me you think it's OK to act like a pig at my table."

I shook my head frantically, "N-no, I just wanted—"

My dad cut me off with a wave of his hand. "Stop. I don't want to have to punish you for lying as well."

He patted the tabletop. "Put your hand on the table."

I shot my mom a terrified look, begging her for help. Her eyes were wide and her face pale. She didn't know how to react, had never seen her husband so cruel or sharp with us. She was speechless, afraid that saying something would antagonize my dad further.

"On the table," my dad repeated, his voice hardening.

Hand shaking, I placed it on the table, palm down. Jay had started to cry next to me, tears dripping from his cheeks.

My dad picked up his fork.

"Henry," my mom whispered, eyes wide.

I looked at my dad, fighting back my own tears, fear choking me.

My father gripped the fork. "You need to understand that—" he stopped suddenly, coughing hard and then gasped in a dry voice, *"Don't you hate the wind in the north?!"*

He dropped the fork on the table and his mouth fell open,

his tongue stretching to his chin. His eye began to twitch rapidly and he rubbed it viciously, closing his mouth and gritting his teeth.

None of us moved, paralyzed by the odd display. I had no idea what he was talking about or why he was acting like this. Something was wrong with him; that much was clear.

After a few seconds, my dad lowered his hand from his face and smiled at all of us. "I think you boys understand now. Remember what I said and we won't have to do that again, OK?"

Jay and I nodded vigorously, desperate to get away from the tension, the table, all of this. I felt like I was stuck in some alternate reality, a nightmare I was just waiting to wake from.

My dad pointed to the floor. "Tommy, could you please clean up that mess?"

As I scrambled to comply, he turned his eyes to my mother, looking her up and down where she sat. He began to twirl a spoon in his hand and got a strange look in his eye. It was as if he was evaluating her as a person, taking in all her physical features.

As I was scraping globs of spaghetti into the trash, I heard my father say, "Jay, can you go around to the back of the house and get me a brick?" I heard my brother get up and open the side door to the outside, the hinges creaking in their familiar way.

"Henry, what's wrong?" I heard my mom ask in a hushed voice. Even as I sponged up the mess, I could hear the fear in her voice.

My dad didn't respond. I finished wiping sauce from the floor just as Jay shuffled back into the house. He held a brick in his hands, dirt staining his fingers. With downcast eyes he brought it to my father and placed it on the table next to him.

My dad turned to the both of us, his voice cold steel. "Now both of you go to your room for the night. I'm going to fuck your mother."

I heard my mom gasp as Jay and I turned away. I took my brother's hand in mine, heart racing. I was terrified. I rarely heard my dad use that kind of language before and never in such an abrasive manner. As we quickly walked to our room, I looked at Jay and saw his face was a mess of snot, drool, and tear-streaked terror. His eyes were wet and wide with confusion. He didn't understand any of this, didn't understand why his father was being so mean to him. I didn't either and so I gave his hand a little squeeze, unsure of what else to do.

We closed the door to our bedroom and stared at each other. We could hear our dad yelling loudly in the kitchen, his voice rising. Jay covered his ears and ran to his bed, collapsing into his pillow. I went to him and put a hand on his back as he cried, his sobs muffled in the cotton.

Then I heard my mom start to scream.

I felt tears spill from my eyes and I began to hyperventilate, each breath a desperate attempt for oxygen. I covered my ears and squeezed my eyes shut as something crashed to the floor in the kitchen. More banging followed and all the while my mother continued to shriek, her voice rising to an inhuman level. There was agony in her cries along with fear, and I kept waiting for her to stop.

But she didn't.

It kept going.

And going.

And going.

And going.

Jay was weeping now, shaking his head into his pillow, trying to block out the sound. His whole body was shaking and it sounded like he was having trouble breathing. I laid down next to him and clutched his body to mine, my own tears spilling into his hair. I didn't know what to do, didn't know when this horrible nightmare would end.

I heard another crash as something shattered in the kitchen. I heard my mother howling and the screech of table legs on the hardwood floor. I heard Jay praying to God, his voice trembling. I clutched him tighter, realizing that I was sobbing as well. My whole body felt like it was a quivering mass of Jell-O, my muscles weak and useless. I was more terrified than I had ever been in my life.

Finally, my mother stopped screaming. A soft hush fell over the house. I didn't hear anything except the blood pumping in my ears. Jay had quieted to a series of soft sniffles, his face still buried in the pillow. I looked up from the bed, staring at the closed bedroom door. I begged it to remain shut.

I heard movement in the house, footsteps that came down the hall and stopped on the other side of the wall, in my parents' bedroom. I heard shuffling and then a door shut. I waited. I prayed.

Jay shifted next to me and I told him to be quiet, wiping tears from his face and holding him close. More footsteps in the house, heavy, slow paces. I thought for sure my mom was dead. People didn't scream like that and live.

Our bedroom door opened.

Jay let out a little scream and shrank into me as my dad entered.

He was crawling on all fours, his mouth hanging open, drool running down his chin, his eyes rolled back into his head. He shuffled side-to-side across the floor, slowly opening and closing his mouth, spittle leaking from his face. He was blinking rapidly, one of his eyes rolling forward to stare at us.

After a few seconds, he coughed, hacking up phlegm. Growling, he wiped his lips and stood, looking down at us cowering on the bed.

"Come with me," he said, his voice a low rattle in his chest.

I didn't move. Jay shrank further against me. I could feel his body shaking against mine, sweat beading on his skin.

My dad took a step toward us. "Get up, both of you, right now."

"Where's mom?" I asked, voice trembling.

He was standing in front of us now. "She's resting. She's had a long day. Now get up."

Jay shifted against me and then he was sliding to the floor. Without much choice, I followed his example. My dad placed a hand on each of our shoulders and guided us toward the door.

As we were directed through the house, I listened for my mother. What had he done to her? Where was she? Was she dead in the bedroom? I didn't hear anything, no clues as to her condition or where she was.

We entered the kitchen and I saw that the table was pressed against the cabinets and a few of the dinner glasses lay shattered on the floor. I expected to see blood smeared across the floor or dripping down the surfaces, but there was none.

At least, that was until I saw the brick.

It had been placed on the counter by the sink. Half of it was soaked with thick, oozing blood.

When I saw it, I felt my body tense. My dad must have felt the change in my stance because his grip tightened on my shoulder. Jay was sniffling beside me, his eyes cast down, refusing to look up and potentially see the horrors my father had bestowed on my mother.

My dad pushed us outside through the side door. The night air was humid and sticky on my skin. A fat, yellow moon hung in the sky like an out-of-place Christmas ornament. Stars twinkled across the black canvas and my ears were filled with the sound of chirping night critters. Contrary to inside, everything felt alive out here, pulsing in unison to the night's dark heartbeat.

We were led around to the back of the house toward our old shed. My dad didn't keep much out there, just a few tools and the rickety lawn mower, both of which weren't used much throughout the year. I didn't like the shed; something about it always haunted me. At night, as I lay in bed, I would imagine some creature hiding inside, waiting until I fell asleep before emerging and creeping into my room to watch me.

Jay and I jerked to a halt as my dad squeezed our shoulders.

"Wait here," he said, his voice sounding far away and strange. I glanced over my shoulder and saw he was rubbing his eyes.

"I want to go back in, I want mom," Jay sobbed, wiping his nose with the back of his hand.

"You can go in when—*came up and traveled in the wind,*" my dad said, his sentence fracturing into two nonsensical statements. He coughed hard and stuck his tongue out like he had a bad taste on it. I saw a shudder wrack his body and he looked like he was about to gag. He gained control of himself with a quick shake of his head, closing his mouth so hard his teeth clicked together.

I watched as he came around us and walked toward the shed. He looked back, making sure we were obeying, and then went inside. Jay looked at me, his eyes full of fear. He expected me to have some kind of explanation, an answer to the madness that surrounded us. I couldn't summon the words to comfort him, didn't know what combination of soothing syllables I could possibly string together to calm his terror.

"What is he going to do to us?" he whispered, the warm moonlight shining in his eyes.

"It's going to be OK," I said softly, the words tasting like a lie.

We heard movement from the shed, our father's actions hidden behind the closed door. A warm breeze stirred the distant trees and the night was filled with the sound of rustling leaves. My hair danced across my forehead in the wind and I begged to blow away with it. Jay and I remained frozen in place, neither of us knowing which would be worse: facing whatever my father was preparing or running away and facing the wrath that came after. It's not like we had anywhere to run; where could we possibly go? Whom could we flee to? Our minds were trapped inside our youth, doomed to the almighty authority of our father.

The shed door opened, snapping me out of my thoughts. My dad stepped back into the night, his figure draped in shadow and dark moonlight.

"Both of you get inside," he ordered.

Jay grasped my arm as we shuffled forward, our father stepping aside to let us pass. The smell of rotting wood and old grass assaulted my senses and I rubbed my hand across my nose, trying to scrub the stench away. My dad had illuminated the cramped space with an old electric lantern. It sat on the workbench on the right, our small lawnmower catching the light on its dull metal surface. Tools piled around the lantern, an array of rusted hammers, screwdrivers, and pliers. I couldn't remember the last time my dad had actually used any of them.

But all of that was seen with a passing glance. That wasn't what held my attention. Something else did, my eyes drawn to it like fire and gasoline. Jay's fingernails dug into my skin as he saw it, too, his breath catching in his lungs.

A noose hung from the crossbeam, dangling down into the empty space. The rope was knotted tight, the twisting cords more menacing than anything on the workbench.

My dad entered behind us, shutting the door .

He went and stood by the noose, motioning me forward. "Come on now, Tommy, let's get this over with."

"D-dad," I croaked, mouth dry and voice cracking like a dead twig, "w-what are you going to d-do?" My heart was pressed against my ribs, throwing itself against bone, a wild beast in my chest.

Dad traced the hanging loop with this fingers. "You're going to be my wind chime, son. I need to know when the wind will blow north. I think you'll make a good chime once I empty your insides out. But I'll do that after."

"Why are you doing this, daddy?" Jay cried, wet tears rolling down his cheeks.

He didn't answer, just waited for me to go to him. I didn't move, didn't know what to do. Was he serious about going through with this? He couldn't be; this was my father! He loved me, he would never do anything to seriously hurt me.

At that age, blind trust is a dangerous thing. It filled me, the memories and kindness my dad had shown me over the years. I trusted him. He was my father. But that darkness in his eyes, that black spark, it terrified me. Reality and faith collided together in my mind like oil and water, the mixture turning my stomach in sick horror.

My father gripped the hanging rope. "If you don't come over here right now, I'm going to use Jay instead."

I felt my brother bury his face into my side, weeping "no, no, no, no, no" over and over again, his tears damp on my shirt. I wrapped an arm around his head, feeling his sweaty hair brush over my skin. My heart was audible in my ears, my lips cracked and dry, breath coming in stuttering heaves.

"D-dad," I cried, feeling myself begin to cry, "dad, I don't want to. Please, dad…" My face was flushed as the fear came bubbling out of my face in wet streaks.

My father suddenly reached out and grabbed me, gripping my arm and yanking me toward the rope. I let out a cry and fell toward him, his hands hard and strong. He pushed and shoved me, positioning me under the rope, its shadow a dark halo over my head.

Jay was screaming openly, his face red and terrified. He just stood there helpless as my father pulled the noose down and slid it over my head.

Dad's going to hang me.

The thought hit me like a knife to the heart. My knees were weak and knocked together, my whole body trembling in horrific anticipation. The rope around my neck scratched and rubbed against my skin, coarse and itchy. This was really about to happen. Up until this point, I didn't believe my father was capable of such sins, especially to his own son. My dad was my hero, a strong supportive pillar and example to my brother and I.

And now I waited with bated breath for him to kill me.

"Here we go," dad said, positioning himself behind me and grabbing the dangling end of the rope that hung from the crossbeam.

I heard a tightening of cords, the rope stretching and straining.

Suddenly my throat was clamped with hot fire, a burning agony that cut up into my chin as I was lifted off my feet. I kicked my legs frantically, impossibly helpless, my hands grabbing at my neck.

I couldn't get my fingers between the rope and my skin, the tension denying any space to dig my nails into.

My head swelled and I felt the blood in my face ready to pop out of my eyes and mouth. I hacked and coughed, horrible gagging retches exploding from my lips as I tried to breathe. My vision began to swim and colors began to blend.

I felt myself *dying.*

Suddenly, the pain was gone, the halo of fire around my throat vanishing. I felt my knees hit the hard floor and I crumpled into myself. I sucked in deep lungfuls of air, the oxygen never tasting any sweeter in my life.

As the world began to focus again, I realized my father was

screaming. I blinked back the dizziness and focused my eyes, pushing the shadows away.

My father was against the back wall, clutching his side and howling as blood bubbled from his shirt. Jay stood next to him, weeping, screaming, his right arm soaked with blood up to his elbow.

He was holding a rusty box cutter, its blade dripping.

"Don't hurt Tommy!" Jay was howling through wet eyes. "Don't hurt him, dad!"

Hand pressed to his side, my dad swiped at Jay, trying to snatch the box cutter. Jay jerked back and almost tripped over himself, letting out another shriek.

"Look what you did to me!" my dad grimaced, pulling his hand away and revealing a deep gash in his side, his shirt tattered and red.

I struggled to my feet, reaching out and pulling Jay toward me. I took the box cutter from him and put a hand on my throbbing head.

"I'm OK, it's going to be OK," I tried to reassure him.

Suddenly, my dad lunged for me, pushing himself off the wall using his back. Without thinking, I slashed at him, a purely defensive reaction.

Time seemed to slow as I watched the blade catch my dad in the arm, the blade eating into his skin. It cut through the flesh like soft butter, parting his wrist like a bloody zipper. Blood squirted into my eyes and I heard my dad scream, pulling his arm back and cradling it on his chest.

He slumped to the floor, his face pale and full of fury. He was breathing hard and I could tell it wouldn't be long before he steadied himself and was at us again.

I grabbed Jay and ran from the shed, the night behind us filling with howls of rage.

As the air hit our tear-stained faces, I suddenly noticed trucks roaring down the road and up our driveway. They were bulky and loud, the diesel engines growling toward us. Blinding white lights cut paths through the night, shining across my bloody face as two, three, then four of them stopped in front of our house.

They were camouflaged. Even at that age, I knew they were military.

What is going on? my exhausted, terrified mind asked.

I pulled Jay close to me and advanced on them, unsure what they were doing here, but desperate for help.

Two men emerged from a white van dressed in Haz-Mat suits. They sent a shiver of fear coursing through me as they charged Jay and I, yelling and waving their arms. I froze in the yard, Jay trembling beside me.

Men in uniform poured from the other vehicles, guns drawn, all pointed at us. They all had gas masks on and it gave them a chilling, inhuman look in the moonlight.

Everyone was shouting as the men in the HazMat suits approached Jay and me. I backed up a step as they got close, gripping the box cutter in my bloody hand. I didn't know who these people were or why they were pointing guns at us. I needed to protect Jay. He had been through enough; we both had.

"It's OK kid, it's OK!" one of the men in the suits said, raising his hands. The other one had a pistol drawn, scanning the yard.

"Where is he?" the one with the pistol asked.

I stammered, mind blanking in fear and confusion.

"Your dad, where's your dad, kid?" the first one asked.

"He's in there!" Jay cried, pointing to the shed. "He wanted to hurt Tommy so I cut him! I had to! I'm sorry, I didn't want Tommy to die!"

The first one looked at the one with the pistol and gave a quick nod. I watched as he trotted over to the shed and peeked inside. He looked back and gave the three of us a wave and then a thumbs-up to the men in gas masks.

Then he entered the shed.

And I heard him kill my father.

The gunshot exploded in the night and I jumped, the finality of it deafening.

I stood there, dumbfounded, bloody, confused, and terrified. I didn't know who these men were, what they were doing here, or why they had just shot my dad. I clutched Jay to my side; he was staring up at me with giant round eyes.

"Did…did that man just kill dad?" he asked, his voice a shaky whisper.

The man in the HazMat suit shook his head. "Son, you don't have anything to worry about. It's going to be OK now. He won't try to hurt you anymore."

Someone was yelling behind him, and I glanced over his shoulder to see that the men in masks had gone into our house. One of them was calling for a medic, frantically waving his hand to get inside.

My mother. I prayed she was OK, that these men could help her. I didn't know what my father had done to her, but I remembered the screams.

"W-what… what is going *on*?" I whispered as I watched

the man with the pistol exit the shed. He was yelling toward the soldiers, asking for something, my ears not registering his calls. My world was crashing down around me in inky patches of disbelief and shock.

The man knelt down in front of us, placing a hand on each of our shoulders. "Boys, I really shouldn't be the one to tell you this, especially not right now."

I looked at him with moist eyes. "My dad just tried to hang me...please..."

I could see shock ripple across his eyes through the Haz-Mat visor. He looked at both of us, struggling with himself.

"Please," I begged, desperate to make any kind of sense of the madness.

The man sighed, "Boys...something horrible happened today. I really don't think I should be the one to tell you...but..." He looked at us again. "Boys, something bad happened by the bank where your dad worked. There was some kind of earthquake. Very minor, but it cut a deep gash in the earth. It opened up a pocket of...something...that we've never seen before. Some kind of gas. The wind carried it toward town and..." He looked to the ground, shaking his head. "It killed a lot of people. *A lot* of people. We're trying to contain it, keep whatever it is from spreading."

"Is that why you shot dad?" Jay asked quietly, sniffling and rubbing his nose. "'Cause he got the bad wind on him?"

The man looked up at both of us, his eyes fearful, "Boys...your dad died this morning along with everyone else at the bank. We took his body to containment. They're performing an autopsy on him as we speak. I'm really sorry."

I felt my brain bend back on itself, a mess of knotted

thoughts and emotions, the words hitting me like bullets. What was this man talking about? Dad died this morning? That wasn't possible; he came home from work just like every other day. My dad's body was lying dead in the shed. This man was lying; he had to be.

"Then who's...who's in there?" I finally asked, the question coming out in a weak dribble.

The man shook his head, "Son, whatever is lying dead in that shed...it isn't your father. You see...something else came out of the earth this morning. Something other than the poisonous gas. Something that crawled up to the surface and got out. Something that, for whatever reason, took the form of your father and drove home to you all. Witnesses saw him, it, leaving, the only one to get out. When we found your dad's body, we didn't know what to make of it. We still don't. That thing in there," he said, pointing to the shed, "we don't know what it is or what it was trying to do. But that is not your father." He shook his head. "Shit, I'm really sorry, kids, I really shouldn't be telling you all this. I'm sorry about your dad, I really am." He stood up. "Come on, we need to get you to a hospital and have you checked out. It's going to be OK, I promise."

I barely heard him as Jay and I were led to the trucks. I saw men carrying my mother out of the house on a stretcher. She was alive and barely conscious, but when she saw us she reached out and called our names.

Jay started crying again and sprinted to her. I wanted to as well but found I didn't have the strength.

Everything the man had told me twisted and coiled around my mind. None of it made sense. None of it could possibly be real. It couldn't be. How could my entire life change so drastically in one night? What was going to happen to us now? Where were they taking us? Were we going to be OK? At the time, I didn't know.

I felt someone grasp something out of my hand and I realized one of the soldiers was trying to pry the box cutter out of my grip. I let go, the rusty metal peeling away from my palm, blood staining it in sticky red splotches.

What had happened tonight?

I looked back and saw the men in HazMat suits pulling my dad's dead body from the shed and zipping it up in a clear plastic body bag.

A final thought ripped through the madness.

What the hell is that thing?

6

Feed The Pig

I slowly opened my eyes. My head was swimming and a dull pain surrounded my throat. I was thirsty. That was the first thing I noticed. I licked my dry lips as my surroundings faded into focus. My body ached and I realized it was because I was tightly bound to a metal chair in the middle of an empty room. The barren concrete walls were stained and dirty. The floor beneath my bare feet was cold and slightly wet.

A single bulb lit the room, dangling from the ceiling by a string. It cast moving shadows and I blinked back darkness. An open door stood before me, but I couldn't see anything but the wall of a hallway.

I tried to clear my head, tried to remember how I got here. I squeezed my eyes shut and forced myself not to panic. I slowed my breathing and focused my thoughts, desperately trying to summon some recollection of why I was here.

I couldn't remember anything.

I opened my eyes and exhaled, my parched throat throbbing. I could hear sound echoing off the hallway walls outside the door. Screaming, clanging, howling, all very distant but that did nothing to help calm my nerves.

"Hello?!" I cried, the word tearing at my vocal cords. I felt my chest hitch in pain but I cleared my throat and yelled again.

"Is anyone there!? Hello!?"

The dark hallway remained silent except for the constant echoes. I shut my mouth and tried to wriggle free of my bindings, but the rope was knotted impossibly tight. I fought back against my imagination as it flooded my mind with horrific scenarios of what awaited me. If I could only remember!

Suddenly, footsteps erupted from outside the door, a rapid patter of small feet. My hopes rose and I trained my attention on the door, praying it was help.

A young boy ran into the room dressed in a red onesie, complete with padded feet. Stretched over his face was a plastic Devil mask. The eyeholes revealed massive blue eyes that greeted me curiously. Taken aback, I opened my mouth to speak, but that's when I noticed something was off. His eyes were huge, impossibly round, and bulging from their sockets. It sent a shiver of unease down my spine, but I shook it off. This child might be able to free me.

"Hey!" I hissed, urgently. "Hey, kid, can you get me out of here?!"

The boy took a step closer, cocking his head, but remaining silent.

I rattled my bound arms against the chair. "Cut me free, please, I shouldn't be here, this is some kind of mistake!"

The boy eyed me behind his strange mask and stopped directly in front of me. He leaned in close and whispered, his voice like wet silk, "You did a bad thing…"

Confused, I shook my head. "No! No, this is a mistake! I didn't do anything!"

The boy's enormous blue eyes suddenly filled with sadness. "Oh, you did a really, really bad thing…"

I shook my head again, violently. "No! I'm sorry! I don't remember, just please get me out of this chair!"

Suddenly, before either of us could speak again, a man came charging into the room. He was overweight and dressed in overalls, his grizzled face twisted in seething anger. He was holding a sawed-off shotgun in his arms.

"I didn't do anything!" I cried as he advanced on us, my voice cracking. "I'm not supposed to be here!"

The big man ignored me and instead grabbed the kid and shoved him hard against the wall. The boy grunted as his back struck the concrete and his eyes rose to meet the grizzled man's.

Wordlessly, the man raised his shotgun, placed it against the boy's forehead, and blew his head off. Chunks of gore splattered the wall as shock slugged me in the stomach like an iron fist. My ears rang and time seemed to slow as I watched in horror as the headless body crumpled to the ground.

My breath rushed back into my lungs and time seemed to readjust.

"Jesus fucking CHRIST!" I screamed, straining against the ropes, my eyes bulging in horrific shock. "WHAT THE FUCK!?"

The man ignored my screams as he bent down and picked up the boy. He slung the ruined corpse over his shoulder and walked out the doorway.

Suddenly, the hallway erupted with malicious laughter, a chorus of voices all howling in glee. I shut my eyes, the noise deafening, as absolute terror filled my every pore.

After a few moments, the laughter faded and I cautiously opened my eyes, unable to believe what I had just witnessed.

"Hello."

I jumped as I realized there was another man standing before me. He was dressed in a simple white button-down shirt and jeans. His brown hair was cut short and he appeared to be in his early thirties. His green eyes were dull and lifeless, his full lips pulled down at the corners.

"What is going on!? Where am I!?" I cried, new fear pooling in my stomach like hot blood.

The man crossed his arms. "So you're the new one, huh?" He shook his head. "You people disgust me."

Questions bubbled on my lips, but he waved them off with a sharp chop of his hand, slicing the air and demanding my silence.

He ran his tongue over his teeth, sneering, "You look like you've already seen some of the horrors this place holds, huh? Yes, I can tell by the look in your eyes. You're terrified. You've seen something, haven't you? It doesn't seem all that bad now, does it, looking back? You've been here five minutes and already you're shitting your pants."

"Where am I?" I gasped, unable to hold back any longer. "What do you people want?"

The man crossed his arms behind his back. "I bet you want to get out of here don't you? I bet you'd like to go back to your home, your family, everything."

"Please," I interrupted. "Whatever I did to you…I'm sorry, I really am, but I don't remember!"

The man rolled his eyes. "You didn't do *anything* to me. You did it to *yourself.* You really don't remember anything?"

I shook my head and felt tears brimming in my eyes.

The man looked at me with contempt. "You waited until

your wife left for work and then you went out to the woodshed and hung yourself. You're dead."

The recent memory rose in my mind like a monster from a bog. My eyes went wide. As much as I wanted to deny it...he was right. I had killed myself. The incident tore through my brain like a bullet train and left me reeling.

"I'm Danny, by the way," the man said, ignoring the shocked look on my face, "and I'm number two here. I run the orientation process. I want to make this quick because I'm tired of repeating this fucking thing to you pathetic Suicidals. You get one question before I begin."

He stared down at me and I scrambled to organize my thoughts into something cohesive. This was all horrifying. Why had I killed myself? I fought against the fog and panic and the mists of confusion slowly began to lift. I had just lost my job. Yes...that was the start. I squeezed my eyes shut and forced more of the memory to emerge. I had lost my job and I was about to lose the house. My wife...Tess...she found out and was going to leave me. I didn't have any way out, didn't have any options. Getting fired had come out of the blue and I didn't have much in savings. I was broke, soon to be homeless, and my wife hated me for it. There was something else...yes...that's right. She had been cheating on me. I had seen texts on her phone while she slept one night and confirmed my suspicions. My life had degraded to shit and I had run out of options. Humiliated and ashamed, I had decided death was my only option.

"Hey, fucker, do you have a question or not?" Danny said, snapping his fingers in front of my face.

I was sucked back into reality and I asked the only question that mattered.

"Is this hell?"

Danny snorted, "That's always what you people ask." He began to pace back and forth in front of me. "No. This is not hell. It's not heaven, either. This is the Black Farm. And no, I didn't name it that. This is where God sends the souls who have ended their own life. Suicidals. You see, he doesn't really know what to do with you…and neither does the Devil. There are genuinely good people who kill themselves. Seems cruel to banish them to hell for all eternity for a moment of weakness, right? Personally, I think God and the Devil were just tired of arguing about it. And so they send them here, to the Black Farm."

"Did…did God create this place?" I asked, growing more and more confused.

Danny spit on the floor, chuckling. "Sure, at some point. But he lost control of it when he put The Pig in charge."

"What's The Pig?" I asked, unsure I wanted to know the answer.

Danny held up a hand, annoyed. "Can I fucking finish? God created this place eons ago, put The Pig in charge, and then forgot about it for a while. Well, when his back was turned, The Pig decided to use his new powers to try to create his own little world. This mess you see around you is the fractured remains of that experiment. The Black Farm used to be a lot nicer, but The Pig wanted things to be different. He wanted to create his own vision. These people you see, these monsters? They are The Pig's attempts at creating functioning life. Instead of mirroring God's Earth, these mutated horrible creations are full of sin and hatred. They run rampant here, unabashed. This place is chaos. The Black Farm is a circus of freaks and monsters. And it's your eternity."

Fear boiled in my gut like thick oil. No. No this couldn't be my end. I didn't believe in stuff like this. This wasn't real! I would wake up soon and realize I was just having a nightmare! That had to be it!

Danny stood before me and lightly slapped my face. "Hey, hey! Don't go into hysterics on me. I haven't finished yet."

I raised my teary eyes to meet his.

Danny smiled. "You can always Feed the Pig."

My breath pushed from my lungs like burning steam. "W-what does that mean?"

Danny spread his hands, still smiling, "It's as simple as that. Feed the Pig. If you do so, there's a chance he'll send you back to your life."

"A-and w-what happens if it doesn't?" I bumbled.

"You get sent to hell. So flip a coin if you have one. Stay here with us or Feed the Pig. If you choose to stay, I'll let you go...I'll let you go out there," he said, pointing toward the door, "but let me assure you...what awaits you at the end of the hallway...well...let's just say hell isn't that much worse."

I swallowed hard, trying my best to digest everything. Why wouldn't I try Feeding the Pig? Whatever that meant. If there was even a sliver of hope, I would take it. An eternity in this place, the Black Farm, be sent to hell, or...or Feed the Pig? I would do anything for a chance to go back. This nightmare made my problems seem like nothing in comparison.

Danny raised a hand before I could speak. "I'll let you think on it a while. I'll be back later."

"I want to Feed the Pig!" I cried, not wanting to spend another second in this awful room. I could hear a woman screaming down the hallway, her cries rising as something meaty pounded into her. My breath came in sharp pulls and my throat burned. Danny noticed the noise and grinned.

"Sounds pretty bad, huh?" he said softly as the woman's voice creaked with agony. Something was still slamming into her, the sound of beaten flesh igniting my imagination with horrors.

"Please," I gasped, breathless, "just...just let me Feed the Pig. I don't want to stay here any longer."

Danny turned away from me. "I'll be back later. Enjoy your time alone. Really think about your situation. Weigh your options. And remember...you put yourself here."

And with that he was gone, leaving me in the dim room.

Tears streamed down my face.

The woman didn't stop screaming for hours.

At some point, I fell into a semi-sleep. The darkness in the room seemed to press in on me and my eyes fluttered shut. My body ached and my throat was a halo of fire. Thirst raked at my windpipe like sharp glass. My lips felt like crumpled paper. My head thundered like a drum. The room swam in and out of focus and my mind drifted toward the horrific sounds that never ended.

I was lost in a haze, unaware that something was sliding into the room until I felt a sharp prick on my big toe. I jolted out of my daze as my bare foot ignited with pain. I screamed and tried to move, but my bindings held me tight.

The room rushed back into focus and I blinked in agony

as I felt blood trickle between my toes. I looked down for the source of pain and I felt a scream claw up my throat.

Staring up at me was an armless man. He slithered on the floor like a worm, his bald head scabbed and filthy. His legs were wrapped together in barbed wire, forcing him to wriggle his body to move. His eyes were lidless and wide, two bloodshot white orbs that stared up at me with hungry intensity. His teeth had been removed and replaced with long screws which jutted from his bleeding gums like a broken rock formation.

Around his neck was a chain leash, which I followed across the floor to the open door. The end of the leash was held by a tall, naked man. His body was hairless and flabby, covered in similar scabs like his pet. A dirty bag was pulled over his head that hid his features except for a single red eye that peeked out at me from a crude cut in the cloth.

He stared at me and groped his engorged penis, his breath heavy and labored. As the armless man wriggled toward me again, his master started to masturbate. I screamed as the screw-filled mouth bit at me again and my cries seemed to stimulate the naked man even more.

"Get off of me! Stop it!" I screamed, horrified. I tried to kick at the man, doing my best to avoid his sharp metal teeth. I brought my heel down on his head and he screamed as his face bounced off the floor.

A moan of pleasure escaped the bagged man's mouth and I turned away as a mist of black sprayed out onto the floor. There was a rattle of chains and I turned back to see the two of them leaving, the armless man dragged by his neck out the door. I looked at where the bagged man had ejaculated and saw a puddle of dead ants. I vomited onto myself, thick chunky curtains of bile and slime.

"GET ME OUT OF HERE!" I screamed, strands of puke running down my chin. "I DON'T BELONG HERE!"

I listened to the two men retreat down the hallway, the clank of chains accompanied by the sound of flesh being dragged across the concrete. I screamed again, but I knew no one was going to help me. I spit a wad of phlegm and bile onto the floor, ridding my mouth of its sourness. I forced myself to calm down. It wasn't easy.

After some time, I heard someone else approaching. I had been in a miserable lull, my mind a blank canvas of dark despair, but the noise roused me from my trance-like state. The muscles in my arms burned from being restrained for so long and I shifted them desperately, trying my best to prepare myself for whatever horror was about to walk through the door.

Footsteps drew closer and then a woman walked into the room. She stopped at the doorway and looked at me. One of her eyes was missing, a dark cavernous hole in her skull. Her hair was ratty and wild, a brown tangle like a forgotten nest. Her skin was pale and filthy and she was dressed in rags. I couldn't tell how old she was, but there was maturity in her one good eye.

"Still thinking?" she asked, her voice course and brittle.

"What?"

She took a step closer. "Are you still deciding whether you're going to Feed the Pig or not?"

I looked at her cautiously. "Yeah…I am. Who are you? What do you want?"

"I was once where you are now," she said, "trying to decide my fate. I couldn't believe that this was what happened…what happened after we die. It wasn't what I was taught…religion didn't warn me about this place."

I tested my bindings again before asking, "You killed yourself, too? You're a person like me? You're not one of those…those creations?"

She snorted, "Breaks my heart you have to ask," she touched the hole where her eye should have been, "though I can understand your caution. Yeah, I'm a Suicidal. I've been here a long, long time. But that was my choice. I decided to chance it here."

I motioned with my head toward the door, "What's out there? What is all this?"

She exhaled heavily and leaned against the wall. "I can't even begin to describe this place. It's like nothing you've ever seen. You walk down that hallway and go out…into it…and…" she swallowed, "You'd have to see it to understand."

"How bad is it? Why are all these mutated people hurting and killing each other?" I asked.

She let her head loll back against the wall. "It would take years for you to fully understand this place. Years you don't have. Right now you have to make a decision. Stay or Feed the Pig. They tell me hell is worse than here, but it can't be by much. Monsters and Suicidals roam the Black Farm…killing, raping, brutalizing…and then you wake up and wonder how long you can survive before something else kills you. It's an endless cycle."

"So why did you stay?" I pressed. "Why didn't you Feed the

ELIAS WITHEROW

Pig? I don't even know what that means, but I would do anything for a chance to go back. I can't stay here, I...I just can't!"

She smiled sadly at me. "Why? Why did I choose this? It's simple, really. I'm a coward. I was a coward when I was alive and I'm a coward in death. When it came down to it, when the moment presented itself, I chose to stay here. I didn't know what awaited me outside. It boiled down to a simple choice fueled by my own fear."

"What is The Pig? What does it do to you?" I pressed.

She suddenly turned to go. "I'm afraid that's for you to find out. But let me warn you. Think hard before you make a decision. Sometimes suffering through your fear is better than suffering for eternity. Be brave."

"What do I do!?" I yelled, shaking in my chair as she walked out the door.

She paused and took one last look over her shoulder. Her eye darted around and she dropped her voice to a whisper, "Feed the Pig."

And with that she was gone.

I sat in silence once again. My mind was spinning, desperately turning over my options. I still couldn't fully understand the situation I was in. It was too much, too overwhelming. The other side of death wasn't supposed to be like this. I didn't know what I had expected, but it wasn't this nightmare. Questions crashed over my mind like cold waves onto a sinking ship. How was I supposed to make a choice when I didn't even know what my actions entailed?

This place, the Black Farm...I couldn't stay here. But what if I went to hell? What if I didn't get sent back? I would be out of the fire and into the frying pan. My existence would forever be damned to unending misery. Here, though…here there were people like me. Suicidals. It wasn't all monsters and mutilated murderers. Maybe I could hole up somewhere with them, try to scrape together a passable existence. Surely that would be better than getting sent to hell!

No. No, this wasn't going to be how I spent my eternity. I refused to let it be. If there was even the slightest sliver of hope, I would take it. I didn't want to wonder what could have been. I didn't want to be tormented by doubt. I would Feed the Pig and accept whatever fate chose for me. When I boiled it down, that was the only option left.

I would Feed the Pig.

"Hey! Hello!? Danny!" I yelled, rattling in my chair. "I've made my decision! Danny!"

After a couple seconds, I heard footsteps echo down the hall toward me.

Danny walked through the doorway, an annoyed look on his face.

"I've made my choice," I said. "I'm going to Feed the Pig."

"Sounds like you've really thought a lot about it since I left you," Danny said sarcastically.

I licked my lips. "You'd do the same thing if you were in my place."

Danny walked behind me. "I was in your place once. And I chose differently." My eyes widened and then Danny wrapped my entire head with a strip of thin cloth, blinding me. I sucked in as much air as I could, but each lungful felt empty.

I felt Danny cut me free from the chair, and my body sighed as my stiff muscles were released. I rolled my shoulders as my hands were released and I moaned with relief. I dug my fingers into my back and I stretched, my bones creaking.

"Keep your blindfold on and follow me," Danny said, pulling me up.

My legs shook as I put weight on them, my thighs trembling after their long-cemented position. I groped blindly in front of me and found Danny's shoulder. I rested my hand on it as he walked us out of the room.

As we entered the hallway, I could suddenly hear sound I hadn't before. The clank of metal, a long fleshy tearing noise, something vomiting...these sounds sprang to life in my ears, painting the darkness before my eyes with imaginary scenes of horror. I gripped Danny's shoulder tighter, stumbling behind him, my heart thundering.

I heard something trailing behind us, but Danny didn't seem to notice. Or if he did, he didn't care. Flesh slapped the concrete mere inches behind me and I suddenly felt hot breath on my neck and the click of a wet tongue against gums. My breathing became even more labored as fear choked me.

"Goin' ta feed da piggy are ya?" Something whispered in my ear. I felt something press against the back of my head and I tried not to think about what it might be. It was wet and slimy and I heard the thing chuckle.

"Ee's a 'ungry piggy, you make shor' ee gets iz meal now," the thing whispered again, its voice low and unlike anything I had ever heard before. It was like a series of grunts and moans jumbled together to form broken words.

To my relief, I heard the thing retreat back to wherever it had come from and I continued to follow Danny. He remained silent as we walked and I could feel shifts in the air.

The thick heat gave way to a cooler, almost pleasant temperature, but then it kept decreasing and soon I was shivering violently against the cold. I couldn't see anything but I felt a breeze on my face, like we were outside. I didn't hear Danny open any doors, but nothing about this place was natural. It was like reality blurred and bled into itself, like reels of film melting together.

Teeth chattering, I was suddenly blasted with intense heat and I gasped. My feet tripped over themselves as the terrain changed and I was suddenly walking on what felt like warm iron. My ears were filled with the sound of blazing furnaces and the clash of working machinery. I couldn't see it, but I felt like there was a vast open expanse overhead. I smelled ash and tasted dirt on my tongue, sweat already forming along my spine.

Suddenly, I crashed into Danny as he came to a halt. I backed up a few paces and muttered my apologies. I could hear movement in front of us, a rustle of chains and an odd clicking sound on the metal floor. Something else too...something...snorting.

And then the room filled with the deafening sound of an immense pig squealing. I covered my ears, head splitting at the high-pitched wail. I gritted my teeth as the noise echoed off the metal and faded into a series of snorts and grunts.

It sounded absolutely enormous.

"I've brought another one," Danny announced, a slight tinge of respect lining his voice. "He wants to Feed the Pig."

I waited, expecting to hear some answer, the cloth around my eyes sealing my sight to darkness. I realized my knees were shaking and my back was coated in sweat. I was terrified.

"If that is what you wish," Danny said and I felt him bow under my hand. Apparently some unseen conversation had just happened and Danny took my wrist and pushed me forward.

"Approach The Pig," he instructed.

My whole body trembled and my knees locked into place. Robbed from sight, I raised my hands, trying to get my bearings, the heat and ash filling my head with nausea. I felt like I was going to throw up, my stomach rolling like a dead sea. I didn't know where I was or what horror lay before me. I felt lost and tiny, a fresh splash of tears dripping from my eyes and soaking into the cloth around my face.

"P-please," I begged, "let me see what's happening."

Danny was suddenly behind me, pushing me forward. He guided my hands toward something as we stepped together in unison. Even with the cloth around my face, I could see a giant mass of towering darkness before me. It was a spot of black on an already darkened canvas.

As we walked forward, I was suddenly assaulted by a horrendous smell and I gagged, turning away. Danny's grip tightened and forced me to continue. I could sense something just in front of me, a living, shifting mass of flesh. The smell increased to a wretched level and I gagged again. Then hot air was being blown on my face, a blast of heat that came in repeated short bursts.

I vomited into my cloth, the source of the smell stemming from the hot air. I choked as the bile gushed over the fabric, soaking it and momentarily cutting off my oxygen. Danny slapped my hands away and I took a few seconds to steady my breathing again. I was openly crying now, fear and misery collapsing my willpower.

The wet cloth stunk as I sucked in soggy breaths. My own stomach acid coated my skin and I begged for all of this to be over.

And then something squealed directly in front of me.

I felt my bladder go. I was standing before The Pig.

It was the source of darkness in my obscured vision—a fat, titanic creature that filled my senses with every breath it blew into my face.

Danny raised my hands and suddenly I was touching The Pig's snout. I recoiled immediately, but Danny forced my hands back. Its fur was stiff and brittle and as my shaking hands explored up its nose, the size of the animal became clear to me.

It was gigantic and had to weigh over a ton. Its flesh wiggled under my sweating hands and it opened its mouth slightly. My fingers curled around teeth the size of kitchen knives and I realized its mouth was absolutely cavernous.

The Pig squealed again and I heard its hooves clack against the ground. It sounded like thunder rolling across an open field in the middle of summer.

"Take this blindfold off, please," I begged, my legs turning to jelly.

Danny had taken a few steps back and I heard reverence in his voice. "You don't want to do that."

I jumped as The Pig nudged me with its nose, the wet circle of flesh squishing against the length of my face. I shuddered away, raising my hands and emitting a cry of fear.

"Feed the Pig," Danny instructed, his voice like cold steel

now. "You made your choice. Now live with it. It's the only chance you have of going back. Or maybe The Pig won't like how you taste and send you to hell. Only one way to find out."

My eyes widened behind the vomit-soaked cloth. "Won't…like…how I taste?!"

"Climb into its mouth."

My bladder let go again and I felt warm piss run down my leg. "N-no…no, you can't mean…"

Danny's voice hardened. "Climb into its mouth and don't stop crawling forward until it's done with you."

"P-please," I begged, turning toward Danny's voice, reaching out blindly. "Please, there has to be some other way…don't make me do this!" I was a mess of snot and tears, my words bumbling from my mouth like a toddler.

Danny stepped forward and spun me back to face The Pig. "DO IT! You made your choice! It will all be over soon! This is your only CHANCE!"

I could feel The Pig breathing onto my face, its snout mere inches from mine. The smell and heat it emitted made me want to vomit again, but I held it back. This was insane; this wasn't happening. My mind spun and twisted in chaos and fear. There had to be some other way. I couldn't do this, I COULD NOT do this!

Suddenly I remembered the words of the woman: *Sometimes suffering through your fear is better than suffering for eternity. Be brave.*

This was my only chance to get back to the world of the living. I had made such a terrible mistake in killing myself. If I could go back and change my life, I wouldn't have to spend eternity here. I could change my ways, ensure a spot somewhere else. Somewhere away from The Pig. But what if it decided to send me to hell? How much more suffering could I endure?

I had to take the chance.

"Please, God," I whispered, taking a step forward, "if you can hear me…please…have *mercy* on me."

My shaking hands reached out for The Pig and I grasped its thick fur. I felt it slowly lower its head and open its mouth. It was waiting for me, its thick, hot breath stinking in my nostrils. This was it. No turning back now.

I slowly gripped its teeth and pulled myself forward into its jaws. Its head was at a downward angle and so I immediately fell onto my stomach at a forty-five-degree angle. Its wet tongue squished under me and I was shaking so hard I could barely breathe. Tears soaked my blindfold and my heart crunched against my ribs.

I slowly reached forward and found another tooth to grab onto. Gritting my teeth, I pulled my body inward past my knees. The Pig raised its head and I was suddenly completely horizontal on its tongue.

Saliva and mucus dripped around me and the heat was so intense I almost blacked out. My knees clacked against its front teeth as I pulled myself even deeper. Its inner cheeks pressed in around me, squeezing my body like a soaking fleshy coffin.

Crying, terrified, I reached ahead of me and found more teeth. I pulled myself deeper into its mouth and I felt my feet slide past its lips. My whole body was coated in slime and I openly wept, grasping in the darkness for another tooth.

And that's when The Pig started to chew on me.

I screamed in crushing agony as my body was compressed between its massive teeth. I heard my legs snap instantly and felt wet bone pop from my skin. I shook violently as my body spasmed in shock, a mangled twist of blood and pain.

Its tongue shifted me in its mouth and I felt it bite down on my shoulder. My eyes bulged in their sockets as I howled, a hot pillar crunching down on my collarbone. I threw up violently, unable to control myself, the pain overwhelming.

Keep crawling.

Screaming, bloodshot eyes rolling wildly, I reached forward with my good arm, wetly searching for another tooth. I grit my teeth, blood squirting between them as my fingers wrapped around something solid.

The Pig bit down again, its tongue twisting my body so its molars could snap down on my knees. The pain brought darkness, but my howling screams forced my eyes to remain open.

"JESUS, MAKE IT STOP!" I bellowed, my trembling hand still gripping the tooth ahead of me. "PLEASE MAKE IT FUCKING STOP!"

I ground my teeth together so hard they cracked, screaming as I slowly pulled my body deeper into the mouth.

Something was changing, the tight walls of its throat squeezed my head and I realized I was almost through.

"COME ON, YOU MOTHERFUCKER! COME ON!" I begged, vocal cords cracking. I reached ahead of me and grabbed onto a thick wad of flesh. My head felt like it was splitting, and The Pig bit down on me again.

I gasped, blood exploding from my mouth in a great gush of red.

It had pierced through my stomach, obliterating my insides

like bloated noodles. Darkness rushed in on me and I was in too much shock to even scream.

With the last of my strength, right as the blackness took me, I pulled myself forward one last time and felt myself slide down its throat.

Darkness. Falling…screaming. I was screaming. Heat. Heat so intense I thought I would melt. Clanging. Something was hammering on metal. Colors and images flew past me so quickly I could only make out their shape. Blood poured into my eyes.

I felt like I would keep falling forever.

Suddenly, my eyes snapped open and I was falling, my breath rushing back into my lungs in a great wave of purity. My face bounced off a wood floor and I cried out as I felt my nose break. I tasted blood and saw stars.

I had stopped falling.

There was a ring of burning fire around my throat and I felt impossibly thirsty.

I was lying on the floor.

I slowly opened my eyes again and the darkness began to fade like morning mist under a hot sun. Colors blended together and shapes came into focus.

I was in my woodshed.

I reached up around my throat and grasped at the source of heat. It was the rope I had hung myself with, but now it was severed, releasing me from the grip of death.

Relief rolled over me in overwhelming waves of thanks. I curled up on the floor and sobbed, tears dripping from my eyes onto the dirty floor. My body shook, unbroken as I wept, wet hoarse cries rising from my quivering lips.

I had been spared. I was alive again.

From my spot on the floor, I turned my eyes upward, my voice cracking. "Thank you God. Oh *thank you.*" I fell into another fit of uncontrollable sobbing. "I promise I won't waste my life again. I promise I'll make things right, I'll fix everything."

I don't know how long it was before I got up. Time seemed to stretch for eternity. My mind refused to rebuild, the horrors of what I had just witnessed crushing me.

But I knew I would do everything I could to make the most out of my life. I was going to live every day to the fullest. I would devote myself to helping others in dark times. I would reach out to as many Suicidals as I could and try to save them from what awaited on the other side.

I didn't want anyone else to have to witness the horrors of suicide.

I didn't want anyone else to have to Feed the Pig.

7

Ten Days, Ten Pills

Day 1

I'm trying a new medication. My doctor recommended it. Said it would help with things. It's a new drug, still in the testing phase, so they're putting me on a ten-day trial. Minimal side effects. Really no risk, so they say.

My doctor said I should document any changes I feel, good or bad, regarding my behavior. So I started this little diary. I feel kind of silly; I've never been the journal type. I just got home from the doc's about twenty minutes ago. I'm about to take one of these little pills. I feel a little nervous, despite his reassurances. I'm probably just paranoid, as usual.

Anyway…here we go.

Day 2

Well, I didn't sleep very well. I had headaches all night. The doctor said that was a possible side effect. Other than that, I haven't noticed any other differences. I took some Advil around four and that seems to be helping.

I'm about to make lunch. They say I should take these pills on a full stomach. I'm glad I don't have to go into work today.

I think after lunch I'm going to take a nap. I'm tired and my head has finally stopped killing me.

It's funny; this is the second entry I've written today. Maybe I actually like doing this? Anyway, I'm about to go to bed. Earlier, I ate lunch, took my pill, and then passed out on the couch. I had weird dreams. It's strange because I NEVER have dreams.

Anyway, it's almost midnight and I need to get some sleep. I'm going to try to make the most of my Sunday and get an early start, maybe go down to the lake. Hopefully it doesn't rain.

Day 3

I had a weird day today. Everything was fine until I went to the lake. I took my pill around noon before I went. I don't know if that has anything to do with what happened (I don't see how it could) but regardless, the whole point of this journal is to record anything out of the ordinary while on this trial.

So, I went to the lake around three. I brought my book and towel and laid out on the shore. It was sunny and warm, a nice day. There were a few families there, mostly little kids and a few teenagers.

Everything was going OK until…well…I heard this…horn.

Now, you have to understand this lake is out in the middle of nowhere. It's a local secret. You have to take this awful dirt road through the woods to even get there. But once you're there it's beautiful. A year ago, some of the locals dumped sand along the shore and have kept it groomed since then. It's like being at the ocean in the middle of a forest.

So anyway, it's about six o'clock and the sun is going down and this…horn…starts blaring from the woods. It's distant and low, rumbling across the water from the far bank. It reminded me of one of those old Viking horns.

Bewildered, I realized I was the only one who seemed to hear it. I looked around, tearing my sunglasses off, and no one even blinked at the sudden noise. After about three minutes, the horn finally stopped.

After that, I decided it was time to leave. I started packing up my car and froze, one hand on the driver's-side door.

Across the lake, three figures were watching me at the water's edge. They were far away, too far to make out their features. It looked like three men, but I couldn't be sure. Something was wrong with their faces, but no matter how hard I squinted, I couldn't see clearly.

Scared, I pulled my door open and hopped in my car. As I drove away, I could feel their gaze in my rearview mirror.

Day 4

I don't know what to make of all this. I'm going to call my doctor. I had more dreams last night. My head hurts. I took my pill a little before breakfast, but I'm wondering if I should have held off. It seems to make these headaches worse.

I went to work today but couldn't seem to concentrate. I felt like someone was watching me.

I feel like there's someone watching me now.

It's four in the morning. I just woke up from a nightmare. I heard that horn again. I don't know if it was outside or in my dream, but it woke me up. I'm sweating like crazy; it scared the shit out of me. I keep thinking I see things move past my window.

Day 5

Well, today was much better. I called my doctor and told him about all the strange stuff. He told me the headaches and dreams were probably just a side effect, nothing to worry about. He seemed skeptical about the other stuff, though. I told him everything and, God bless him, he listened to my ramblings. He assured me it was probably just stress-related, but to contact him if it got worse. He reminded me that this wasn't an approved drug, but it was the best chance we had of helping me.

I'm just going to suck it up. He said I just had to finish the ten-day trial and then we could reevaluate. I'm halfway there.

Day 6

More dreams last night. I dreamed something was sliding around my floor, like a shadow under my feet. Every time I tried to move away from it, it would zip back under me. I crawled up on my bed and it slid up the wall like a dark piece of paper. Right before I woke up, I thought I heard giggling under my bed.

When I got home from work today, something didn't seem right in my apartment, either. My closet door in my bedroom was wide open. I don't remember opening it this morning, but

I guess I could have forgotten about it. I made sure to close it tight.

It's four in the morning. I'm fucking terrified. Something is giggling in my bedroom closet. I don't know why, but every ounce of me is telling me to just ignore it and it'll go away. I'm writing this down to keep myself from going into a full-blown panic.

Day 7

I'm sitting on my couch, wondering whether I need to call my doctor or not. I don't feel good. I took my pill. I don't know why.

I have this feeling that if I just make it through the ten days, everything will return to normal. I called out of work. I closed all the blinds. I just want to sit in the dark and not fall asleep. My head is still killing me. Something is really wrong with me.

I think there's something standing on my balcony.

Day 8

It's midnight. I haven't fallen asleep yet. I'm on my couch, haven't moved since yesterday except to take my pill.

I can hear that horn again. It's distant, barely audible, but there.

I think something is giggling in my bedroom.

Day 9

I called my doctor today. I told him about all the horrible things that have been happening. You know what he said? He said I had to finish the ten-day trial, that I needed to, or they would come get me. When I asked who, he hung up. He seemed flustered, scared. What the fuck is going on? Who's doing this to me and why?

I'm still sitting on my couch. I don't want to move. Work keeps calling me, but I don't care. I just need to finish this trial. Just be done with it.

I think there's something in my bedroom. I can't see it because my door is closed, but I can hear it. It walks around on heavy feet and then giggles. I feel like if I just ignore it, it can't hurt me.

Day 10

It's three in the morning. I'm still on the couch. Something just opened the bedroom door. I can feel it staring at me, but I refuse to look at it. I'm writing this down to keep my eyes away from it. My heart is beating so fast I feel like I'm going to throw up.

The apartment is dark, but I can see the long black of its form out of the corner of my eye. It's just standing there like it's waiting for me to acknowledge it.

It's going to kill me if I do. I know it will.

It just giggled at me, the childlike sound ripping through the darkness. What eight-foot thing makes a sound like that? Why won't it move? What does it want from me!?

There's something behind me, too. I won't look, I won't look, I won't look. I need to keep my hands busy and focused on this so I won't look.

It sounds like there's...three...behind me...

I just need to make it until morning...just need to make it until the sun comes up...

Day 11

I...made it. I suppose. I...I don't even know what to say.

I called my doctor. Told him I finished the ten-day trial...told him about my horrible nighttime visitors...and...and do you know what he fucking did?

He started laughing at me.

Big, loud, gut-busting laughter. Once he got himself under control a little bit, he told me that the pills were harmless.

He told me the pills were Tylenol.

I sputtered, my mind expanding with possible reasons to this revelation and reaction from him. He started laughing again and I asked what the hell he was talking about.

He said the whole trial was bullshit.

He said it was a little game he had concocted for me.

He said there was no hope for me.

He told me that a paranoid schizophrenic like myself who suffered from chronic hallucinations deserved to be in an asylum.

He told me that there was no helping me and that he just wanted to play off my illness, really wind me up, before recommending me to be institutionalized.

I hung up to his howling laughter. My hands were shaking, sweating.

I couldn't fucking comprehend it. I couldn't wrap my head around why he would do something like that.

I thought I was getting better...

The sane are an entirely different kind of sick...

8

Red West

I watched as my son splashed around in the waves, the sun reflecting off the cool green water. Sean laughed as the waves crashed around his ankles and chased him up the shore. The ocean then pulled away, leaving trembling patches of sea foam that shuddered in the wind. The hot sand sighed with brief respite as the great walls of water curled in on themselves and fell, cooling the earth.

My son Sean was five and I smiled as he screamed with delight, another wave chasing him up the beach and collapsing at his feet. The sun lit a cloudless sky and the water danced in its light. The sky was empty and blue, a vast stretch of perfect color.

And it was all for us.

I looked behind me at my wife, sunbathing in the glorious heat. She had her sunglasses on so I couldn't see if she was looking my way, but I gave her a little wave from the water's edge just the same. I turned back to my son, grateful I had paid the hefty sum to get this exclusive stretch of beach.

And why not? We certainly could afford it, my recent success in the stock market fueling this celebratory vacation. I wanted my family to live like royalty, and a private beach thirty miles from everything was certainly a step in the right direction.

I looked back at the house behind me and grinned. It really was incredible. It was painted a soft blue and faced the oceanfront. Massive windows let in the breathtaking views, the modern design a series of hard angles that layered over one another to form a staggering feat of architecture. A two-level deck wrapped itself around the house, a stage to admire the melting evening colors as the sun set over the water. It was perfect.

In fact, everything was perfect. I scanned the area around us, still grinning, taking in the exclusive isolation my money had gotten us. Money really can buy happiness.

I looked at my watch and realized it was almost time to start making dinner. I called out to Sean and waved him over. He took another couple of big leaps in the crashing waves and then sprinted over to me, his face split into a big smile.

I asked him if he was hungry and he said he was "staaaaarving," so I instructed him to gather his toys and shovels and start packing up for the day. He ran to obey and I walked over to my wife, Rose, and told her I was going to take Sean up to the house and start grilling burgers. She asked if I minded if she stayed a little while longer and I swooped down and kissed her, telling her I didn't mind at all.

Sean and I stomped our way up to the house and rinsed our feet in the outside shower. That was something my wife insisted we do before we went inside. I watched as the sand swirled off our toes before I turned the water off, asking Sean if he could take my towel and hang it up to dry on the deck.

As he bounded up the stairs to comply, I walked to the front of the house to fire up the grill. I intended to burn off any residue before cooking the burgers, but as I rounded the corner of the house, I stopped.

There was a man standing in the driveway. He was big,

maybe six-four, with dirty blond hair that fell to his shoulders. He looked like he was in his late thirties, maybe early forties. He was wearing a brown leather jacket and a white T-shirt underneath. His pants were dirty and stained, the faded jeans looking well worn.

His sparkling blue eyes met mine.

He smiled and nodded. "Evening."

I took a hesitant step forward. "Can I help you?" I looked around—where had this guy come from? There wasn't another house for miles. The road leading to our secluded get-away was barren as well. All the stores and gas stations were dozens of miles down the street.

He pointed at the beach house. "Nice place you have here."

I cocked an eyebrow at him. "Thank you. Is there something you need?"

He smiled slightly, his eyes looking almost sad. He shoved his hands into his coat pockets and looked up into the sky. He didn't say anything, just stared at the mixing colors that swirled in the evening light.

I took a step toward him, unease worming its way into my stomach. The man wasn't acting hostile, but something about him put me on edge.

"I asked you if there was something you needed," I restated, my voice firm.

He looked back at me, his blond hair spilling across his shoulders, "Oh, I'm sorry. Can you tell me what time it is?"

I didn't know how to respond to his strange request and so I quickly checked my watch, wondering why the time was so important he had to walk all this way to ask me. I told him it was almost seven.

He looked up at the sky again. "I'm afraid that's not long."

My unease and caution bubbled up in my throat and I took an aggressive step toward him. "Look, buddy, I don't know who you are, but you're on private property right now. I'm going to have to ask you to leave."

Those bright blue eyes met mine again and I saw...kindness in them. A soft, apologetic look that told me he knew his presence was upsetting me. He pulled his hands out of his pockets and raised them at me, a sign of surrender.

"I'm sorry," he said. His voice was soothing, a gentle rumble, a deep cut of smooth silk.

He stuck his hand out for me to shake. "My name is Weston. I promise I mean you no ill will. I need to tell you something. Something important."

What the hell? I thought. After a moment's pause, I shook his hand, "I'm Dillon."

Weston smiled, his white teeth glowing in the setting sun. "Good to meet you, Dillon. I'm...afraid I have some bad news."

Here it comes, I thought. *I knew I wasn't being paranoid for no reason.*

Weston continued, "You and your family are in danger here. You need to leave."

I stared at the big man for a second before snorting in disbelief. "You're joking, right? You want us to leave? Do you know how much I paid to get this place? Do you know how long of a drive it was to get here? No, I'm sorry, buddy, but my family and I aren't going anywhere. Now are you going to explain to me what you're talking about or do I need to call the police? Because that sort of sounded like a threat."

Weston shook his head. "It's not a threat. I told you, I mean you no harm. I'm here to *warn* you."

I blinked at him. "Warn me about what?"

His eyes turned dark. "Something terrible is coming."

The way he said it made goosebumps pop out on my arms. I shook my head. "I don't understand. What's coming?"

He returned his gaze to the sky. "The Red West."

I snorted again. I had had just about enough of this guy. I wasn't sure if he was crazy or just a weirdo, but either way, it was time to get rid of him.

"Listen, buddy," I said, splaying my hands out in front of me, "my family and I are on vacation. We don't want any trouble. We just want to be left alone to enjoy our time away. OK? You get what I'm saying?"

He looked sideways at me. "You don't believe me, do you?" He looked back to the sky. "Of course you don't. Hell, I wouldn't believe me. I don't know if there is anything I can do to get you to leave; there probably isn't, but I had to try."

I pointed down the road. "Please just leave us."

Weston sighed. "It's coming soon. You don't want to be here when it arrives. I've traveled a long way for this. Please, take your family and go."

I jerked my finger toward the road. "Go! Now! Please!"

Weston stared at me for a moment longer and I saw a flash of something behind his eyes. Violence. Wordlessly, he jammed his hands into his coat pockets and turned. I watched him walk down the driveway, feeling my pulse slow. I wasn't sure what had just transpired, but I felt relief as he reached the road and kept walking.

I turned back to the beach house.

What a strange guy, I thought.

———

I scooped sizzling meat onto a plate, stomach growling as the hot cheese oozed down the sides of the patties. Sean was sitting at the table, clanging his fork against his glass in noisy anticipation. Rose placed a salad down and told him to stop making such a racket.

"Did you enjoy your quiet time alone?" I asked her, coming to the table and setting the stack of burgers down.

Rose placed her hand over Sean's, lowering his fork. "Yes, it was wonderful. I wish I could live on this beach. It looked like there was a storm coming, but hopefully it'll blow over by morning. I'm looking forward to another perfect day."

I took my place at the table. "Ooo, maybe we can turn off the lights and watch the lightning. Wouldn't that be cool, Sean?"

Sean shrugged. "I guess. I get to sit with mom, though."

I laughed and started preparing a burger for him. "Nope, you have to sit outside!"

Sean rolled his eyes. "Daaaaaaad, I'd die!"

Rose plated the salad and gave me a smile. "You just have to run faster than the lightning!"

The big bay windows lit up as lightning flashed across the sky leaving trails of thick, white afterglow.

"Whoa!" Sean exclaimed.

I passed him his burger. "Here, buddy, eat up. Can't outrun

the storm if you don't have food in you." As he took it, thunder rumbled overhead—a deep, bellowing growl.

"Sounds like it's going to be a big one," I said.

Rose speared salad with her fork. "You should have seen the sky on the horizon. It looked nasty."

The conversation lulled as we began to eat. I watched Sean as he munched away, his focus entirely on his food. It seemed like just yesterday he had been born.

It's scary the way time flies and how one day you look around and wonder what happened. It's like driving down a road where the surroundings gradually change, bit by tiny bit. As you drive, you don't even notice that the trees are getting taller, the foliage a little thicker. Before you know it, you're in a jungle and you don't even know how you got there.

I looked at Sean and wondered how much deeper into the jungle I had to drive before he started to resent me. It was bound to happen during those awkward teenage years. I knew I had hated my parents. Maybe Sean would be different. I was hoping I could just skip over that teen angst and get to the part where we'd be friends again.

I noticed Rose was watching me and I offered her a little smile. She returned it and I knew she understood my thoughts. That was something she had always been able to do. Back when I met her, she would tease me because of it. She had a little game where she would try to guess what I was thinking at random times. We could be on a date, visiting our parents, having sex; it didn't matter. No activity was safe from her.

When our relationship was still in the early phases I would sometimes lie and tell her she had guessed correctly. I did it because I wanted to see her laugh and flash that beautiful smile at me. That smile held me captive and was one of the first things I fell in love with.

Rose was the first woman to make me feel important to her, like I was someone special. She admired me, admired my mind. She looked up to me. She and Sean both did. I was their provider, their protector. I took that role very seriously and always looked out for their well being before my own. Isn't that what a good father and husband does? Puts the needs of his family before his own?

As I took another bite of my burger, I vowed I would never let anything bad happen to my family.

And that's when someone knocked on the front door.

Rose looked up from her plate, cocking an eyebrow at me. Thunder rumbled in the distance and I heard the first splatters of rain on the roof.

"Who's knocking?" Sean asked around a mouthful of food.

I stood, pushing my plate away.

"Are we expecting someone?" Rose asked, looking puzzled.

"I have a feeling I know who this is," I said. "There was a man walking around earlier while you were still at the beach. I sent him away, but..." I trailed off. "Look, both of you just stay here."

Through the windows I saw a bolt of lightning snake down from the sky and light the dark ocean, a freeze frame of silent violence. I turned my back to it and went to the front door.

I opened it and felt my stomach sink.

"I thought I told you to leave," I hissed.

Weston loomed in the doorway, his brown leather jacket crunching as he shifted his hands in his pockets.

"I'm really sorry," he said, his eyes two liquid blue crystals, "but this is where it's going to happen. I want to keep you and your family safe if I can."

"What the hell are you talking about?!" I asked as thunder boomed from the black. The spatter of rain on the earth uprooted a pleasant smell that filled the night air. It swirled in the rising wind and filled my senses as the prelude to the storm gained intensity.

Weston shifted his weight, his face urgent. "I know how this sounds, I know how this looks, and I'll be the first to tell you that you have every right to be suspicious of me. But I'm telling you, I want to help. It's almost here, it's too late to run." He pointed to the sky as more thunder cracked through it. "This is no ordinary storm coming."

I blinked at him, disbelief masking my face with its skeptical fingers. "Why can't you just leave us alone?! Do I need to call the police? Because I'm about to!"

Weston reached out and gripped my shoulder, a plea in his eyes. "Listen—Dillon, was it? Have you looked out across the ocean? Have you seen what this storm looks like? Please, just go look. You'll understand. Just look out at the ocean, look to the west."

I grabbed the front door, "OK, it looks like I'm calling—"

Weston stopped me from shutting the door, one big hand on the frame. "Please! If you don't believe me after you look, I'll go! I promise! I'm trying to save your family! I'm trying to protect them!"

I paused, his words striking a chord with me. I gritted my teeth, fighting internally with myself. I guess it couldn't hurt to look. After all, he said he'd leave afterward.

"Wait right here," I growled. I shut the door and stormed back into the house. My family looked to me with questions in their eyes. I waved them away, shaking my head, frustrated and annoyed that our vacation was being interrupted.

I went to the big bay windows and looked out into the black. I scanned the horizon, muttering under my breath. Everything looked…normal.

I was about to turn away when I paused, something catching my attention. Far out against the backdrop of black sky and dark ocean, something red and yellow began to flicker in the clouds. I pressed close to the window, cupping my hands around my face so I could see better.

The red and yellow light danced inside an enormous wall of bubbling, tar-black thunderheads, the veil of ebony smog tumbling from the sky in puffy, bloated waves to meet with the surface of the ocean. Lightning flashed around the mass of gloom, sparking and snaking in and out of the billowing pillar of darkness. Inside the immense vortex, the flares of red and yellow continued, pulsating like some kind of silent heartbeat.

It was unlike anything I had ever seen before.

And it filled me with creeping horror.

I backed away from the window, mouth going dry. The wind picked up and began slamming sheets of rain against the pane as if to get my attention at what was brewing on the horizon.

"What is it? What's going on?" Rose asked from behind me, concern in her voice.

I said nothing. I turned and stared at her blankly, my face a pale mask of fear. Thunder erupted overhead and Sean visibly jumped.

"W-we might have an issue," I stuttered, going back to the front door. Rose called out behind me, but I couldn't deal with her questions right now. I didn't have any answers to give.

I flung the door open and Weston was waiting for me.

"You see now?" he asked quietly, his tone somber. "You see what's coming?"

"Why didn't we hear about this on the news?" I asked, licking my lips. "A storm like this...we should have been warned!"

Weston shook his head. "Satellites and radar can't detect this. There was no way of knowing unless you've been following it from its inception. This storm...didn't come from here."

"What am I supposed to do? I have to protect my family!" I cried in a low whisper.

Weston's eyes shifted in shadow. "Yes...it will. But I can help you, if you'll let me. I've been following this for a long, long time now."

"What IS it? What kind of storm is this?" I asked.

"It's not the storm you need to fear," Weston said quietly, "it's what's inside the storm that should scare you." He pointed inside. "May I come in? We don't have much time."

I bit my lip and then waved him in, closing the door behind us. We walked back into the dining room and Rose and Sean were at the window, mouths agape, staring out at the coming storm. Violent clouds bubbled into each other like infected blisters, expanding and then popping in flashes of red and yellow while lightning cracked around it.

It was getting closer.

The rain was relentless now, throwing itself against the house in heaves of anger, the wind screaming in agony as

Mother Nature howled. Thunder shook the walls and the lights flickered once, then twice.

Sean was clutching his mother, his little hands tangled in her clothes in terrified bunches. They both turned around as we entered the room.

"Dillon, have you seen this? And who is this?" Rose asked.

Before I could answer, Weston strode forward, pulling his hands from his brown leather jacket. He reached out to my wife and shook her hand.

"I'm Weston. It's nice to meet you. Don't worry, I'm going to try and help you all weather this storm. I know it looks nasty, but I'm going to do my best to get us all through this, OK?"

He then squatted next to Rose and gave Sean a little fist bump. "Hey there, champ. You doing OK? I know this is probably pretty scary, but it's going to be all right." Sean blushed and squirmed against his mom.

Rose looked up at me, confused as to whom this man was and what he was doing in our house. I just stared at her, trying to find the words, but ended up just shutting my mouth.

"You look like you're a pretty tough kid," Weston was saying, still crouched next to Sean. "Do you think you could do me a favor, bud?"

Sean grinned awkwardly and shrugged.

Weston smiled back. "Can you be brave for me tonight?"

Sean looked at up at Rose and then back at Weston and nodded, "Yeah, I'm a pretty brave kid."

Weston laughed and tousled Sean's hair before standing back up. He loomed over Rose, but there was nothing threatening about his demeanor. For whatever reason, I found myself trusting this man.

"Good kid you have there," he said to Rose.

"I don't mean to be rude," Rose said, "but what are you doing here? Who are you exactly?"

Weston looked back at me and then at Rose. "I'm just someone who's trying to help a family in need. I knew this is where the…storm…would hit land and I knew there was a house here. I was hoping it wouldn't be occupied when I got here, but unfortunately, you're in this now."

"In *what*?!" Rose asked, clearly getting upset.

Before he could answer, something from outside silenced us all.

From the west, echoing across the churning water and infectious clouds, something *ROARED*. It was deafening, the noise shaking the foundation of the house. The lights flickered as we all slammed our hands over our ears, our terrified, bewildered eyes meeting one another. Sean screamed and wrapped himself around Rose's legs, burying his face against her.

The blast faded, the deep rumble retreating back into the frothing storm.

We all took a moment to recover, searching each other's faces for signs of comfort.

Except for Weston. He was staring out into the darkness, his face carved from cold stone but white as fresh snow.

"W-what the hell was that?" I finally whispered, blinking rapidly.

Weston didn't reply for a moment; he just continued to stare out into the night. Finally, after giving himself a little shake, he turned to address me. "We need to get you all downstairs right now."

"Dillon, what's going on?" Rose cried, panic in her eyes. "What was that?"

Weston placed a hand on her shoulder. "He doesn't have the answers; now let's go downstairs please."

I let him usher us toward the stairs and as we descended, my mind pulsed and reeled with disbelief at what was happening. Everything was moving so fast. Where had this storm come from? What did the strange light mean? What had made that noise?

Weston seemed to know what was going on but didn't seem too eager to share. I wasn't sure if I wanted to know. The most important thing right now was to keep my family safe, and Weston seemed to be of the same mindset. I didn't know who he was or where he had come from, but in that moment, I was grateful for his presence. He seemed to be in control of himself, seemed to know what we needed to do. I didn't know how he could help us, but I felt slightly more calm with him around.

Thunder boomed and the wind continued to howl against the house as we made it to the basement. We entered the den area, populated by a large sectional couch and a massive plasma TV. The ground level, the one we were currently on, wasn't underground, but I felt a little safer just the same. There was a sliding glass door that looked out on the ocean, but the view was obscured by a pair of drawn blinds.

Weston went to the door and peeked out, his watchful eyes scanning the darkness, waiting for a flash of lightning so he could see the beach.

"What are we supposed to do?" I asked, feeling helpless.

Rose had picked up Sean and was holding him tight, looking frightened. I went to them both and wrapped my arms around them, waiting for Weston to instruct us.

Not moving, he answered from his post at the door. "Just sit tight for now. It's getting closer. Won't be long now."

I felt sick, my stomach rolling in on itself as questions rose in my throat like bubbling water, but I swallowed them back down and waited. It wouldn't do any good to start saying things that would scare Rose and Sean.

I sat my wife and son down on the couch and kissed Rose on the head. I walked to Weston and dropped my voice to a soft whisper.

"Weston, listen, I need you to be straight with me. With whatever is out there...with whatever is coming...are...a-are we going to make it through this?"

Weston glanced at me and I saw fear in his eyes. "I hope so. We just need to wait."

"What are you waiting for?" I asked, shooting a look over my shoulder. Sean was quiet and curled up on my wife's lap, his eyes closed as Rose stroked his hair.

Weston pulled the blinds apart a little wider. "For it to make landfall."

I peeked outside and saw the towering column of darkness was fast approaching. It rose out of the ocean like a tightly coiled snake, thick and squirming with inky black energy. Its enormous mass reached for the stormy skies and tangled with the clouds, rising and getting lost in the night. The red and yellow lights continued to pulse and throb as pockets of neon smog burst along the coal-black pillar.

I turned away and sat with my family, leaving Weston to keep watch. I didn't know what I was looking for anyway. The air was filled with an ominous dread, a heavy blanket of hot fear. I let my wife lean into me, her head resting on my shoulder.

"I'm scared," she whispered.

"So am I."

I placed a hand on Sean's arm, letting him know that his dad was with him. We sat like that for a while, waiting, listening to the clash of thunder and rain outside. The walls shuddered as the wind came screaming off the ocean, the gale gaining intensity.

I watched Weston. He didn't move from his spot, his face a pale picture of grim uncertainty. His eyes remained locked to the outside, silent and waiting like the rest of us. My heart was tripping over itself in my chest, a clumsy drumbeat of nervous anxiety.

Suddenly, Weston slapped an open palm against the wall and leaned into the glass door, straining to see between the blinds. From my spot on the couch, I saw his eyes were wide and bloodshot.

"What is it?" I asked.

He didn't move and answered in a hard whisper, "It's here."

Suddenly, the night erupted as another deafening roar shook the house. It was deep and powerful, a long, howling cry of violent anger that shattered the air with splintering intensity.

Sean cried out and buried his face in my wife's lap. I clutched them both, my breath coming in short gasps, until the roaring howl passed and echoed around the house. Fear filled every ounce of me, and I had to fight not to join my son in a cry of terror.

Whatever was out there sounded massive and *furious*.

Weston took a couple steps back from the door, clearly shaken. He looked to us on the couch and then back out into the darkness. He was breathing heavily and he visibly fought to get himself under control.

"What is it!?" I hissed, urgency lacing my voice.

He swallowed hard. "It's emerging from the storm."

No sooner had he spoken then I felt slight tremors run through the earth. They were spaced apart and just intense enough to feel a physical registration. It felt like…footsteps. Like something colossal was walking toward us from the storm.

"Weston!" I cried, unable to hold in my fear any longer. "What do we do!? What is coming!?"

Rose was shaking against me, the terror infecting her. She held Sean close to her and whispered soothing words of reassurance into his ear as he continued to cry.

"Weston!" I pleaded.

Instead of answering, Weston stood in front of the door and visibly calmed himself. He closed his eyes and took a few slow, deep breaths.

Then he took off his leather jacket and tossed it to the floor. Without stopping, he peeled off his white T-shirt and flung it aside.

I blinked as I took in this strange display. His body was a mass of coiled muscle, thick and powerful, his toned flesh rippling with years of conditioning. His blond hair fell across his bulging shoulders as he closed his eyes and stepped toward the door.

"Weston!" I cried. "W-what are you doing!?"

He paused, one hand on the door. He turned to look at me and I saw burning violence in his electric blue eyes.

His voice grated in his throat like a blazing furnace. "I'm going to go kill that thing."

Without waiting for a response, he pulled open the sliding door. The wind and rain came barreling in, a sudden cold energy exploding from the night. Weston didn't even seem to notice as he stepped out into the darkness, pulling the door close behind him.

And then we were alone.

My wife and I looked at each other, my own shock and disbelief mirrored on her face. I felt like I should say something, but my throat clogged with fear and doubt. The tremors underfoot were gaining intensity and I felt my stomach bubble with despair.

As the minutes ticked by, I kept waiting for Weston to come back inside, but the door remained firmly shut. Thunder slammed against our ears and the torrential downpour added to the night's brutality.

It felt like the violence outside was building toward something.

I stood, unable to remain still any longer, and went to the door. I pulled the blinds apart and cupped my face to the glass.

I waited for lightning to illuminate the night and when it finally did, what I saw took my breath away.

Weston was standing motionless on the beach, facing the ocean. The wind and rain beat against his bare chest, but he remained an iron pillar in the storm, a mountain of grim determination. His hands were balled into fists, his rain-soaked hair dancing in the gale.

Something *titanic* in size loomed before him, drawing

closer with each earth-quaking step as red and yellow light flashed around it.

I turned away from the scene and felt sick, a deep horrified nausea eating away at my insides. I looked at Rose, feeling sweat trickle down my spine. What was going on? *What was that thing?!*

I flinched as a new noise cut through the night. It sounded like a cannon blast, the deep boom coming from the beach. As soon as the noise cracked the air, the windows flared with bright red light, a blinding blaze.

Another roar, this time sounding different. It sounded like a cry of pain. The light fixtures shook as the crimson light faded, overtaken once again by stormy darkness. The ground shook as another blast jolted the earth, the cannon-like explosion causing my ears to ring.

"What is going on out there!?" Rose cried, pulling her feet up onto the couch and wrapping herself around Sean.

Trembling, I turned to look outside as the sky flared in a blinding glow of red. I covered my eyes and steadied myself against the wall as the ground shook, the cannon-blast explosions growing more and more frequent.

And there was a new sound.

Behind the roar of the immense entity, my ears picked up the distinct sound of heavy gears grinding together. The two twisted and mixed together, the animalistic howling followed by the chug of working machinery. A moment later it sounded like gears shifting, which flowed seamlessly into the deafening howl of a biological being.

I pulled the blinds apart and stared out at the beach, knees weak.

I couldn't see much, the rain-streaked glass obscuring any clarity. Red and yellow lights pulsed along the beach, rising impossibly high into the night sky. Lightning flashed across the dark canopy and I caught a glimpse of... of *impossibility*.

Weston was rocketing up from the ground toward the colossal monster like a missile, a pale smudge against a black canvas. I watched in absolute amazement as he made contact with the creature, powering his fist into it with all his might.

I jumped as the familiar *boom!* followed, the sound of his knuckles cracking into the flashing black mass. Following the blow, the sky broke out in blinding crimson and I turned away from the scene, mouth agape.

Weston was fighting the monster.

I slumped down and leaned against the wall, trying to catch my breath. A barrage of cannon-blast explosions shook the foundation of the house and I shut my eyes against the vibrations. The thing outside bellowed in pain and fury, the bizarre howl seamlessly interlocked with the panting of a gigantic machine.

I don't know how long I sat there listening to the battle.

The windows pulsated with color, the storm screamed around us, and the deafening cries from outside engulfed my senses. I kept my eyes shut, silent prayer pouring from my mouth. The house shook and swayed, the groan of wood against wind and water.

The night bled with violence, the never-ending blasts ringing in my ears and rattling my teeth. My head ached with it, my bones shook with it.

I listened to the storm inside the storm, the clash of inhuman power that overshadowed reality. Something dark and evil had entered our plane of existence, something had slithered through the cracks of space and time and found our world. Something had emerged from the great mystery of the unknown and had arrived with a devastating anger.

This isn't happening, my mind pleaded, *this can't be real.*

Suddenly, the sliding glass door erupted in an explosion of brutality as something was flung through it at a terrifying speed.

Weston smashed into the far wall, a mass of blood and muscle, partially caving it in. His head whipped back in agony as he made contact, his body crushing through the sheetrock.

Rose and Sean screamed, covering themselves as the glass and plaster rained down around us. The wind screamed through the broken door, bringing with it a torrent of stinging rain.

I jumped to my feet, heart thundering, assessing Weston's condition as he slowly pulled himself from the wall. He gritted his teeth as blood leaked from his mouth, his face a twisted, bloody mess of pain. His chest was cut, blood dripping onto the carpet in thick wet drops. His hair was a tangled mess of soaking clumps plastered to his face.

He got to his feet and wiped the blood from his chin. He looked at me and I felt my blood run cold.

To this day, I have never seen eyes sparkle with such violence and fury. I took a step back as he flexed his shoulders. He pulled his hair back from his face, his knuckles swollen and split, blood running down his fingers.

"I can't kill it like this," he growled, looking at me. "I hurt it bad, but this won't kill it."

My legs were shaking and I fought to calm my panic. "Weston, what is it? Why is this happening?"

He sucked in long lungfuls of air. "It's The Red West. It was never supposed to make it this far. I didn't think it could. But somehow it made it onto this plane of existence, it broke through the walls of possibility."

"Where did it *come* from?" I asked, voice shaking. I wrapped my arms around myself, the wind blasting through the shattered door.

Weston met my eyes. "Home. It came from home."

"But where is that? How is any of this possible?" I cried, my mind straining to make sense of this impossibility.

Weston put a hand on my shoulder, his voice ragged. "The Red West is a horrible phenomenon that occurs where I come from. We've only had it occur two other times in the vast stretch of our existence. But it's supposed to be isolated to our reality. It shouldn't have been able to come here. I've been following it for a long time, watching it develop and grow. But then it began to move. That's why I had to come here, that's why I have to stop it. This is our problem, not yours. Your world shouldn't have to suffer from the horrors in ours."

As his words washed over me, a vociferous roar of raw rage blasted from the night.

It was waiting for Weston.

I looked up at the big man, looked at his bruised and bloody body, and said the only words that I could.

"Please...*save us.*"

Weston looked at my wife and son, who were curled up on the couch crying. He looked at me. His eyes melted into soft puddles of blue warmth.

"That's why I came," he said. "There's only one more thing for me to do now. For me to end this."

He gripped my arm. "Take care of yourself. Watch over your family. I hope to meet you again one day."

And with that, he released me and I saw his body begin to pulse with a dark energy. His skin began to radiate a deep red color and as I took in his sudden change, Weston charged back out into the storm.

I stepped into the shattered door frame and looked out into the night.

I'll never forget what I saw.

Weston's feet churned the sand, his body glowing with a brilliant bright energy. He was screaming, running at full speed, fists clenched at his sides. The towering mass of black and red loomed before him, blinking its strange neon colors. It stepped toward him, howling with ferocious anger as his opponent rushed to meet him.

Lightning lit the sky, the thick white veins illuminating the battlefield. Thunder crashed overhead as the two foes met at the water's edge.

Weston crouched at a full run and then rocketed from the ground, leaving the earth with such force that a shock wave sprayed sand and earth into the sky. He was a blazing red comet, a crimson bullet that soared toward the heavens, toward the head of the titanic entity.

I could hear him screaming with vengeful determination as he made contact with the tremendous mass of darkness.

The sky exploded with color, a cloud of red mushrooming out from the impact followed by a shock wave that was so powerful it knocked me off my feet and sent me tumbling into the far wall. Sand and earth exploded into the house from the broken door, showering us with wet clumps.

My ears rang as reality ripped, a screeching flash of pulsing colors, the sky twisting in on itself. A sound deafened my ears, a great screeching groan that rippled through the night and crashed down around us.

A moment later, everything went silent and I lost consciousness.

Darkness welcomed me…

Darkness…

Dark…

––––––––––

How do you make sense of impossibility? How do you settle your mind after witnessing such devastating horror?

I haven't seen Weston in four years. I probably won't ever seen him again. My family and I still haven't recovered from the terror of that night.

After the blast, I…don't remember much. When I woke up the sun was rising. Rose and Sean were lying on the floor and when I saw them I thought they were dead. I crawled over to them and shook them awake, breathing a sigh of relief as they opened their eyes. I remember tears were running down my cheeks.

We were covered in sand and dirt and I took us outside to breathe the clean air.

The beach was…gone. The earth looked like God had

struck it with an almighty hammer. It was…terrifying to behold.

Weston was nowhere to be seen. Both him and the entity were gone.

The sun was just creeping up the horizon and the beauty of it brought me to my knees. I couldn't believe I was alive to see it. My family joined me and we all wept, so completely shaken by the night's events that we couldn't do anything but cry. We clung to each other, feeling the wind rush through our dirty hair and across our exhausted bodies.

We had made it. We had survived.

I write this with hopes that somehow, someway, it will reach Weston.

I pray that he's alive somewhere, that he lived through the blast. I hope that whatever reality he may exist in, that these words reach him.

We owe you *everything*. No amount of thanks can even come close to what you are deserved, but from the bottom of my heart: Thank you.

Weston…*thank you.*

9

Blackout

I pulled into the bar parking lot and stopped the car. I sat there for a moment, letting the engine idle as I thought about what I was doing. I knew my wife and kids were at home waiting for me, but I just couldn't bear to face them right now. The thought of spending another evening with them while avoiding the elephant in the room made me physically sick. I closed my eyes and cursed myself.

Everything was going to shit. My wife was pregnant with our fourth child and I simply wasn't making enough money to support us. Over the past six months our quality of life had slowly declined and it was becoming harder and harder to explain to the kids what was happening. My wife and I loved each other, but the financial difficulties sprouted endless arguments that could last late into the night.

In truth, I was getting scared. I didn't know what was going to happen to us. I didn't know how to pull my family out of this terrifying nosedive. I couldn't stop thinking about it, couldn't stop thinking about that day when we'd be kicked out of our house.

I started having trouble sleeping and my mood worsened. I would find myself snapping at the kids over little things. One night just a few weeks ago, I had smashed a coffee mug in a rage. I'll never forget the looks on my kids' faces. I hate myself for that.

So instead of taking out my fear and frustrations on my family, I started to drink after work. At first it was just a beer or two, something to take the edge off. But after a month I began to stay later and later, drinking more and more. It was time I needed to think. It was a few moments of peace before going home and shamefully explaining to my family why we were eating beans and rice for the third time that week.

My wife hated my habit and I didn't blame her. She never argued with me about it, but when I came home reeking of beer and whiskey, she'd get a look in her eye. That look said everything: *You're not the man I married.*

I never really was a drinking man before I fell on hard times. Even in college I never drank much—certainly never to the point of being seriously drunk. I just didn't see the point. I hated feeling inebriated and usually only sipped on beer at parties so I'd fit in.

But now that my life was crumbling before my eyes, I found comfort in it. It was a space I could enter and push my thoughts to the edge of my tired mind. It was a momentary breath of air in a smoke-choked sky.

And tonight, I needed a drink.

Before leaving work, my boss told me they were conducting layoffs in the coming weeks. He didn't go into detail, but as I sat in my car, I realized he was unofficially informing me that I would soon be jobless.

I felt sick.

What the hell was I going to do? How was I going to provide for my family? Growing up, I never expected this. It wasn't what we were told. Poverty was something other people suffer through, not me.

The thought of my kids made me terribly depressed. They depended on me, they looked up to me. How was I supposed to tell them that their father was a failure? How was I supposed to tell them that we were going to have to move because daddy couldn't pay the bills?

I pulled my car door open and forced my mind to settle. I licked my lips. I needed a *few* tonight. I almost ran into the bar.

Music droned somewhere above me as my eyes roamed around the room. Neon beer signs lined the walls and their colors trailed in the air as I sipped my sixth rum and Coke. My head was floating above my shoulders and the conversation around me slurred and streaked like wet paint. I licked my lips and they felt bloated on my face. I blinked lazily and realized I was breathing heavily.

I shifted on my barstool and almost fell off. My mind exploded with dizziness and my stomach churned uncomfortably. How many beers had I had before starting the endless rum and Cokes? I couldn't remember.

The bar was surprisingly full, but I couldn't focus on individual faces. They piled around me, trying to get in drink orders, and I felt like a rock sticking out in the middle of a moving stream. I raised my glass to my lips and drained the last of its contents.

"Hey, Jack, you should go home, buddy," the bartender said, leaning in toward me out of the pool of mixing colors.

"Maybe one more and then I'll head out," I mumbled, raising my head to meet his gaze. His face swam before me and I closed one eye to stop it from moving.

"I think you're done, buddy. Come on, go home to your family."

I could feel darkness swirling around the edge of my vision.

I snorted and the bartender shook his head. "Want me to call you a cab, Jack?"

For some reason, I found this incredibly offensive and I shook my head violently, "Ah, piss off. I'll be fine." My head felt like a bloated boulder. I dug into my pocket and pulled out a wad of crumbled cash. I threw it on the bar and stumbled toward the door.

I felt like I was walking through a movie scene I wasn't supposed to be in. People turned to stare at me and I heard mutterings and snickers directed at my intoxicated state. I was too drunk to register shame and I shoved some punk kid aside and pushed myself out the front door.

The world rocked beneath my feet and I felt a sudden urge to vomit. I exhaled slowly and dragged my feet toward my car. I was in no state to drive. I gritted my teeth and checked my watch. It was after ten. Shit. I banged into my car, still looking at my watch, and let out an angry grunt. I ran my hands over the door until I found the handle and pulled it open. I didn't dare look at my phone to see how many missed calls I had.

I sighed as I climbed into the driver's seat. I needed to rest for a moment, settle my head. Then I'd drive home and apologize to my wife. I'd wait to tell her about the inevitable layoffs.

But first I needed to sleep.

I closed my eyes and darkness rushed me.

"Hey there, slick."

THE WORST KIND OF MONSTERS

I pulled my eyes open. Blinding sunlight immediately forced them shut again and I rubbed my face, trying to clear my mind. To my surprise, I felt all right. In fact, I felt fantastic. I opened my eyes again and cheery sunbeams warmed my face.

I blinked.

I was sitting in a sprawling green meadow. Birds chirped overhead and green grass rustled beneath me, a pleasant breeze chuckling through the air. I was sitting against a tree in a circular clearing with swaying forest that wrapped around a sparkling pond. Lily pads spotted the crystal surface like green paint on an artist's palette.

It was breathtaking.

For the first time in months, I felt peace settle in around me. The blue sky overhead was cloudless and I closed my eyes as I raised my face to absorb the gentle sunlight.

"Beautiful, ain't it?"

I snapped out of my trance and shot a look over to my left where the sudden voice had come from.

There was a man sitting against a tree not five feet from where I sat. He was in his mid-forties and was wearing a tan suit. A silver watch glittered on his wrist and his sports jacket wrinkled against the bark. His green eyes sparkled underneath the brim of a blue baseball cap that was pulled low.

"Where am I?" I finally asked. The last thing I remembered was passing out in my car, drunk off my ass.

The man smiled to reveal perfect teeth. "Ah, don't worry about that. Ain't no use in it. Just relax and enjoy all this." His slight Southern accent added to the pleasing atmosphere and I unexplainably found myself comfortable around this stranger.

"My wife, I need to get back to her and my kids," I said without much conviction. It was just so impossibly gorgeous here. I knew I needed to get home, but the overwhelming calm I felt made it hard to put action behind my words.

"They ain't going nowhere, slick," the man said, closing his eyes and taking a deep breath through his nose. "Just take a load off, enjoy yourself."

Bewildered, I leaned back against my tree and ran my hands through the blades of grass. The woods filled my head with an earthy scent, a combination of dirt and fresh rain on wood. The pond before me glittered like a mirror filled with diamonds and I found myself smiling.

Whatever this place was, I never wanted to leave.

All my worries seemed so trivial here. The overbearing stress I had felt earlier was gone, leaving in its place a warm comforting feeling, almost like happy nostalgia.

"I'm Russ, by the way," the man said suddenly from his spot. I turned and saw his eyes were still closed, but a small smile lined his lips.

"I'm Jack," I answered, watching a silver fish jump from the surface of the pond to snatch a bug.

Russ chuckled. "Oh, I know who you are, slick."

I cocked my head at him. "Who...who are you? What is this place?"

Russ adjusted the ball cap on his head before answering, "I just told you, I'm Russ. And this," he spread his hands, "this is just a little slice of peace, buddy. Ain't nothing more."

"Can I stay here?" I asked after some time.

Russ snorted, but there was no malice in it. "'Fraid not,

partner. That wouldn't be good. This place isn't meant for that. Not anymore."

I raised an eyebrow. "Not anymore?"

Before he could answer, a noise echoed in the forest around us. It was distant and low, a single deep note that crawled up the sky and fell upon us.

It sounded like the beat of a great drum.

Russ pulled his cap up and sat a little straighter.

"What was that?" I asked as the sound faded.

Russ looked at me, his eyes uneasy. "That's why you can't stay here for very long."

Suddenly, the drum sounded again…and again…and again…a constant beat that filled the woods with a single ominous note.

And for some reason, it filled me with creeping dread.

"Not good," Russ mumbled under his breath.

"What is it?" I stressed, feeling uneasy.

Russ stood up, brushing himself off. "It's the Whistlin' Man. Oh, he's bad news, slick. You don't want to be around if he shows up."

I wasn't following anything he said and it must have shown on my face because he raised his hands.

"Listen, you need to leave," he said as the drum slowly began to grow louder.

"Why? What will happen?" I asked.

Russ waved me off. "Nothing good, slick, I'll tell you that much. You can come back, but not when he's around."

"B-but where IS here?!" I sputtered as Russ advanced on me.

Before he could answer, the forest filled with a piercing cry, a sharp whistle that cut through the sky and echoed all around us. I slammed my hands over my ears as the deafening note danced across the sun rays and exploded across the meadow.

As the wavering echo faded, another whistle followed, this time lower, a kind of haunting melody that chilled me instantly. The drum was growing louder and I thought I felt the earth shiver slightly beneath my feet.

Russ turned to me, his eyes wide. "Get out of here! GO!"

He shoved me backward and I stumbled, tripping over my feet—

—and woke up gasping in my car.

I immediately opened the door and vomited into the parking lot, a great gush of hot stomach bile and gurgling rum. Tears leaked from my bloodshot eyes as I sat up and wiped my mouth. My head was splitting and I was desperately thirsty. I looked at my watch and groaned. It was a little after midnight. I took a few seconds to collect myself, thinking back on what I had just experienced.

What had just happened?

I could still hear the echoing shrill note of that chilling whistle. Or did I? I ran my hands over my face, the consequences of my nighttime drinking churning my stomach again. How was I going to explain this to my family? What would I tell my wife?

She was going to be furious.

I suddenly wished I was back in the meadow. The serene peace it had offered upon arrival was intoxicating. No worries, no stress, no responsibilities. Just warm sun and beautiful, accepting nature.

As I started my car, I made a decision.

I would do anything to go back. And now...I thought I knew how to get there.

The next two days were a waking hell. As expected (and rightly so), my wife was pissed. She wasn't a woman who yelled or threw things. I almost wished she were. Instead, she turned to ice, barely acknowledging my existence until my due sentence was up...whenever that was. I tried to be extra active with the kids, even taking them out for ice cream, but that wasn't enough to get my dear wife to warm to me.

It was the weekend and every minute seemed like a chore. On the outside, I was Super Dad, making sure to always wear a smile and engage my kids in conversation and playful fun. None of this thawed my wife out and I felt the thirst return to me with a vengeance. I still hadn't told her about the inevitable layoffs and judging by her mood, I wouldn't until her fury had passed.

When Sunday night rolled around and she still wasn't talking to me, I decided that after work the following day, I would return to the bar and get shitfaced again. I needed to see if I could go back to that meadow. I needed it in the worst kind of way. My sanctuary of peace.

I knew it was the worst thing I could do, but the frustrations of the weekend pushed logic out of my frazzled mind. She didn't fully understand the stress and worry I was going through. She didn't know the weight I carried every day. It wasn't her fault, but I expected her to cut me some slack.

As I slid into bed that night, my wife silently turning her back to me, I licked my lips and focused on tomorrow. The need was so great I almost got up and left right then and there.

What little reason I still possessed forced my eyes closed and I tried to summon the vision of the meadow.

I could almost feel it, waiting for me right behind my eyes. If I focused hard enough, I thought I could smell the greenery swirling through the swaying forest. If I shut everything out, I thought I could hear the frogs croaking at the edge of the water. Was that Russ? I was sure I had just heard him speaking to me, his Southern accent melting the air like warm butter over steamed corn.

But it was all just out of reach.

For whatever reason, I couldn't quite access that special place. I needed a catalyst.

I needed a goddamned drink.

And that's how I found myself slumped over the bar the following night. The day had seemed like an eternity, the clock indifferent to my desperation. On the way to work that morning I had almost stopped at the liquor store but had managed to hold off.

My boss didn't say anything to me, which I took as a good sign, and I diligently plowed through my day's duties. My wife still wasn't talking to me, barely looking my way as she prepared the kids for school. I had tried to give her a hug goodbye, but she brushed me off, muttering that she had to finish packing lunches.

This sparked an anger in me and I wordlessly left the house, clamping my teeth shut so I wouldn't say anything stupid. I knew getting wasted tonight wasn't going to repair our teetering marriage, but I had been pushed to my limit. If she wasn't going to forgive me, then what was the point? Her morning coldness had cemented my resolve to go out tonight and I barely felt any guilt. I justified it in my mind with little effort and as I pulled into the bar parking lot, I felt a cool blanket of relief sweep over me. This was where I could let go a little. This was where I didn't have to think about my problems. This was my much-needed breath in a life devoid of oxygen.

I tipped the glass to my lips and sucked the rum off the ice cubes. I hadn't bothered mixing my drinks tonight. I had a destination in mind and I wanted to get back there as soon as possible. Judging by the way the room swam, I was doing a pretty good job of it, too.

The bar was relatively empty and I was relieved for it. A quiet tune played from the retro jukebox in the corner and I hummed along as I tapped the bar for another refill. The usual bartender, Kenny, was off tonight, and I was grateful for it. He had a tendency to cut me off and I didn't want that tonight.

I smiled at the young lady, my drink server for the evening, and muttered my thanks as she placed a fresh rum in front of me. I was trying my best to maintain my composure, and the lack of people helped my cause. I didn't want to stop drinking until I couldn't see.

I downed half the rum in one swig and felt it slam into my stomach like a derailed train. I burped behind my hand and felt my eyelids flutter as if they were suddenly swollen. I smacked the taste from my lips and my tongue burned with alcohol. My thoughts had become hard to control, the booze filling my mind like a sinking ship.

I had been here for three hours and I felt like if I tried to stand, there was no guarantee my legs would obey.

I tipped the glass to my lips one last time and that was

ELIAS WITHEROW

enough to cloud my vision with a heavy fog. Blackness pressed
in on my sloshed brain and I ran a hand over my face. It felt
like there was a face over my face. I giggled at the thought but
was suddenly overcome with sadness. I blinked a few times
and decided it was time.

I cashed out with a mumbled thanks to the bartender and
very carefully walked out to my car. The world rocked beneath
my feet and the full moon was so bright I had to shut one eye
against it. My head felt thick and every breath tasted like ice
and spiced rum.

I stumbled to my car and managed to get the door open
before collapsing into the driver's seat. I rolled my head back
and shut my eyes, a small smile on my lips. I waited for it to
happen.

It didn't take long.

"Well howdy there, slick."

I opened my eyes and gentle sunlight lit my vision. Stunning greens and blues melted together to form breathtaking
beauty and my senses filled with the peaceful, now familiar
meadow before me.

I was back.

The dense forest encircling this pocket of paradise swayed
gently in the breeze, the leaves rustling together to form a
serene soundtrack to the majesty of this hidden nature.

The grass was soft beneath me, like cool blades of emerald
silk. I ran my hands through it and leaned comfortably against
the tree I sat under. The pond before me was captivating in its
stillness, a plate of shining silver.

I turned and saw Russ sitting a few trees over, his blue baseball cap resting high on his head. His tan suit jacket was balled behind his head and he leaned comfortably against it.

"I had to come back," I said. "This place…" I trailed off, trying to find the words.

"It's somethin' special, ain't it?" Russ grinned, crossing his feet in front of him.

"You got that right."

Silence passed between us and I sighed heavily, a smile filling my lips. My head emptied of worries and was filled with complete tranquility. The secluded isolation added to the calming magic of the meadow and pleasant bird songs danced between the trees.

Again, I was filled with the desire to never leave this place. Everything was just so perfect. It made life seem unfair in comparison. Why were things so hard? Why did misfortune and approaching despair plague my every day? Why couldn't I just stay here, away from all that, and close my eyes in peace? This was all I needed.

"You know," Russ said from his spot, "as much as I enjoy your company…I worry about you."

I snorted and looked over at him. "Oh, yeah? Why's that?"

Russ adjusted his baseball cap. "You know why. Don't make me say it, slick."

"Can you just let me enjoy the quiet?" I asked, shutting my eyes.

Russ grinned. "Of course, pal. Of course. But I need you to know something."

Before he could continue, a distant drum began to beat.

Boom…boom…boom…

I opened my eyes.

Russ pointed out into the woods toward the noise. "That."

I shifted, trying to block out the sound. It twisted my stomach with unease.

"What about it?" I asked softly.

Russ stared at me under the brim of his cap. "That didn't used to be here."

I nodded toward the distant drum. "That? The drum?"

His green eyes bore into my skull. "Not just the drum...*HIM*."

I licked my lips. "Who?"

Russ's voice dropped to a whisper. "The Whistlin' Man. You can tell when he's around when the drum starts. He's looking for you, slick. And he ain't ever going to stop."

I shifted uncomfortably. "Who is he...what does he want?"

Russ stared out into the forest. "Do you really have to ask?"

I suddenly threw my hands up in frustration. "What are you talking about?!"

Before he could respond, the air filled with a shrieking note, a long high whistle that bore into my head like a screaming drill. Swarms of birds erupted from the trees and took flight, escaping the sound.

Russ jumped to his feet, fear written across his face. "You better scram, slick; it sounds like he's close."

"I don't want to!" I shouted, climbing to my feet. "I don't care who he is, I don't care what he wants! Anything is better than going back to...to...out there!" I finished, jabbing my finger toward the sky.

Russ approached me as the drumbeat grew louder, another whistle slicing through the meadow like a razor blade. It was the same low note as last time, the strange melody chilling me to the bone. But despite that, the thought of leaving made me want to weep. I had only just arrived, I couldn't leave yet; I couldn't face what awaited me on the other side.

"He doesn't have to be here!" Russ said urgently, shooting a look over his shoulder. "You have to get rid of him! It wasn't always like this!"

"What the FUCK are you talking about!?" I cried. The drum was deafening at this point and I felt the soil beneath my feet begin to tremble.

Russ opened his mouth to speak, but a new voice erupted from inside the forest, a horrible deep bellow of rage.

"JAAAAAAAAAACKIE! WHERE ARE YOU, JACKIE!?"

Another series of long whistles followed, cracking the air like a bullwhip.

Russ's eyes went wide and the blood drained from his face. He took a step forward and raised his hands to me.

"GO! GOOO!"

He shoved me hard, and I went sprawling backward—

—and woke with a jolt inside my car.

Nausea tossed my stomach like a rotten salad and I slammed the door open and emptied my gut onto the asphalt.

"NO!" I screamed, wiping my face and pounding on the steering wheel. "No no no! I can't be here! Let me go back!" The horror of being back in the waking world faced once again with my looming, life-ruining problems filled me with absolute panic.

The night air filled with indifferent moonlight and I raised my eyes to the sky. "I can't do this anymore! Russ! Let me come back!" I thought I could feel his presence, a tickle in the back of my head. I focused on it, begging to be swept away to the calming meadow. I didn't care about this Whistlin' Man, I didn't care about what he wanted. I couldn't face my family right now. I didn't want to think about work or money. I just wanted to go back!

"Help me!" I cried, slamming my fist into the dashboard. "Take me BACK!"

I sat there for a moment, trembling, bloodshot eyes catching focus on everything, then nothing.

I wiped my face. "You can't do this to me," I muttered. "You can't make me stay here." I checked my watch and saw that it was midnight. Last call wasn't for another hour and a half.

I licked my lips and ran a hand through my hair. I felt like shit. I knew I probably looked like shit, too, but that wasn't going to stop me.

"I'm coming back," I growled, stepping out of my car, avoiding the puddle of vomit, "and I'm not going to let you send me away this time."

My legs wobbled as I carefully made my way back inside the bar. I steadied my breathing and summoned as much willpower as I could. It wasn't easy. My throat burned and my eyes were watering. The world rocked and swayed beneath me and I gritted my teeth against it.

I pushed the bar doors open and slowly made my way back to my stool. I motioned for the bartender and she returned to me, an eyebrow cocked. She told me she was surprised to see me back and I told her my car wasn't working. I told her a friend was coming to give me a lift and I was just coming back in to kill some time. I spaced out my words and tried my best not to slur. I asked her if she could load me up a beer and a shot.

She chewed her lip for a moment and I could see her thinking, my intoxicated state apparent no matter how good an actor I thought I was. I reached into my pocket and slid her two twenties, tipping her a wink.

"For taking such good care of me tonight," I said.

The money shattered any moral disputes she had been fighting against, and she immediately cracked the top off a beer. She filled a shot glass and placed it in front of me, telling me to behave myself. I thanked her and assured her I would.

When she turned away, I slammed the shot, gasping at the sudden charge of heat. Whatever edge I had lost from vomiting returned as the rum hit my system. I snatched the beer up and sucked it down, exhaling heavily as the last drops slid onto my tongue.

I felt sick, like a soaked sponge left on the counter. I stank and my already upset stomach fought against the booze. I looked around, the room tilting and swaying, and saw there were only two other patrons. They were over in the corner not paying attention, and to my delight I saw them wave over the bartender. It looked like they knew her. She shot a quick look at me and then went over to them.

Heart racing, consciousness blinking, I quickly leaned forward and snatched a half-full bottle of rum from the counter. I chanced a look over my shoulder and saw that my act had gone unnoticed.

"You can't get rid of me," I mumbled, tipping the bottle to my lips. "You can't make me stay here."

I closed my eyes and drank.

I didn't stop until everything went dark.

I gasped and opened my eyes. I was on my stomach, soft clovers tickling my face. I breathed them in and sighed, relief running through me. I got to my knees, pulling myself up, and surveyed the meadow.

Something was wrong.

The sun was hidden behind thick gray clouds, a blanket of dark cotton. I craned my neck and was met with nothing but silent gloom. The woods were quiet, the usual chorus of birds and bugs eerily absent. I could hear my heart hammering in my chest, a rush of beating blood in my ears.

I looked to my left, scanning the tree line, and suddenly felt sick as my eyes focused on the scene before me, a deep fear sparking in my chest.

The forest was ripped in half, leaving a dark corridor of splintered ruin. It looked like an immense train had exploded through the woods, obliterating everything in its path. Fractured trees and uprooted underbrush spilled out into the clearing, the remains of nature's vicious goring.

"What is going on?" I whispered, voice tainted with fear.

I suddenly spotted something in the pond, floating on the surface. It bobbed slightly and as I squinted to try and make out what it was, my eyes went wide and panic foamed in my throat.

"Oh no, no, no," I cried, charging toward the water's edge. I splashed into the shallows at full speed, tripping and then pulling myself up. I shoved lily pads aside and sloshed deeper, the horror before me gaining clarity.

"RUSS!" I screamed, reaching out for his motionless body. The water was up to my waist as I grabbed at him, pulling him up from under. He was dead weight in my arms, his head rolling against my chest as I dragged him toward shore.

"Come on, come on," I begged, gritting my teeth, heart racing, muscles groaning. His eyes were closed and he didn't move.

Gasping, I finally got us onto the grass, where we collapsed in a rush of weight and water. I struggled to regain my breath as I got to my knees and flipped Russ over on his back.

My heart sank.

His face was a mess of cuts and dark bruises. His clothes were a tangled jumble of torn fabric and tattered cloth.

"What happened to you!?" I cried, brushing strands of wet hair from his face. "Who did this to you!?"

I felt like I already knew the answer.

I shifted myself over him, fighting panic. I placed my hands over his chest and began administering CPR.

"Please wake up," I begged, pumping his chest. "Please, you have to wake up, don't do this, please!"

I leaned down and blew into his mouth, tears starting to leak from my eyes. I felt helpless, alone, and filled with overwhelming despair. Why did everything always have to go to shit? Why did I always end up making things worse? Why couldn't I escape the never-ending stream of misfortune?

"PLEASE!" I screamed, now beating on Russ's chest. "PLEASE DON'T DO THIS!"

Suddenly, in a rush of urgency, Russ's eyes snapped open and he vomited up a great spout of pond water. He coughed and sputtered, emptying his stomach as his body convulsed.

I leaned back on my knees, unable to believe it. Relief swept over me as I exhaled, a cackle escaping my lips.

"Ha! You're alive! Oh my God, you're alive!" I cried, gripping Russ's shoulder as he wiped his mouth and lay on his back.

Russ kept his eyes shut, his voice terribly weak. "Hey, slick. You just can't seem to stay away, can you?"

"What happened to you? Why is everything different?" I asked.

Russ tenderly touched his beaten face before answering. "He found me. He found me with you already gone. He didn't like that."

"Who?" I already knew the answer.

Boom...boom...boom...

I jerked my head to the woods, the sound of the drum robbing my attention. *No. Not now. Please, not now.*

Russ sighed, broken and defeated. "He's coming back to finish the job. And if you're here, he's going to get you, too."

Boom...boom...boom...

The drum was getting louder.

I leaned down and grabbed Russ's arm. "What does he want? Why is he doing this?"

Russ closed one eye and looked painfully at me with the other one. "He's not doing this, Jack. You are."

My body went cold and I said nothing, throat going dry.

Suddenly, a long rising whistle rose from the forest, first high, then dipping low. The notes bounced off the dark clouds and echoed across the meadow, filling me with dread.

Russ tried to sit up, grasping at my arm. "You can't keep doing this," he growled, desperation filling his voice. "You can't keep coming here like this. He's going to kill you!"

My eyes lined with tears and they spilled down my face. My

lips trembled and I looked down at Russ. "I'm sorry. I'm so sorry." I put my hands over my face, sobbing, "Jesus, what have I done?"

"JAAAAAAAAAACKIE!"

The voice cracked through the air like a clap of thunder and my heart tripped into my ribcage, a flutter of crippling fear spreading across my chest.

BOOM...BOOM...BOOM...

Another shrieking whistle, a sharp drill in my ears, boring into my skull.

The ground shook beneath my feet and I suddenly heard a roar of exploding wood and crashing underbrush from the forest. The sound was distant but approached the meadow at a tremendous speed.

"The Whistlin' Man," I whispered, my breath sour on my tongue.

I stood up and faced the tree line. Sweat coated my spine with cold fear and I licked my lips, face pale and gaunt.

"Don't let him get you," Russ said from the ground.

Tears ran down my cheeks as the cacophony of sound rose around me in a deafening crescendo. I closed my eyes as the drum and constant whistle blasted around me. I could hear trees crashing to the earth as the Whistlin' Man rocketed toward me from the woods. I felt helpless and terrified, a lone man against a tsunami of power and devastation.

The Whistlin' Man exploded from the tree line and into the meadow.

Immediately, everything went silent.

My heart counted the seconds against my chest. I squeezed my eyelids shut even tighter.

I suddenly felt the presence of someone standing directly in front of me, hot breath on my face.

"Been looking for you, Jackie," something said, inches from my face. The voice was a low rumble like thunder in the summer.

I kept my eyes firmly shut. My knees were shaking and I felt my bladder release in a rush of terror. My lips quivered and tears dripped down my chin.

"Go away," I croaked, my voice a dry rasp.

I felt a heavy hand rest on my shoulder, followed by a low chuckle. "Go away? Ah, Jack, why would you want that? You brought me here."

I shook my head, squeezing my eyes shut even tighter. "Not anymore."

A hand gripped my chin. "Look at me. Open your eyes. Look at what you've created."

"Please," I sobbed, spittle spraying. "Just leave me alone."

"Open your eyes, Jackie."

Weeping, I slowly pried my bloodshot eyes open and the breath rushed from my lungs in a haunting wave of horror.

I was staring into my own face.

The Whistlin' Man grinned as the recognition twisted my face with shock.

"You see?" he growled. "There ain't nothing to be afraid of. This is just who you are."

I took a step back, shaking, trembling. "No...no, this isn't who I am."

He chuckled and took a step closer. "Oh...yes it is, Jack."

I violently shook my head, "No! NO! I'm a good person! I'm NOTHING like you! I'M NOTHING LIKE YOU!"

The Whistlin' Man suddenly stepped forward and grabbed me by the throat, his grip deadly and impossibly strong. "It's time we finally settled this, Jackie."

"J-just leave me alone!" I gurgled as his grip tightened around my throat.

He leaned into me, grinning, and squeezed darkness into my vision. "It's over, Jack."

Stars swam around me and the world began to fade.

With one last gasp, I whispered, "P-please…just let me go home."

Right as I was about to pass out, as blackness ate my eyes, the iron grip around my throat was removed.

I gasped and fell to my knees, the meadow rushing back into focus. Color and clarity realigned and I coughed and sputtered, clutching my aching throat.

I looked up in relieved confusion and my eyes went wide.

Russ was holding the Whistlin' Man from behind, one arm wrapped around his throat in a chokehold. He had his other arm over the Whistlin' Man's face with his hand shoved inside his mouth, gripping his upper jaw with commanding strength.

Sweat stood out on Russ's face, his eyes two coals of burning fire. His voice crackled like a blazing furnace. "HE DOESN'T NEED YOU ANYMORE! LEAVE HIM ALONE, GOD-DAMN IT!"

The Whistlin' Man growled around Russ's hand, fury shaking him. "I AM HIM!"

Russ's neck muscles strained as he began to pull the Whistlin' Man's head backward, howling with deafening authority, "NOT…ANY…MORE!"

Screaming with exhausted effort, Russ ripped the Whistlin' Man's head back between his shoulder blades in an explosion of blood and bone. I heard a sickening pop as his spine shattered, blood gushing from the now lifeless mouth.

Gasping, Russ pulled his bloody hand from the Whistlin' Man's jaws and shoved the dead man to the ground. Breathing heavily, he looked at me, chest heaving.

"You OK, slick?"

Shock rooted me to the ground, complete disbelief freezing me where I sat.

"Jack?"

Crying, I got to my feet and embraced him, weeping into his chest. Russ stroked my hair and let me cry into him, his heart beating against my chest.

"Thank you," I wept. "I'm so sorry. I'm so fucking sorry for doing this."

Russ pulled me away and took me by the shoulders. "You're a lot stronger than you think, Jack. Never forget that."

I wiped tears from my face, unable to stop more from coming. "I won't forget. I promise I won't. Thank you."

Russ nodded. "Are you ready to go back?"

I nodded, sniffing.

Russ closed his eyes. "Good luck to you, slick. I'm proud of you."

And with that, he pushed me backward—

—and I awoke with a start on the bar floor.

Faces were looking down at me, a blur of color and noise. I blinked and then everything rushed into focus. It was the bartender and the two men she had been talking to. Their faces were filled with concern and I realized they were talking to me.

"Hey, you OK?" one of the men asked, getting down on one knee and helping me sit up.

Relief washed over me in a suffocating wave and I gritted my teeth as my eyes filled with tears.

I smiled up at the three of them, my head clear and focused, all traces of a hangover gone. "I'm all right, thank you. Must have slipped in my stool and bumped my head is all."

The bartender told me they had heard a crash and looked over to see me lying on the floor, unmoving. She said it had taken them a little bit to wake me, almost to the point of calling an ambulance.

I assured them I was OK, climbing to my feet and brushing myself off. My inexplicably calm demeanor clearly confused them to the point of not pressing me further. I thanked them for their concern and told them I was going to call a cab and go home.

After making sure I was really OK, they told me to take care of myself.

I smiled. "I will."

That was three years ago. It's been a long, hard road since that night, but I'm doing well. It took months for my wife to get over that horrific act of selfishness, but I've proven to her since then that I will never be that man again. I can't believe she didn't leave me, and it fills me with eternal gratitude.

I've spent this time proving to my family that they can rely on me. I've shown them my resolve and we've grown closer, making it through those horrible early months of uncertainty.

But we're stronger now and life has begun to show promise of happiness.

I did end up losing my job, but my boss was able to secure me another job with a sister company. It was an act of kindness I wasn't expecting, and it furthered me down the path of positivity.

It's taken three years to rebuild my life to a point of hesitant optimism.

And it's been three years since I had a drink.

I'm not going to lie to you and tell you it was easy, because it wasn't. It was hard, impossibly hard, even after everything I went through. There were days I almost gave in to the temptation, but I would open up to my wife during those times of weakness and she got me through them. She gave me hope that I could change. But I had to face what I had become first.

And I will never go back to being that man.

I'll find my own way to the meadow.

I know it's out there, waiting for me, the path to its peaceful serenity growing more clear the longer I walk the road of recovery.

And even though I've come so far and made so much progress…I'm still filled with fear.

Because I know he's out there waiting for me.

He'll always be there.

The Whistlin' Man.

10

Where Is My Son?

My son has gone missing.

It's been three weeks. The police can't find him. The detectives I've talked to inform me they haven't found anything, but they won't give up. My neighbors are constantly ringing my doorbell, offering support, offering help in any way they can. My daughter, Lily, misses her older brother. At just five, she doesn't understand what's going on. What's happening.

My wife is a mess. She's drunk herself stupid, keeping the blinds closed and wandering aimlessly about the house. My life is a mess. My world has shattered, every day feeling like a nauseous dream. I can't sleep. I can't eat. I can't even think. My little boy. My little man. Where did he go?

Justin is eight years old, loved by all, charismatic and full of kind words. He's an angel. He is my everything. And he's gone. Where? There's not an easy answer for that. The only thing I do know is that the story I told the police fell on deaf ears and raised more than one eyebrow.

It was three weeks ago. Everything was normal. Everything was how it should be. The kids had come home from school and I had taken Justin to soccer practice. I had watched him play, talking with the other parents around me, humbly thanking them for their praise as they watched my son dribble the ball like he was born to do it. It was cool that night, a relief from the August heat. I felt at peace. I was happy.

Later, after practice, I had taken Justin to get ice cream. We laughed and I joked with him that one day he'd have more girls chasing him than he knew what to do with. He made a face and told me girls were gross. He was eight; he wasn't thinking about girls. He was thinking about sports, about becoming a star player. Just like he should be.

We went home, our stomachs bursting with sweet sugar, and I instructed him to take a shower. As he showered, I played with my daughter, Lily. She loved me and she loved her brother. She was quiet, unlike Justin, and had a gentle sweetness that I prayed she would hold onto as she grew. She didn't get it from her mother, that's for sure.

My wife Tess was a hard woman. After Lily was born, she began to despise everything. The kids took up most of her time, her freedom, and she didn't like that. I had talked to her many times, begged her to stop yelling at the kids, and asked her to soften her heart and words. But she hadn't. She had started drinking instead. More times than I can remember, I would come home and find her slumped over on the couch, an empty vodka bottle next to her.

My heart grew heavy. I loved this woman. I wanted to see her smile, to see her live and love. I wanted her to love me. But her anger just seemed to grow the more I pressed her to be that way. Did I go about it the wrong way? Probably. But I knew that behind all of it, she knew I loved her and knew I wanted what was best for her. I wanted our family to be happy.

It got worse. She kept spiraling down the dark hole of alcoholism, growing worse and worse every day. As she sank, I found myself shrinking into myself. I found myself spending as much time as I could with the kids, away from the house. Away from her. Away from the screaming, the anger, the bitterness. If she wanted her freedom, fine; I needed my kids and I needed to be a good father to them. I wanted them to grow up and remember a happy childhood. I wanted them to smile.

Why didn't I just leave her? Take the kids and get out? Because she was my wife. She was the mother of my kids. I couldn't. I wouldn't. I was stubborn and I desperately believed things could change.

And they had.

But not the way I expected. That night after practice, after putting my little angels to bed, I climbed into my own bed, next to my wife who was already snoring off her day's dose of alcohol.

I awoke to Lily frantically shaking me, her tiny face inches from mine. She looked terrified. She was crying.

"What is it?" I asked. "What's wrong?"

"Justin's gone," she sobbed softly, rubbing tears from her eyes.

I bolted up, taking her by the shoulders. "What?"

She looked up at me, lip quivering. "He got taken down the hole."

I charged into my son's bedroom, heart thundering, praying my daughter had some nightmare, that my son would be fast asleep in his bed.

His room was empty. The sheets on his bed were cast aside, his race-car nightlight was off, and the room was unusually hot.

I turned on the light, feeling fear throttle my senses. My

hands shook as I dropped to my knees and looked under the bed, convinced I'd see him under it. Nothing.

I heard crying behind me and I spun to see Lily walking into the room. I went to her, crouching down to her level, and grabbed her, voice cracking with hysteria.

"Where did he go, baby? Where's Justin?"

She pointed toward his walk-in closet. I turned, seeing the door slightly ajar. I went to it, my mind spewing a thousand desperate prayers, and flung the door open.

My breath was robbed from my lungs. My legs melted and I crashed to my knees, eyes bugging in my skull.

There was a dark hole torn into the floor just big enough for a small boy to fit inside. Written on the wall in front of me in a dark ashy scrawl were the words:

He's My Son Now.

I scrambled to the edge of the hole and peered down. I could feel heat rising up from its depths and sweat popped out on my forehead. I screamed for Justin, my voice gaining an echo as it cascaded down into the depths. I screamed and screamed until my throat was raw. What was this? What was happening? Who had done this? Where was my boy?!

I turned and saw Lily sobbing, sitting on her brother's bed with her knees pulled up to her chin. I went to her and took her tear-soaked face in my hands.

"Who took Justin? Where is he?"

Lily just shook her head, crying harder.

I tilted her chin to look up at me, feeling my own tears form as panic gripped me in a way only parents can feel when their child is missing.

"Lily Pad," I said, forcing the hysteria out of my voice, "who took your brother?"

She looked into my eyes, her soft voice shaking.

"The monster with the big horns, Daddy."

And that's what I told the police. They all thought I was hysterical, and I was, but I didn't care what they thought of me. I just wanted them to find my son. Anything that would help. I didn't know what my daughter meant, what she saw, but I knew she was telling me what she saw in the way she understood it.

The police didn't know what to make of the message on the wall or the hole. They had investigated but couldn't make heads or tails of it. It was too small an opening to send someone down into it, so instead they had dropped glow sticks down into the darkness. We watched as they disappeared, swallowed by the black, straight down, impossibly, terribly far down into the ground. They walked around our small one-story house searching for an exit hole but came up empty. They had nothing to go on. They had no leads. Forensics came and swept the entire house but came up empty. The only thing they deciphered was that the message on the wall was written in ash. That's it. They boarded up the hole and told me they'd keep looking.

It was as if my son had ceased to exist.

I felt useless. I felt like a failure. I wanted to lock myself in my bathroom and weep. I wanted to pull my hair out until blood poured from my skull. I wanted to scream. What had happened to my son? What was that hole? Had someone tunneled under our house and grabbed Justin while he slept? None of it made sense. Things like this didn't happen to people like me. To people like us. What was that hole? And what was that message scrawled on the wall? What did it mean? Who would do such a thing?

Or was it something else?

Was it something…more terrible?

My daughter's words kept coming back to me.

"The monster with the big horns…"

Lily was at school and I sat on the couch, watching my wife pour herself another drink. I felt irritation bubbling up inside of me as she took a swig, her eyes meeting mine over the glass rim. It was only noon but she was on her third drink of the day.

"Don't you think you should take it easy?" I said, already knowing it was pointless.

She snorted, "Why? So I can sit there and be miserable like you? My boy is missing, too. And I hurt. I ache. This helps."

"'Cause you didn't drink before he went missing?" I spat.

She slammed the glass down on the countertop. "What the hell is that supposed to mean?"

I rubbed my hands over my face, feeling my rough, unshaven skin grate against my palms. "Never mind. Drink away. The hell do I care?"

She took a step toward me. "You think I don't care about him, is that it?"

I balled my fists. "Not today. Please. Let's not do this today.

I can't take feeling any worse than I already do. I don't want to fight."

"You brought it up!" she yelled.

"Just drop it. Do what you want."

She sneered at me. "Look at yourself. What are YOU doing to find our son? You sit on that couch day in and day out, staring at the walls. Are you trying to wish him back? You call yourself a man. Why don't you get out there and look for him!"

I stood up and advanced on her, shaking with a sudden fury. "Shut the fuck UP! I've looked! I've spent days and days looking, hoping, praying for him to show up again! Don't you dare say I haven't!"

She took another drink, our faces inches apart. She smacked her lips. "You want to hit me, is that it? Storming up in my face, screaming at me? Go ahead. Hit me if that makes you feel more like a man. A big strong man who hits his wife. Go ahead, do it!"

My teeth ground together like pieces of rusted iron. I took a deep breath and turned away, forcing my anger down.

"That's what I thought," she muttered. "What a coward."

I snapped. I grabbed the coffee table in front of me and threw it with all my might against the wall. If exploded in a shower of splinters and I turned on my wife. "Enough with your POISON! I miss our BOY! I die every day he's not here! We're supposed to support each other! How the FUCK are we going to get through this if we're at each other's throats?!"

Tess stared at me, a small smile on her lips. She glanced at her watch, then turned and walked away, calling back over her shoulder. "Don't forget to pick up Lily in an hour."

God bless me for not beating the *fuck* out of her.

We had eaten a silent dinner and when the sun was safely tucked in for the night, I put Lily to bed. She asked about Justin and I told her we still didn't know where he was. She nodded sadly and I could tell her little heart was breaking along with mine. I kissed her on the head and tucked her in.

Back in my own room I found my wife fast asleep. Thank Jesus. Not wanting to even be near her, I grabbed my pillow and a blanket from the closet and went to sleep on the couch.

I stared at the ceiling, our dark house silent, and felt the tears coming before they even reached my eyes. What did I do to deserve this? I tried so hard to be a good person, a good husband, a good parent. Why was this happening to my family? I squeezed my eyes shut and, not for the first time, begged God to bring my son back. I wasn't a religious man, never had been, but it's funny how we find ourselves on our knees in times of hardship.

"Please bring him back," I cried, staring up into the darkness. "Please tell me where he is…I beg you…" I wiped my nose and waited.

Nothing.

"I'll do whatever you want me to," I continued, openly sobbing now. "Just please God…help me…I need you…I need you so bad right now…"

Silence.

I ground my teeth together, jaw locking, anger suddenly burning in my chest, "No answer? Then what fucking good are you? Sleep tight, you malicious fuck."

Sleep did not come quick.

My dreams blurred and shifted, voices and noises rising and falling around me. I swam in a sea of images, all of which were just out of focus. I heard Justin screaming for me. I thought I could see him, surrounded in a haze of red and black. He was reaching out toward me, pleading with me to help him. The air swallowed me up, pulling me back away from him. I strained and fought, but the dream wouldn't allow it. I screamed his name, screamed for him to tell me where he was.

Just as he disappeared, something huge and black loomed over me. Heat enveloped my body and I choked on ash and smoke, eyes watering.

A long, clawed hand reached out toward me, finger extended, pointing down at me.

And then a voice erupted, deep and sinister.

"He is no longer yours."

I was driving Lily to preschool, trying not to fall asleep at the wheel. The nightmares had continued until I cracked my eyes open at dawn, not sure which reality was worse. I glanced in the mirror at my daughter in her booster seat and saw she was frowning.

"What's wrong, honey?" I asked.

"I had bad dreams last night and they made me sad," she said quietly.

"What dreams?"

Her lip began to tremble. "About Justin. He…he said he wanted to hurt me. And it made me sad."

"Aw honey," I said, reaching an arm behind the seat and

rubbing her leg, "Justin would never hurt you. He loves you very much just like Mommy and Daddy."

She was silent for a moment, then said softly, "He looked scary."

The memories of my own nightmares, still fresh in my mind, made me ask, "Why was he scary?"

She looked up into the mirror, her eyes meeting mine. "He had horns on him."

After I dropped her off at school, I went to get a coffee down the street. The fresh air felt good, the morning still clinging to a slight chill before the afternoon heat. I saw a few parents who had also just dropped their little ones off and I was greeted with the sad looks I had grown accustomed to. What was worse were the questions. *How are you and Tess holding up, have you heard anything, how's Lily?* And then came the false positivity, the hand gripping my arm as a sign of support, the assurances that we were in their prayers.

I bit back my anger at the last part, instead smothering my face with a big phony smile and thanking them. They meant well; they really did. What else could they say? I was so tired, my mind sloshing like a slop bucket of pain and misery. I didn't want to go home to my wife. I didn't want to watch her drink today. I didn't want to do anything. If I could, I would have stood there, hot coffee steaming in my hand, and stared at it until it was time to pick Lily up.

I could have gone back to work, but the thought of being in that environment made me sick. I would be useless anyway. My boss had told me to take as much time as I needed until things got resolved one way or another.

I ended up sitting down on a bench, watching the cars go by. I sipped my coffee and then threw the cup away. I watched everyone around me go about their normal lives. They didn't know what pain was. They didn't understand my suffering.

I ended up sleeping on the couch again that night. I had gotten into another argument with Tess after I brought Lily home. Everything was just so broken. I felt like my life had shattered before me and when I tried to pick up one piece, another three fell from my grip.

I didn't talk to God that night. I just tossed and turned, my beaten mind refusing to shut up. My heart ached and I wondered where my son was sleeping tonight. If he was sleeping. If he was alive. It had been so long since I had seen him, since I had heard his cheerful voice. I felt tears forming, but I didn't cry. I didn't have the energy. I didn't have anything left in me.

I don't know what time it was, but the moon was high in the sky, beaming brightly through the windows when I woke. I heard...something.

Voices. Soft, gentle voices down the hall toward my daughter's bedroom. It sounded like children. Rubbing my eyes, I sat up, making sure I wasn't imagining it or asleep. I strained my ears in the darkness. There it was again. Was that Lily?

I stood and made my way to her door. Before I opened it, I noticed how hot it was. In just the dozen or so steps down the hall, the temperature had increased significantly. I paused. There they were again. The voices.

Quietly, I opened Lily's door and my eyes widened, heart freezing in my chest.

There was Justin.

No. Not just one. Three of him.

They all stood around Lily's bed, one on each side and one at the foot of it. They were all muttering something I couldn't make out.

As I was about to speak, cry out, make sense of what I was seeing, all three turned toward me and smiled. Dark circles ringed their eyes and their mouths twisted into sick smiles. Their hair was matted with sweat and they all breathed in unison, tiny puffs of smoke escaping their lips.

They spoke as one.

"She's next, Dad."

I blinked.

They were gone.

I sat by my daughter's bed until dawn, bloodshot eyes darting around the room in a daze. I didn't know what to make of the horror I had seen. I didn't know if it was a hallucination brought on by lack of sleep or if I had actually dreamed the whole thing. But I was scared.

It was at this point that I began to realize things were very, very wrong.

I took Lily to school in silence, my shell-shocked mind replaying what I saw over and over again. My eyes were glazed over with exhaustion and I had to actively blink to stay awake. My head was swirling, my conscious state beaten to a pulp. I felt dead. Was I losing my mind or was something more sinister actually happening to my family? I couldn't deny the…dare I say it…the satanic signs that had begun to sprout their wings over my life. My mouth was dry and felt dirty, my unwashed hair was in greasy tatters down my face, and my clothes stunk. I was sinking. I was being eaten alive by depression and exhaustion, their duel jaws hungrily chomping away at me.

I walked my daughter into her school and drove home. I don't remember a single detail from that drive back. I walked into my house and blinked a few times. I heard my wife crying.

I went to Justin's bedroom and saw her sitting on his bed, cross-legged, with a bottle of vodka wedged between her thighs. Her eyes were red and tear-streaked as she looked up at me.

"Where is he?" she cried.

I let my body fall, sitting next to her and letting out a long, tired breath. "I don't know. I don't know where he is, Tess. God knows I wish I did." I didn't mention what I had seen last night, not sure how I would even go about explaining it.

"He's dead, isn't he?" she asked, pulling the cap off the bottle.

I placed a gentle hand over hers, stopping the bottle from reaching her lips. "Please, honey…not today. I'm so tired…I can't even think straight anymore. I need you today, I need you with me."

She looked at me. "You need me?" She jerked the bottle away from my hand. "You need me?! Why don't you man up? Our son needs you! You're supposed to be strong, you're supposed to be the head of the house. You don't want me to drink? Why? Because you need me? Grow a backbone and get out there. Get out there and do something!"

I felt my eyes fluttering, my chest heaving with sorrow and desperation, "Tess, I'm so beaten down. I'm so weary of this. I'm so, so, so weary of this. I need my wife…I need…" I felt tears begin to form. "I need you to tell me everything is going to be OK…I need you to love me today…please…" I was crying now, unable to stop the floodgates of sadness and defeat I felt.

Tess shook her head at me, disgusted. "I've never met a more pathetic man. Wipe your face, you look a mess. Why did I marry such a spineless child?" She took a long pull from the bottle. "I'm not going to tell you everything is going to be OK. Not until it is. Not until you do something to find our son."

I looked at her, pleading, eyes red and puffy. "I don't know what else I can do! You have to believe me I've tried everything! I…I just don't know what happened to our little boy and I hate myself so much for that."

Tess stood up, taking the bottle. "Good. You should." She walked out of the room without looking back. I crumbled in Justin's bed and lay there, crying silently, wishing it would end.

I was in my bed. The clock read two AM. Tess was asleep beside me, stinking of alcohol. Despite my body screaming for sleep, it just wouldn't come. I lay there in the darkness, listening to the tiny snores from down the hall. At least Lily was sleeping well tonight. My little angel. What a trouper she was. She didn't understand any of this, didn't know the true extent of turmoil her family was in. So innocent.

I turned over on my side toward the dark open doorway,

exhaling. *Please fall asleep,* I thought, *I can't go through another day without sleep.* My eyes had heavy, dark bags drooping from them, looking like I had been punched in the face. I decided to take a shower and shave tomorrow, clean myself. Maybe that would make me feel better, if only a little.

I closed my bloodshot eyes and let my thoughts wander on their own. I don't know how long I stayed like that. I told myself I wouldn't open my eyes until I felt the morning sun on them. Ever so slowly, I began to feel the warm blanket of sleep cover me. My breathing steadied, my mind slowed, and the world started to fade.

"Daddy."

Groaning, almost crying, I forced my eyes back open. I had been so close. I rubbed my face, tearing away the grip of exhaustion. It was Lily, standing in my doorway, her little frame nothing but a dark shadow against a darker black.

"What is it, baby?" I croaked, reaching out to her.

She padded closer and I saw she was dragging something behind her. She stopped a foot away from the bed and held out what she was holding.

"Daddy, Justin said to give this to you."

I jolted awake, a spark of adrenaline igniting my mind, and then horror clawed its way up my throat and I bit back a scream.

Lily was holding a severed goat head.

Blood ran down her arms and stained her pajamas as she held it out for me to take. "He told me you would like it. Do you like it, Daddy?"

I steadied my breathing, forcing myself not to yell, not

wanting to scare my daughter. I was amazed she wasn't crying at the sight of it, disgusted by the gore.

Heart thundering, I took it from her, glancing over my shoulder at my wife who remained unconscious in a state of drunkenness. Good. I looked down at Lily.

"When did he give this to you?" I asked, a tremble entering my voice.

Lily wiped her hands on her chest. "Just right now. I was asleep and dreaming about him and when I opened my eyes, he was sitting on my bed. He said he had a present for you and gave me that. He said he has one for me, too, but I have to wait."

Jesus Christ, I'm losing my mind, I thought, *what do I do here? What the hell do I do?*

I nodded and forced a smile. "Wow, what a neat present. Hey, why don't we clean you up, huh? Let's get that nastiness off your hands and clothes, OK?"

She smiled. "OK, Daddy."

I got off the bed and walked her out of the room, closing the door behind me. I held the goat head away from me by one of its horns. Its fur still felt warm. I breathed through my mouth, eating the outburst of terror I felt in my gut. *Just stay calm, don't scare Lily,* I told myself.

"Honey, go into the bathroom and start washing your hands," I said, nodding down the hall. "I'm going to…go put this someplace special."

I watched her pad down the hall and turn on the light in the bathroom. I waited until I heard the water running before I sprinted outside and threw the head into the trashcan by the side of the house. I slammed the lid closed and put my hands on my knees, bent over and gasping.

"What the hell is going on?" I said, letting myself feel the stomach-churning fear I was keeping locked up. "What is happening, what is happening, what is fucking happening?"

I took another few seconds to calm myself and went back inside. I needed to throw Lily's clothes away and instruct her not to say anything to anyone. The last thing I needed was for Tess to find out. God knows what she'd do.

I closed the front door behind me and paused. I didn't hear the water running. I didn't hear anything. I walked toward the hall and looked down it. The bathroom light was off.

Heart racing, I walked toward the bathroom door. "Lily? Honey, are you done washing your hands?"

I turned the corner and looked inside.

Justin was holding Lily up by her ankles, drowning her in the toilet face-first.

"She had a little blood on her face," Justin said, grinning, his voice deep and manly.

"STOP IT!" I screamed, darting forward and knocking him away from his sister, back into the shower. He fell with a thud, hitting his head against the wall.

I grabbed Lily and pulled her up. She came out of the water screaming, gasping for air as water splashed around us.

I quickly wiped her face, hands shaking uncontrollably. "Baby! Lily! Are you OK? Breathe, baby, breathe!"

She threw up a mouthful of murky water and sobbed into my chest, her whole body shaking like a rag doll. "Why did he do that?" she screamed.

I looked up and saw Justin stand in the shower, not smiling

anymore. He looked different; he didn't look like my son. I stared into his face and I was overcome with fear.

A dark, twisted horn protruded from his left eye, curving up past his forehead. Blood leaked from where it had punctured through and the black bone shined with it. Another horn snaked out of his forehead above his right eye, the skin bloody from where it had exited his head.

He put one foot up on the bathtub's rim and leaned forward. "Come down with me, Dad. It's so much better down there."

"You're not my son," I said shaking, my voice weak.

Justin stood up straight, shock cracking his face. "Why would you say that, Dad?" His voice was his own again, innocent and young, "Don't you love me, Dad?"

Chest heaving, still stroking my daughter's crying face, I nodded, "Of course I do! Of course I love you! I love you so much. Please...come back to me, Justin...come be with us again."

Justin threw his head back and laughed, his voice dropping back into that horrible deep rumble. "You don't love me like he loves me." He reached out and patted my face. "I'll be waiting for you, Dad."

I blinked. He was gone.

I spent the next twenty minutes trying to calm my daughter, trying to wrap my shaken mind around what had just happened. I didn't know what to do. I didn't know whom to go to. I didn't know what was happening. I just sat there on the floor, stroking my daughter's tear-stained face, telling her it was OK over and over again.

What was I going to do? Should I leave? Would it matter?

Should I go to a church and talk to a priest, beg him for help? I knew the police wouldn't take me seriously. This kind of thing didn't happen. This kind of thing didn't exist. My reality bled from a dark, beating heart and I felt chaotic terror seep from its open chest.

Eventually, I picked Lily up and brought her back into her room. I laid her down and curled up next to her. I didn't know what else to do. I kept stroking her hair until she fell asleep, her little body shivering against mine. I had to protect her. I had to stop this. I needed to do whatever I could to make this nightmare stop.

As I lay there, I began to feel myself fall asleep. I fought against it, but I had long surpassed the point where I could fight it any longer. I drifted off into a light sleep, my fleeting dreams plagued with dark and bloody shapes moving just out of sight.

I woke two hours later, morning's first light sneaking in through the windows. I groaned and forced my eyes open. I wasn't ready for today. I wasn't ready for the choices I had to make. My mind was a cloud of dark haze. I felt dirty, unwashed, and hot. My head was killing me, a thick throb pulsing against my forehead. I felt as if my head would split open from the pain. I shifted on Lily's bed, forcing my body to move, forcing blood through my dead muscles.

Something wasn't right.

Lily was gone.

I sprang up, my body howling in revolt, my head hurting so bad I thought it would explode. My sleep-crusted eyes stared at the empty bed.

She was just…gone.

"Lily!" I screamed, pulse quickening. No, no, no, please God I beg of you, not her! Lily, where are you?!" I yelled again, searching under the bed, in her closet, tearing her room apart in a panic. She wasn't there.

Chest heaving, I ran through the house, screaming her name, searching every nook and cranny, tearing apart every room. Nothing.

Finally, I burst into my bedroom. Tess sat up rubbing her eyes.

"What the hell are you screaming about?" she asked, her voice hard and irritated from being woken up.

"Tess, it's Lily! She's gone!" I yelled, my body contorting against the heavy grip of fear and utter exhaustion I felt.

Tess bolted up. "What do you mean she's gone?"

"She's gone! She's disappeared!" I screamed, pulling at my hair.

Tess shook her head, eyes wide, and stormed out of the room. She went to Lily's room and when she came up empty she searched the house just like I had. I followed her, wringing my hands together, feeling myself die under an avalanche of sorrow and terror. *Not my baby girl. Not her. Please.*

After we had gone through the house a second time, Tess stopped in the kitchen, facing me. "How did this happen? Where's my daughter!?!"

I swallowed, putting a hand to my head, and tried to rub away the sharp pain. It was so bad I felt dizzy. My limbs felt like they were made of stone, dragging me to the ground.

"She had a nightmare last night and I got up with her," I lied through my teeth. "I put her back to bed and stayed with her. I woke up this morning and...and she was gone!"

Tess stood there, breathing hard. Her hands balled up into fists and I saw fire in her eyes. She took a step toward me, slamming her hand down on the countertop. "You mean to tell me that someone came and took her away right out from under you?"

I was helpless before her, beaten and defeated. I started to cry, just staring at her with big wet tears running down my face.

Tess grabbed a coffee mug off the counter and threw it at my head, screaming, "Stop crying, you fucking worthless piece of shit! How could you let this happen!? How could you let them take our children?!"

The mug hit me full in the face, shattering across my nose. I reeled, hands clutching my face as the glass cut my skin. I felt warmth trickle through my fingers and I blinked back blackness.

Tess grabbed another mug, shaking it at me. "You lay there sleeping as someone stole our daughter away from us! How could you be any more pathetic!?" She threw the mug and I managed to stumble and avoid it, wiping away the blood on my face.

"Someone out there has our babies!" she continued, now snatching a plate off the counter. "Someone has our children and you stand here crying about it!" She advanced on me. "Crying about it instead of getting them back! You're a worm, you're a dirty fucking worm!" She spit in my face. I flinched away as it hit my eye.

A dark murderous fire erupted in my chest.

This. Fucking. *Cunt.*

I caught her wrist as she swung the plate at my face.

Surprised, she let out a yelp, my grip like iron.

I pulled her close, spittle spraying her face as I hissed through gritted teeth, "I wouldn't do that if I were you." My head howled and I felt like my brain was going to split my skull at the seams. My vision swam and the weeks of exhausted, depressed, crushing sadness all came collapsing down on me in that instant.

Tess saw my tired, beaten eyes and her mouth twisted in hatred. "Or what? You're a worm." And she spit in my face again, spraying me.

Without even wiping it off, I cocked my fist back and blasted her in the face. She screamed and fell back against the counter, holding onto it for support. She looked up at me, her eyes wide with shock, her nose bleeding profusely.

"I warned you," I said darkly, my whole body trembling with years of suppressed rage and hatred for this miserable bitch. I felt the weight and misery for my children crush my senses. I had taken the brunt of this whole ordeal on my own shoulders, desperately trying to keep sane, fighting every ounce of my being to not just curl up and die from the sadness.

"You just made the biggest mistake of your life!" she screamed, the fight still burning in her. "I'm going to make your life hell for that!"

I sprang forward and grabbed her by the throat, squeezing with fury. "You want to see hell?" I whispered, my face inches from hers, raw and burning. "I'll show you the Devil."

I slammed her face down into the counter and was

rewarded with a scream of pain as her teeth shattered. Before she could slump to the floor, I grabbed her by the hair and dragged her across the kitchen. With a heave, I threw her face-first into the wall.

With a thud, she smashed into it, partially caving it in, and went down, her eyes rolling. I slowly walked over to her, watching her gasp for air. I grabbed a half-empty handle of vodka off the counter and knelt over her, knees pinning her sides.

"Why don't you have a drink, babe?" I hissed, the blood from my own face dripping down and mixing with hers. "I know you could probably use one right now."

I ripped the top off and shoved the neck of the bottle down her throat, cracking the fragmented remains of her teeth. "Drink up, you fucking bitch!" I howled, slowly pushing down on the bottle, forcing it deeper and deeper into her mouth. I watched as the sides of her mouth split as she deep-throated past the neck.

I suddenly pulled the bottle out. "Ah ah ah! Not too much now! I know you have a drinking problem and I don't want to..." I trailed off, searching for the words, twirling a finger in the air. "I don't want to encourage that kind of behavior."

I brought the bottle smashing down over her face. Her forehead split open in an angry red line and the glass shattered around her face. I picked up two pieces of glass about three inches long, one in each hand.

I rammed them into her forehead.

"Look at that!" I screamed with mad euphoria, feeling my sanity drift away in a tide of sleep deprivation and pain, "You have horns now! Just like our little devil son! Did you know that he tried to kill our daughter last night? You didn't, did you!? Of course not! That's because you don't give a FUCK about anyone but yourself!"

I got off her, staring down at my dead wife.

I had killed her. Jesus Christ, I had murdered her.

I smiled.

Nothing mattered anymore. My world was over. My children were gone, my wife was dead. I had nothing left. And I didn't care.

I was just too goddamn tired.

I rubbed my aching head, feeling the pain hit me in waves, feeling my body about to buckle under the mental and physical torture I had gone through the past few weeks. It was all over. It was finished. I was done trying to make sense of it all, done trying to hold my family together. I was beaten.

I looked down at Tess, her face a bloody mess.

"I'm going to be with my children now," I said. "I think I know where they are."

I walked into Justin's room, toward his closet, and flung it open. I ripped up the board the police had used to cover it, feeling a blast of heat hit my face.

The hole was bigger now and I could see a faint red glow far below. I looked up and on the wall across from me, in big black letters, were the words:

Come home, Daddy.

I'm sitting on my son's bed now. I'm writing this all out so that someone knows what has happened. So that someone knows why my wife is lying dead in the kitchen. She didn't deserve to die, but I don't regret doing it. I'm free of her and I can go be with my children.

When you find this, when you read this, I ask only that you cover up the hole. Fill it with cement, dirt, I don't care. Just seal it away so that nothing else can get out. So that no one else has to go through what I have. Best of luck to you, and sorry about the mess.

Now if you'll excuse me, I'm going to go find my kids.

11

Texts From My Brother

PART 1

Last weekend, something happened to my brother. After I write this, I'm going to go find him. If something happens to me, let this stand as a testimony to the events surrounding my disappearance.

My brother Mike is younger than me by two years. He goes to college two states over, but despite that we've remained close. We talk frequently, maintaining our brotherly bond through phone calls and tons of text messages. Suffice it to say, I love my brother.

And that's why I'm so worried about him.

Last Friday I was at a bar drinking with my friends. It was early, around six, when I received a phone call from Mike. I was taking a piss in the bathroom, trying to hold the phone against my ear with my face as I unzipped my pants. My brother Mike told me he was going out with two of his friends, Jason and Tim. Apparently, Jason had found something while hiking a week ago and wanted to show them. He wouldn't say what, but my brother seemed nervous, unsure if Jason was going to play some prank on him and Tim. He said he was going to text me updates as the night progressed because he was deathly afraid of the woods. (He always had been, ever since he was little.)

As he explained this to me, my phone slipped from my ear and splashed into the toilet. Crying out, I quickly scooped it up, but the damage was done. I couldn't get it to turn back on. Sighing, I wiped it off and put it back in my pocket.

I didn't get it fixed until Monday.

And when I did, I received a flood of backlogged texts from my brother. As I read them, my stomach turned to ice and my mouth went dry.

This is the last known communication with my brother:

6:13pm
Dude what happened? Your phone just cut off.

6:22pm
Alright man, whatever, I tried calling you back but it's just going to voicemail. I'm in the car with Tim and Jason. Jason seems pretty excited, but he won't tell us where we're going. Tim seems skeptical. I'm a little nervous. You know I hate the woods.

6:58pm
We're driving on this little road through the mountains. It's getting dark. Why do we have to do this when it's dark? Glad Jason brought flashlights. Answer me you asshole!

7:15pm
Ug, Jason's music sucks. I wish we'd just get to wherever we're going. Still driving through the mountains on this little road. Haven't passed a single car.

7:41pm

Parking the car now. Completely dark and spooky. We're about to go into the woods. Hopefully I still get some reception lol

7:55pm

Jason keeps saying "wait until you see it" and Tim is giving him shit. We're both wondering what the big surprise is.

8:12pm

Dude, walking through the woods at night is literally the scariest thing ever, even with the flashlights

8:34pm

Getting close. Jason is getting more excited. Still won't tell us what's out here. If I wasn't such good friends with this loser, I'd be totally sketched out right now. Are you getting these texts?

8:59pm

The woods are so quiet. I've tripped over so many damn rocks. Feels like we've been walking forever. Tim is complaining. I don't blame him. This is kinda lame. And all these dark woods are freaking me out.

9:16pm

Jason says it's just ahead. I'll keep you posted.

9:27pm

Holy shit

9:27pm

Dude...

9:28pm

Jason was right. This is...

9:29pm

Bro, we're in a clearing in the middle of the forest. It's insanely foggy here. In the center of the clearing there's this...rope...hanging from the sky...dude this is fucking weird.

9:34pm

Standing around the rope. Jason and Tim are captivated. I'm kinda freaked out. It's so foggy...I can't see what this rope is tied to. It just goes up and up and up into the night mist...I've never seen anything like it. There's nothing up there but sky...

9:48pm

Jason wants us to climb up. Something about this place is seriously creeping me out. I wish you'd answer my texts, I'm getting scared.

9:59pm

Jason is going to climb up. I can't talk him out of it. Tim thinks this whole thing is cool. I know I'm scared of the woods, but there's something wrong with this place

10:02pm

Jason is climbing up. Fuck.

10:09pm

I can hear Jason calling down to us. He sounds so high up. Can't make out what he's saying.

10:38pm

Haven't heard anything from Jason in 30min. He's still up there somewhere. WTF.

11:03pm

Fuck man, something is so wrong. Jason's been gone for over an hour. Tim is worried but he's trying to play it cool. WHERE'S JASON

11:22pm

Still nothing. Jesus the fog is thick

11:31pm

Tim's freaking out now too. Wants to go up after Jason. I don't know what the hell is going on. I'm so fucking scared. I feel like there's something out there in the woods. Something bad.

11:40pm

Tim's going to climb the rope. I begged him not to, but he won't listen. I'm going to be alone down here. DUDE PLEASE ANSWER ME I'M FUCKING SCARED

11:43pm

I'm alone now. I can still hear Tim, but he's lost above me in the fog. I'm shaking. It's getting cold.

12:01am

I am freaking out. Tim's gone.

12:04am

I can hear something in the woods circling the clearing. It sounds huge. I'm crying now, bro, please, if you can see this come get me

12:08am

Please come get me

12:10am

I can hear screeching from the woods. Like heavy steel being dragged across a metal floor. How is that even possible?! It keeps screeching over and over…WHAT THE FUCK IS THIS PLACE

12:13am

I'm going to climb the rope. Whatever is up there can't be worse than whatever is in the woods. That fucking screeching is getting louder.

12:15am

God help me. I'm going up now. Whatever is circling the clearing sounds…like it's about to do something. I hope I can find Jason and Tim. I hope they're waiting for me up there somewhere…goodbye brother, I hope you read this.

4:13am

//////////////{HEL}

4:19am

[HEL]{XTXTXTXT} (ZCZ)

4:22am

[DAEDMAIDAEDMAIDAEDMAIDAEDMAIDAEDMAI]

That was the final text from him. I have no idea what the last three meant, if anything, and it fills me with uneasy fear. I've tried calling him, tried to text him, but I can't seem to reach him. It's been two days since he went up into the mountains with his friends.

I'm scared. I hope I'm not too late.

I'm going to go look for him.

I'm going to try to find that strange clearing with the rope in the fog.

I'm going to see where it leads.

PART 2

Entry #1

9:48am

I'm writing this all down in case something happens to me. I'm determined to find my brother. Hopefully this will shed some light on my discoveries (if any). Because of the unsettling nature of his last communication with me, I'm going to be frequently updating this log.

Last night, I drove the two hours to Mike's college (my brother). As far as I know, this is the last place he was seen.

I've spent all morning asking around about him. He seems to be pretty popular, because most of the students know him.

I inquired to see if anyone knew where he was headed on the night he disappeared. Most of Mike's friend's didn't know, but this one guy, Paul, seemed to have an idea. After struggling to give me directions, he decided to come with me. Apparently, he's pretty good friends with Mike and is concerned after I showed him the texts I received.

But first things first. We're going to go talk to the police and park rangers. Hopefully they can assist us.

Entry #2

3:21pm

Today is not going as I expected it to. I'm worried about Mike and so maybe that's stirring this strange paranoia that's risen in me.

Paul and I went to the police and park rangers, told them about my brother and his friends disappearing, showed them the texts...and...I don't know how to explain this. Both the police and park rangers reacted the same. Wary, uneasy looks were exchanged followed by an unenthusiastic missing person's report. They seemed to just be going through the motions, an unheard conversation passing silently between the officers and rangers.

I asked if they knew where this clearing with the rope was, asked if they were going to help me look for Mike and his friends. They informed me they'd do a perimeter check in the morning. What the hell does that mean? These woods are endless! How do they expect to find him just by walking along the outskirts?

I voiced my concern but was sternly cut off by an officer. He said they'd do everything they could to help find my brother, but that I should stay OUT of the woods. When I asked why, he looked at the floor and told me "it was for the best."

Paul kept me from going into hysterics, practically dragging me out of the station. He told me we didn't need them, that we could go look ourselves. I don't understand why the authorities are being so unhelpful and it's infuriating.

What are they so afraid of?

Entry #3

6:01pm

Paul's driving as I write. We loaded up on gear and food after we left the police station. I don't think we'll need most of this stuff, but I'd like to be prepared, just in case. Paul has a general idea of what mountain my brother and his friends were going to. He didn't remember exactly what trail they were taking, but at least we have something to go on. I'm glad Paul decided to help me look for Mike. I feel like I'd be a mess right now if he wasn't here. I barely know the guy, but I'm happy for his company. I can understand why my brother is friends with him.

Anyway, I'll update once we get there. Shouldn't be long.

Entry #4

7:21pm

We found the mountain (I hope). Paul's double-checking everything before we head out. I'm nervous. The sun has almost set. I don't have the deep-rooted fear my brother does of the woods. But right now I don't want to think about those weird texts he sent. God, please be ok Mike.

Alright, Paul is ready to go. We picked a mountain trail at

random, hoping it's the correct one. I'm going to check my flashlight batteries and then we'll be off.

Fuck, I'm nervous.

Entry #5

10:48pm

Taking a break. Paul and I have been walking for hours. No sign of Mike along the trail so far. I've tried calling out to him, but the mountain remains silent. The woods are thick along the trail, almost like they're trying to devour us. There's no moon and so we're relying solely on our flashlights.

After walking this far, I've begun to doubt myself. What am I doing out here? Do I really expect to find Mike out here? These woods are seemingly endless and we have no way of knowing how close we are to where he might be.

What am I talking about? I have to try. I can't just leave him out here. He needs my help. I won't abandon him. I will NOT do that.

Paul's ready to keep moving. He seems uneasy.

Entry #6

1:12am

Taking another breather. Still haven't found any clues. I'm tired. The minimal conversation between Paul and I has died to nothing. I think the seriousness of our situation is weighing heavily on him. Neither of us want to think about what might be waiting for us out here. What if we find Mike, Tim, and Jason all dead? Makes me sick to think about.

Something about these woods…doesn't feel right.

Time to keep moving.

Entry #7

2:01am

We found something. Paul tripped over it as he walked off the path to take a leak. He called me over and I shined my light on it. As soon as the object illuminated under my flashlight, I felt my stomach twist in on itself.

It was a small black stone, pressed into the earth, rising from the soil by about a foot. It was blacker than the night and rough to touch.

It looked like a gravestone.

Carved into it was: /////[HEL] —>

Paul and I looked at each other, eyes full of eerie unease. We both recognized the strange word.

It was one of the last things my brother texted me.

Carved next to the word was an arrow that pointed off the path and into the dark woods. I didn't even have to argue with Paul. We've agreed to follow the sign and see where it leads.

So far, it's the only clue we've seen.

Entry #8

2:21am

We've found another three stones, all similar to the first. I don't know how far off the path we've wandered. This is crazy. Where are these stones taking us? Paul keeps muttering under his breath. He's scared. We both are.

Entry #9

2:44am

Seven stones now, leading us deeper and deeper into the mountain.

Entry #10

3:01am

We've stopped. We can hear something. It sounds like metal being dragged across a metal floor. The screeching echoes across the sky like some kind of enraged animal. Paul is starting to panic.

We both remember my brother's texts. He heard this, too.

We must be close.

Entry #11

3:22am

We're following the stones again. The screeching is following us, too. I can hear the source crashing through the underbrush a couple hundred yards away. Find the next stone. Keep moving. Paul is openly talking to himself. He doesn't seem right.

Entry #12

3:48am

Paul's gone. He ran off into the woods. Something was wrong with his eyes.

The screeching has stopped. Fog is rolling in and I'm cold.

What the fuck is this place?

Entry #13

4:01am

Jesus Christ. I've found it.

I kept following the stones…they've led me to a field, a massive clearing in the middle of the forest. The fog is so thick I can barely see. Wait…

What the fuck…?

Jesus Christ, there's DOZENS of ropes, all hanging from the foggy sky like balloon strings. What the hell is this place?! Is this where my brother disappeared?

I tried calling out for him. I tried until my throat went raw. No answer.

But the screeching has returned. It's close, circling the clearing, watching me. I see the shadow of something absolutely enormous shifting between the trees.

I can't see where the ropes lead, the dangling cords disappearing far up into the fog and night sky.

I'm going to climb up.

But how do I decide which one is the right one? Is there a right one?

And what the hell is waiting for me up there?

I'm shaking. Something is so wrong with this place. Please God.

Don't let this be the end.

Entry???

????

///[HEL]{>>>>>>}
>>>>>>>>ENOGGNIHTYREVE>>[HEL]

Entry???

????

\\\\\\\\\\\9TH666/////////////{MIHDNUOF}/////[HEL]>>>>>

PART 3

What follows is a transcript of an audio log recorded by Officer Michael Trenton, recovered at XXXXXXXX:

3:32pm

"This is Officer Trenton. It's about three-thirty on Wednesday the 18th. I'm…I'm assuming this tape will be the last thing the living world hears from me. I don't think I'll be coming back from this. But I don't care. I've had enough. I can't live with this guilt anymore.

clears throat

Two days ago, some young men came to our police station seeking help. They told us their friends had disappeared into the mountains. They had a series of disturbing texts from one of their brothers who was missing. They were looking for him. We turned them away. I suspect they went to look on their own, which means they're probably gone, too.

You see…something is wrong with those mountains. We all know it. The rangers, the police, all of us. But we don't talk about it. We don't like to. It makes us…nervous. Some of us have seen the ropes, hanging in the clearings…the fog and cold choking the courage right out of us. A few have heard that…thing…as well…that screeching darkness that resides by the ropes.

None of us knows what it means. None of us wants to talk about it. For some reason, I feel like we shouldn't. Something just ain't right about that place.

But those boys…they needed our help and we turned them away. It wasn't right. We shouldn't have done that. We're all scared of those woods, but they came to us for help! I tried talking to the others about it, a couple of the rangers, but they wouldn't join me. So I'm on my own. I'm going to try and find those kids, I have to. I haven't slept properly since they showed me those texts. They're out there…it's my duty to help them."

4:19pm

"Officer Trenton here. I'm on my way to the location. This tape recorder will hopefully serve as my eyes and ears. I want people to know what's up here. Maybe then they'll stay away. Maybe then no one will get hurt. Maybe I can prevent some of this…ah shit…you know what I mean."

unintelligible mumbling

"I'm about twenty minutes from the mountain. I brought a flashlight. I wish I could do this in the daylight…but it doesn't work like that.

Not if I want to see the ropes."

4:45pm

"Trenton here. I made it. I'm at the start of the trail. The mountain is looming before me in the fading light. It's so…quiet. I'd be lying to you if I said I wasn't scared. Standing here, looking into these woods…I'll tell you, it drains the courage right out of me.

But those boys need help.

And I have to try."

6:29pm

heavy panting

"So far, so good. All's quiet. Been walking for about two hours now. These woods…they feel like they're changing…moving…or maybe that's just my own paranoia. Either way, I feel…unhinged. It's been a long time since I've been here. And now I'm remembering why I stayed away for so long. I hope I haven't forgotten the way. Christ, these woods are quiet."

8:44pm

"I feel like I should have found the spot by now. I've been walking for four hours. I don't remember it taking so long. I'm moving slower now that it's dark, but still. Something feels off. More than normal."

9:58pm

"I shouldn't be here. Maybe this was a mistake. I feel like I'm getting lost."

10:39pm

rustling

"I found one of the stones. Almost tripped over the damn thing. There's an arrow on it with some strange markings. I don't remember the markings. Maybe they're new. I must be getting close. I need to keep following the stones. They'll take me to the ropes."

11:14pm

whispering

"It found me. The monster. Christ, it's fucking horrible. I can hear it…screeching and groaning out there in the darkness. It's following me. What the fuck is it? What does it want? It sounds enormous, a lumbering shadow that's blacker than the deepest darkness.

I think it wants me to keep moving."

12:01am

"Jesus…I've found them…"

static

"It's…it's been so long since I've seen the ropes…they look like empty balloon strings, dangling from the fog-choked sky. I'm standing in a field, circled by towering trees. That thing, that grinding, scraping noise, it's behind me in the trees. It's watching me. I feel cold, terrified. I'm shaking, the fog wrapping around my skin like an icy husk. I can see my breath pluming from my mouth as I speak.

Jesus, can you hear that thing? Listen!"

distant screeching

"Can you hear that!? It's getting impatient. God…there's so many ropes. Those boys…they're up there somewhere…

Fuck, now that I'm standing here, I don't know if I can

do this. I'm so fucking scared. This place, whatever it is…it shouldn't exist."

loud screeching

"Jesus SHIT. You can hear that, right? Fuck fuck fuck FUCK!"

heavy breathing

"I don't have a choice. I have to go up. God, if you're listening…please help me…"

???

unintelligible noises in the background

"I think I made it to the top…my God…if you could see this…"

???

"This place…this place shouldn't exist. It's not possible. It's so cold up here. There's fog everywhere. Darkness. I can see the moon, but it's…different. It looks…elongated. Warped, like there's a wavering film over it. I'm in some kind of woods, but the trees are bare and the branches are all bent, as if they're craning backwards to stare at that eerie moon.

I've been following a noise. It sounds like a person calling me.

I think it's one of those boys."

???

whispering

"I've found another clearing. I haven't gone into it yet. I'm hiding behind a tree. Jesus, if you could see what I'm seeing…

Something huge is standing in the middle. I can't seem to focus on its shape. It looks human but…not. It's shifting, a mass of darkness. I can make out legs, arms, and a dark head with a long snout. Fog is rolling off of it in thick waves.

It's…it's pointing at the moon, motionless, a long ebony finger stretching into the dark sky.

Christ!

There's people! Tons of people! How did I not see them before!? They're circling the massive black form, all staring up at that weird, horrible moon. They look…

Fucking hell, they look terrified. Holy SHIT…I see them. I see the two young men who came into the police station! I fucking see them! They're in that circle, looking at the moon. Christ. I want to leave, I'm fucking horrified. There is something evil going on here. It's churning my stomach. What is this insanity? Where am I?!

What is this place?!

What the fuck…there's something wrong with their necks…they're…growing…expanding from their shoulders like fleshy worms. What the fuck what the fuck what the fuck…

Stretching toward that twisted, warped moon!

There! They're all whispering something! I can barely make it out…it sounds like they're saying…'Shimmer…Shimmer…'

What does that mean?!

Are they…are they worshiping this thing?

JESUS CHRIST THEY SEE ME THEY SEE ME THEY SEE M—

static

END LOG.

12

Shimmer

My girlfriend and I unpacked the groceries from my car and walked them inside the cabin. We had gotten about a week's worth of food because the drive into the closest town was over thirty miles. It was a pleasant drive, the long winding road taking us through Vermont's lovely countryside, but not one we wanted to make daily. We came out here to get away from all that, to enjoy her recently inherited lake house and each other's company.

Jenny, my girlfriend, had been the sole remaining relative to her grandmother, and while they hadn't been close, she had received quite a sum of money plus the house as a result of her passing a couple months ago.

We decided to spend a few weeks of our summer vacation here, exploring nature and the mountains, before going back to college in the fall. We had been looking forward to this and it had given us the extra willpower to get through the brutal college finals.

The lake house was beautiful. A three-bedroom master-piece of woodwork and architecture. The wood interior was polished to a shine, the cozy thick rugs were clean and inviting, and a massive fireplace sat directly in the middle of the living room.

The house faced an expansive lake, a neatly kept green

lawn stretching for fifty yards to meet the water's edge. Dense woods crowded around the rest of the house, barely giving way to the long driveway that snaked up to a two-car garage. It was everything we could have hoped for.

"You got everything?" Jenny asked, hoisting a couple bags.

"That's the last of it," I said, struggling to close the trunk and not drop the food I was juggling.

We walked into the house and began putting everything away, a mood of excited freedom sparking our conversation. After everything was in its place, I fired up the grill on the front porch and began cooking up some steaks. Jen came out and cracked a beer for me, smiling and tilting her own toward mine.

"Cheers, babe, here's to a month of adventure."

I clinked bottles then leaned in and kissed her, letting it last. She pulled away and went inside, throwing me a wink over her shoulder. Life was good.

That was before the nightmares began.

It was the first night, both of us slightly drunk and giggly, and we had sex in the master bedroom. The two of us were so alone, more alone than we had been all year, and it sparked a playful coyness in my girlfriend. It was definitely a night to remember.

After I rolled off her, we lay breathing, both of us smiling and looking at each other. I reached out and wiped a trickle of sweat off her forehead.

"Worked for that one, huh?" I said, teasing.

She laughed and rolled over to rest her chin on my chest,

her big blue eyes meeting mine. "I'd say that goes in our top three."

I mocked shock. "What do you mean OUR top three? How about 'of all time'?"

She bit my chest playfully. "You know you're my only one."

I leaned down and kissed the top of her head. "Yeah I wish. I love you, Jenny."

She kissed me. "I love you too."

Soon after we were fast asleep, a bright moon rising and spilling its soft glow across the lake. A gentle breeze added to the symphony of night noises, lost to us in peaceful slumber.

I awoke slowly, not quite sure what my reason for waking was. Then I heard Jenny quietly muttering in her sleep. She kept rolling over, a stray leg or arm bumping me. She was covered in sweat and her face was bunched in a worried expression. At first I thought she was trying to tell me something, but I realized she was still passed out.

As I was about to gently calm her, I caught what she was saying. It was the same word over and over again.

"Shimmer…shimmer…shimmer…"

I figured she was probably having a strange dream and I carefully placed an arm around her shoulders and pulled her close. I stroked her hair and kissed her head.

"Shhhh, baby, it's OK. Shhhhh…you're just having a bad dream. I'm right here."

After a couple minutes her body relaxed and she went silent, the nightmare releasing her mind. We both slept soundly until morning.

It was a stunning June day and the bright sun practically

sang out over the deep blue sky. As I made us breakfast, I asked Jenny if she remembered having nightmares. She said she didn't, that she slept like a rock, so I let it go and we took our food outside and ate on the porch, enjoying the morning air.

As we ate, we discussed our plans for the day. There were so many options. Do we go hiking? Swimming? Lay out in the sun and read? We decided the lake looked inviting and so after we cleaned up the breakfast dishes, we changed and went charging toward the water screaming and laughing like little kids.

It was a wonderful day, the weather warming and encouraging us to take multiple swims between suntanning. At lunch, Jenny walked up the front lawn and came back a few minutes later with the chicken wings we bought yesterday and a couple of beers. We sat on the shore, eating and drying off, the cold beer underlying how perfect it all felt. After lunch I fell asleep. The warm rays trickled down the sky and stroked my skin as I slept.

Three hours later I woke with a smile. I stretched and stared into the blue. I had needed that, the long drive yesterday exhausting me. I felt refreshed and I pulled myself up from my towel, scanning the yard for Jenny. I didn't see her so I rolled over on my back and wiped the grogginess from my face.

Eventually, I got up and went up to the house. I called out for Jenny as I entered the front door, but there was no response. I figured she went for a walk in the woods and began making us dinner. I wanted to do something romantic, given this time to surprise her, and so I cooked stuffed chicken, the one thing I could make with some finesse. Time ticked by and as I was putting the last dish on the table, Jenny returned.

"Oh, look at you," she said, kicking off her shoes and taking the glass of wine I was pouring for dinner. "Don't you just know how to spoil a girl?"

I gave her a kiss. "You didn't give me time to go find some flower petals I could sprinkle over the table."

She laughed and surveyed the steaming food. "Looks like you did pretty well, regardless."

"Where'd you go?" I asked, pulling a chair out for her to sit.

She took another sip of wine and sat down. "Just out into the woods for a little exploring. Didn't know how long you were going to be asleep for."

I sat across from her and started to fill her plate. "Find anything good?"

She picked up her fork. "Not really, just a lot of trees and bugs. This looks amazing by the way, thank you."

Right before she took her first bite, her fork froze and very quietly, she muttered something in rapid succession.

"Shimmer shimmer shimmer shine."

I looked up. "What was that?"

She took a bite and her eyes rolled back. "Oh my God, this is so tasty. What? I didn't say anything, love. But I will say you're turning into quite the chef."

I stared at her for another second then dug in, discarding what had surely been my imagination.

After dinner we started a fire and sat cuddled together drinking wine and talking about the past semester. The evening slowly bloomed into darkness and the moon returned, climbing its star-studded ladder into the sky. The fire started to die and the sounds of late night began to chirp all around us.

Draining the last bits of wine from our glasses and the bottle, we slowly made our way to bed, turning the lights out and making sure all the doors were locked. After brushing our teeth and stripping, we climbed into bed and fell asleep cuddling.

I woke up. I glanced at the clock on the stand next to me and saw it was a little after two. Jenny was kicking me again, slowly tossing from one side to the other. She was an oven. Through the window, the moonlight showed a sheen of sweat covering her face. She was talking, her voice strained, almost scared. I couldn't make out what she was saying at first, but then I leaned in closer.

"Shimmer…shine…shine…shimmer…"

Again with this, I thought. *I knew I heard her at dinner. What the hell?*

I reached out to wake her when her eyes snapped open and she looked directly at me.

"It's in here. It's over there in the corner."

I paused, her words chilling me. I glanced over at the far corner of the room which was empty…and saw nothing.

"Honey, you're having a nightmare, there's nothing there. Everything is OK," I said.

She didn't move an inch, her eyes huge and bulging. "I can see it. It's there. It's looking at you."

Her words made my heart race, the sureness in her voice chilling me. I knew she was asleep; she had sleepwalked before in school so this was nothing new. But I had never heard such anxious seriousness in her voice before.

I glanced again at the dark corner, the shadows from the moon twisting the black. There was nothing.

"Jen, wake up," I said, grabbing her shoulders.

She remained the same, those eyes drilling into mine. "It scares me. It really, really scares me. Make it go away...NO! NO, DON'T LOOK AT ME!" She suddenly screamed, turning to look into the corner. She pulled the sheets over her head, her voice shattering the last bit of bravery I had. I leaned up and snapped the light on.

There was nothing in the corner.

"Look!" I said, trying to pulled the covers down. "Look, there's nothing there! It's OK!"

Jenny stopped screaming, her breath slowing, and she very cautiously peeked out. She closed her eyes and sighed, "It's gone back to the shimmer..." and then she was fast asleep as if nothing had happened.

"What the hell," I whispered, shaken from the whole thing. Clearly she was having some horrible nightmare, but being in a new house out in the middle of nowhere did nothing to help calm my shocked nerves. Making sure she was asleep, I quietly got out of bed and went to sit on the porch outside. I needed the night air to clear my head.

I leaned back in my chair, watching the way the water rippled in the moonlight. I looked to my right, toward the tree line, and scanned the looming woods. All was quiet and still. I sighed deeply, running my hands over my face. What a night. I decided I was going to talk to Jenny in the morning, ask her what this shimmer nonsense was all about. It weirded me out, the soft passive way she kept saying it. I'd never heard her mention having nightmares before either, not for as long as I had known her. It must be the new place, I reasoned; unfamiliarity can breed fear.

I took another deep breath, the crisp air cleansing my thoughts. As I was about to get up, I paused, my eyes going toward the waterfront.

I could feel something watching at me. Right by the shore. I didn't see anything, but the hairs on the back of my neck stood up and goosebumps rose on my arms.

No.

There was more than one.

"What is going on?" I whispered to myself, dread creeping down my spine.

I strained my eyes, trying to pick up shapes or movement. There was nothing, just the gentle sound of small ripples hitting the gravel sand.

Slowly I stood, taking the three steps down the porch to the front lawn. I dared not go any further. Nothing happened, nothing moved, nothing breathed. Then I heard a loud snap come from the woods on my right.

I spun, heart pumping red-hot adrenaline through my bloodstream. The trees swayed slightly in a gentle breeze, the sound of rustling leaves clogging my ears. I begged them to stop, my eyes darting back and forth, half-expecting some dark being of the night to come charging out. But nothing did.

"OK, time to go back inside," I said, turning. I stopped.

Whatever was watching me from the shore had moved closer. I could feel some kind of weird energy and heat flowing in my direction. Or was I just imagining it, paranoid by my girlfriend's nightmares?

Not sticking around to find out, I bounded up the steps and

back into the safety of the house. I locked the door and turned on the porch lights. Trying to slow my heart rate, I went back into the bedroom and tucked myself in next to Jenny. When sleep finally came, it was restless and full of moving shadows.

Both of us slept until almost noon, our bodies tired from the night activity. A warm sun peeked in the windows and eventually we got up. We were quiet as we started the day, murmuring good morning to each other and making coffee. When it was finished, we took it outside to the porch, Jenny sitting on my lap with her head resting on mine.

I took a cautious sip from my mug and swallowed the hot liquid before asking, "You remember any nightmares you had last night?"

Jenny looked at me, puzzled. "Nightmares? No, why? Was I keeping you up?"

I shrugged. "You were talking in your sleep a little bit. Sounded like you thought something was in our room. Scared the shit out of me, to be honest."

She pinched my cheek, smiling. "Awww, don't worry I'll protect you from the monsters under the bed."

I shrugged her hand away and took another sip of coffee. "I was just worried about you. You were tossing and turning the first night, too, all sweaty and muttering stuff."

"What was I saying?"

I took a moment, collecting my thoughts. "Well, it's weird…you kept saying these two words…in fact, I'm pretty sure you said them last night at dinner. You kept repeating, 'shimmer' and 'shine.' And last night when I was trying to get you to calm down you said, 'It's gone back to the shimmer.'"

Jenny ran her tongue over her teeth. "That's sounds crazy as a crab cake, buddy. Next time just kick me and tell me to shut up," she giggled and leaned down, kissing me. "Just not too hard, mister."

I wasn't about to let it go so easily. "Look, baby, it really freaked me out. You would have been scared, too, if you heard the things you were saying."

She stuck her bottom lip out at me. "I'm sorry. Maybe I should drink some tea tonight before bed. You do look pretty tired."

I wrapped my arms around her. "I'm just worried about my girl, that's all."

She stroked my hair. "You're a good boyfriend."

We sat like that for a while, finishing our coffee and watching the water. Seeing the lake in the daylight made me feel kind of silly about last night. Of course there had been nothing there. Still, I decided to keep that part of the story to myself, not wanting to add fuel to any potential nightmares.

"What do you want to do today?" I asked after a while.

Jenny shrugged. "Anything you want. You decide."

I motioned my head toward the woods. "You wanna take a walk? Check out the woods; see if we can't find something cool?"

I felt Jenny shrink ever so slightly into me. "I'd rather not. At least not today, if that's all right."

"Hey you said I could decide," I teased.

"I know," she said. "I went for a walk yesterday, though. I walked pretty far back and," she paused, her words coming slowly, "there's nothing out there."

I sighed, pretending to be crushed, "Fine…I guess I can think of one other thing I'd like to do all day…I guess."

She perked up. "Oh? What's that?"

I picked her up and marched us into the bedroom, Jenny playfully resisting and laughing the whole way.

Once again the moonlight filled our bedroom, a peaceful silence cooling the air. It had been a fantastic day. Jenny was already asleep and breathing softly next to me. I looked over at the clock and saw it was midnight.

"Holy shit," I muttered, "how is it so late already?" I rested my head down on my pillow, feeling my muscles ache. They had certainly gotten a workout today. I smiled, thinking about the hours before. I had complete confidence she would sleep like a baby tonight.

Not quite ready to turn in myself, I crept out of the room and pulled a beer from the fridge. I plopped myself down on the couch in the dark house and pulled out my phone. I scanned the news and my other usual sites, feeling content and worn out.

About halfway through my third beer, I began to feel the day's activities catching up with me and I began nodding off. Just as I was about to enter the comfort of deep sleep, I heard something.

"Baby?"

I forced my eyes open, trying to adjust my vision in the darkness.

"Baby, where are you?"

Jenny. I prayed she hadn't had another nightmare.

"I'm right here, hon," I said loudly, waving my arm behind

my head toward the bedroom door. "I fell asleep on the couch I think. I'm sorry. Come over here."

I heard her stumble through the bedroom and walk out into the living room, her footsteps softly rounding the side of the couch over toward me.

"I'm over here," I said, squinting, trying to make out her shape.

My blood froze in my veins.

That wasn't Jenny.

I scrambled for my phone and hastily swiped the screen, shining the light where her voice was coming from.

Nothing. I was alone in the living room.

"What the fuck?" I croaked, voice shaking. I stood up, heart beating like a hammer against my chest, and walked around the couch into the bedroom. The sheets were cast aside and the bed lay empty.

Jenny was gone.

"Jenny!?" I cried, fist slamming into the wall and flicking the light on. "Jenny, where are you!?" I scanned the room, feeling panic rise, and saw the window wide open.

I ran to it, tripping on my shoes at the foot of the bed and going down hard. Cursing and gasping, I hoisted myself up and went to look out the window. Dark night and a claustrophobic tree line were all I saw, the moon rays unable to break through the dense woods.

I ran to the front door, throwing it open and putting my hands to my mouth, screaming for Jenny. I ran out onto the lawn, cool dew splashing on my bare feet. I looked toward the water's edge, desperately searching for some sign of where she could be. Nothing.

"JENNY!" I screamed, voice cracking. I could feel terror wrapping a cold hand around my mind as I spun three hundred and sixty degrees, eyes poking at every shadow.

I saw her.

She was standing motionless by the tree line on the right side of the house, unmoving, and staring into the black woods.

I sprinted to her, breath coming in sharp bursts of panic. I grabbed her by the shoulders and spun her toward me.

"Jenny, what are you doing out here!?" I gasped.

She shook me off and turned back to the woods, raising a finger to her lips. "Listen."

Confused, I stood there only hearing the blood pumping in my ears. Then...I heard it.

Screaming.

The noise echoed back to us from deep, deep inside the woods. A man's voice.

Jenny glanced at me, her voice barely audible. "Do you hear that?"

I swallowed hard, chest rattling. "What the hell is that?"

She said nothing and we both were trapped in horror as the screaming continued, a raw, penetrating howl that buried itself deep in my ears. And then it began to get closer.

"We need to get back inside," I said, trying to grab her again.

"Wait!" she hissed, head cocked. "Listen. He's saying something."

I wrapped my arms around myself, biting back the fear.

The voice was screaming for help.

And then my eyes grew wide as I realized something.

That was my voice.

"Jenny! NOW!" I said, practically dragging her back inside the house. I slammed the front door and turned on every light I could find, my terrified, confused mind soaring in crippled chaos. I went to get my phone and call someone, anyone, when I heard Jenny speak.

She was standing by the front window, nose practically touching the glass. "Shimmer, shimmer, shine, we all shine….look at them all…" she repeated over and over again. I ran to her and spun her to face me. Her eyes were clouded and I realized she was asleep.

I slapped her hard. "Stop it! Stop saying that! Wake UP!"

She stumbled back, hitting the wall and almost falling. She blinked and tears began to form. Her cheek glowed from where I had stuck her and her eyes met mine. Confused and clear, she began to cry.

"What are you DOING!?" she sobbed, sitting down against the wall. "What is happening? Why am I in the living room?"

Oh shit, I thought, *too hard.* I quickly crouched down, trying to comfort her, but she battered me away. "You asshole, you hit me!" Big tears rolled down her cheeks and I went from being scared out of my mind to feeling horrible.

"Jen, baby, I'm sorry! You were sleepwalking and I had to wake you up! You were walking around outside, I think you were going to go into the woods! I'm so sorry, I didn't mean to hit you that hard!"

"You're such a meanie," she said, crying harder and wiping her eyes. She stood up and stormed into the bedroom, slamming the door hard enough to splinter the wood. And my heart.

I stood there, feeling awful, heart racing. I shook my head. "Fuck me."

I didn't know what to do. I was still paralyzed with confusion as to what was happening. Feeling like I was wading through a dream, I sat down on the couch and stared into the dead fireplace. Thoughts came and went like a passing summer storm. My eyes felt heavy and tired, but my mind kept them open, afraid that if they shut I would see monsters behind my eyelids. What had happened here tonight? I couldn't make sense of it and my stomach slowly soured as I replayed everything in my mind. I didn't feel safe here anymore. We needed to go into town and talk to someone. To talk to the police, animal control, anyone. I had too many questions that held no logical answers.

I lost track of time, everything floating around me in a haze. Before I knew it, the sky was beginning to color, a splash of purple and orange spilling across the horizon. I looked toward the windows expecting to see twisted faces staring back at me. Nothing. Of course there wasn't anything. Exhausted, I wondered if I was losing my mind.

I went to the bedroom door and quietly opened it. Jenny was asleep, her back to me. I crept toward her and slid between the sheets. Sleep came softly and I welcomed it.

I woke to pressure on my face. I opened my eyes and Jenny was leaning over me, her finger pressing against the tip of my nose. She looked tired, her hair spilling over my face and tickling my cheeks. I gave her a small smile.

"Morning. I'm sorry," I said, shifting so she could scoot closer.

She lay her head down on my chest. "I might have overreacted. I know you wouldn't do that normally."

"Everything was just...out of control last night," I said brushing her hair with my hand. "I was so scared. You ran outside, I couldn't find you, we heard noises in the woods..." I trailed off.

Jenny was silent for a while, then, "I really ran outside?" she giggled. "Wow, that'll be a story for the kids."

I looked down at her. "Jenny, this is serious. There's something weird going on. Ever since that first night I've felt like something is wrong. You've been acting strange, I'm hearing voices, I keep thinking something is watching me...I'm getting freaked out."

She rolled on top of me. "Can't take much more of your crazy girlfriend?"

"No, no," I said. "It's more than just your nightmares and sleepwalking...something is wrong out here."

"Don't tell me you want to go back already," she said, sitting up.

I propped myself up on my elbows. "Well...no...but I'd feel better if we went into town and talked to someone. Like the police. Just to be sure there's no crazy hillbillies running around killing people or whatever."

She collapsed onto her back with a groan. "Oh, please don't make me sit in the car again!"

I could feel myself getting frustrated. "Look, I'm just worried about keeping us safe and last night I did not feel safe, OK?"

She rolled over and looked at me, her big blue eyes widening. "Can we pleeeeease just stay here today and have a good day together? Please? Can't you just call or something?"

I closed my mouth and turned everything over in my mind. I would much rather talk to someone face to face, if only to get away from the house for a few hours, but calling did make more sense. Jenny stared at me as I made up my mind, fluttering her eyelashes at me and pouting. I groaned internally.

"Fine, I'll call. But you're making breakfast this morning," I said, caving.

She laughed and hit me with a pillow. "Fine, just don't start beating me again if I burn your toast."

"Har har."

Jenny bounded off the bed and went to prepare for the day. I didn't move for another couple minutes, feeling like a bitch. Finally, I got up and took a shower, the hot water and steam purging my bad feelings and filling me with optimism.

After breakfast, I went outside with my phone, watching as Jenny sprinted past me toward the water in her swimsuit. I told her I'd join her in a moment and looked up the local sheriff's department, dialing the number.

The phone rang a couple times, then was answered by a man with a high, young-sounding voice. I told him I needed to talk to the sheriff and he told me I was speaking to him.

I told him my name and where we were staying and described what happened last night, going over the weird feeling of being watched, the screaming, the voices, everything.

"I know this all sounds crazy," I said for the hundredth time, "but I'm telling you exactly as it happened, OK?"

Silence grew on the other line, then finally, "You said you were up by the lake?"

"Yeah."

"You're quite a ways from us. Quite a ways from everything, matter of fact." The sheriff paused and I could hear him sucking his teeth. "Listen, there's a lot of weird noises up here. Especially if you aren't used to the woods. Animals can make all kinds of sounds that sound human. You know a fox can sound like a crying baby? Creepiest thing you'll ever hear."

I shifted the phone to my other ear, watching Jen dive into the water from the pier. "Listen, I know I didn't grow up around here, but I know what a human voice sounds like. And a fox can't scream, 'Help me,' can it? Unless you're going to tell me that was a fucking owl." I could feel my temper rising, the frustration of being talked down to heating me.

The sheriff's tone shifted. "Don't get smart with me; you're the one calling me for help, right?"

"You're not helping!" I yelled, throwing my hand up in the air.

"You wanna know what I really think?" he said, quieting.

"Please!"

His voice filled my ear, his mouth pressing against the receiver. "I think you should stay the fuck out of those woods." And then he hung up.

I blinked and stared at my screen. What did he say? Stay out of the woods? Why? Gritting my teeth, I shoved my phone in my pocket and walked down to the pier. I was pissed. I had no answers and I was torn as to what to do.

Jenny swam over and asked me about the call. I waved a hand at her, dismissively telling her they didn't know what I was talking about.

She gave me a big grin and said, "See? Everything is fine. Now can you please stop moping and come in here with me?"

Reluctantly, I pulled my shirt off and wrapped my phone in it. I slipped into the cold water and told myself that if things went weird again tonight, we would leave. Screw the trip, screw the plans, we could go anywhere, the summer was just starting.

Having made that decision, I found it easier to relax and have fun. I felt the tension bleed out of me and the knots in my neck began to loosen. Soon I found myself laughing and splashing around, chasing Jenny through the water and dunking her, then letting her dunk me.

The sun crawled across the sky like a dying man in a desert. As evening dawned, clouds began to bump into each other and form a thick overcast blanket above us. The sunset was lost in its thick weave and darkness began to move in early.

As the light dimmed, we went back up into the house and began preparing a huge dinner. We joked about how much food we were making, but we were both starving. I played music loudly over my phone and we danced in the kitchen, a delicious aroma swirling with us.

Finally, around nine o'clock, everything was ready. With great anticipation, I poured two large glasses of wine and we took our seats at the table.

"This is going to be glorious," I said, raising my glass.

"Amen to that," Jenny said, raising her own. We let the crystal touch and then we drank, the warmth of the alcohol spreading in my chest.

Jenny stabbed a piece of meat from her plate and as she raised it to her mouth, she paused, her eyes glazing over.

"Shimmer…shine…," she whispered.

I froze. I looked up at her and she was staring at me. No. She was staring behind me toward the windows.

Her eyes expanded, clear again, and her face twisted in terror.

Her voice trembled as she spoke, "They're all watching us."

All the lights went out.

Before I could even cry out in surprise, the front door behind me exploded inward with brutal violence. Splinters of wood hit the back of my neck and I heard the rush of heavy footsteps rush us. Jenny screamed as we were both knocked to the floor, the table upended as something slammed into it. I heard dishes shatter on the floor and the clatter of our chairs as they were kicked out from beneath us.

In the darkness, I reeled, trying to focus, my head erupting in pain as it bounced off the hard floor. Behind the sound of screaming, I heard the quick shuffle of feet. I shook my head against the stars dancing around my vision and tried to focus, looking for Jenny in the chaos.

I felt a hand grip my ankle, then loosen and release.

"They're taking me! HELP ME, THEY'RE TAKING ME!" Jenny howled, her voice piercing through the fog.

My eyes cleared and my breath seized in my throat. Something was dragging Jenny out the front door, her legs held by some invisible force. She was reaching toward me, her nails digging into the floor. Terror burned in her eyes.

"Jenny!" I yelled, attempting to stand. Something hard slammed into the side of my head and I crashed to the ground again, feeling blood fill my mouth. For a few seconds the world was a slideshow of still images as I shook the dizziness away.

Get up, I thought. *Help. Her.*

Breathing heavily, I spit a wad of blood and saliva and raised myself up on shaking arms. I couldn't see Jenny anymore, but I could hear her screams outside.

Right as I was about to get to my feet, I felt something hot in my ear and then,

"Shimmer with us...shine...with us."

Screaming, I spun onto my back, fist soaring toward where the sound had come from. I felt my knuckles connect with something meaty and wet, and a screeching howl shook the walls of the house. Panicking, I backed myself up to the couch and listened as footsteps hastily retreated out the front door.

Sucking in air, I stood. Jenny's screams were more distant, but her voice reached me and filled me with blood-curling horror.

"They're taking me into the woods! They're taking me into the woods! HELP MEEEEE!"

I sprang into action. I dashed out the door and onto the lawn, the dark clouds overhead giving me no indication of where she was. I scanned the tree line, trying to decipher where her voice was coming from. My heart thundered in my chest, my mouth dry, the blood in my mouth cracking around my lips. Jesus Christ, this wasn't happening. This was a nightmare. This wasn't real.

Wake up, I thought, *please let me wake up.*

I ran toward the woods. I crashed through the trees, each breath a labored effort, each noise I made a distraction from Jenny's screams.

I didn't stop, the thick foliage reaching out with dark fingers, tripping, scratching, grabbing, trying to pull me to the earth. My shoeless feet bled and scraped against stone and wood, branches rising up out of the black to claw at my face. I bounced off trees, stumbled over roots, battered my toes, bloodied my arms as I ran, every breath of air pulled out of the claustrophobia and rammed down my throat.

Gasping, I stopped finally, leaning over, drinking in oxygen, listening again for Jenny. To my right, screaming, close now. As I was about to start again, I heard something behind me.

"Jenny, I'm coming!"

It was my voice.

And then, seconds after, a deep rumbling laugh, long and echoing through the trees around me.

"This is a nightmare," I sobbed. "Please, God, let it stop..."

I ran. She was getting closer, the woods beginning to thin. I engaged the last burst of energy I had and charged, half-falling, half-sprinting, hearing the loud snap of branches not far in front of me.

I went sprawling, a rock catching my ankle hard, and I went down, bursting through the trees into a clearing and landing on soft grass.

"HELP ME!" Jenny screamed.

I looked up, my eyes adjusting, and saw we were in a circular clearing about twenty yards from side to side. Jenny was kneeling at the far end across from me, struggling viciously against something. I could tell in the darkness she was sobbing, her voice ragged.

And then, as I looked toward the middle of the clearing, I saw something.

At first, I thought my eyes were playing tricks on me, but

at that moment the clouds parted and the moon shone down, illuminating the world.

The air…shimmered and a shape began to take form. It was a sphere about five feet in diameter, floating in the air. I could see through it, but it was like looking through a glass of water. My eyes strained as I tried to make sense of it.

And then something whispered behind me, a voice so soft I almost didn't hear it.

"See with ussssss…"

The shimmering sphere suddenly exploded in light, blinding me, my eyes slamming shut against the glare. I felt my head rumbling and behind the darkness of my eyes, my world shook and reformed.

Gasping, I opened my eyes again, the light from the sphere going out just as quickly as it had come.

And then I screamed. I screamed until I couldn't anymore.

Filling the clearing were dozens of twisted, human-shaped monsters. They stood on two legs, their arms long and dragging on the ground, their joints contorted at horrifying angles. Their bodies were slender and human-like, pink skin stretching over naked torsos. Their necks were stretched to an impossible length, twisting and coiling like snakes.

And each of them had a human face. Their mouths were pulled up into grotesque smiles and their hair hanged down in wild disarray. Their eyes glowed like jack-o'-lanterns, beams of light visibly shooting out from their sockets, all of them staring at me.

But that wasn't what I was screaming at.

The sphere had returned to its original shimmering state,

but something was sitting on the ground behind it, holding it in giant black hands.

My neck strained as I looked up, my eyes taking in the towering creature, its body a pulsing mass of black oozing horror. It had no skin. Its exposed muscle was wrapped tightly with thin rope, acting as a skeletal structure holding its organs in. It crisscrossed up its body, the threads biting into its mass, the rope tied so tightly that its muscles rose around it like a pieces of bound meat.

Its legs were splayed out before it, its huge hands gently cupping the shimmering sphere. My eyes reached its face and I felt fear devour me like never before.

Its skull was exposed, white bone contrasting the darkness of its body. A long snout protruded from its face, long teeth shining in the moonlight. A thick, greasy tangle of black hair formed at the base of its neck and ran to the top of its head, spilling down and covering most of its face.

Except for one eye. It was huge and unblinking, rolling in its socket, yellow with a bright red iris. It was bloodshot and agitated, giving it a wild, crazed look that haunted me.

This reality peeled itself back in the blink of an eye and came crashing down onto my senses with the force of a tsunami.

Suddenly, slimy hands pinned my shoulder down and something heavy pressed into my back. I craned my neck and saw one of the elongated monsters holding me down, its crooked smile and shining eyes glowing down at me.

I struggled, grunting in cold fear, but it was immensely strong, its hands gripping me tighter. I looked back toward Jenny and saw her being dragged in front of the colossal beast, kicking and screaming. Two of the creatures held her tight as she was forced to kneel in front of the shimmering sphere.

The monsters suddenly started whispering in unison, their voices high and excited, chattering with an inhuman rhythm.

"Feed her…feed…her…feedherfeedher…feed…"

They began to draw closer, their shining yellow eyes trained on the sphere.

"Jenny!" I screamed, redoubling my efforts to get away. A strong hand grabbed a handful of my hair and my head was jerked around, viciously slamming it into the ground. Then it was yanked up again.

My vision swam and my head pounded as I watched the giant beast holding the sphere slowly lift its hand and dip a long clawed finger into the top of the shimmering orb.

The globe turned a soft white and it seemed to vibrate in the air. The monsters holding my girlfriend grabbed her face and forced her mouth open, blood leaking down the side of her mouth from the force.

I watched, unable to move, as fist-sized bubbles began to float out of the sphere, filled with a swirling black and red liquid. They moved in a perfect line, drifting through the air, bobbing slightly, one right after the other.

With no strength left in her, Jenny feebly wept and tried to close her mouth, but the creatures held her firmly in place.

In helpless agony, I watched the bubbles stuff themselves down Jenny's throat, pumping into her like a row of marbles. She gurgled and gagged, vomiting violently around them and down her chin, her eyes rolling back in her head.

After a few moments, the bubbles stopped and the sphere

returned to its colorless shimmer, the light fading from the center.

The monsters released Jenny and she collapsed to the ground, shaking and convulsing. They stood watching, whispering.

"What are you doing to her? STOP IT!" I screamed.

They all looked at me, their heads swimming through the air on slimy, twisting necks. One of them arched its head back, its neck extending to the sky, its throat puffing out.

"Stop it!" it howled in my voice. They all let out harsh, barking laughs and turned back to Jenny who now lay motionless.

"Jenny, baby, I'm right here, it's going to be OK!" I yelled, tears spilling down my face.

Then she jerked again, her limbs flailing out. She began to cough, a thick wet sound, and she tried to stand up. She fell back to the ground and grabbed her arm, howling.

With a sickening crack, I watched as both her arms extended and popped, seeming to grow and bend on their own. Then her torso twisted and tore upward, growing and stretching, like her ribcage had grown new bones. Still screaming, her legs and neck began to follow, her face contorted in searing pain as her neck sprouted from her shoulders like a giant worm.

She lay there, suddenly silent, sucking in air. The monsters around us went silent as well, the only sound the drum of my heart.

Then two bright beams of light shot out of her eyes and she howled, her voice a chorus of nightmares. The creatures around me whooped and hooted, jumping up and down excitedly as Jenny stood and became one of them.

"No," I sobbed. "No this isn't happening. Jenny...JENNY!" I gritted my teeth and wept, staring as her mouth grew a demented smile, her long neck twisting to look at me with eyes that shined with light not of this world.

Then I felt myself being dragged forward. Dragged toward the shimmering sphere.

"No, NO!" I screamed, terror consuming me.

"Feedhimfeedhimfeedhim," they chanted.

I looked up at the looming beast that held the orb, its bulging eye meeting my own. I felt my bladder release as I was forced to my knees in front of it.

No. No, no, no, I wasn't going to let them do this to me. I wasn't. I couldn't be one of them. Please, God, NO!

I suddenly threw my head back and smashed it into the creature holding me. Howling and taken by surprise, it loosened its grip for just a second.

That was all I needed.

Fear powered me as I stood, turned, and sprinted for the woods.

A deafening screech filled the air and I felt the earth vibrate as they ran for me. I felt the grasp of their fingers reach for me, trying to snatch my clothes, my hair, anything they could get their hands on. My feet churned the dirt and I ran like I never had before. The wind whipped around me and filled my ears and I could feel them just inches behind me.

I burst into the woods like I was shot from a cannon, tearing through the underbrush like a madman. The night echoed with furious howling and I put on an extra burst of speed.

I don't know how long I ran. I changed directions dozens of times, trying to separate myself from the screams of my pursuers. My lungs burned like a blazing inferno, my legs ached like hot fire, my vision was blurry from tears pouring from my eyes, my body ripped and cut by a thousand dark splinters.

After what felt like an eternity, moments away from collapsing in exhaustion, I broke free of the woods. I broke free by the lake house. By some miracle, I had run back to it. Stumbling, still hearing the crash of foliage behind me, I made a dash toward the car.

I raced across the lawn, leaving a trail of bloody footprints behind me. Wheezing, I reached the car and threw open the door, diving inside. I reached down and grabbed the keys from the cup holder right where I left them the day we had arrived.

I turned the ignition, watching in frenzied terror as the monsters broke through the trees, eyes shining in rage that their prey was escaping.

The car started and I slammed it into reverse, tires smoking. I spun it in a tight half-circle and gunned it. I reached the main road doing seventy and the world around me began to slow down.

My breathing steadied and some form of clarity washed over me. I gripped the steering wheel with trembling bloody hands, catching a glimpse of someone I didn't recognize in the mirror. My face was cut beyond recognition from my flight, blood and leaves stuck to my face like some kind of camouflage.

I felt misery and deep anguish wash over me and as I sped toward town and wept, big heaving screams filling the car.

Jenny.

I had left Jenny.

She was gone.

It's been a week since everything happened. I'm in a hospital bed writing this all out for you as a warning. My heart aches and the shame and sadness of the past few days are almost too much to bear. My dear Jenny…she's gone. Out there somewhere, one of them. I'm so, so sorry.…

I was interrogated by the police multiple times. I gave them my story, the whole thing, and I could see the looks they shared between themselves. The FBI was called in and a search party was formed to look for Jenny, but they haven't found anything yet.

They found the clearing. It was empty.

One of the officers told me that the ground had been matted down, like hundreds of feet had walked over it. I said nothing. He knew my story and I knew he didn't believe me. The sheriff I had talked to on the phone was there. He didn't say anything to me, keeping his distance and shooting me wary looks.

They've all left for the day and I'm alone again.

If the shimmering sphere was in that clearing, they all would have seen the nightmares that surrounded it just like Jenny did when she took that walk in the woods while I slept.

Did she see the monsters then?

Was she in some kind of trance after that?

Why didn't she say anything?

I know I'll never have the answers and they will continue to haunt me for as long as I live.

There is one thing that I keep coming back to that sends a shiver down my spine.

Where did the monsters go? Where did that beast take the sphere? Where did they all come from?

I don't have the answers for you. But I am afraid. I am very, very afraid.

Let me leave you with a warning…if you wake at night and feel like something is in your room watching you…well…I'm afraid that's because something is.

13

Chrome Sunset

Your entire life can change in a day. That's a scary thought, isn't it? And yet we never really expect change. We get up, go to work, come home, and expect the constant flow of normality to maintain its predictable pace. We feel like we are in control of our lives, navigating through its many channels, guiding our minds and bodies through the jungle gym of working society. We set our alarms, we lock our doors, we buy our food. We establish these pillars of control, these decisions that give us the illusion that we're dominating our destiny.

But what if the power goes out and the alarm never goes off? What if someone breaks into your house? What if your food goes bad?

What if something else is ultimately in control of your life?

What if we are merely pawns in a much grander plan?

What would you do if your entire life changed for the worse?

I don't tell you these things to scare you, I tell you these things to prepare you. Don't try to outsmart the cosmic forces that hover all around us. Don't try to get ahead of the disaster. Don't bother locking your door. Don't worry about setting your alarm.

Because in the end, none of that is going to matter. We're all going to die and it's coming sooner than you think. It may come tomorrow, it may come a year from now, but every second you're alive, death takes another step closer.

And there's nothing you can do about it.

I've come to realize these morbid lessons. I've been shown the brutal blade of unpredictability. I was like you once, going through life, expecting every day to mirror the last. I didn't plan for…what happened…but in my defense…how could I?

And that's what I'm trying to tell you. There will be random events of horror that happen in your life that you cannot prepare for. There are evils creeping closer to you that you cannot stop. So instead of blinding yourself to their existence with false security, open your mind up and expect the worst. Expect a loved one to die, count on your wife leaving you, expect misery and sadness. Because if you do, when life decides to stab you in the heart, at least you'll be wearing some armor. It will still hurt, you might still bleed, but it won't kill you…it won't kill you…

Now, you might be reading this and thinking my outlook on life is a little grim. You might think I'm overreacting to the possibility of tragedy. Well…let me tell you…if you've been through what I've been through, you'd be saying the same thing.

But you haven't and so you're going to blow my warning off.

You're not going to take this seriously.

You're not going to be ready.

And that's because you haven't seen a Chrome Sunset.

I wiped sweat from my forehead and scanned my brother's farmland. The golden sun crawled down the sky, leaving streaks of twilight color that oozed across the land like melting rainbows. Purples and pinks splashed into each other amid brilliant orange, and the cloudless sky sighed with a warm breeze.

I looked across the fields, stabbing my pitchfork into the soft earth toward the house. I could see Pete and Ashley scampering up to the porch where they were met by their father, my brother Charlie. I smiled, content and happy with the day's work. I found myself unexpectedly pleased with my decision to come to help my brother after my divorce. His own wife had died three years back and mine had just left me. We were lonely men with few things in common, most of which were bad luck and heartbreak. He was a gentle man, my brother, and it had taken him a long time to recover from his wife's death. The kids had adapted as well as could be expected, Pete doing his best to comfort his younger sister through those hard times.

They were good people. Charlie was a year younger than me, always the quiet one. My heart broke along with his when his wife died. He didn't deserve such sadness. He had always done the right thing his whole life. He was my constant voice of reason, my moral compass at life's crossroads. When my wife left me, he opened up his home to me until I recovered from the anger and despair that had rocked my state of mind.

His two kids, Pete and Ashley, mirrored their father's moral integrity. Pete was ten now, a strong young farm boy with an ever-present spark in his blue eyes. He took care of his little sister, who was six, and I knew their bond would last for years to come. It was good to see them all bond together, supporting one another through the hard times they had undergone.

Sighing, I checked my watch and saw that it was a little after seven. My stomach grumbled and I started walking back toward the house. The barn to my right reflected the sun's brilliance off its new coat of red paint. Last week I had helped Charlie redo the whole thing and I was pleased to see how well our efforts had turned out.

To my left were the cornfields, stretching out for acres in rows of rolling green. They caught the sun in their swaying stalks and reached out for more, gently cracking in the warm wind. I walked between the barn and corn, along the strip of crispy grass that rolled to the front door like a red carpet. My feet crunched over it and I breathed in the silent country air. I never knew I liked isolation until I moved out here, away from the city, away from everything.

I finally made it to the porch and climbed the stairs, the dying sun hot on my back. I went inside and saw Charlie pouring lemonade. He looked up at me and smiled, holding out a glass that clinked with ice and sweet lemon. I accepted it gratefully and took a sip, the cold liquid washing down the dryness in my mouth.

With a satisfied sigh, I asked him if he wanted me to make dinner tonight, but he waved my offer away. He said he was going to grill some steaks out back for us while Ashley prepared some vegetables. She might have been only six, but that little girl had a knack for cooking. She got it from her mother, rest her soul.

The kids ran into the kitchen and Charlie poured them lemonade. He asked Ashley if she would get the broccoli out of the fridge and then asked Peter if he would feed the horses in the barn before dinner. Groaning, Peter complied and as he walked toward the door, I ruffled his hair and told him not to tell the horses we were having steak.

I asked Charlie if he needed help with anything, but he pointed to the front door and told me to sit out on the porch and take it easy. I raised my glass to him as a sign of thanks and took my tired body outside.

Exhaling heavily, I plopped myself down in a rocking chair and kicked my feet out in front of me. I took another sip of lemonade as I watched Pete walk to the barn. I smiled. All this hard work and sunshine was going to do him good in his later years; he just didn't know it yet. It's one of those things you don't realize as a kid—the benefits of chores your parents make you do. They slowly turn into good habits that get stuck in your mind, forming you into a better person. But when you're a kid, it's just annoying work.

I watched as the sun dipped under the horizon, a half-circle of burning light that watched me from beyond the distant hills. The breeze picked up and rustled through the cornfields to my right, stirring them from the earth. It was a pleasant sound and I let it wash over me in waves of contentment.

I heard Ashley in the kitchen preparing the side dishes, quietly singing to herself. I grinned, her little voice carrying through the screen door toward me. What a character she was.

I drained my lemonade and set the glass down. Everything just felt so…right.

And that's when I noticed something in the sky.

I blinked in the fading light, bringing a hand up to shade

my eyes so I could see better. It was distant, scraping the roof of the sky almost like a cloud.

But it wasn't a cloud.

It looked like a small circle of paint being gently swirled, its chrome color shining in the evening air, almost like the sky had opened up to reveal something behind it. From this distance, it was the size of a dime, but as I continued to watch, it gradually grew bigger and began extending down like a funnel.

I felt unease tickle my stomach. It was climbing down the sky, its eerie liquid texture reaching for the earth like a long wet finger. Immediately, I thought it was a tornado, except it was brilliant silver and I didn't notice a change in the wind. In fact, the weather didn't change at all. The sun fell behind the horizon, its beautiful color lighting the sky like colored ink.

The chrome funnel continued its descent, widening and expanding. My heart began to race as I watched the odd surface of the liquid funnel drip closer to the earth. It didn't bend in the middle like a twister might, but instead it remained perfectly straight like a pillar.

I felt the need to call Charlie, but I was held captive by the bizarre spectacle. I heard him inside, gathering the steaks to grill out back and giving instructions to Ashley, but I didn't move. The funnel had almost reached the ground.

I held my breath, waiting.

The tip of the chrome pillar dipped to the earth, and as it made contact, I felt a soft rumble beneath my feet.

I gripped the arms of the rocking chair, the shining tower of liquid two hundred yards directly in front of me, two hundred yards of grass separating us. I waited for another tremor, but none came.

I looked up toward the top and realized that I couldn't see it, the stretch of silver extending beyond my eyesight.

"What the hell?" I muttered.

I was about to call Charlie when the air rippled with a deafening sound.

I covered my ears as a deep bellow echoed from the pillar. The air seemed to shimmer around me and my head howled in pain. It sounded like a boat horn, like a freighter coming into harbor, its low cry chilling me to the bone. My vision swam and I blinked away dancing color.

I heard Ashley drop something in the kitchen and Charlie burst through the back door to see what was going on.

My mouth went dry, a feeling of dread creeping up my throat.

Something began to emerge from the chrome tower.

I stood up, heart hammering against my ribs as I watched.

It was human in shape and size, made from the same shimmering silver liquid. It looked like a person, but it had no hands or feet, just rounded nubs. Its head widened up from the chin to reveal an open top with smoke pouring from it like a smokestack.

It didn't move as it morphed out of the liquid, but instead glided into the open air like it was on an invisible conveyor belt. It was hundreds of feet up, but I could see its strange, funnel-shaped head billowing silver smoke.

Suddenly, Charlie burst through the screen door, mouth open in confusion as to what was happening. He stopped dead in his tracks when he saw the soaring tower of chrome liquid. He turned to look at me, eyes wide, and I could offer him no explanation. The human-shaped creature that had emerged from the column was slowly floating toward the ground, still immobile.

From behind the screen door, I heard Ashley gasp. Questions flowed from her mouth, but Charlie and I remained silent, the scene before us robbing our minds of reason.

The strange chrome figure had almost reached the ground. I felt Charlie tense up next to me and I couldn't help but feel a sickening anxiety. What was happening? What was this eerie phenomenon? I calmed my racing heart, licking my lips and flexing my fingers.

The silver figure's rounded nubs touched earth.

And it came to life.

I gasped as it moved, taking a slow step in our direction, its body leaning forward as if it was fighting against a strong wind. Smoke poured from its open head, thick silver cotton that swirled up in the gentle wind. It was a couple hundred yards away, but the distance didn't make me feel any safer. This thing was coming for us. I didn't know what it was or what its intentions were, and that filled me with uneasy fear.

I heard Charlie speaking urgently to Ashley, but I barely heard him. Something was happening again with the chrome cylindrical tower. The air seemed to hum and move around it, distorting like it was emitting intense heat. The smooth surface rippled slightly and I felt my breath die in my lungs.

More of the strange figures were morphing out of the column, all frozen in the air like they were products on a moving belt. That strange smoke poured from their heads, a wispy heartbeat of unknown meaning.

They began to descend, all gently gliding toward the earth like wet statues. I swallowed hard as I counted twelve of them in total, including the one slowly making its way toward us. They looked like mannequins, but with thicker appendages and no visible joints or features. Their fingerless rounded arms and legs ended in smooth nubs that reminded me of giant pinballs.

Blinking back shock, I realized that Ashley was yelling at Charlie and me. I hadn't even realized Charlie was still next to me. I snapped out of my trance and turned to Ashley, gripping Charlie's arm and shaking him slightly. He looked at me with complete disbelief and I saw panic pooling in his eyes.

I turned to Ashley, asking her what she was trying to tell us. She pushed the screen door open and told us to follow her quickly. Charlie and I did, the two of us moving like shell-shocked zombies. We clambered through the house, following Ashley through the kitchen and out the back door.

As we pushed through the door, I froze and felt a cold fist of fear slam into my stomach.

Another chrome funnel was extending from the sky behind the house.

Suddenly, Charlie was shaking me, his eyes wide and his breath stinking with panic.

"Oh my God, Peter's in the barn! We need to get him now!"

I felt my guts sink, kicking myself for not realizing it sooner. The spectacle had held me captive, erasing all sense from my mind. I ran into the house, not waiting for Charlie. I crashed through the front door but skidded to a stop. The shimmering creatures had all landed and were now slowly walking toward the house, their bodies bend forward like they were walking uphill.

And then I saw Pete step out of the barn, not fifty yards

from the leading figure. From where I stood, I could hear his cry of shocked fear. Immediately, the forms turned to look at him, alerted by his outburst.

Oh, no.

They turned and started walking toward the barn. I cupped my hands to my mouth and shouted for Peter to get back inside, to hide and stay put until I could get to him. They were going to get there before I could, and then...and then who knows what they'd do?

Charlie almost knocked me over as he charged onto the porch and I grabbed him before he reached the steps. I spun him around and pointed to Ashley, who was behind us. Big tears rolled down her cheeks and she reached up for her father, fear engulfing her. I told Charlie I'd go get Peter, that he needed to keep his daughter safe and to lock up the back door. I could see he was torn, indecision cementing him where he stood, and so I pushed him toward Ashley. He scooped her up in his arms and she cried into his shoulder.

"Where's the shotgun?" I asked, knowing he had one.

He jerked his head. "Follow me and hurry!"

We rushed back inside and he placed Ashley on the kitchen counter. He took a quick glance out the back door before slamming it shut and locking it. Before he did, I could see figures gliding to the earth. Charlie rushed to the pantry and tore the door open. He reached up behind the door frame and pulled down his shotgun. He tossed it to me and I checked the feed.

"It's loaded," he said, going to Ashley and picking her up again. "Now go, hurry, please!"

Wordlessly, I charged out the front door, the barrel of the

gun cold in my hands. The light had almost faded from the sky, the last remnants of dark purple bleeding into black. But I could see the shining figures, the rising moon illuminating their silver bodies.

They were almost to the barn and I saw that Peter had gone back inside and closed the big door. The figures were gathering before it, their odd arms prodding the wood, examining the strange red barrier.

I quickly took stock of my options, the barn before me, and then ran down the steps and off to the left, planning to circle around to the far end of the barn. I kept my distance, praying to make it before the figures got inside. I kept them in constant eyesight, watching as they ran their smooth arms across the door. I was about twenty yards behind them, their smoking heads creating a thick smog as they all clustered together. My feet quietly swung me around toward the side of the barn, holding my breath as I passed parallel to the creatures on my right. They didn't seem to notice me and I breathed a sigh of relief as they became obscured from view by the side of the barn.

I raced to the small door at the far end, going at full sprint now that I was out of their line of vision. The full moon glowed overhead, its light reflected by the strange towering column. I felt relieved that more figures weren't morphing out of its liquid walls.

Breathless, I reached the door and pulled it open. The familiar smell of straw and animals filled my nose as I quickly stepped inside, closed the door, and let my eyes adjust to the darkness.

"Pete!" I hissed urgently. I heard movement to my left and

I swung the shotgun up and found myself staring at Peter's terrified face. I lowered the gun and embraced him in a hug, telling him I was glad he was OK. He asked what was going on, what was happening, and I admitted I had no clue. He was scared, but not hysterical. I admired him for that.

I took his hand and pulled him toward the door. I opened it and let out a scream, stumbling backward.

One of the creatures stood before me, its shining chrome body a solid foot taller than myself. It must have seen me and followed me back here!

I pushed Peter behind me and brought the shotgun up. Without pause, I pulled the trigger and the gun bucked in my hands, the report deafening in the enclosed space. The buckshot rocketed into the figure, tearing half of its spout-like head in half. Thick smoke bled from the open wound as a silver substance splattered onto the ground in wet chunks. The creature let out a loud cry from its gaping hole and sunk to its knees, that familiar boat-horn sound slamming into my ears.

I took a step back as its body crashed to the earth, where it remained motionless. Slowly, its body began to seep into the dirt and hay, evaporating where it lay.

"The rest must have heard that," I said, breathless. "Come on, Pete, we need to move, now!"

We exited the barn, the night humming with the echo of night bugs. I peeked around the corner of the barn and my throat tightened with fear. The creatures were walking toward us, following the noise of the gunshot.

I grabbed Pete's arm and pulled him after me, racing around the opposite side of the barn, back toward the house.

I looked over my shoulder at the looming chrome tower and slowed my pace, unable to help myself.

It was pulsing with white color like a lighthouse. Its glow illuminated the night in brief flashes of blinding brilliance and I suddenly felt the ground tremble beneath my feet. About a hundred feet up, I saw the surface of the liquid tower begin to shimmer.

"Oh no..." I muttered, a trickle of sweat running down my spine. Pete was frozen next to me, his breath hoarse in the wind.

Another of the figures emerged, gliding out from the surface as if breaking the calm of a still pond.

"It's regenerating," I said, shaking my head.

Suddenly, I heard Ashley scream from inside the house and I snapped out of my trance. I grabbed Peter again and dragged him along behind me. As we raced toward the house, I could see the second tower glaring over the roof at us.

God, what is happening? I thought, my mind ragged.

We ran up the porch steps and charged through the front door. I had the shotgun raised, ready to blast away anything that wasn't my family. Charlie was dragging the kitchen table over to the back door, sweat standing out on his forehead. Something on the other side was pounding against it, the wood groaning from the force. Ashley let out another scream as we entered the house, but relief calmed her features and she ran into her brother's arms.

I closed and locked the front door and ran to help Charlie, placing the shotgun on the kitchen counter.

"There has to be another twelve of them out there!" he cried as we barricaded the back door. "What are we supposed to do?!"

I winced as the figures pounded on the blocked door. "I don't think we can kill them. I shot one of them and it melted. But a couple seconds later it morphed back out of that weird tower!"

Peter called to us from the front window, Ashley tangled in his arms. We rushed to them both and I looked out to where Peter was pointing. I felt my stomach sink. The figures from the first tower were walking toward the house, their bodies leaning forward as if it took considerable effort.

I looked at Charlie and his eyes met mine. Neither of us had a plan.

Suddenly, we all jumped as something crashed upstairs. It sounded like something falling from the ceiling, an eruption of wood and splinter.

"Oh no," I whispered, feeling my skin go cold. I ran to the counter and picked up the shotgun, chambering a round. I instructed Charlie and the kids to go into the living room as we heard heavy feet thump across the ceiling toward the stairs. The figures had climbed the roof and smashed their way in.

As Charlie herded the children into the other room, I flinched, a large silver arm crashing through the back door. I turned the shotgun toward the hole and pulled the trigger as a large smoking head peered inside. I was rewarded by a long howling horn, a sure sign I had seriously hurt it.

I swung around, a sudden noise catching my attention.

Two of the creatures were at the top of the stairs, silver fumes leaking from their heads and drifting along the ceiling toward me.

I raised my gun and blasted one of them in the knees. Immediately, the volume of smoke increased drastically as it fell, tumbling down the stairs. I tried to jump out of the way, but its wide head thumped into my legs and I went sprawling. My face bounced against the hard floor and I saw stars.

I could hear the thing squirming and moaning behind me and I grit my teeth.

Get up, get up!

I heaved myself to my feet, vision swimming, and heard the front door begin to shake with heavy blows.

We're never getting out of here, I thought.

And then another part of me ignited, a defiance to the impossible situation I was in, a fire in my chest that spread and boiled my blood.

This would *not* be our end.

Something swung into my legs again and I caught myself on the counter, breaking my fall. The figure with the blown-out knees was swinging its silver nubs at me. I coughed and felt my eyes water as the kitchen filled with smoke. I scrambled, looking for the shotgun, knowing I had seconds before the second one was on me.

The creature swatted at my legs again, but I jumped aside, grabbing onto a kitchen chair.

Enough was enough.

I grabbed the chair and hoisted it over my head, screaming, and brought it crashing down into the chrome being. Wood exploded across the floor as the chair shattered and I grabbed a fragmented leg. Howling, eyes wild, I drove it down into the thing's face.

My ears creaked as a dying howl erupted from the figure and smoke immediately ceased pouring from its head.

Without stopping, I snapped my eyes up and saw that the second one had reached the foot of the stairs. Its sudden appearance startled me and I stumbled back, falling on my ass. I felt something hard against my hand; I saw that it was the shotgun, shoved along the side of the counter.

I snatched it up and pointed it at the advancing silver statue.

I blew the bastard to hell and back again, the roar of the shotgun cracking in the thick air. As it fell, I watched as the bodies slowly evaporated, disappearing back into whatever substance they were birthed from.

Charlie was screaming from the living room. I swung around and saw him and Pete shoving the couch against the front door as the figures beat against it from outside. It wasn't going to hold out much longer. A noise behind me drew my attention and I swung the barrel of the shotgun toward the back door just as it gave way. The kitchen table was pushed aside as the silver-skinned monsters crowded the doorway, all pushing to get in.

I emptied the shotgun into them, yelling for Charlie, and when the gun clicked dry, I flipped it around and began to beat them with the stock. Three went down, blasted apart by the shells, and another two staggered back against my onslaught. I was sweating, screaming, my muscles tight as I brought the gun around and smashed it into one of their smoking heads. It fell to the side, crashing into the doorframe before sliding to its knees. I swung the gun like a baseball bat, crushing its featureless face.

The howling horn of death followed.

Charlie was at my side gripping a leg from the broken chair. He battered the beings as they continued to pour into the house, a desperate energy igniting us. He stabbed one in the face like I had earlier, and it fell back, leaving a splash of wet silver on the sharp wood.

Ashley was screaming behind us and I heard the front door start to give. My heart hammered in my chest as I listened to the wood splinter. I shot a look over my shoulder and Peter was standing on the couch, pressed against the door, trying to slow their progress.

I heard heavy footsteps from upstairs.

More were coming.

"Charlie, I need more shells!" I screamed, swinging the gun around and crushing another one in the face. It stumbled backward into another two and fell, stunned.

"They're upstairs in my bedroom!" Charlie yelled, running behind me to help Peter. Ashley was in the corner, crying and clutching her knees to her chest, wet tears flowing down her distraught face.

No good, I thought. *They'll be all over me.*

I whipped around, ready to help Peter at the door, and froze as two more came walking down the stairs in front of me. Smoke filled the air as they turned away from me and toward Ashley.

Screaming, I charged them. One of them spun, brought its arm up, and swung at me. Surprised, I tried to duck but the blow caught me across the nose. It was like getting hit with cold iron and my nose erupted in a fountain of blood as I fell back, dazed. They turned away from me and kept walking toward Ashley.

I blinked back darkness, gritting my teeth.

Not the kids, I thought, hauling myself up.

I charged again and slammed into one of them, tackling it to the ground with a heavy crash. Its body was ice cold under me as I rolled up on top of it. I laced my fingers together to form a giant fist and brought it down into the thing's face. As I made contact, I heard Charlie rocket into the second one, smashing it against the wall, screaming for Ashley to get away.

The creature under me swung at me, clearly slowed by my blow, and I grunted as its silver nub plowed into my ribs. I thought I heard something crack, and the wind was robbed from my lungs.

I didn't stop beating it, though, bringing my now-bleeding fists into its face over and over again. I took another shot to the ribs, but I managed to twist away in time so that my shoulder took the brunt.

Suddenly, Peter was looming over us and I jumped back as he brought a lamp down into the thing's face. It howled and I rolled away as he did it again, silencing the monster. Without stopping, I scrambled to my feet and went to help Charlie who was pinned under the creature and taking a beating. His face was bloody, but I saw fire in his eyes.

I took a giant step and punted the thing under its face, cracking its head up and tumbling it off of Charlie. I pulled him to his feet and then stood over the stunned creature.

Panting, roaring, I stomped on its face until the horn of death sounded.

The front door exploded inward.

Six of the creatures pushed their way inside, turning to face us.

Footsteps thundered above us as more piled in from upstairs.

My ribs hurt and blood ran down my face. I was gasping, holding my side, exhausted. I looked at Charlie and we looked behind us at the kids.

We charged the figures, roaring.

I wrapped my arms around the front two as I plowed into them, bringing them down with me. Charlie soared over me, slamming his body into the other four like a human cannon-ball.

Sucking in hungry lungfuls of smoky air, I hammered my fists into anything that glowed silver. I winced as something thudded into my back, but I kept focused on the one beneath me. My knuckles were bloody lumps of mangled bone and flesh, but I never stopped beating on them.

Suddenly, something crashed into me, sending me air-borne. I thudded into the far wall, air forced from my body in an agonized exhale of blood and sweat. I slid to the floor and fought a blackout. My head ached, my back screamed, and red dripped into my eyes.

I blinked, vision swimming, and looked up.

Two of the figures tore Charlie in half at the waist.

My body hitched in disbelief as blood pooled onto the floor and my brother's guts spilled around his ripped body.

No.

Please God, no.

The two creatures dropped the halves of my brother and advanced on Ashley.

Peter crashed into them, screaming, tears running down his face.

I tried standing, darkness filling my vision.

The two creatures battered Peter away and then stood over him.

"YOU LEAVE HIM ALONE, YOU GODLESS FUCKS!" I screamed, spitting out a mouthful of blood, crawling to them. My hands left bloody prints on the floor as I inched my way toward them.

The two creatures looked at me and then at each other. For the first time, they seemed to communicate with one another, exchanging sound and smoke in short bursts of what I could only assume was their language.

Then they knelt in front of Peter, pinning him to the ground.

"DON'T YOU FUCKING TOUCH HIM!" I howled, hacking up a mouthful of blood. I couldn't move, my body giving up. My mutilated hands shook as I begged them to pull me closer, but I was completely expended.

The two creatures placed their nubs over Peter's splayed-out body. In unison, they emitted a new sound, a low ping that deafened me. I squeezed my eyes shut as the sound continued, blasting through my skull like sharp knives hammered in through my ears.

I coughed as smoke crawled down my throat, felt my eyes water, and blood drip from my chin. I blinked through the haze, trying to see what they were doing.

What I saw brought a scream blasting up my throat.

Peter was covered in their silver liquid, his body cocooned in the chrome substance. But it was sliding off of him, pulling itself up his body from his feet like a curtain being raised.

And what it left behind ripped horror from my chest.

Peter was slowly being turned into a tangled mass of working machinery.

As the silver substance rose up his legs, it left behind coiled wires and humming steel. His legs were not legs anymore, but instead, one long block of thrumming, blinking machinery. Red and blue lights flashed from the twisted construction, hundreds of parts shifting and adjusting to lightning-quick calculations and adjustments.

I watched helpless as Peter screamed, the chrome liquid pulling up his waist to his chest. It left in its wake the same impossible apparatus, a contorted engine of unknown workings. The automaton purred with life, using Peter's body as a vessel.

And then it covered his face, leaving in its wake a still screaming child, his features covered by the living machine.

The creatures stood, looking down at their work. Peter's body was barely recognizable, a heap of steel and smoke, blinking lights and throbbing parts, all moving and working to the heartbeat of their own making.

And yet, Peter was still screaming, his voice cutting though the hum of machinery.

He was still alive.

I fought to move, fought to do something, but I could feel my body shutting down. Everything ached in severe pain, but there was nothing to be done. I dragged my face across the floor to look at Ashley, who was curled up in the corner, eyes wide, face deathly pale.

She wasn't screaming anymore, her mind trapped in shock. I could see her blue lips moving, but no sound came out. Her eyes slowly altered between her dead father and her screaming, metal brother.

The figures filling the house looked down at the two of us, their eyeless heads puffing hot smoke. Slowly, they turned away and began to leave.

I couldn't believe it, couldn't accept it. Why were they leaving, what had been the point of all this? What had they done to Peter? Why weren't they killing me?!

As they walked back through the front door, I turned my head to look out the front window, into the night.

The towering column of chrome was blinking with light, a steady throb of pulsing white. The creatures walked back to it, their bodies leaning forward as thick plumes of smoke darkened the night.

The tower was pulsing in rhythm with the lights on Peter's body.

As I opened my mouth to call out to Ashley, darkness rushed in on me and swept away my consciousness.

I fell into it.

The empty arms of the great black.

When I woke up, I was in the hospital. I was confused, distorted, and immediately asked where Ashley was. The doctors told me she was being taken care of and she was OK.

When I asked for Peter, they didn't answer, instead shooting one another a knowing look. My whole body was killing me, a mass of knotted pain. I tried to get up, screaming, roaring for answers, asking where my nephew was, but I was quickly silenced as a nurse jabbed a needle into my arm.

That was…three months ago.

Apparently at some point that night, Ashley had called 911. I don't remember any of that—the police, the ambulance, the paramedics, nothing. I can't imagine what they thought when they walked into that house. When they saw Charlie.

When they found Peter, still screaming.

Recovering from that night hasn't been easy, both mentally and physically. I'm doing physical therapy, each day a painful reminder of the horror I've seen. Ashley is doing better, but I know there are parts of her that will never heal. Going through something like that at such a young age opens bloody wounds that will never close.

I was questioned about the events that night. Over and over again I was questioned…

No one really believes me, no one really understands what we've been through. No one believes in the possibility of horrors from another plane of existence splicing into our world. After all, there was no evidence of them besides the wreckage of the house. Their bodies just…evaporated back into that fucking tower. And then the tower evaporated into the night sky.

They didn't completely discredit my story, though.

Apparently, others had seen the two silver pillars rising into the sky.

They're calling it a Chrome Sunset, a never-before-seen natural phenomenon.

They don't know what the fuck they're talking about.

But I believe that deep down, they know I'm telling the

truth. They know that something inhuman invaded our little house in the country. They know because they won't let me see Peter.

I don't know where they took him, what has happened to him, but I bet you he's still screaming around that mass of machinery.

It doesn't matter. None of it does.

You see…I think I know what those monsters did to my dear nephew.

And if I'm right, we're all fucked.

Because I think they created a living, breathing, tracking device.

I think they marked him so they know where to come back.

14

My Father, My Monster

I had a hard childhood. I had a really hard childhood. Each day felt like survival. Thinking back, I'm surprised I'm alive. There are some things no one should have to go through. There are some things that are better left in the past.

But here I am. Writing this all out. Why? I don't know…I feel like by doing this, by telling you all this, I can finally purge my mind of these memories. I know they will always be there, lurking behind my most lonely days…but they won't have the bite they do now. By telling you this, I hope to take their fangs away.

So let me start with some things you need to understand.

My mother died when I was two. I'm still not entirely sure how, but I think it had to do with drugs. I was her only child, leaving me in the care of my father, Richard. I don't remember my mother at all. Not even her face. I've never seen a picture of her, never heard a story told about her…nothing. My father just told me she died when I was two.

My father, Richard, was the hardest of men. He worked construction and I didn't see him much. I grew up in a two-bedroom apartment, fending for myself, mostly abandoned. I had to find ways to feed myself, wash, and survive. I didn't go out much for the first couple years. I just stayed in my room or wandered around the filthy space, hoping my dad left something for me to eat.

It wasn't abuse at that point, at least not compared to what came later. It was neglect. He didn't harm me, he didn't yell at me, he just hardly acknowledged my existence. He went to work and then came home, maybe muttering a few drunken words to me as he went to collapse in his bed.

At that point, I wasn't unhappy. It was my life, it was all I knew. I thought that's what everybody's lives were like. Thinking about that now makes me sick, but then? Then it was just the way it was.

But you spend all that time alone...it does things to you.

When I was six, I created Ryan. Ryan was older than me by a couple years. He was my friend. I talked to him, confided in him, cried to him. He was my imaginary buddy. He was a part of me. He was a projection of a strength I longed for.

And Ryan *hated* my father.

I tried not to talk to Ryan when my dad was home. It was hard, though, because the more I invested into the fantasy, the more real he became. Even now, I can picture exactly what Ryan looked like.

When my father started catching on that I had an imaginary friend, that Ryan existed, that's when things became...bad. If he caught me talking to Ryan he would hit me, tell me to "stop being such a little faggot."

He was worse when he drank, like all fathers are.

He'd bring women home and tell me to stay hidden in my room while he had sex with them. Sometimes, though, he'd drink too much and couldn't perform...and when that happened he would get furious. That's when the beatings were the worst. He'd kick out whatever unlucky woman he had convinced to go home with him and then come stumbling into my room. The stink of rum on his breath, the dark silhouette, the deep rumbling in his chest.

Yes. Those were the worst nights.

Ryan would watch, fists clenched, fury boiling from every pore until it was over. Then he'd come hold me as I cried, wipe the blood from my face, and tell me to hold on. He would cry with me, shaking his head, my agony one with his.

It went on like this until I was eleven.

That's where I'll start my story...that's where I think the deepest darkness dwells.

I watched the land flow past me as I stared out the window. The sun was spilling its soft pink warmth over the horizon and I longed to be swallowed up by its light.

I gripped my lunch box in my fist, wondering why I even needed it. All it held was a single banana, my lunch for the day. I didn't dare complain, though. It wasn't worth it. I was used to it. Feeling hungry was better than feeling my dad's anger.

I glanced up at him, noticing the way he gripped the steering wheel, his knuckles white. He wasn't in a good mood this morning. He was hung over and I could smell last night's liquor on his breath. Heavy bags dripped from his bloodshot eyes. After he dropped me off, he was headed to work. I wasn't looking forward to whatever mood he came back with tonight.

I said nothing, just impatient to get to school before he found a reason to yell at me. I hated the yelling. I hated the way he made me feel when he was mad at me: stupid, small, a bother to everyone, an inconvenience he had to deal with.

I didn't have friends at school, but I didn't have any enemies, either. When my dad was hung over, I was his enemy.

"He stinks today, doesn't he?" Ryan commented from the back seat.

I said nothing, didn't even look behind me.

We pulled into my school and my dad stopped the car at the front entrance. He didn't look at me, didn't say anything, just stared straight ahead and waited to be rid of me. I fumbled with my seat belt and then opened the door, pulling my backpack along with me.

I shot a look over my shoulder. "OK, see ya dad," I said softly.

He leaned over and grabbed the door from the inside and slammed it shut before speeding off. I sighed.

Ryan placed a hand on my shoulder. "Fuck him. Come on dude, let's go in."

I hefted my battered backpack up onto my shoulders and made my way inside.

School passed in a blur of gray and black. Moving from classroom to classroom, long walks down crowded hallways, the chatter of my fellow students floating just above my head. It was all just part of the scene, a movie I could watch but wasn't allowed to be part of. No one talked to me, no one bullied me, no one even seemed to acknowledge my existence. I was the weird kid, the poor loner who was avoided. Even the teachers didn't talk to me any more than they had to.

I was a ghost, a pale boy with a sad face.

Ryan kept me company, though. He would comment throughout the day, yell at kids he thought were assholes, and whisper answers to me from behind my desk. I was grateful to him and his constant support. He got me through those dark times in more ways than one.

When school was over, I climbed onto the bus and took it home. I sat in the back and stared out the window, ignoring everything that was happening in front of me. I watched the road pass underneath, the white painted lines zipping by. I pretended they were lasers just missing our spaceship.

When I got home I unlocked the front door of the apartment with my key and put my stuff in my room. I went to the kitchen and opened up the fridge, my stomach growling. I spotted a half-eaten burger from a fast-food place down the street. It was partially wrapped and I snatched it up, tearing away the remaining paper. I didn't even microwave it, just stuffed the burger down my throat, hardly chewing.

After I had licked my fingers, I went to my room and pulled out my notebook. During these quiet moments, I would draw. It was a way for me to release and detach myself from reality. I would lie in my room for hours, sketching anything I could think of. I wasn't very good, but I wasn't bad, either. Dragons, spaceships, warriors, swords, guns—nothing was safe from the point of my pen. Sometimes I would create stories around my pictures, simple paragraphs about whatever I had drawn. Ryan would watch me, fascinated, and give me suggestions on what to do next.

I was just putting the final touches on a sea monster when I heard the front door crash open. I jumped, the sudden noise shattering the still quiet. I looked at my clock and saw that it was almost midnight. I couldn't believe it; how had I been drawing so long? My stomach snarled and confirmed the late hour. I put my pen down, my fingers stiff from the hours of creativity.

My father wasn't alone. I could hear him talking and laughing with another person. A woman.

"Sounds like he made a friend," Ryan said darkly.

I slipped off my bed and went to my door. I peeked out from the crack and saw my dad leading a blonde lady into his bedroom. He sounded drunk; they both did. He must have picked her up at a bar after his shift. I watched him put something down on the counter, what looked like more beer, and stumble into his room.

"What does he do with them?" Ryan asked, leaning over me to stare out the door.

"Adult things," I muttered, closing the door. This was a familiar situation. My dad brought women home on a regular basis, mostly drunk, and took them into his bedroom. I knew they kissed and stuff, but there were other noises that made me think they were doing more. I didn't know what, but it seemed to make them happy.

My father was usually in a good mood the day after such events. It was these days he'd actually talk to me. It wasn't much, but it was something and I clung to those times. I wanted to talk with him, wanted him to like me, even love me. I didn't understand why he was always so mad at me. Other kids at school didn't have bruises on them. They didn't talk about how their dads hit them.

I felt like there was something wrong with me. That I, as a person, had some deep-seated flaw that rendered me unlovable. I figured my dad could see it and that's why he was always so mean to me. I used to cry about it a lot, but as I got older I just accepted it. There was something wrong with me and one day I'd understand what that was.

"Boy!"

My heart froze in my chest.

Was that my dad? Why was my father calling me?

I turned to Ryan, eyes wide and terrified. "What do I do?"

Ryan shrugged, looking equally confused. I was a ghost when my father brought home his friends. I was to stay in my room and not come out. I was dead until they left.

"Come here!"

I shot another terrified look at Ryan and then opened the door with a shaking hand. My heart sputtered like a wild drum.

I walked down the hall, mouth dry, and pushed open my dad's bedroom door. It was dark inside and I couldn't see his face. He and the woman were on the bed, two shadows with gray washed skin.

"Y-yeah dad?" I asked, the words clogging in my throat.

I heard my dad shifting on the bed, a dark smudge in moving black. "Bring me the beer on the counter, now."

The woman giggled and there was more movement. My father's words were slurred and wet, the familiar alcohol-soaked speech of a night out. It was a language I was used to, its alien accent becoming more and more understandable as I got older.

Wordlessly, I padded into the kitchen, heart still thundering. I spotted the six-pack sitting on the counter. I grabbed it, shooting Ryan an uneasy look. I walked back to the bedroom and stopped in the door. I didn't know what to do now.

From the darkness, a hand motioned me forward. "Well, bring it here!"

I walked to the foot of the bed, beer extended. The woman leaned forward out of the black, completely naked, and scooped it from my grasp. She giggled and patted my head.

"You have a cute kid," she said, speaking with the same slurred accent. She placed the beer down on the bed and leaned forward again, her breath hot and stinking.

"Do you want to stay and watch?" she asked, reaching out to touch my face.

I jerked away from her hand, appalled and disgusted by her. I didn't know what she was talking about, but I knew I wanted no part in it. She laughed as I recoiled and retreated into the shadows with my father.

As I turned to leave, my dad's voice cut through the air. "Stop!"

I gulped and slowly turned around. "Y-yeah, dad?"

"Why didn't you bring a glass for the lady?" His voice was heavy, a boiled rumble coming from his chest.

"I-I'm sorry dad," I stuttered.

Suddenly a beer bottle exploded across my head, the pain sudden and fierce. I howled and clutched my skull as sharp glass and warm beer rained down on me. I fell to the floor, vision going blurry, my head pulsing with intense agony.

"Leave him alone," Ryan growled from the doorway, his fists clenched.

I scrubbed the stinging spot on my head and stood slowly, beer dripping from my bangs. Before I could get my bearings, I felt a hand grab the back of my neck.

I stumbled, my father's grip like iron, and blinked against the pain as he led me out of the room. I was bumbling apologies, a useless stream of regret that fell on deaf ears.

He dragged me into the kitchen and threw me against the refrigerator. I cried out as my shoulder took the brunt of it, a jolt of pain snaking its way through my muscles. I tried to stand but my father was in front of me, grabbing me by the hair and pulling my head up to look at him.

"If you embarrass me again, it's not going to end well for you," he growled, his voice like burning coals.

Ryan's face was a gaunt mask of pale fury, sweat standing out on his skin and a vein bulging in his forehead. He leaned in and snarled into my father's ear, "Get your hands off of him, you repulsive motherfucker."

My father pulled me up, my mind in a haze, and grabbed my shoulder. "Now go get the beer while I fetch a glass."

He pushed me toward the bedroom and I tripped and almost fell over. I steadied myself and blinked, rubbing my shoulder. Ryan was at my side, one arm around me, helping me. I felt tears running down my cheeks. I gritted my teeth and sniffled, confused and miserable.

Ryan looked down at me and I could see the hurt in his eyes when he saw the fresh tears on my face. His body tightened against mine and I felt him begin to shake with fury.

I entered my dad's room and went to the bed. I groped

around and found the six-pack. The woman was lying on her stomach, watching me, a distant look on her face like she had never seen a child before. She didn't say anything, just watched as I pulled the beers to my chest and left the room.

As I left, I felt a sharp pain prick the bottom of my foot and I fell with a sharp cry. The beer I had been holding soared into the hallway and smashed against the far wall in an explosion of foam and glass. I rolled on the floor, clutching my foot, gritting my teeth, fighting back more tears. I had stepped on a broken piece of glass, the remains of the bottle that had been smashed over my head.

"What the in fucking hell!?" I heard my dad roar as he charged toward me. He stopped as his eyes washed over the mess, his mouth open in shock.

"I-I'm s-sorry dad, it was an accident," I said weakly, getting to my feet, dread flooding my guts.

"Don't apologize," Ryan said, helping me up.

"Quite the clumsy kid you have," the woman droned from the bedroom behind me.

My dad lunged forward and grabbed me by the throat, dragging me down the hall toward the front door. Now that he was away from the woman, he threw me against the door and backhanded me across the mouth.

I cried and collapsed to the ground, blood splashing across my tongue. I saw stars and heard Ryan screaming at my father. I felt like this was it. My father was going to kill me. My short life was about to come to an abrupt end as he beat me to death in a drunken rage.

"What is wrong with you?" he yelled, leaning down to

scream in my face. "I ask you to do one thing, one goddamn thing!"

"I'M GOING TO RIP YOUR FUCKING THROAT OUT IF YOU TOUCH HIM AGAIN!" Ryan roared at my father, spittle spraying from his lips.

My dad grabbed me and dragged me to my feet. He slammed me against the door, one hand on my throat, choking me. I sputtered, my breath wheezing through my enclosed throat in short, desperate pulls.

"Now, I'm going to go to the store to get more and you're coming with me," my dad said, his hot breath blasting my face with traces of beer and rum.

He let me go and I went to the floor in a pile. I grabbed my throat and sobbed, big wet tears hitting the ground like falling diamonds. Ryan squatted next to me, rubbing my back and whispering that it was going to be OK. He was here; he would see me through this. I sniffed and pulled my shoes on. I could hear my dad telling his lady friend that he would be right back, that he was going to get some more alcohol for them.

He came out of the darkness in a T-shirt and jeans. He grabbed the car keys and stumbled toward me. I sidestepped his approach and he pulled the front door open. He turned around and pointed for me to go.

Afraid he was going to hit me, I covered my head, still crying, and shuffled quickly past him. He said nothing to me as we made our way to the car, his steps staggered and drunk. I knew he wasn't supposed to drive like this, but I didn't dare bring this up as I quickly climbed into the passenger's-side seat.

He turned on the car and sped us down the street. He rolled the window down as we turned onto the main road, letting the cool air wash over us. I glanced at him and saw him blinking rapidly and opening his eyes wide. I gripped my seat as the car drifted from side to side, my father doing his best in his altered state.

"He's going to kill us," Ryan said from behind me. "He's going to fucking kill us." I heard panic in his voice.

My dad was mumbling and kept rubbing his hand over his face, as if he was trying to pull something from his skin. Thankfully, there weren't many cars out this late and the road was mostly our own.

I shivered as the wind whipped through the open windows and licked my exposed skin with a cold tongue. My head was throbbing from where it had been struck, my whole body aching in unison.

After a few minutes of silent driving, my dad pulled into a gas station. He left the car running as he fumbled for his wallet. I swallowed hard, noticing that we were the only ones around. I could see the clerk from inside looking at us through the window.

"God DAMN it!" my dad roared suddenly.

I shrank into my seat, trying to disappear, trying to melt into the fabric. I couldn't take anymore tonight; my body and mind were at their limits. My face was soaked with tears and my lip stung from where I had been struck. Ryan reached out from behind me and squeezed my arm reassuringly.

"Of course I leave my fucking wallet," my dad was mumbling, shaking his head, rage building in his eyes. "Of all the nights for you to act like a fucking moron!" my dad growled, turning toward me. "You smashed the beer and you're ruining my chances with this woman. Why do you have to be such a goddamn FUCKup?!"

I didn't say anything, just huddled into myself, crying silently. I didn't know why I was such a fuckup, why I couldn't just make him happy. I wanted to, God knows I wanted to. But no matter what I did, I couldn't seem to win his affection.

"Open the glove box," my dad said, slapping the back of my head. "Open it, hurry up."

"I'm fucking warning you," Ryan said through gritted teeth. He was staring death at my dad through the rearview mirror.

I wiped my face and pulled open the glove box.

A gun.

A revolver.

I stared at it, eyes growing wide, heart beginning to beat faster in my chest. I looked up at my dad, my face a mask of fear.

"Take that and go get me some goddamn beer," he said, pointing inside.

Every ounce of me screamed not to. I felt panic and acid horror rising in my throat. He wanted me to rob the place. No...no, I couldn't.

"D-dad, I can't..." I trailed off weakly.

My father leaned forward and snatched the gun out of the glove box and shoved it into my hands. He gripped my face in his rough hand and pulled my eyes to meet his.

"Get in there and get me my beer. You have to make this right. Don't you know that when you do something bad, you have to make it right?"

I didn't know what to say. I knew this was wrong.

Ryan leaned forward, his eyes bright and savage. "You can end all this right now…blow his fucking brains out." His voice was a sharp whisper. "You put that gun in his eye and you pull the goddamn trigger. Put a bullet through the back of his skull."

"GO!" my dad roared, shoving me against the door.

I got out, knees shaking. The gun was heavy in my hands, the cold steel glowing under a full moon. I couldn't do this. I couldn't do this.

I knew that if I didn't try, my father would kill me himself. That wasn't a question or a possibility; it was a reality. There was a dark edge in my father's eyes tonight, a hard hatred that I had seen growing more and more the past couple of months. It wasn't all about me; it was about the world, his job, his lot in life, everything. A few times I had heard him talking to himself, claiming the deck was stacked against him, that he just couldn't seem to get ahead of things.

I walked into the gas station, a little bell announcing my arrival with a pleasant jingle. I hid the guy by my side, keeping an eye on the clerk. He was an older man, maybe late sixties. He cocked an eyebrow at me, taking in my appearance. I didn't think about it, how my face looked, and I turned toward the coolers. I opened one at random and the gentle cold washed over my beaten features. I paused, closing my eyes, enjoying the small comfort.

"Just grab one and let's get this over with," Ryan said softly, throwing a look over his shoulder.

I grabbed a six-pack and let the frosted door swing shut. My heart was smashing itself against my ribs, my breathing coming out in staggered gasps. The gun shook in my hand.

I walked to the front slowly. I kept the revolver hidden behind my back. Not looking at the clerk, I turned toward the door.

"What are you doing, son?" the man asked, clearly not concerned.

I didn't say anything, just kept walking. Almost to the door.

"Hey, stop!" the man yelled, the recognizable tone of adult authority freezing me in place. I gulped, sweat trickling down my spine.

I spun, bringing the gun up. I pointed it at the clerk, paralyzing him in his place. My hand shook and the grip was coated in sweat.

"My dad needs this," I sputtered, the words fumbling off my tongue. "I-I'm really sorry…I didn't want to do this."

The man raised his hands, eyes wide. "Whoa, whoa, easy boy, easy. It's OK, I'm not going to do anything."

I pushed the door open with the beer. "I didn't want to do this," I was crying now. "Don't call the police…please…"

I dashed out of the gas station. Tears flowed from my face, my vision blurred and dark. My eyes stung as I hopped back into the car, slamming my door.

My dad let out a whoop of delight and floored it. The car peeled out, the smell of burning rubber mixed with self-loathing and despair. I wiped my face, trying to stop myself from crying anymore, but I couldn't seem to stop. I hated myself, hated what my dad had made me do.

My father was whistling to himself, oblivious to my sorrows. He rolled down the window a little more and the night air made my eyes sting. Ryan was silent in the back seat, not knowing what to do or say.

After a little bit, we pulled into our apartment complex and my father parked the car. He pulled the keys out of the ignition and turned to me, snatching the beer from my lap. He paused, the six-pack dangling in front of my face.

"What the hell is this?"

Stomach churning, I looked up at him, at the beer.

"W-what's wrong?" I asked, wiping my face with the back of my hand.

"What's...wrong?" my dad growled, dropping the beer back onto my lap. "I hate this kind of beer. How do you not know that? I don't drink this shit!" He smacked the back of my head and knocked a couple more tears from my eyes.

"Are you doing this on purpose?!" he roared suddenly. "Do you think this is funny? Is that it?!" He grabbed me by the neck and slammed my head against the side of the car. Pain ignited across my skull and stars bloomed like distant fireworks.

"Stop hitting him!" Ryan yelled from the back.

My dad was shaking me, throttling me. "It's like you're retarded or something! Are you a retard!? ARE YOU!?"

"STOP IT!" Ryan bellowed.

My dad's hands were burning a halo of fire into my throat. I hacked and gagged, desperate for air, my vision starting to darken. Maybe it was better this way. Maybe I did deserve to die. Maybe everyone would be happier like this.

"ENOUGH!" Ryan screamed.

He grabbed my hand with his, the hand I was still holding the gun with, and pointed it at my father's face.

"I said leave him the FUCK ALONE!" Ryan howled, his voice deafening.

My dad's eyes widened and he immediately retreated to his side of the car. His hands went up and he licked his lips, the sudden aggression catching him off-guard. I had never done anything like this before, never stood my ground against his onslaught of abuse.

"Are you ready to die, you fucking miserable piece of goddamn garbage?!" Ryan snarled, his eyes wild, his finger pressing mine to the trigger.

My dad seemed to relax slightly. "Huh…you going to shoot me, boy? Is that it? Going to kill your old man?"

"You're goddamn right I am," Ryan spat, his voice hot iron.

"Go ahead," my dad said, a small smile on his lips. "Go ahead and pull the trigger. Just do it."

"I've been waiting a long time to do this," Ryan growled.

I felt Ryan squeeze my finger around the trigger.

"NO!" I screamed, "Ryan, STOP!"

Big, wet tears streamed from my face, my mind shattered into shards of hopeless sorrow and suffering.

I jerked the gun away from Ryan and I saw my dad snort and almost look disappointed.

Weeping, I put the gun to my own head.

"Is this what you want!?" I screamed, an ocean of sadness rising in my chest, filling me. "Will this make you happy!?"

The small smile fell from my dad's face. His eyes grew wide, a sudden unease welling in his features.

"Why can't I do anything to make you happy!?" I howled, voice cracking in suffocating hurt. "Why don't you love me!? What did I do!? WHAT DID I DO!?" The gun barrel was shaking against my temple, my finger wrapped around the trigger like a snake ready to strike.

"WHY DO YOU HATE ME SO MUCH, DAD!?" I wept, openly sobbing, snot and tears flooding my face.

I saw something come over my father. His features grew soft and he raised his hands to me. "Hey...hey, it's OK..." his voice was quiet, but shocked. "Please...put the gun down...please..."

"You'll be happier if I'm dead!" I screamed. "I won't be such a bother to you anymore!" I grit my teeth against the hoarse sobs racking my chest.

"Son...don't do this...please..." His voice was gentle, his eyes sober and concerned, something I had never seen before from him.

I dragged the back of my hand across my eyes. "You don't care about me, you hate me! Well, I'm sorry! I'm sorry for making you so miserable! I just wanted you to love me! I JUST WANTED YOU TO LOVE ME!"

My body shook as grief choked me. The gun dug into my skin and I closed my eyes, sobbing.

A hand touched my shoulder, gentle and reassuring.

My father's voice was barely a whisper, emotion lacing every word, "I-I'm sorry...I'm sorry for doing this to you...it's OK...it's going to be OK..." He trailed off, his hand going to the gun.

Weeping, I let him slowly pull it from my temple.

"Why can't you love me?" I whimpered, staring into my father's eyes.

A deep hurt wrinkled my dad's features, a sudden human pain that filled his eyes. He took me by the shoulders and pulled me to his chest, stroking my hair.

"Shhhh..." he cooed. "It's going to be OK, son. I'm here.

Shhhhh." I felt something drip onto my head and I realized my father was crying as well.

I closed my eyes and hugged him, my body warm against his.

We stayed like that for a long time.

———————

He never hit me again after that night. After some time we went inside and he kicked the woman out and went to bed. We didn't speak about what happened.

That night in the car changed my father, opened me up to him in a way I didn't think possible. He saw me differently, saw my suffering and how deeply it had damaged me.

Our relationship has changed since then. We'll never be close, but it's not as bad as it used to be. He's getting older and I have started my first year of college. I don't see him much, but when I do, we manage to hold a conversation.

I don't see Ryan anymore. He simply disappeared after that night. Whatever my young mind needed from him had been filled. There were times I missed him and tried to talk to him, but I always found myself speaking in empty space.

I have scars, both mentally and physically, that can never be healed. The horrible memories my father burned into my mind will never go away. He created a fear in me I can never be rid of.

I don't think my father will ever love me the way I long for. I don't think he has the capacity. I've come to terms with that. I'm OK with that now. Writing this out will hopefully purge the remaining anger I have against him. I'm not sure if that's possible, but I needed to try.

I'm tired.

I don't want to be angry.

I'm tired of thinking about him.

My father, my monster.

15

Behind Hell

I'm a huge horror-game fan and when I heard about a new one floating around the Internet, I was excited. On forums and chat rooms it was touted as one of the scariest experiences someone could play. Naturally, I was dying to get my hands on it. Despite all my searching, though, I couldn't find anything about it other than the name. It was called *Behind Hell.*

After a couple days with no luck, I began to ask around online. Most people said they couldn't find it either and you needed some kind of special access from the creators to play it on a locked site. This frustrated me and I refused to give up, diving deeper and deeper, desperate to play it.

I finally found someone who told me that I would have to email the creators and he gave me the address. He told me that he had been invited to beta-test it before release, but after getting in contact with the creators, he had declined to test it. I asked him why and he told me that the kind of feedback they wanted was "disturbing and unethical." I asked him what he meant, but he refused to go into details.

I ended the chat and pulled up my email. I sent a quick message to the creators, telling them I had heard about their game and I was chomping at the bit to play it. I gave them a few details about myself, what kind of games I played, what kind of horror I found the most terrifying, and then sent the email.

It was only a few minutes later when I was notified I had received a new email. Excited, I pulled it up and saw that it was a response from the creators. I quickly opened it and read:

Thank you for your interest in our game "Behind Hell." We appreciate your enthusiasm to the horror genre and it's because of fans like yourself that we make games. Below you'll find a link to the game site where you can play it. Your code is "Bunny." If you enjoy our product please consider donating to the site. Now turn off the lights and enjoy!

Sincerely,
Behind Hell Studios

I couldn't believe it. After days of searching, I was finally going to get to play the game! I obediently turned off all the lights in my apartment, sat down in my computer chair, put on my headphones, and clicked the link.

The page that popped up had a black background and a single button prompt that read "Play Behind Hell." Smiling to myself, I took a deep breath and pressed it. My whole screen faded slowly to black and then a clock face appeared. It read two AM. I checked my watch and saw that it was actually two AM.

Cool, I thought. *Off to a neat start.*

Then the game began. It started off from first-person perspective, my screen displaying the view through my character's eyes. The man I was controlling slowly rolled off a dirty bed in a sparsely furnished room. Everything looked plain and bare, the walls holding no windows and the floor was filthy. The room was dark and a flashlight was lying on the ground by a closed door, its white beam the only source of light. The graphics weren't anything special, but they were serviceable for this kind of game.

I played around with the controls a little bit, getting used to the sensitivity and stiff animations. I walked over to the flashlight and I was prompted to pick it up. My character stooped and grabbed it, then spoke.

"I need to find the door."

I started to feel the first pangs of disappointment. I had played so many games like this, where you needed to run away and find the exit while some monster chases you. I pushed those thoughts aside and told myself to give it a chance. I had just started.

I pushed the door open and found myself standing in a long, dark hallway. Once again the only light was from my flashlight. I began exploring and soon found myself lost in a labyrinth of plain concrete floors and matching walls. The only sound was from my character's footsteps and I lost count of all the left and right turns I was making. Finally, after five or six minutes, I stumbled upon a room with a wooden desk in the corner. I approached it and saw there was a note on it. I picked it up and it read:

We must seal the door. We only have a few days left before the Tahlo returns. Everyone else has died. It's just me again. If you're reading this, please come find me. I will tell you what you need to do to be free of this place. I will tell you how to save yourself. How to save everyone.

—The Old Man

Interesting, I thought. *At least this game has some story. Now if we could switch up the environment a bit, that'd be great.*

I chose a branching hallway at random and once again found myself pushing through another dark maze. I noticed the sound had changed slightly and I could hear something else, something faint. I took my hands off the keyboard and pressed my headphones against my ears, listening. It sounded like something smacking its lips rapidly. *Weird.* I kept going and suddenly I was in another room like the last, but someone was leaning against the wall at the far end.

I approached him and saw it was an old man. He looked up at me and as I stood before him, he sighed heavily.

"Thank God. I didn't think anyone else would come before time ran out. I know you're probably confused, but I need you to listen to me. There's a door in here; you'll know it when you see it. You need to seal it. Once you do that, you'll be free of this place. Free of everything."

Suddenly, text popped up on the screen and I saw I could choose how to reply. I scanned my options and pressed the one I needed answering the most.

My character spoke: "How do I seal the door?"

"You'll know as you continue on."

A puzzle, I thought to myself. *This better not be some stupid "find five keys to win" bullshit.*

I chose another text option: "What is the Tahlo?"

"He is the creator of the world behind hell," The Old Man whispered, leaning toward the screen.

My character answered for me: "I don't understand."

The Old Man folded his arms and leaned against the wall, sighing again, "Before God and the Devil, before heaven and hell, there was only the Tahlo. He created God. He created the Devil. He made them rivals and watched them clash, watched them fight over…well, everything. Eventually, he grew sick of their bickering, no longer entertained by their conflict. He made heaven and hell and banished both of them to their kingdoms. But then God created Earth. He created it as a loophole. You see, God couldn't go to hell, but he could go down to Earth. But what did he find? His people already corrupted by the Devil. The Devil was fast in turning God's creations against him. I'm sure you're familiar with how things went from there, eh?

He continued, "The Tahlo had turned its back on them eons ago, instead focusing on other creations and experiments. But he has taken notice again. He has seen how HIS creations have snuck around his cosmic rules. And now…now he is furious and is coming back to wipe out everything."

I leaned back in my computer chair, taking this all in. This seemed like a pretty detailed story for a cheaply made online horror game.

My character spoke: "So find the door and seal it before he returns. Is that really going to keep him back? One door?"

The old man spoke again: "It isn't as easy as that. But yes. You will see. Now hurry on."

I pushed a couple buttons, trying to get more dialogue out of the old man, but he just grunted at me and pointed toward another hallway. I pressed on. As I walked I noticed the cement textures had changed to wood floors. Eventually, after another series of patience-testing turns and endless walking, I came upon a door at the end of the hallway. It was plain wood with a golden handle. This couldn't be the door I had to seal, was it? Couldn't be; I hadn't been playing for that long.

I prompted my character to open the door, and he went inside. The room was bare except for a single light bulb hanging from the ceiling. And something sitting under it. I approached and saw that it was a dog chained to a metal spike that had been driven into the floorboards. It barked as I got closer and it looked to be a golden retriever. A button prompt came onto the screen: Pet the Dog.

I pressed the key and as my character reached out his hand and stroked its head, a voice boomed into my headset.

"KILL IT."

I paused, hands hovering over my keyboard. *Really? They want me to kill it? That's a downer.* I noticed something off to the side, barely illuminated by the circle of dim light.

It was a baseball bat.

I sighed. "Well, game, you're a bastard for making me do this."

My character picked up the bat, automatically turning back to face the dog who was looking at me, head cocked. I tried to execute an action but nothing was responding to my input. That's when I noticed the little microphone icon in the bottom right corner of the screen.

"KILL IT," the deep, rumbling voice repeated.

My character spoke then: "Come on, tell me to hit it."

"This is getting strange," I said out loud.

"What did you say? I couldn't understand you," my character said.

I blinked at my screen. "What the hell?"

"What did you say? I couldn't understand you."

My mind caught up. I was supposed to use voice commands to tell my character what to do. I grimaced, not wanting to say anything. I knew it was just a game, but I had a special love for dogs, and I really didn't want to do it any harm. But I had done a lot of digging to find this game and I would be damned if I didn't see it to the end.

I cleared my throat and spoke into my headset's mic, "Hit the dog."

Immediately, my character brought the bat down onto the dog's back. The dog screamed and went down, rolling and howling at its spine fractured. My character didn't move and the dog fell into a series of pathetic whimpers.

"KILL IT."

I pulled a hand down over my face and looked at the screen. I was starting to feel uncomfortable. The dog in the game looked up into the screen and continued to whimper loudly.

"Hit the dog," I said again, feeling my stomach churn slightly. Making me say it out loud was way worse than silently hitting a series of key commands.

My character brought the bat down again over the dog's body and I saw bone explode out from the dog's side, low-resolution blood staining its fur. The dog screamed again and arched its body, howling at the ceiling.

"For Christ's SAKE, HIT IT ON ITS HEAD!" I yelled, feeling awful.

The bat came down over the dog's head and silenced it with a sickening crunch. My character dropped the bat onto the floor and watched it roll into the shadows, leaving a bloody trail. The microphone icon in the corner of the screen disappeared.

"For fuck's sake," I said, breathing heavily, slightly upset over what I had just done. I let my heart rate slow and sat watching the screen. I could understand now why that guy hadn't wanted to beta-test the game. There's horror and then there's just plain cruel.

As I placed my fingers on the keyboard to continue playing, another voice echoed in the room. It was a woman's voice.

"Bunny has awoken."

"Whatever the hell that means," I said to myself.

My character pulled his flashlight out and I saw a door on the other end of the room. I gladly went for it, wanting to get past the scene I had just experienced. As I pushed through it, I jumped as The Old Man stood directly in front of me.

"Cheap," I muttered.

The Old Man was blocking my path and so I prompted him to speak.

"I know that wasn't easy, but you've done well. You're getting closer now. You need to be careful. Bunny has awoken. He has felt what you've done and he wants nothing more than to stop you. If you see him, run. He has ended so many lives, I don't want yours added to the pile. And with so little time left before the Tahlo returns, I feel you're our last chance."

Text options appeared before me again and I selected one.

My character spoke: "Who's Bunny?"

The Old Man leaned against the wall, shaking his head.

"Something the Tahlo created a long, long time ago. It put him here as a safety measure in case anyone tried to seal the door between dimensions. Between our reality and the many of the Tahlo. Bunny will hunt you. If he catches you, he will kill you. He wants to see his creator again and will let nothing stand between that. Now go, we don't have much time."

I crackled my knuckles across the keyboard and shifted my headphones over my ears. OK. Bad Bunny, stay away, keep moving, seal the door. Got it.

I moved my character past The Old Man and down another hallway. I noticed that the wood textures on the floor were getting lighter and the width of the hallway was expanding. About every thirty steps or so I would come across a square room, empty, with three other pathways extending from it excluding the one I had just come from. I pressed on, hoping I wasn't looping back on myself, hoping the next hallway would lead to something other than an empty space. The darkness seemed to deepen and I noticed a whirring sound repeating in my ears. It sounded like a giant fan rotating over and over again. I hoped this was a sign of progression and that I was getting closer to reaching my objective.

So far I wasn't impressed with the gameplay. It was fairly standard for this sort of thing, with repeating hallways, darkness, a light source, and a first-person perspective. But the intrigue of what I was learning about the game world kept me going. I was curious as to how this ended.

I reached yet another empty room and as I scanned my options as to what hallway I was going to go down next, I had my first real scare.

The beam of my flashlight swept past one of the entranceways and something was standing in it, looking directly at me. My heart exploded in my chest as I refocused my light on it.

It stood about nine feet tall, with the body of a man, completely naked. Its fingernails were grown out and extended into sinister-looking claws, its body was scarred and muscular.

And its face...

Starting at the neck, dark veins popped from under the skin, black and angry, snaking up under its chin. Its head was that of a bunny, its ears long and stiff, its fur black as hot tar. Its lower jaw had been completely ripped off and it was missing an eye, its empty socket staring blanking into the screen. Its good eye was completely white, with no iris. Its teeth were yellow and the two dominant front ones extended down from its gum line, reaching its chest.

It stood there, visibly breathing, its body expanding and compressing. Then it shrieked and charged me.

Screaming in terror at my computer, I fumbled over my keyboard and mouse, directing my character to flee. I reached for the sprint button and took off down the hallway, blood thundering in my ears and heart drumming in my chest.

I lost myself in the maze, charging down whatever corridor was closest, hearing the terrifying shrieks of the Bunny right behind me. Left, right, left, left, left, right, straight, endlessly. I started to hear my character suck in breath and begin to slow.

"No, no, no, no don't you stop!" I yelled at my screen, hammering down on the sprint button.

I chanced a quick mouse flick to view over my shoulder and saw the Bunny just a few feet behind me, on all fours, screaming and crashing down the hall toward me.

I rounded another corner and saw a door, just like the one with the dog behind it. My character crashed into it and burst through, going into an automatic animation of him slamming it closed behind him. He leaned against it, sucking in air, his voice raw in my ears. The screen shook as the Bunny slammed into the wood, roaring angrily that his prey had escaped. After a few seconds I heard it snarl and scurry away, back the way it had come.

"Jesus," I exhaled, leaning back in my chair for a moment. "That was close." I rubbed my eyes and refocused as the screen shifted and my character looked toward the center of the room.

It was identical to the one with the dog, a lone bulb hanging from the ceiling, spilling a gloomy glow at what lay under it.

It was a child. A boy.

There was a sack over his head that was tied at the neck with rope. He was bound to a wooden pole that had been hammered into the ground. He was struggling weakly against the ropes, crying softly.

"Oh, shit, oh, come on," I said, shaking my head. "Don't…just…please don't."

The voice from earlier erupted in my headphones.

"KILL HIM."

The microphone icon appeared in the corner of the screen and I vainly tapped my keys. No response.

"This is just sick," I said, not knowing what to do.

My character spoke, "Tell me to kill him."

"Oh fuck you, you sicko," I said.

"What did you say? I couldn't understand you."

"Shut up!" I yelled.

"What did you say? I couldn't understand you."

I exhaled slowly. This was a horror game. Just a game. I was playing it alone in my empty apartment. No one had to see the horrible human being I was about to be. I closed my eyes and licked my lips.

"Kill him."

My character walked behind the wooden pole and picked up an axe that had been resting against it.

"Oh, come on!" I said, leaning forward in my seat. The kid struggled, hearing the noise, feeling what was about to happen. He cried louder and fought against his bindings, desperately trying to get away.

My character circled the pole and stood in front of the child. He spoke.

"Say it again."

I felt nauseous. This game was purposefully fucking with me now. I gritted my teeth, preparing the words on my tongue.

"Kill the boy."

In one swift motion, I watched as the axe was brought down, watched it from the eyes of the killer. There was a grisly *thunk* sound as he planted it directly into the kid's skull. Blood exploded from his head and splattered onto the screen, leaving red streaks. The boy died instantly.

I took off my headphones and rubbed my eyes, clearing them of the image. I ran a hand through my hair and stared at the screen. This was gross. I was sure there were some people out there who would have no problem doing what I just did, but it didn't feel right to me. Even though it was just a game, I had just simulated murdering a child with my own voice. *This is a horror game,* I told myself, *there's a reason this isn't available to the public, what did you expect?* And I really did want to keep playing, to see this thing to the end. If nothing else, to do it because so few had. This game was an exclusive experience and I wanted to be one of the few to play it to completion.

I put my headset back on and my fingers found their familiar places on the keyboard. I continued.

I walked my character out the door on the other side of the room. Once again, The Old Man greeted me. I didn't jump this time, expecting his presence.

He was leaning against the wall and looked up at me. "Almost done, son. Only one more room to go. You've gotten further than most, I'll give you that. Most strangers that come through here have been killed by Bunny by now. Not you, though. Don't give into despair, don't give up. You're nearing the end."

He heaved himself off the wall and with a nod walked into the room I came from, the door closing behind him. I took a deep breath and began to walk.

The hall looked different. The high walls were stained with a black substance and the floor beneath my feet looked slimy, covered in patches of red ooze. The audio had changed again as well, a deep human humming noise repeating in my ears. The high ceiling was gone, replaced with open sky, tiny white stars winking down at me.

I took a moment and trained my character's head to look up at them. I watched them for a few moments, examining the way they glowed and shifted slightly in the great dark canvas of night. As I was about to move on, I heard something in the hall in front of me.

Three sharp bangs. Then silence. After a few tense seconds, it repeated, and I saw the wall to my right begin to bow as something behind it tried to get through.

"Time to go," my character said.

"Couldn't agree more," I muttered and led him quickly down the hall, passing the source of noise. More dark empty passages greeted me and I continued through the now familiar process. As I went, the banging in the walls followed me. And they were growing more frantic.

Where's this last door? I asked myself, hoping something wasn't going to kill me this close to the end.

Suddenly, as I entered another hall leading off from one of the square rooms, the banging hit twice in front of me and then the wall exploded, a huge clawed human hand reaching out. It was followed by the large grotesque head of Bunny, pulling himself slowly from behind the wall.

"Oh shit, go, go, go!" I yelled, turning my character around and taking him back into the square room. I quickly chose another path and slammed my finger down on the sprint button.

Behind me I heard heavy footsteps thudding toward me, along with a high-pitched animalistic snarl. I swallowed hard and watched as my character tore down the black hallways, his light ray bouncing as he ran. As soon as I could make out a corner, I quickly instructed my character to turn down it, feeling Bunny right behind.

Without warning, the screen flashed red and I heard a scream. My character slowed, looking down at his leg, and we both saw a nasty gash torn from his calf.

"Don't you die!" I yelled, urging him forward. I spun my character's head around and saw Bunny, slowly walking toward me, his long, claw-like nails dripping red. He was a towering horror looming over me, illuminated only by my flashlight.

"Go!" I screamed, tapping to sprint, over and over. With agonizing effort, I limped down the hall, turned left, and saw it.

A door!

"Go, you bastard!" I yelled, leaning closer to my monitor. I heard Bunny behind me chattering, a sharp flurry of high-pitched noise. Almost there, just a little further! My character was dragging his leg behind him now and breathing hard, blood staining the floor. Only another twenty feet, come on!

Suddenly I went down. My character sprawled on the floor gasping, flashlight bouncing down the hall and spinning to shine in my face. He was sucking in air, deep raw breaths that ripped down his throat.

"NO! GET UP!" I screamed, pounding on my keyboard.

My character was suddenly flipped onto his back and I was staring directly into the mutilated face of Bunny.

It leaned down and roared, exposing a dark throat and long black tongue that hung limply on its chin. Its long teeth inches from my face, it reached out and grabbed me by the throat, lifting me from the floor, its sharp claws wrapping around my throat. I could hear my character begin to gurgle as he stared into the empty eye socket of his attacker.

"DO SOMETHING!" I screamed, hands pounding down on keys, hoping for some response.

Suddenly my character's arm flew up and his fist slammed into the giant white remaining eye of Bunny, completely rupturing it. White slime and blood exploded onto the screen as his knuckles sank into Bunny's face.

Screaming, Bunny dropped my character to the ground and clutched its face, reeling.

"YES!" I screamed. "Now run!"

Audibly gasping, my character began crawling toward the door, the environments pulsing through a blurry lens. He got to one knee and picked up the flashlight with a gore-soaked hand. I chanced one look back to see Bunny on his knees, screaming and holding his face, and then commanded my character to take the final steps to the door.

And then I was through. I breathed a deep sigh of relief as the door closed behind my character and the sound of Bunny faded.

But then I saw what lie in front of me.

Once again, the room mirrored the last, dimly lit by a single bulb hanging overhead. This time though, an older woman, probably sixty, was lying stretched out on a table, her head covered and bound by a dirty sack. Her arms and legs were tied to the four corners. I could hear her raspy voice sucking in air and she slowly twisted her wrists, testing her bindings.

"Hello?" she croaked. "Is someone there? Please, get me out of here!"

My character automatically walked to the end of the table by her feet and stared down at her. I waited.

Then the voice came, blasting like deep fire into my ears.

"RAPE HER."

My mouth dropped open and my eyes widened. No. No, no, no, no. Are you kidding me? What kind of sickness was this?

This wasn't something you put into games. You just don't do this. No.

"Just do it," my character told me as the microphone icon appeared in the lower right corner of my screen.

I sat in silence. This was the end, wasn't it? The last room? Christ…why this? I didn't want to do it. Having to say those words out loud, even in a game, sickened me. Just rolling the syllables around in my mind made me feel disgusting.

"We're so close," my character said quietly.

I was torn. It was just a game. But how twisted was I to even have to simulate something like this? I covered my face in my hands. *Just walk away. You're done with this. You've had your fun, this is sick, just turn it off.* But that little part of me refused to. I was almost done. I wanted to beat this damn thing. I wanted to see the end.

"Rape her," I said quietly. I turned away from the screen and took my headphones off. I sat in the darkness of my living room and felt disgusted. I felt nauseous. I chanced a look at the screen and turned away quickly. It wasn't over.

"Fuck, who comes up with this?" I said aloud, shaking my head. I checked my phone and saw it was almost three in the morning. I had only been playing for an hour. It felt much, much longer.

After another couple minutes I put my headphones back on and turned to the screen. The woman was sobbing softly, the sack on her face forming around her mouth as she took desperate breaths.

My character was standing at the foot of the table again, motionless. The microphone icon was still displayed on the screen.

"What the hell do you want me to do now?" I asked, beginning to feel a deep hatred for the person I was playing.

The voice followed.

"KILL HER."

I dropped my hands to my sides, feeling them go numb against my chair. I stared, shaking my head slowly back and forth, a look of disgust plastered to my face.

"You're a sick motherfucker," I spat.

"What did you say? I couldn't understand you."

"JUST KILL HER!" I screamed, throwing my hands up.

I watched as my character climbed on top of the table and crawled over the woman, sitting on her chest. He reached down and began to strangle her.

The noise was almost too much for me. She cried out and then the gurgling began. It took what seemed like an eternity. Finally, my character climbed off her and stood motionless. The microphone symbol vanished.

"Only one more thing now," my character said.

I slammed a fist down on my desk, "What?! I thought this was the end?! Do I have to keep playing this shit? How many more sick things do I have to do!? This was supposed to be the end! You fucking asshole, I'm done with this, I can't kill any more dogs or axe any more children! It's been enough! Fuck you and fuck this game!"

With that, I hit the Esc. button, bringing up a pause menu, and threw my headphones onto the floor. I'd had my fill. I couldn't do it anymore. I stood up, shaking my head angrily, and pointed a finger at the screen.

"That was some sick shit. I don't want any more of this.

That was the last thing I'm doing for you! I'm not going to sit here until sunrise torturing any more people!"

I stormed out of my living room into my small bathroom. I turned the faucet on and splashed water over my face, horrified at what I had just played. Why didn't I just stop? If anyone knew I had played through that, God only knew what kind of judgment they would cast on me. I dried my face, tried not to look in the mirror, and went to bed.

My apartment was quiet in the deep of night and my sheets were cool and soothing. I took a few moments and forced the game out of my mind. I directed my thoughts to happier things and memories.

In the darkness, I pulled out my iPod and popped some earbuds in. I needed some relaxing music to wash away the filth I had just played. Sighing deeply, I pulled my covers over me and steadied my breathing, letting the music lull me closer and closer to sleep.

"Bunny has awoken."

My eyes flew open. What did I just hear? I glanced at my iPod and hit pause. The words had come from my earbuds. Silence. I checked the song that had just been playing. Nothing out of the ordinary. What the hell?

My heart was thundering and I tossed my iPod to the side, sitting up in bed. I had just imagined that voice, right? It had just been an audio memory replaying in my subconscious…it had to be.

Then I heard something.

Something down the hall in my bathroom.

Splashing.

I calmed the storm in my chest and got out of bed. What the fuck was happening?

I turned on the hallway light and listened. Splashing.

I crept toward the bathroom door, sweat popping out on my forehead. I reached the door and peeked inside.

Bunny screamed at me as it struggled to pull the rest of its body out of the toilet, his upper half leaning over the rim, claws digging into the floor. Its empty eye sockets dripped as water poured from them and its teeth extended down and cut into the linoleum floor.

I screamed, falling back and reeling in terror, away from the pawing grasp of this monster clawing its way out of my toilet. I turned and sprinted into my bedroom, slamming the door as I heard the heavy *thunk* as Bunny pulled free.

My breath came in long burning gulps and my mind raced to make sense of what was happening. I knew I only had seconds. What the fuck was going on!? I needed to get out of here, needed to get to my car and drive away from this nightmare. What was it doing here?! *HOW* was it here!?

Footsteps thudded outside my door and I closed my eyes, whimpering and praying for help. Sweat ran down my face and I licked my lips, face contorted in agonized fear. Behind me, I could feel Bunny tracing his big human hands over the wood, blind and angry. Then it kicked the door.

I fell to the floor from the impact, sprawling in front of my bed. The wood shattered and blew inward, the hinges knocked clean off. I rolled to my side and under my bed as the door came crashing down where I had just been lying.

The nine-foot giant ducked its head and entered the room. I lay wheezing, tears forming in my eyes, holding back a scream that was rocketing through my body. I watched his feet take two steps forward, then stop. I put a hand to my mouth, trying to shove any noise back down my throat. With both eyes gone, Bunny began to sniff the air, taking long pulls and growling. Slowly, it knelt and got down on all fours. I watched, pulling myself away, as it lowered its head to look under the bed directly at me.

The hollow eye sockets were two patches of dark ink, its fur ruffled and messy, its long teeth glowing in the night. It took one quick sniff and then roared, a huge hand shooting out to grab me, claws whistling toward my face.

I screamed, my pathetic hiding spot blown. I rolled out from under the bed and jumped onto the mattress. Without pausing, I dove for the door, my knee catching Bunny's face as it looked up. It howled and pain exploded down my leg. I crashed awkwardly through the door and then I was up, sprinting toward the front door.

I grabbed my keys and phone from the counter and practically tore the front door off its hinges, escaping out into the hall. My car sat parked just a few feet behind the building and without looking behind me, I ran for it, blasting the unlock button on my keychain with my thumb.

Once inside my car, I turned it on, almost snapping the key in half. As I was about to back up, I looked up and saw Bunny thundering toward me on all fours, his long teeth sparking against the pavement as he ran. I shifted into gear and hit the gas, propelling my car forward with a screech.

Bunny slammed into the side of the car with all its might, howling furiously. I felt whiplash shock my senses, and pain erupted in my arm as the driver's-side door caved inward slightly from the impact. I never let off the gas, gritting my teeth and feeling blood leaking between them. I tore out of the parking lot, leaving the deformed monster behind.

I pulled my phone out with a shaking hand, mind spinning in shock, and called my parents. They lived only a few miles down the road on the same street, in the house I grew up in. *Please answer,* I begged, *I need help, please, please, please.* It went to voicemail and I heard my dad instruct me to leave a message.

I screamed into phone, "Mom, dad, call the police, there's something chasing me! I'm hurt and I need help! Call the fucking police NOW! I'm on my way over! I'll be there in a few minutes!" I threw my phone down on the seat next to me and glanced in the rearview mirror. I didn't see it following me.

It was the middle of the night so the streets were empty. I silently flew down the road, the street lamps casting rapid shadows across my vision, making me jump at every one. My eyes darted from the road to my mirrors at a rapid pace, fully expecting to see Bunny right behind me. How was it here? Why was this happening?!

As I approached my parents' house, I saw the street bathed in blue light. The cops were already there waiting for me. There must have been ten cop cars lining the street, sur-rounded by fire trucks and ambulances. Officers swarmed my parents' lawn and I spotted my dad sitting on the curb.

He looked up as I came screeching to a halt in front of him. I kicked my door open and got out, immediately embraced by my father. He hugged me tight and pulled me close, burying his face in my neck.

"I'm so glad to see you," he said, his voice weak and cracking. He pulled away and I saw his eyes were red and bloodshot.

"Dad, something weird is going on, you're not going to believe what I'm about to tell you," I said, the words fumbling out of my mouth in a rushed frenzy.

"Listen to me," he said softly, sorrowfully.

He took me by the shoulders, his eyes swollen and brimming with tears.

"Your mother is dead," he croaked, mouth trembling. "She was..." he gritted his teeth and shook his head, now weeping. "She was murdered and—" ...tears poured from his eyes... "—and they raped her...goddamn it they raped my wife, my angel."

I felt the blood leave my face. My stomach rotted in on itself. The breath was punched from my lungs. I staggered, looking at my father, and felt myself stumble into my car behind me as my knees disintegrated. I gasped for air.

"W-w....what did you say?" I mumbled, barely aware of my surroundings, the world growing dark corners.

"I'm so sorry, son," my dad said, his whole body shaking as more tears fell. "There's more."

No. No, please God.

He wiped his eyes, "Your little brother, Lyle...Jesus Christ...they fucking killed him, they killed my boy!" My father collapsed to the ground, sitting down hard on the pavement, covering his hands with his face. "I was sleeping on the couch...I...I didn't hear anything." He looked up at me pleading, "I could have saved them..."

I sucked in air, the world spinning. Lyle...my brother...dead. It couldn't be true. There's just no way. Please.

I suddenly bent over, pulverized by the shock and grief, and screamed. I shrunk to the pavement as mucus bubbled out of my nose and drool dripped from my chin. I screamed hard, my whole body convulsing as the crushing reality of my father's words hit me. I sobbed and rocked on the pavement, eyes squeezed closed so tightly I saw stars. I don't know how long I lay there weeping and screaming, but as my energy drained I felt a hand on my shoulder.

I opened my eyes, the face looking down on me blurry and I cleared my vision with the back of my hand. It was the chief of police.

"I can't tell you how sorry I am," he said gently. "If there's anything I can do, please ask and I'll do it."

"W-why?" I cried, looking up at him.

"I don't know," he said, sighing heavily. "I wish I had an answer for you. Sometimes people just do bad things."

I sat up and pushed myself so my back was resting against my car. "Who did this? Who did this to my mother and brother?!"

The chief shook his head. "We don't know. But we'll catch them. I promise you. We will get the bastards who did this."

I paused, "Them?"

He sat down next to me, glancing at my father across from us on the curb who had stopped crying and was listening.

"There's been a pattern of these incidents," he said. "Two people: One watches, the other acts. We don't know why they do it. But it's always the same, a mother and a son. They even kill the fucking dog."

And that's when the horrible, sick realization dawned on me with the force of a thousand suns. That game. That fucking game had done this. Somehow, someway, my actions had controlled the hands of fate in this waking night terror.

I leaned over and threw up on the ground. And then I threw up again. I felt dizzy and numb, my consciousness fading in and out, threatening to abandon me.

What have I done?

The police chief put a hand on my shoulder, a look of deep sympathy on his face. He remained silent and we all sat there for what seemed like forever. The police streamed in and out of my parents' house, pushing past paramedics and detectives, all talking and looking grim.

And that's when my phone rang.

It was still in my car on the passenger's seat and I didn't hear it at first until my father nodded his head at me and said in a delirious voice, "That's your phone going off."

I staggered up, the police officer leaving us in privacy, and reached through the shattered window of my car. I looked at the screen and saw the incoming call was blocked.

I numbly answered it, "What?"

"Get back to your computer and finish what you started."

I blinked, feeling like I was floating above myself. That voice.

"Only a few have made it so far, please, the entirety of existence depends on it, you must go back!"

"Old Man?" I said incredulously.

"Yes!" he said, his voice rising. "Please, I know your loss is great tonight, but the Tahlo has almost completely turned his vengeful gaze upon us. You need to go back and finish! The door is down one last hallway! That's it! Then we are safe, then we all survive!"

As he talked, I felt a burning inferno rising in my chest. "You know what, go FUCK yourself, you sick, twisted bastard! I'm done with your fucking game, I'm done with this whole nightmare! It's a fucking GAME!"

My father and a few officers looked my way, hearing me yell. I turned away from them, walking behind my car.

"This isn't real, none of this can be real, my fucking family is DEAD!" I screamed. I looked over at my father and saw him covering up his dead dog on the lawn. I hadn't even noticed it. I lowered the phone from my ear. I saw its face just before my dad covered it with a blanket. It looked like it had been pulverized.

"Jesus Christ," I whispered, pain sprouting from my chest. I raised the phone back to my ear. "What is this?" I asked. "What is fucking happening?"

The Old Man answered in a hushed tone, "Without meaningful sacrifice, the sealing of the door will not hold. The blood of an animal, a child, and a broken mother is required. That's just the way it is. That's just the rules. I'm sorry, I really am, but you have to believe that the Tahlo is coming, this hurricane of violence is approaching!"

"And why the FUCK should I believe anything you say?" I snarled. "Because of you my family is shattered. Because of you, my family is dead!"

"Bunny has entered your world, hasn't he?" The Old Man said softly. "He's trying desperately to kill you, isn't he?" He paused, the silence stretching between us. "I thought so. I know this is madness to you, but you are the only person who has made it as long as you have after the third room. Please. All you need to do is go back to your computer and walk down the last hallway. Please. I n—" he suddenly stopped, the line going quiet.

Then, "Oh, heaven help me, Bunny is here. He's found me. Just go! Not for me but for what family you have left! GO!" The line went dead.

I stood there in the night, seeing nothing. What had happened? When was I going to wake up? I looked at the somber buzz of people before me and then I cast my eyes to the stars. Tears dripped down my face silently and I breathed.

"Fuck you," I whispered.

I quietly climbed into my car and drove away, seeing my father walk into the road behind me and stare, his face red in my tail lights.

I didn't think about anything, my body shutting down and going into autopilot. My mouth was closed, jawbones creaking as my teeth ground together. This was my nightmare.

I pulled into my apartment building and marched straight back inside to my apartment. I slammed the door behind me and locked it, flipping on the lights as I went back to my computer. Silently I sat back down in front of my screen. The game was still paused.

I put on my headphones and gripped the mouse. I resumed.

"Where were you?" my character asked, his voice shaking.

"Go to hell," I growled. I moved him forward toward the door in the back of the room I was in. The dead woman's body still lay motionless on the table. My mother.

My character pushed the door open, the familiar gloom of the hallway meeting us.

The Old Man lay dead on the ground before me.

It looked like he had been ripped to shreds in a torrent of fury.

My character and I remained silent. At the end of the hallway I saw light. We moved toward it, the echo of my character's footsteps vibrating off the walls. My heart was a sinking ship, my mind a melted sculpture. Just. Finish. The. Game.

As we stepped past The Old Man and walked down the hall, the passage widened again and as we reached the source of light I saw that it was a glowing white door. Above it was written in ashy black: **THE END.**

As I approached the knob, the game took over and my character went into an automatic animation. His hands appeared, covered in thick dripping blood, and he slowly dragged them across the clean white surface of the door, making an X pattern. He then knelt in front of it, his hands clasped together in front of him.

He spoke, his voice soft, "Please, oh God, hide your creations from the coming storm. Save us from the coming wrath. You have given us life, now please, we beg of you, shelter us from extinction. Cast your shadow upon the world so as to hide us from the Tahlo. This we pray, this we plead. Amen."

And then the screen faded to darkness.

It's been three days now. I sit here writing this out, the pain and sadness in my heart threatening to devour me. My father has tried to call me, visit me, but I can't talk to anyone. The blackness in my mind is growing greater. What did this all mean? What was it that I did? I haven't tried to contact the creators of the game, but I have a feeling that even if I did, I'd find no trace of them. And no trace of the game.

Did I murder my family?

Did I save the world from some cosmic apocalypse?

And, God help me…where is Bunny?

16

Horse/8min

It was an incredibly hot day when I heard the knock on my door—one of those days where you close the blinds and crank the AC, trying to find relief in darkness. It had been like that all week, each day growing more and more unbearable. I was upset at whomever was knocking at my door because that meant I was going to have to get up and open that door, letting the crushing heat in.

I quick-saved my work on the computer as I always do before leaving my station and walked to the door, my mind still filled with thoughts of paints and borders. I have the fortune of working from home. I'm an artist and I draw backgrounds for various cartoons and animations both on television and the Internet. I had almost finished my day's work and so it was especially irritating to be interrupted and break the flow I had been enjoying.

I reached the front door and opened it, raising a hand to my eyes against the sudden sunlight. I felt the warmth of the day drape itself around me like a heavy blanket and I could feel myself begin to sweat.

No one was at the door. I stared out at the empty street and could feel my irritation grow. Some kind of joke? That's when I looked down and saw that someone had left me a small package. I quickly bent down and picked it up, bringing it inside. I walked over to my work station, turning over the small box in my hand. There was nothing written on it. No address, no name, nothing. I weighed it slowly in my hands and it felt like there might not even be anything inside. Sitting down in my desk chair, I began opening the mysterious package. Inside, wrapped in some old newspaper, was a single DVD. I tossed the box aside and held the disc up to the light. Written sloppily on the disc were the words "horse/8min."

I wondered what the hell that meant and saw that the disc was really scratched up, as if it had been played over and over again. I sat there for a few moments, figured what the hell, and popped open the computer's disc tray. I wasn't sure if it would actually read the DVD considering what poor shape it was in, but after a few seconds, the player popped open on the screen and the video began.

What I'm about to describe does not give justice to what was on that disc. I'll do my best to convey what it was I was seeing as the first few seconds ticked by.

The video was grainy and shot in a very dark room with deep maroon lighting pushing only the darkest shadows off the screen. In the middle of the frame was a person, sitting down with their back to the camera. I could only see from the shoulders up and the person's arms were resting on the armrests, just out of sight. The person appeared to be wearing some kind of dark winter jacket. Instead of a human head, though, it was the head of a horse. Its mane was grown out and looked almost like human hair. It was black and greasy and fell down to its shoulders. Its head was turned, looking slightly behind itself toward the camera. The one eye that I could see was completely white and severely bloodshot. Its mouth was twisted and almost ripped back to form a smile that looked both painful and amused. Its lips were pulled up almost to its eyes and the gums were black and irritated.

The initial shock of what I was looking at caused me to jump. What the hell was this? What was I looking at?

I sat, captivated, feeling both creeped-out and curious. The thing didn't move, it just sat there, staring, unblinking, at the camera. Its shoulders seemed to heave with almost desperate, heavy gasps, but there was no sound of breathing.

I cranked the volume to max, listening for anything. About every twenty seconds, I thought I could hear a single bark somewhere offscreen. But it didn't sound like a dog barking. It was the sound a person makes when trying to imitate a dog bark.

It was so faint that I put my ear to the speaker, trying to catch it and decipher some sort of clue as to what I was looking at. Another twenty seconds passed and something barked again, ever so faintly. ?I leaned back in my seat and pushed the mouse around the screen. I was seven minutes in and nothing had changed. The figure continued to stare at the camera, smiling its sick smile, teeth clamped together. Its shoulders rose and fell, neither gaining nor losing intensity.

I scrolled over to the pause button and clicked it. Nothing happened. I tried it again but got the same result. I clicked to exit out of the video player, but my computer seemed frozen while the video played.

That's when the horse head moved.

In one terrifyingly quick moment, the thing spun toward the camera and let out one loud bark. It was the same sound I had been hearing on loop, but much louder now. As soon as it barked, the video ended.

I sat, stunned at what I had just witnessed. I didn't know what to make of it. I realized my heart was racing and despite the AC, I was sweating. A deep uneasiness filled me and I quickly stood up and opened the curtains to reveal a setting sun. I turned on all the lights in the house, knowing I was being stupid.

Questions raced through my mind. Who had sent this to me? Why? What did it all mean? Was someone messing with me? Something about the deeply serious nature of the video haunted me. I felt an almost intimate recognition of what I had just seen. I was shaken.

I went outside and sat on the porch until the night put the day to bed. The open air calmed me slightly. I even began to feel rather foolish. Eventually I went inside and started to wind down for sleep.

It's 1:57 AM. Something woke me up a few minutes ago. At first I wasn't sure why I was awake. I lay there in silence, taking account of my situation. Then I heard it.

Something was barking outside. One single bark about every twenty seconds. That awful, skin-curling human bark from the video. Now I lay paralyzed in fear, just listening, hoping that the sound will stop. It's distant, but present.

I'm writing this on a pad I keep by my bed in hopes someone finds it. Something is going to happen to me tonight. I know it and I am so scared I'm crying. The noise keeps repeating. Please. If you ever come across the dvd labeled "horse/8min," I beg you, do not watch it.

The barking outside stopped.
Now it's outside my bedroom door.

17

Deep, Deep Down

I arrived at the Pine Palaces a week ago. It was as beautiful as the website boasted. This high up in the West Virginia mountains, where the air was untouched by cities and smog, you could feel the purity in every breath. The cabins I would be maintaining, along with the other two summer workers, weren't quite palaces, but they were elegant in a natural sort of way. Each log cabin was decked out in all the usual outdoor décor. Animal heads hung silently on the walls, polished exposed wood filled the interiors with a delightful smell, and a fireplace sat ready to burn the neatly stacked pile of wood that rested beside it.

There were eight cabins in total—six for the guests, one for the workers, and one for the owner of the retreat, Ken, who lived there year-round. They formed a semicircle along the parameter of tall trees, where space had been made for a giant fire pit in the center.

Half a mile down the dirt road there was a lake that Ken rented out paddle boats for the guests to use. I had asked him upon arrival if employees could use them free of charge and he had winked and told me if he liked his workers.

Behind the cabins, down a path that led into the woods about four hundred feet from the clearing, was where our maintenance supplies were kept. Rakes, leaf blowers, a couple axes, a chainsaw—the usual upkeep wares. I remember on the first day when Ken showed us the old shed, one of my fellow workers, Carter, had asked why he kept the supplies so far back. Ken had chuckled and told us that we'd understand once we got married and went on vacation with our families. He slung his arm around my shoulder and said that he had never seen people fight worse than up here where most modern amenities were unavailable.

"Wouldn't put it past one of 'em to take the chainsaw to their significant other," he had said, throwing Penny a wink. Penny, the last piece to our trinity of workers, looked at Carter and then at me, her face unsure and a little nervous.

"Don't you worry," Ken had said, "I've never had trouble up here. Real trouble anyway. Most folks are good people just looking to get away from all the nonsense. They come up here and roast their marshmallows, eat their hot dogs, and listen to the silence."

After that, we all went back to the cabins and Ken began instructing us on our daily duties for the summer, and we prepared the site for the arrival of our first wave of visitors the next day.

Three days later I found that I enjoyed being up in the mountains more than I had anticipated—the quiet days, the chirps, squeaks and groans of nature, the warm yellow sun, and the explosion of bright crystal stars that lit the night.

Carter, Penny, and myself all got along very well and it felt weird that we had only known each other for three days. We were all outgoing, inspired, and wanted something a little different to fill our time between semesters. We wanted to go back to college in the fall and have unique experiences and adventures to tell our friends.

And then there was Ken. Ken had been running the place for twenty-eight years. His dad built it, and when he passed away, Ken took over. He was proud of it; you could tell by the way he worked, the way he moved, and the way he talked to the guests. He was about sixty but had the mentality of a man in his early twenties. He was energetic, kind, and made everyone feel welcome. He insisted all the visitors call him Grandpa Ken and if anyone wanted, he'd tell stories at sundown about the history of the mountains and land around us. It was charming and I found myself looking forward to that time of the day.

That was all before I found that fucking well.

I pulled the paddle boat behind Ken's cabin and wiped the sweat off my face with a dirty hand.

"That's the last of them," I said to Carter. "Everyone is in for the day. Penny should be done stacking the wood for tonight's fire. Do you wanna see if she wants to go for a swim?"

Carter, tall and thin, sporting glasses and blond hair that he was always pushing away from his lenses, nodded. "Yeah, that sounds good. I feel like I'm going to melt. It's hot as hay fever today, isn't it?"

I snorted, "Got that right. You go check out with Ken, let him know we're finished for the day, make sure he doesn't need anything. I'll go help Penny put the tools away."

"OK."

I brushed my hands on my jeans and walked around to the front of the cabin. A couple of guests were sitting on their porches, enjoying the shade and winding down for the evening. I spotted Penny by the fire pit stacking the last few pieces of wood.

"All done?" I asked.

She looked up at me. "Yeah, that should do it. I hope that's enough." Penny was a cute girl. Nothing to write home about, but her charm came not from her looks, but from the adorable way she always worried she was going to get into trouble.

I smiled back. "It's fine. You really think Ken has the capacity to yell at you even if it's not?"

She shrugged. "I just want it to be right."

"It is. Now do you want to go swimming with Carter and I? He's letting Ken know right now."

She lit up. "Oh, that sounds fantastic! Can you put the axe back in the shed while I go suit up?"

"Sure thing," I said, bending and picking it up.

"Thanks, I'll meet you back here," she said and scampered off to our cabin to change.

I slung the axe over my shoulder and made my way to the path that led into the woods, nodding my hellos to the guests I passed. The woods were quiet today, a low hum of wildlife getting lost in the gentle sway of trees that danced back and forth in the sunlight. My boots kicked up dry dirt as I walked, and I wondered when was the last time it had rained.

As I was about to round the final bend to the shed, something caught my eye. About thirty or forty steps to my left, off the path, I spotted something coming out of the ground. Curiosity took over and I began to make my way toward it. I wondered why I hadn't noticed in my previous trips back here, but I had been more concentrated on sticking to the path and not getting myself lost.

As I walked closer, I saw that it was a well, its stone sides rising up out of the ground in the center of a big clearing. I broke through the tree line and stopped dead in my tracks.

A heaviness came over me. A thick unease bubbled in my stomach. Something was making my skin crawl and I felt goosebumps form on my arms. I licked my suddenly dry lips and swallowed hard. A warning light was going off in my mind and my unease turned to panicked nausea.

Suddenly, I didn't even want to look at the well. I turned my eyes away and stood there, unable to move.

I tried to tell myself to snap out of it, but the unbearable avalanche of horror that filled me when I tried to look at the well wouldn't allow it.

I needed to leave. I felt my hands shaking at my sides and I realized that I had dropped the axe. I couldn't even will myself to pick it up.

Why are you being such a baby? I asked myself, still not moving. As soon as the thought crossed my mind, I knew the answer.

Because there's something down there.

I ran. The terror turned to a feeling of haunting danger and I fled.

I crashed back down the path and back to the cabins, my sudden disruption causing a few of the visitors to look my way curiously. I looked at them and offered a weak smile. Shaking my head and feeling slightly stupid, I went to find Penny and Carter. The terror was fading quickly now that I was back around people, and I was starting to feel ridiculous about the whole incident. My breath steadied and my heart rate slowed. I shook my head, rolling my eyes. *Get a grip, man.*

I found Carter and Penny and we all strolled down to the lake and went swimming, the cool water washing the dirt and sweat from us. I decided not to say anything to either of them about the well, but I made a mental note to ask Ken what the deal was after his nighttime stories.

"Sleep tight, folks, and thanks for listening," Ken said as the guests offered him a genuine round of applause. We were all sitting around a roaring fire and Ken had just finished telling us about how this place was built. For such a mundane story, Ken had filled it with practiced flair and charm that only old men seem to be gifted with when telling a tale.

As the visitors thanked Ken and lifted sleeping children over their shoulders to bed, I approached Ken: "Can I ask you about something real quick?"

Ken, still sitting at his bench in front of the fire, patted the space next to him. "Sure thing, kiddo, have a seat." He pulled out a cigar and cut the tip off, striking a match against the wood bench.

I took my place, watching as the last of the guests retreated to their cabins for the evening. Carter and Penny looked at us inquisitively and came over, curious as to what I was going to ask.

I took a deep breath. "What's the deal with the well back by the supply shed?"

Ken froze, his match hovering inches from the tip of his unlit cigar. After a second, he lit it and took a couple of deep puffs from it before answering.

"What do you mean, son?"

Carter and Penny had taken a seat on the bench next to us and Carter piped up. "What well? There's a well back there?"

"Yeah, it's in a clearing a little off the path," I said, pointing in the direction it was in.

Ken turned his head and looked directly at me. "Don't go near there, you understand me?" The seriousness in his voice shook me. His grandpa persona was gone and his eyes were cold black rock. "I mean it, son. Ain't nothing good back there. Just steer clear of it, OK?"

"What's wrong with it?" Penny asked.

Ken took another drag, obviously uncomfortable with the conversation, before answering. "It's dangerous. There's something wrong with it. I don't know what it is, but I know for a fact that…well, that people aren't supposed to be around it. There's something…unnatural about it. Best you all keep your distance."

Carter leaned forward, his eyes lighting up. "Is it haunted or something?" I could hear the excitement in his voice.

Ken shook his head. "No. Ain't no such things as ghosts, kid. But there are other…forces of nature that humankind just aren't meant to find."

I swallowed hard, remembering the terror from earlier. "Ken…is there something down there?"

Ken was silent for a moment, the crack of the fire popping sparks around us. Then he whispered, "Yes."

"What is it?" Carter pressed. "Have you ever looked down there?"

Ken shook his head. "Can't bring myself to get near the thing, truth be told." Suddenly his head whipped around and he was looking hard at me again. "You didn't look down it, did you?!"

I shook my head: "No. Honestly, I got spooked just being around it. That's why I asked; it seemed so jarring compared to the peace these mountains hold."

Ken let out a sigh, but Carter wasn't done asking questions. "How do you know something's down there then?"

Ken tapped his cigar and a hearty piece of ash floated to the ground. "I had a horse back when I first took over the camp," he started, then looked at Penny and cleared his throat. "I don't want to go scaring Penny; just take my word on this and stay away."

"I want to hear," Penny said. I didn't blame her; something about the sober tone in Ken's voice begged for explanation.

"I suppose you're all adults," Ken said, staring into the fire, "but let me warn you that what I'm about to tell you is rather...unsettling." With a giant sigh, he continued, summoning the old memories. "Back when I took over this place I had a horse. I named her Cherry. Beautiful creature. For the first couple weeks, it was just me and Cherry. I was working on fixing the place up and getting it ready again for guests. During the evenings I would ride Cherry all through these mountains," he said, sweeping his hand across the dark horizon. "Let me tell you, you haven't seen a sunset 'til you've seen one up here when the leaves are changing. Anyway, one evening I tied up Cherry to that tree over there," he said, pointing toward the path that led back into the woods. "We were about to go for our evening trot. I went inside to wash my face and change out of my trousers. Wasn't gone but five minutes. When I came out, Cherry was gone. I didn't see her anywhere. But I could hear her," he said, his voice quieting and shaking slightly, "and she was screaming."

"Screaming?" Penny asked softly, eyes wide.

"I ain't ever heard anything like it before," Ken continued, "but I took off down the path toward where I heard her. And that's when I found the well for the first time." He paused, silently puffing on his cigar. After a few moments, he continued, "Cherry was trying to force her way down the well. She was too big, though. She was stuck, her rump sticking up in the air, her head down the hole. And let me tell you...she was going mad. Her hind legs were kicking and scraping against the stone walls of the well, trying her hardest to push the rest of her body inside. She was thrashing and wriggling about, all the while screaming down into that hole," his voice started shaking again, "but there was nothing I could do for her. I was too afraid. Something was keeping me from getting close to that well. I could feel the hairs on the back of my neck rising. Pretty sure I wet my trousers at some point as I stood there watching. Oh, I was frightened," he said softly.

"What happened then?" Carter said quietly.

Ken looked around at all three of us, then said, "She eventually squeezed down into the blackness. Took her the better part of an hour to do it. She wriggled and kicked 'til she scraped off her skin and she fit. I ain't seen so much blood before in my life. How she was still alive, I don't know. But I stood there and watched, paralyzed, as she grated herself against the stone 'til eventually, she slipped down inside and immediately she stopped screaming."

We were all quiet as he finished. Ken idly flicked more ash from his cigar and stared at the ground. The unbelievable events he had just shared with us chilled me. I remembered the feeling of being close to the well. I shivered.

"It's getting late," Ken eventually said, standing and tossing his cigar into the fire. "Why don't you kids get some sleep, huh? Going to be hot tomorrow, I think a lot of the guests are going to want to use the paddle boats."

We all stood up and wished him a good night, all of us somber and a little rattled. Except for Carter. His eyes buzzed with light. We retired to our cabin and began preparing for bed. Penny slept in her own room and after brushing her teeth and washing her face, she bid us goodnight.

Before she closed her door, I asked, "You OK, Pen? You're not freaked out?"

She gave me an uneasy smile. "I'm not sure if I believe everything he said, but it was a pretty creepy story nonetheless. I'll be OK; thanks, though." And with that she shut her door.

I went to the room Carter and I shared and stripped down to my boxers and laid down on my bed. Carter followed and turned the lights off. We were silent for a while and then I heard him sit up.

"Dude, let's go check it out."

I sat up, slightly alarmed. "What? No way, man, you heard Ken. We should stay away from it."

"Oh, come on," he pleaded, "it'll be spooky. You know how great it'll be to tell Penny in the morning that we went and looked down the well?"

I snorted, "Carter, you didn't see it. You weren't there. It creeped me out; no way I'm going back at night. Now just lay down and go to sleep. Please? Just drop it."

After a moment I heard him sigh and lay back down. Relieved, I closed my eyes and stared at the ceiling. Sleep did not come quickly.

I don't know what time it was when my eyes snapped open, but something was wrong. I jerked into a sitting position and let my tired eyes adjust.

Carter was gone.

"Shit, shit, shit, you idiot what the hell," I said, standing and grabbing my clothes. I didn't take Carter as an adventurous person, never mind a brave one. What was he thinking? If he was where I thought he was, then I needed to tell Ken immediately. I had been by the well, I knew the story held truth and I knew that there was something dangerous about it.

I thought about waking Penny but decided against it. I stomped into my boots and flung the door open. The night was calm, a fat white moon dripping its vanilla rays down to meet me. The camp was still and sleep coated the air. I marched down the stairs and turned toward Ken's cabin when something caught my eyes toward the tree line.

Carter was walking toward me. He spotted me and gave me a sly smile. "Well well, change your mind?"

The big fire in the middle of the camp from earlier was almost out, but there was just enough flame that I could make out his features as he approached me.

"What the hell are you doing?" I asked, my voice a harsh whisper.

"Sorry, man," he said, putting his hands in his pockets and shrugging, "I just had to see it for myself. Took me forever to find it."

I paused, cautious. "You…you saw the well?"

He nodded, the smile still on his face.

I licked my lips. "And?"

He slapped me on my shoulder. "Ken's full of crap I'm afraid. It's just a stupid well. There's nothing down there, man."

I released a breath I didn't know I had been holding in. "Wait…really? You actually went and looked down inside?"

He chuckled and rubbed his eyes. "Yep, no ghosts or monsters I'm afraid. Just Ken jerking us around. It was a good story, I'll give him that."

I shook my head. "Well, I guess I'm just a big baby then. Let's tell Penny in the morning; I think she was a little freaked out."

He laughed. "All right. I'm totally busting on Ken, too, for trying to freak us out. Come on, let's go to bed."

As we turned back toward our cabin, the dying fire splashed the last of its light on Carter's face and I noticed that his eyes were incredibly bloodshot. He rubbed them again and we went back inside and slept until morning.

The next day was blistering hot. As predicted, most of the guests wanted to take the paddle boats out onto the lake. Ken, back to his grandpa routine, helped the three of us make sure they were accommodated and happy. He asked if we would take shifts staying down by the water and keep an eye on things. Penny said she'd take the first shift and so Carter and I stayed behind and saw to the daily chores. We had ended up not telling her. We agreed that it was better if she didn't know because of her constant paranoia of getting in trouble. And if she was frightened by Ken's story, she didn't show it as she went about her morning.

Carter was cheerful despite the heat and helped me prepare the wood for the evening's fire. His eyes were still terribly bloodshot and when I asked him about it, he shrugged it off.

"Probably caught me a case of double pink eye. Just my luck. They itch like crazy. You think Ken has something for them? Eyedrops maybe?"

"He might. It looks bad, man," I said, dragging another log over to the chopping block.

He scrubbed at them. "Ah, let's finish this first, shall we?"

Today was cleaning day and after we finished the wood, Carter went to relieve Penny. He ended up not speaking to Ken about his eyes, despite my protests. He said maybe a swim would clear them up and I told him to not touch anyone if he was going to keep itching them.

About a half-hour after Carter left, Penny came strolling up the hill looking hot. She wiped sweat from her forehead. "You would never know that I was in the water ten minutes ago. It is stifling today, isn't it?"

I nodded. "Yeah, I'm looking forward to my shift at the lake. Did you see Carter?"

"Yeah, what's wrong with his eyes?"

"He thinks it's pink eye."

She shivered, "Gross. Poor guy." She scanned the campsite. "So what do we have left? We're cleaning the cabins today, right? Mid-week scrub for the guests?"

I stretched my arms over my head. "Yeah, sounds fun, doesn't it? Ken told me this morning we don't have to go overboard. The deep clean is on Sunday in between arrivals. Just neaten up, make sure the bathrooms are clean, get rid of trash, all that."

"All right, let's get to it then," she said and we both went to gather supplies for our afternoon of upkeep.

Time went quickly with the two of us chatting and cleaning, the work quickly muted to the sound of good conversation and laughs. She was a nice girl and I found myself incapable of growing slightly fond of her. We hadn't gotten much time to talk one-on-one, and I found her to be quite the pleasant person.

As the sun crawled across the sky like a dying man in the desert, we finished up the last of the houses. I blinked sweat out of my eyes and let out a long sigh as I saw Carter trudging up the hill. He saw us and waved, meeting us in the middle of camp. His eyes were still bloodshot, but they looked much better than they had that morning.

"Save any lives?" Penny asked with a smirk. "Any hot moms rescued?"

Carter threw his head back and laughed. "'Fraid not. Nope, just a bunch of whiny kids and drunk dads. You guys finish cleaning?"

"Yeah," I said. "All that's left is to rake the grounds. I'm going to go change and head down for a dip. I mean, to keep an eye on everyone." We all laughed and split ways, Carter and Penny going to retrieve the rakes and myself down to the lake.

The water was cold and wonderful. As the sun slowly dipped into a rainbow of colors, I spent the remainder of the day swimming and having casual conversation with the guests. I couldn't think of a more pleasant way to end the day.

The story that night was about Ken's vision for the camp-site. He told the guests about all the improvements he wanted to make and how he wanted to redo the cabins. He involved the visitors, asking for their feedback and accepting their comments graciously. Most of the people had nothing but good things to say, all of them thanking the four of us for being such wonderful hosts and how they couldn't wait to come back the next year and see the place.

After the conversation dulled to a murmur and the moon rose high, everyone thanked us again and began to turn in for the night. After everyone was inside, Ken informed us that he was tired and he was going to turn in as well. We all wished him a goodnight and we went back to our cabin.

Feeling exhausted myself from the heat and day's activities, I told Carter and Penny I was going to go to bed. They both agreed and we went to our rooms for the night.

"How's your eyes?" I asked Carter, already in my bed with my eyes closed.

He turned off the light next to my bed and crawled under his sheets. "Still itch like crazy, but I don't think they're as pink as they were this morning. Maybe tomorrow it'll be better."

I muttered my agreement and felt the day disappear into slumber.

I awoke with my heart racing. I was bathed in a thick sheen of sweat and my throat was dry. Something wasn't right. My breath rattled past my cracked lips into the dead air. I tried to sit up, but I crashed back down into my bed. Something was restraining me. What the hell?

I wiggled around and found that my wrists and ankles were

tied to the bedposts. Confused and terrified, I fought with them for a few vain seconds before finally giving up.

I raised my head to look over at Carter's bed. He wasn't in it.

"Carter?" I said aloud. "Carter, where are you?"

Silence. And then, "Shhhhh."

The noise came from his side of the room, but I didn't see him. Heart still pounding, I stretched, trying to flick the lamp on next to my bed. My fingertips brushed the switch and I pulled my hand back as the ropes binding me cut into my skin.

"Carter, what the hell is going on? Where are you?" I asked, my voice cracking in panic.

Silence. Then, again, "Shhhh."

I didn't know if he was playing some kind of joke on me and I didn't wanna start screaming and wake all the guests if that was the case, so I stretched my hand out again, fighting the pain that was burning into my wrists from the rope. Just…a little bit…there!

I turned the lamp on and yellow light pushed the shadows back. At first I didn't see Carter, but movement caught my eye.

He was lying under his bed, looking directly at me.

He was smiling and I saw that his eyes were nothing more than two bloody, pulpy, orbs, rubbed so raw that he had cut into them with his fingernails and torn them out.

"They won't stop itching," he said to me, still smiling. And then he was up. Like lightning, he scurried out from under the bed and was on top of me.

I struggled and was about to scream when he shoved a piece of cloth into my mouth, hard. I gagged as his fingers pushed the torn sheet deeper, his thighs holding my body still with an iron clasp.

"Just keep it down, buddy," he said, his breath dry and smelling of bile. His bloody mushed sockets stared down at me and I turned my face away, the gore making me light-headed.

He sat up on me. "Is it gross? It is, isn't it? Here, let me do something about that." He reached beside me and ripped apart the sheet I was sleeping under. He tied it around his eyes and the back of his head, the blood soaking through and appearing to give him two phantom red eyes.

"There," he said calmly. "That's better. I can see better like this anyway. I was hoping you wouldn't wake up, but I decided I needed to tie you up in case you decided to go looking for me again."

I whipped my head around and tried to buck him off me, terror and confusion slamming into me with every word he said. He held on and gripped my body tighter with his legs, pressing down on my chest with his hands.

"Stop that," he said firmly. "You're safe. I'm not going to hurt you. I just need you to stay here, OK?" He lightly slapped my cheek. "Stay."

He was about to get off me when he paused, smiled to himself, and leaned back toward me, whispering into my ear, "But there's something you should know. Do you want to know what it is? You do, don't you?"

I bit down on the cloth in my mouth and nodded.

He licked his lips. "I'm going to go cut Penny's fucking head off."

My eyes widened and I screamed into my gag, thrashing

wildly. He chuckled softly and held me still, waiting patiently until I wore myself out. Panting hard around the cloth, I looked up at him, his smile full of teeth, the glistening red outline of his mutilated eyes bleeding through the linen.

The well.

The thought crashed into my chaotic mind like a truck. It was the well.

He had...seen something down there. Somehow, it had changed him.

Suddenly Carter raised his fists and brought them smashing down into my face, knocking me into darkness.

I awoke again, face swelling and painful. My vision swam. The room was dark again. I was still gagged and I could feel my breath becoming labored as my nose clotted with blood. I was going to suffocate if I didn't get this rag out of my mouth. Slowly, in a daze, I worked my tongue and teeth over it until I finally could spit it out.

Gasping in deep, grateful breaths, I struggled against the ropes that held me. After a few frustrating moments, I finally loosened them enough to get a hand free. A few more minutes of tearing, and I was completely out of my bindings.

Penny.

Oh no, Penny.

I dashed to her room and kicked the door open. Empty.

I felt my heart bubble up into my throat and I stood there trembling. "Oh no, oh no, oh no, please please please." My eyes filled with tears and I crashed out of the cabin. Get Ken, get Ken, NOW.

The night was thick, the air clawing at my skin with humidity.

The moon stared down at me, uncaring and indifferent. The fire had gone out in the middle of the camp and as I about to charge Ken's cabin down at the end of the lot, I heard something.

Screaming.

It was Penny.

I stood, frozen and immobile. It was coming from woods.

I knew where she had been taken.

Biting my lip, my face screwed up in mental agony, I looked at Ken's cabin and then bolted toward the woods.

Toward the well.

She might have seconds to live. If she was still alive, I needed to get to her and stop Carter. *Please God, let her still be OK. Please, please God.*

I crashed down the path, bare feet scraping against stones and branches, my toes slamming into rock and wood. I didn't care, I didn't think about it. I flew as fast as my legs would take me, heart beating faster with every step.

There.

I reached the curve in the path and turned left into the woods. Crashing through the underbrush, I held my hands out in front of me, pushing aside the low-hanging branches and leaves that reached toward my face.

Panting, I broke into the clearing and froze.

Carter had Penny bent over the opening of the well. He was standing behind her with a fist gripping her hair, pulling her head back to expose her throat.

The muscles on his arms strained as he worked a knife into her pale flesh, slowly slicing into her, back and forth, back and forth, deeper and deeper. He paused and looked up, seeing me.

"Oh…hey."

"Penny!" I screamed. In the moonlight, her eyes slowly rolled over to meet mine.

Agony.

"Jesus fucking Christ, Penny, hang on!" I screamed, tears rolling down my face.

Carter ignored my outburst, taking the time to wipe sweat from his face and tightening the cloth around his eyes. "You know, this is a lot harder than you'd think."

"Carter, stop! It's Penny! You're killing her!" I screamed.

He stared at me silently, the blood-stained sheet around his eyes looking black. Finally, he motioned at me with his bloody knife, one hand still gripping Penny's hair. "Come stop me, then."

I swallowed and was about to charge him when I realized…I couldn't. My knees had turned to water and all the strength in my body had drained. The forest seemed to press in on me. My breath came out in little gasps and I was terrified. I felt my bladder release and warmth spread down my legs.

The well.

The fucking well.

I couldn't even look at it. I was filled with such nightmares that I wanted nothing more than to turn and run. Get out of here, get out of these mountains, and get as far away from that fucking well as I could.

Carter was smiling. "You can't, can you? You're terrified." He tapped the top of the well with his knife. "Come on. Come over here. Look down there," his smile grew. "Look down in the well."

"Please," I mumbled, vision blurring with tears and snot bubbling out of my nose. "Please stop this."

Carter shook his head slowly. "No. In fact, I think it's time to finish this."

He raised his knife again and brought it back to Penny's throat. She was slumped over now, but just as he was about to resume cutting, her eyes met mine and she muttered a single word.

"Run."

Hearing her speak, I ripped myself from my terror. Face streaking with tears and mucus, I charged Carter.

Every step toward him, my body seemed to increase in weight, pulling me to the earth. I grit my teeth and steeled my adrenaline, crashing into Carter just as he was turning toward me, mouth agape in surprise.

He slammed into the side of the well hard, knocking the knife out of his hands. We both went down and I hit my head against the stone, stunning me. The world spun and I heard him growling, already beginning to stand.

"You don't know what you're doing, you fucking idiot," he snarled, grabbing me by the hair and slamming my face into the ground. I bit my tongue and howled in pain, feeling blood fill my mouth.

Dizzy, I rolled onto my back and stared up at him.

He stepped on my chest and leaned down, his voice raw. "You can't stop this."

He quickly jumped back and grabbed Penny, pulling her up and across his shoulders. He hoisted them both up onto the lip of the well and silently, they tumbled down into the darkness. They were gone.

"NO!" I screamed, my voice splintering. I scrambled up, sobbing, pleading, and gripped the sides of the well.

I looked down into the blackness. *I looked down into the well.* My eyes went wide and the world stopped.

"Oh no," I whispered.

18

When Hell Comes Knocking

I moved to a new town about a year ago. I was offered a job and was at a point in my life where I felt restless and eager. A new job in a new town was exactly what I had been waiting for. In two weeks' time, after saying goodbye to my friends and family, I packed up and made the four-hour drive to my new apartment.

Turns out, it's tough to make new friends once you're out of college. I settled into the job just fine, my coworkers and daily routine both to my liking. Meeting new people was difficult, though. I didn't go to church, I didn't really go out much, and I wasn't part of any club.

After a couple weeks of maddening isolation, I forced myself to go to a bar, determined not to leave until I met a few locals. I'm glad I went because that's where I met Lydia. I happened to sit down next to her and, after ordering my drink, she turned to me and smiled, commenting on my shirt.

That sparked our conversation and eventually, after a few drinks, I summoned the courage to ask her out to dinner. She said yes and my life was suddenly exciting again. I couldn't stop thinking about her, couldn't spend enough time with her. She was amazing and our date turned into two, then three, until finally she came over to my place for the night. In the morning, there was no question of how we felt about each other.

As the weeks turned into months, our relationship only got better. We never fought, we never argued. Hell, we hardly ever frowned at one other. I knew that we hadn't been dating that long, but even so, everything was so perfect that I was convinced we would stay like this forever.

One thing that did strike me as odd, though, was that she never wanted to spend the night at her place. We always ended up at my apartment, which was fine, but it struck me as kind of strange. I had seen her place only once and it seemed perfectly fine. Her apartment consisted of an entire top floor of a three-story house, fairly old, but well kept.

I asked her about this once or twice, suggesting we end the evening in her bed, but she always wriggled out of it. I didn't press her too much; her excuses were always mildly valid.

Well…all that has changed.

You see, we did end up at her place for the night.

And Christ, I wish I had listened to her.

We were fairly drunk, the energy in the bar slowly winding to a dull murmur. I heard the bartender make last call and I groggily looked at Lydia on the barstool next to me. She gave me a tired, tipsy grin and I asked her if she was ready to go.

She said yes and as we made our way outside, I realized that I was in no condition to drive. My car was parked behind the bar and as we clung to each other for warmth, I voiced my concerns. She told me she was too drunk to drive as well and suggested we call an Uber.

As I thought this over, I realized where we were in correlation to her apartment. I told Lydia that we were only a couple blocks from her apartment, so why couldn't we just crash there? She seemed to be waiting for this, knowing full well how close we were. I had only been there once so my slogged mind had taken some time for that fact to catch up with my brain.

After a long pause, she agreed warily.

It wasn't a long walk; the streets around us were empty except for a few late-night stragglers. She lived pretty close to the center of town and as we walked the brick sidewalk, I asked her how long she had lived at her place. She said three years, but she was looking to move. She wanted to get a place a little quieter, a little more out in the country. I expected her to casually bring up moving in together, but she never did.

After a few blocks, we arrived at her place. It was a large three-story house with each floor rented out individually. She keyed her way into the front door and I followed her up the flight of creaky stairs. At the very top was her door, and after glancing at me, she unlocked it and we went in.

This was only the second time I had been inside and as I looked around, I wondered why. She kept it very clean and organized. The furnishings were elegant and crisp, modern in style, which contrasted with the older building.

I commented on how nice it was and that we should spend more time here. She shrugged off my comment with a "maybe" and we began to settle in for the night.

It was already late, so we cleaned up in the bathroom and retired to her bedroom. As we stripped and climbed into her queen-sized bed, I noticed that she left the door open a crack. I thought that a little funny, seeing as how deliberate the action had been. I said nothing though and gratefully pulled the soft sheets over me.

Lydia curled up next to me, casting a glance at her door, and then settled her head on my chest. I pulled her tight against me and let out a long, happy sigh. I kissed her on the head and I could feel her body relaxing against mine. It didn't take long before the two of us were fast asleep.

It didn't last long.

I jolted awake as someone pounded on the front door of her apartment. I blinked and opened my eyes in the darkness. What time was it? Who the hell was that? I reached over to the nightstand and checked my phone. It was 3:30 AM, way too late for someone to be stopping by unannounced.

I went to sit up, but Lydia clutched my body, her hands trembling against my shoulders. I looked down at her, confused as to why she wasn't letting me up. I asked her who was at the door. She didn't answer and just held me.

Another trio of knocks, louder this time.

I went to sit up again, asking her what was going on, but she looked up at me with fear in her eyes.

"Don't get up," she begged.

I was thoroughly confused now, her reaction puzzling me. Who was at the door? Was she keeping something from me? Was she hiding something? I wondered if this was some ex-boyfriend, drunk and trying his luck. Just the thought of that made me want to get up and go see who it was, size this piece of shit up. Who the hell did he think he was? Lydia was mine and I wanted everyone to know that.

I tried to pry Lydia off me, expressing my thoughts, but

she shook her head, telling me it wasn't an ex. I wasn't sure I believed her, but I could tell that she was terrified regardless. She put her hands over her ears as another pounding on the front door echoed into her apartment.

I took her face in my hands, forcing her to look at me. I told her I needed to go see who it was. Maybe someone was in trouble, maybe something had happened. In truth, I just wanted to make sure it wasn't some asshole ex of hers.

Tears began forming in her eyes and she looked directly at me, bottom lip quivering. "Please…do *not* open that door."

Another loud knock, as furious as the others.

As I lie there, I noticed there was no yelling from the other side of the door. Typically, this late at night, you would think the visitor would announce themselves. It was eerie and the way Lydia was reacting to this encounter, I didn't feel good about the whole thing. It was as if whomever was knocking had malicious intent.

Mercifully, it stopped. I waited, unaware that I was holding my breath, waiting for the pounding to continue. But it didn't. Exhaling loudly, Lydia softened against me. I could tell that whatever had just happened had been a semi-traumatic experience for her.

I tried to question her, but she begged me to just let her sleep. Stuttering, I forced myself to eat the questions crawling up my throat. Instead, I put a comforting arm around her. Soon I heard her breathing steadily into the deep rhythm of sleep.

I stared at the ceiling and wondered what the hell had just transpired.

The next day was Saturday, so neither of us had to work. We woke up late and Lydia got up before me, going to the kitchen. As I enjoyed the warm bed, I began to smell coffee brewing. I smiled and forced myself up.

It was a pleasant morning, both of us lounging on her couch, idly chatting about what we wanted to do that day. I didn't bring up last night's incident, waiting to see if she would. It was obvious she was avoiding the subject, refusing to even acknowledge it.

She seemed to be in a good mood, though, so I decided to keep my mouth shut. When she wanted to talk about it, she would. Until then, I just needed to be a good boyfriend and not press her on it. Though I would be lying if I didn't say every part of me was bursting with irritated curiosity. I just wanted to make sure it wasn't some lover from the past, returned for some late-night action.

As we finished our coffee, it began to rain outside and I suggested we spend the day here, catching up on our TV shows and maybe cooking dinner together tonight. She seemed excited and agreed immediately (much to my surprise).

I went and put on another pot of coffee as she cued up our show on Netflix that we were watching together. Glancing out at the gloomy day, I smiled and snuggled up next to Lydia, ready for our lazy day together.

The hours slowly went by, both of us in full binge-watch mode. As episode after episode played, the day peaked into a cloudy climax and the dark gray outside began to fade into night. Both of us hadn't moved much, perfectly content on the couch, listening to the rain and television.

After one of the episodes ended, she suggested we start

making dinner. I agreed, feeling my stomach rumble, and asked her what she wanted to make. After some discussion we decided to try our hand at homemade Chinese food.

I turned on some music on my phone as she went to the kitchen and began pulling out ingredients. She tossed me an apron with a wink and I laughed as I tied it around my waist. I went to her and took her in my arms, dancing her around the kitchen, lip-syncing the song that was playing. She giggled and told me I was ridiculous but then kissed me, slowing my dance.

We pulled away from each other and she began assembling the food. I wasn't much help, but I kept her entertained as she worked her culinary magic. We laughed and cycled through songs, our conversation light and flirtatious.

After a lot of work, the food was finally done. We took our place on the couch again, piling the delicious-smelling feast in front of us on the coffee table. I cued up another episode and she shot me a smile, telling me today had been amazing. I agreed and kissed her.

Then we dug in with a vengeance. Lydia had outdone herself. I gobbled down a couple of batter-fried pieces of chicken and told her we should do this again tomorrow.

She agreed but said that she'd like to sleep at my place tonight. I cocked an eyebrow at her, swallowing my food, and asked why we wouldn't stay here tonight.

She looked at me over her bowl of lo mein and said we had been here all day, so why not mix things up?

I put my food down and threw an arm over the back of the couch, expressing to her how great it was here today, that we should just put a bow on it and stay here for the night. I was still in my undershirt and boxers, for chrissakes!

She looked at me a little unsteadily, wanting to argue with me but knowing she didn't have a good reason. At least, that's what I thought. I could see her struggling to come up with something, anything, to get us out of here tonight. Eventually, she just sighed and nodded silently.

I smiled and rubbed her shoulder, telling her it was going to be great. As I turned back to my food, I wondered if her reservations about staying here had anything to do with the person at the door last night. But what did she have to be afraid of? I was here and I sure as hell wasn't going to let anything happen to her.

We finished our food and stretched out on the couch, pushing deeper into our show. Lydia laid down on top of me and after a couple hours in that position, I felt myself begin to drift off. I could feel Lydia doing the same, both of us surrendering to the food and steady rain.

Together, they gently lulled us to sleep.

I was startled awake as someone pounded on the front door. Lydia sprang up on top of me, her knee thudding into my ribs. I let out an "Oomf!" as my side spiked in pain, but she slammed her open palm down over my mouth, silencing me. Her eyes were wide and terrified, all traces of sleep gone from her face.

I looked up at her, waiting for her to say something. Instead, she cowered down into me as another series of loud knocks came from her door.

This is insane, I thought. *Someone is clearly terrorizing my girlfriend and she's been too embarrassed or ashamed to tell me about it.*

I forced both of us into a sitting position, despite her frantic efforts to keep me in place. I whispered to her that I was going to answer the door and put a stop to this. I told her someone was stalking her and that after I confronted the person I was going to call the police and put an end to it.

She shook her head wildly, tears budding in her eyes. She told me that it wouldn't do any good, the police couldn't help. She tried to pull me back down on the couch, but I shook her off.

Another round of pounding on the door.

I told her I was going to answer it unless she told me what was going on. She bit her lip, huddled on the couch, horror stretching her face. She said I couldn't answer the door and begged me in hushed whispers to just wait until they went away.

"Who is it?! You have to tell me!" I said in a soft growl, leaning close to her.

She looked up into my eyes, tears staining her cheeks and whispered, "It's the Devil."

The way she said it sent a chill down my spine. What? What did she mean by that?

Three long knocks shook the frame of the door. I looked at my phone and saw it was a little after three in the morning.

For a moment I was completely frozen with indecision. I wanted to protect my girlfriend and confront this head-on, but the way she was looking at me, begging me to just leave it alone, tore my mind in the other direction.

Finally I made an impulse move, taking three long strides to the door as more pounding erupted from the other side.

Seeing me and realizing what I was doing, Lydia leaped from the couch screaming not to open the door, her eyes bulging from their sockets.

As my hand found the doorknob, Lydia sprang toward me, still screaming, and grabbed my arm, jerking me back from the door.

It was too late. I had turned the handle and the door popped open a crack, letting in an empty darkness.

But there was something in that darkness.

Lydia shrieked and tightened her grip on me, dragging me backward into the bedroom, her face swelling with absolute terror. She shoved me into the bedroom, screaming at me, her voice cracking.

Just before she slammed the door shut, I saw something walk into the apartment, dragging shadows behind it.

Lydia locked the bedroom door and leaned against it, sweating and breathing heavily. She looked at me and I saw fear in her eyes I didn't know existed. She met my gaze and slowly shook her head, unable to believe what I had done, panic dripping from every pore.

I didn't know what to say, stunned by her reaction and terror. I stood by the bed, slightly shaken and confused.

Something knocked hard on the bedroom door.

Lydia let out a little shriek and then quickly covered her mouth. She squeezed her eyes shut and I heard her praying quietly.

I didn't know what to do. I stood there stupidly, mouth agape. Someone was in the apartment. I had seen him come in. Reality was slowly sinking in, pushing aside the confusion and filling me with the icy cold of fear.

Someone had walked into her apartment and was now pounding on the bedroom door.

I swallowed hard, that icy fear tickling my stomach.

We could be in serious danger. I needed to call the police, but both of our cell phones were by the couch, discarded where we had fallen asleep. I had to do something. I needed to try to take control of this. I took a deep breath and stepped forward, taking Lydia by the shoulders and moving her away from the door. She fought me for a second until I assured her I wasn't going to open it.

Another sharp rasp on the door.

Heart racing, I pressed my ear against the wood. I didn't hear a sound between the knocks. Not even breathing.

Summoning my courage, I cleared my throat and asked who they were and what they wanted.

A pause.

I jerked back as another assault on the door rattled the hinges.

I stared at Lydia, looking for guidance, hoping she had an answer to this madness. Every second that passed I felt increasingly scared, the gravity of our position sinking deeper and deeper into my mind.

It's the Devil.

I shook my head, disregarding the thought. That was ridiculous, an impossibility I wasn't going to humor. And yet, I felt…something…on the other side of the door. I couldn't explain it, but it was this…feeling…this weight, like there was a black hole sucking me through the wood.

I suddenly heard movement from the other side and I pressed my ear against the door once again. I didn't hear anything and I wondered if maybe, just maybe, the person had left.

Quietly, I got down on my hands and knees and looked under the door.

A large yellow eye and black face was staring back at me from the other side.

As soon as I saw it, pain rocketed through my eye socket. I fell back, clawing at my face as my vision swam and stars exploded in my skull. Lydia screamed and dropped to her knees next to me, asking what was wrong.

After a few seconds, the pain receded and I blinked back tears. Lydia just held me, terrified, and I looked at her, rubbing my eye. Her lip was quivering and I could tell she believed what she had said. That whatever was on the other side of the door…she thought was the Devil.

I realized my own heart was racing and I took a few steady breaths. That eye…I shivered, not even wanting to think about it. I had never seen anything like it, the way it dilated when it saw me, the sick yellow color…what the fuck was in here with us?

Knock, knock, knock!

Lydia curled up into me, tears freely falling from her eyes. I was so confused and scared I just put an arm around her and stared at the bedroom door in the darkness. What was I supposed to do here? God help me, what was I supposed to DO?!

"He's come for me," Lydia wept, sobbing openly now. "I told

him I was his if he would just give me happiness. I was a little girl, my parents were so mean..." her big wet eyes looked up into mine, "I didn't know what I was doing! I'm so sorry!" She covered her face now, "God never answered my prayers and I was so sad...I just...I just wanted to be happy so I thought...oh what have I done!?" she cried, big hoarse sobs racking her slender body.

I took her face in my hands, forcing her to look up at me. Voice shaking, I asked what the hell she was talking about, a deep seed of terror rooting in my gut.

After another bone-shaking series of knocking, she told me that when she was a little girl, her parents abused her. She cried herself to sleep night after night, begging God to send an angel to save her. God didn't seem to be listening and so, finally, she turned to the other side. She promised the Devil he could have her if he would only bring her happiness.

Three days later, her parents died in a car accident and she moved in with her grandparents who loved her deeply.

In the blackness of the bedroom, trapped and afraid, I listened to her story and felt nausea churn my stomach like rotten butter. As the words poured out of her mouth, I couldn't shake the image of the eye, staring back at me from under the door.

BANG BANG BANG!

I jumped as the wood splintered and whatever was behind the door shifted again, a new sound entering the darkness. It sounded like something was dragging nails across the wall just outside the bedroom. Over and over again, the muted scraping sound pierced the pockets of silence.

I pulled Lydia up onto the bed and sat her at the foot of

it. I stood in front of her, sweat trickling down my spine, and asked her what she was *talking* about, asked her if it was true. She started to cry again, hands reaching out for me, but I grabbed them and pulled them to her sides. I asked her again, trying to block out the scraping sound against the wall.

She nodded and said that it was. She told me that for the past six months, if she was home, the knocking would start around three AM. At first, she thought it was an intruder and called the police. But when they didn't find any traces of anyone after four separate visits, they stopped taking her seriously. Eventually, about two weeks in, she said she remembered the deal she had made when she was a little girl. She remembered whom she had made it with.

"I didn't know it would be this soon," she croaked, looking up at me, her face stained with tears.

I shot a nervous glance at the door as the scraping sound was followed by more pounding. I forced myself to breathe. If what she was saying was true, why doesn't…it…just come in? What's stopping it from kicking the door in and snatching my girlfriend? I couldn't make sense of it and turned these questions on Lydia.

Still sobbing, she said she didn't know, either. She said that whenever the knocking started, she would just wait until it stopped. Sometimes it would be a few minutes; other times it would last until morning. She said that she felt that…it…was powerless unless she opened the door and let it in. Something about the doors, the separation of victim and prey, stopped it.

I didn't know if it was some supernatural reason or maybe spiritual, but either way, I was thankful for it.

But now we were trapped with no way out. We were on the

top floor, in the bedroom, with only one window looking out onto the street below. Our cell phones were out there with the thing and we had no way of communicating with anyone from in here.

Again, I didn't know what to do. My mouth was dry and hot, my breath sour on my tongue. Shooting another glance at the door, I went to the window and looked out. Despite being in town, the streets were empty and the sky dark. I tried to open the window but couldn't. My muscles strained as I put all my might into it, but it was no use.

Lydia saw what I was trying to do and came over to help, mumbling that it should open, it always opened. Even with the two of us, we couldn't get it to budge.

Frustrated, I slammed my fist into the pane as the bedroom door shook, accompanied by more scraping across the walls.

It was useless. We were trapped in here.

Lydia collapsed to the floor, backing herself against the wall, covering her ears against the barrage against the door. Exhausted and terrified, I slumped down next to her.

We would have to wait it out.

———————

It's still knocking. Lydia is crying in my lap. We haven't moved. It has to leave us alone; she said it always does eventually. The sun will be up soon. The clock says it's five AM. Almost there. Please let it stop.

***

Why hasn't the sun come up yet? Something is wrong with

my clock; it says it's 3 AM again. That can't be right. There's no one outside. There should be cars on the road, but I haven't seen a soul. God, it's knocking again.

***

I'm so tired. Screaming and pounding on the floor hasn't done any good. No one seems to hear us up here. I still haven't seen anyone outside. I tried breaking the window, but I can't even get it to crack. Something is going on. None of this is making sense. It's still dark outside. Where is the sun? I haven't heard anything from the door in a little while…I'm praying it's over.

***

I'm getting hungry. I don't know how long we've been in here. Lydia is asleep on the bed, cried herself to sleep. The knocking is back. Louder than ever. I can feel it just beyond the door. I'm so goddamn scared. I don't know what to do. Where is everyone? Why hasn't someone come to see what's going on?

***

I CAN'T TAKE THIS FUCKING KNOCKING ANY-MORE.

***

Lydia is crying. She said she's thirsty. I am, too. I feel like we've been in here for days. I feel like I haven't seen the sun in ages. I'm starting to wonder if anyone is going to come for us. Whatever is outside the door, I think it has bent reality around us. I think we might be stuck here. There has to be a way out, though.

***

I fell asleep. When I woke up, Lydia had her hand on the

doorknob. I yanked her away, screaming at her. I can't lose her. We are going to get out of this. When I pulled Lydia away…the thing behind the door…the demon or the Devil or whatever it is…screamed at me. I have never heard such terrifying fury in all my life. God…please help us, please…

***

Lydia is getting sick.

***

We're never getting out of this room unless I do something. We're both dehydrated and Lydia isn't going to make it much longer without some water. It's knocking, each blow crunching into my skull like a drill. Where is everyone?…the clock still says 3 AM.

***

If there is a God, he can't see us in here.

***

Fuck this. We're dying. I need to do something. Lydia has been lying on the bed for hours. I don't remember the last time I saw her move. Should check on her, but I'm so tired. The knocking is constant now. It hasn't stopped in hours. I think I'm going insane.

***

This is it. Lydia needs medical attention or she's going to die within the day. It's still dark out, the clock still says three AM. I feel like I'm going deaf, the constant thundering against the door a relentless assault on my senses.

I'm going to open the door. I have to, or we're going to die. Whatever awaits us on the other side of it can't be much worse than this. I have to try something. I can't just let her die. I can't.

I'm going to open the door.

I can hear it screaming again.

It sounds…excited.

God, if you're out there, I really could use some help.

Please…save us.

I'm going to open the door now.

19

The Worst Kind Of Monsters

I am a murderer. I've killed nine people and I liked it. I don't get any satisfaction from suffering, but I take pleasure in ending the life of another human being. I don't get off on it, but I enjoy it. I like standing over someone and being the reason they don't get to live anymore.

It started with animals, like most people who do what I do. When I was younger I killed insects, watching them pop as I pressed my thumb down over their little bodies. Then I wanted more. I started killing birds and squirrels. I eventually got bored of that and killed cats and dogs. I even killed a cow once. I slit its throat and watched it teeter over, its massive body collapsing in a pool of blood. It was then that I realized I needed to kill a person. I didn't know how, though; I was too afraid of being hunted down, caught, called a freak.

You see, I don't feel like psycho. In fact, I think I'm a pretty normal person. I derive pleasure from all the trinkets and magic that life holds, same as you. I'm not a malicious person. I just like to kill people sometimes.

My passion would not have blossomed into the killing of humans, though, if I had not met Daniel. I met Daniel in college, both of us bonding quickly over a mutual appreciation for the darker side of life. It started with movies, then books, then strange Internet sites. We cautiously skirted around the subject of murder for some time, both of us prodding the other with questions that approached the subject. We would talk long into the night, sitting in his car, drinking beer, smoking, and eventually he began to start making jokes about killing. Those jokes became more frequent and, with my encouraging reactions, he finally admitted to me that he wanted to kill people.

My enthusiasm sparked a fire in him. Now we spent our nights pouring our hearts out to each other, so grateful that another human being understood us. We excitedly discussed what it would be like, made up fake scenarios, and even role-played. It was so freeing.

Then we abducted our first victim. I'm not going to go into the details, but that night I discovered that Daniel was…well…incredibly sadistic. He loved torture. And when I say he loved it…I mean he loved it. He was brutal, unforgiving, and cruel.

I mentioned earlier that I don't get any satisfaction from suffering. This is true. But that doesn't mean I can't tolerate it. We had a deal between us that Daniel would torture the person we captured and I would get to kill them. It was a match made in hell.

It was sloppy and to this day I can't believe we weren't caught. But somehow we got away with it. After Daniel spent an hour with our unfortunate victim, some poor homeless guy, I stabbed him in the chest and killed him. The rush of what we had just done fueled a starving need in us. From that night on, we formed a bond that could not be broken.

What I'm about to tell you is horrific. The story of Daniel and myself, what we did and what has led me to write it all down with trembling hands, is monstrous. I need you to know that I am so sorry. I know what we did was wrong, and I knew it back then. I don't ask you for forgiveness because over the next few pages you will grow to hate me. Just please…know that I am so *goddamned* sorry.

———————

I took a sip of my coffee, enjoying the cool fall breeze on my face. It complimented the hot beverage my sister had bought me and I felt its heat slide down into my chest.

"Good, huh?" Kate said, sitting across from me. The wind blew her dark brown hair across her face and I realized what a pretty lady she had grown up to be. Being only a year older than me, she and I had always been close. After mom and dad died a couple years ago in a car accident, we clung to each other closer than ever.

"You were right," I said, smiling. "This is delicious."

"Glad you were finally able to come hang out for a while," Kate said, taking a cautious sip of her own drink.

I scanned the scattering of tables we were sitting at, outside of the coffee shop. "Yeah, pretty exciting stuff," I joked.

She kicked me under the table. "Shut up, it's good to see you."

I grinned. "You, too. How's the new place?"

"It's great. It's only a few miles from where you live so we better start hanging out more, Bub."

I laughed. "Yeah, right, miss social butterfly over here. You're going to be too busy throwing housewarming parties with all your professional work friends! You can't be seen with the likes of me! Your loser brother who works at the grocery store…oh, how they'll talk!"

Kate rolled her eyes. "Oh stop, you know I'm not like that. And neither are my friends. Don't worry, I'll make time for you between all my hot parties."

"I'll hold you to that."

We were silent for a little while, watching the people around us move about the downtown area. It really was a nice day. Everyone looked so happy. I found myself smiling, realizing how good it was to see Kate again. After college we didn't spend that much time together, both of us trying to find our places in life—she with her business degree and me with my hunger for murder. Those two passions didn't cross paths as much as one might think.

"How are you doing?" Kate asked, breaking the silence.

I shrugged. "I'm fine. You know me, it doesn't take much to put a smile on my face."

She reached out and squeezed my hand. "I'm glad to hear it. I worry about you sometimes."

I shrugged awkwardly. "Ah, I'm OK."

Suddenly my cell phone began to ring. I threw an apologetic look at Kate and pulled it out of my pocket.

"Yo."

"Hey man…I got one."

Daniel.

I glanced at Kate and cleared my throat. "Oh, yeah? Cool, man."

A pause. "Are you with someone?"

"Yeah dude, I'm hanging out with Kate right now," I said. Kate mouthed at me, *Is that Daniel?* I nodded.

"Ask her when she's going to go out with me," Daniel said, chuckling.

"Keep beating that dead horse," I said, shaking my head, "but it's never going to get up and walk."

Daniel's tone suddenly shifted. "OK man, back to what I was really calling you about. You free to get away?"

I felt the stirring inside my chest, the hot anticipation. "Yeah, man. I'm assuming you wanna go to Chester's first?" Chester's was a pub we sometimes went to before a kill, enjoying the buildup of excitement over a cold beer.

"Of course. See you there in an hour?"

"Sounds good."

I hung up the phone and sighed, looking across the table at Kate.

"Let me guess, that was my future husband, Daniel?" she asked.

"Don't make me throw up this expensive coffee," I pleaded.

"You guys meeting up?"

"Yeah."

She stretched and stood up, with me following her lead.

"Well, I got to go anyway," she said, grabbing her purse from the back of the chair. "It was really good to see you." We hugged and she pulled back and smiled at me.

"What?" I asked, cocking an eyebrow.

She pinched my cheek, just like she had her whole life. "You need a haircut."

"OK byyyye," I said, turning to leave and throwing a wave back over my shoulder.

"Talk to you soon!" she called back after me.

I took a sip of my beer, watching the sun set through the pub's dirty windows. Daniel sat on the barstool next to me, spinning his phone on the bar top.

"It's a college kid," he whispered, his dark eyes lighting up. "Nabbed him this morning. No one saw me, no one followed me to the warehouse. I made sure."

I smiled. "Good work. You're really getting good at this."

He slapped me on the back, grinning from ear to ear. "Thanks, pal. I couldn't be more excited. I have plans for this one, let me tell you."

I sighed, "Just don't make me wait too long, OK? Last time I almost fell asleep before you'd let me finish him off."

Daniel chuckled into his beer. "Well, maybe if you'd join in the fun you wouldn't have to wait your turn."

I shook my head. "You know that's not my thing. No matter how much you wish it was."

He nodded, his dark hair bobbing against his shoulders. "I know, I know. But it's about the journey, not the destination, my friend."

I scanned the empty bar, looking down the counter to the bartender at the far end. "Well, my journey is the three seconds it takes them to die as I slip a knife between their ribs."

Daniel snorted and threw back half his beer in one gulp. He was anxious to get to it.

"Is it a guy?" I asked quietly.

Daniel nodded. I smiled. Good. I liked killing males better. Girls were just so…pretty. I had killed a girl, my third murder, and found myself not enjoying the experience. It was like the difference between killing a cow and killing a sweet baby puppy. One of them was kinda cute and made pathetic noises, while the other just mooed and died.

"What's his name?" I asked quietly.

Daniel glanced at me. "Edward. Rich boy name, isn't it? I'm sure his parents will be sobbing for weeks when the police can't find him. I've followed him for a while. He's a real prick. Fairly popular, good-looking, goes to one of those expensive private schools up north. I'm afraid this will be his last fall break. I almost feel bad for the bastard, the night I have planned for him."

"You're not going to go overboard again, are you?" I asked, draining my beer.

Daniel looked at me, slightly irritated. "What are you talking about? I do my thing, you do yours. That's the way we've always done it."

I shrugged. "Makes no difference to me. I've just noticed you're developing a real nasty streak when it comes to your victims."

"Gotta keep it interesting. Fresh. I like to hear the new sounds that come out of their throat as I work them over."

I winked at Daniel. "You sick bastard."

He threw an arm around my shoulder and slammed a twenty down on the bar. "Shall we go, my darling?"

I threw my own arm around his shoulder, mimicking two drunks. "Oi! Let's be off then, eh!?"

Laughing, we left the bar and got into our cars. After lighting a cigarette, I started my old beater and began the long drive out of town and into the mountains where the warehouse was. It was going to be a good night.

1. EDWARD

The moon hung full and fat in the sky, its cold white light illuminating the abandoned warehouse I was parked in front of. The trees pressed in around it, dark and clawing at its rusted walls. Dust swirled in my headlights, kicked up from the dirt road.

I flicked the butt of another cigarette out my open window and turned off the car. I got out and walked to Daniel, who was getting out of his own car. He shot me an excited look as he pulled on his leather jacket and gloves.

"What's that for?" I asked, pointing to a small plastic bag he was holding.

Daniel jostled the bag at me. "Poor guy hasn't eaten all day. Figured I'd bring him some grub."

I put a hand over my heart. "What an angel you are."

He snorted and jerked his head toward the quiet warehouse. "Shall we?"

We crunched over the gravel toward the rusted-out, windowless construction.

We had made every kill in this building. It was an old bastard, indifferent to the screams that echoed through its iron gut. It was also isolated, miles and miles of forest in every direction. No one heard the howls, the clawing, the begging.

Our kill room was in the dank underbelly of the old bastard, down in the basement. It offered plenty of room for experimentation, and the lower ceilings and cement walls helped mute the screams. Not that anyone would hear; it just gets annoying after a while.

We entered the warehouse, Daniel leading the way through the darkness, his giant flashlight cutting back the shadows. We kicked past the old metal piping that had fallen out of the wall, avoided the jutting steel teeth protruding from corners, and trotted down the wide stairs into the basement.

I heard muffled whimpering as a sea of darkness greeted us. Daniel shined his light toward the center of the room and walked toward it. Through the shadows, I watched as he primed the generator and fired up the overhead fluorescents, bathing the room in artificial light.

There was poor Edward. He sat bound to a metal chair in the center of the room, a burlap bag over his head. As soon as he heard us, he started to cry out, shaking back and forth. It sounded like Daniel had gagged him, the man's words coming out in muted cries.

Behind him was Daniel's workbench, littered with all kinds of tools and items he used on his victims. Also, there was a mini fridge, which I had contributed, stocked with beer and food. Sometimes I got hungry while I waited my turn.

Lining the wall in front of Edward was a battered couch, which I plopped myself down on, settling in for the night. Daniel went to the fridge and grabbed a beer, tossing it to me. I caught it and popped it open, guzzling the contents. It was a little warm, the cold from the fridge doing its best during the intervals between generator use.

This was my theater seat to Daniel's torture. I didn't much

care for what he did, but I was always curious to see the ways he would cause suffering. I kicked my feet out in front of me and snuggled down into the worn fabric.

"Hungry, buddy?" Daniel asked, dragging a metal chair away from the wall and placing it in front of the college student.

He sat down, facing Edward, and pulled the sack up to the man's nose, exposing his gagged mouth.

"Yuck, let me get that out of your throat," Daniel said, pulling the old rag out.

Gasping, Edward sucked in breath, immediately babbling, "Please, my dad has a lot of money, he'll pay you, he'll do anything, just let me go!"

Daniel turned toward me, grinning, and bounced his eyebrows before turning back and facing the quivering young man. "I'm sure he does, buddy. We can talk about that later. For now, let's get some food in you, yeah? You hungry?"

"T-thirsty," Edward sputtered.

Daniel fished in his bag and pulled out two cans of soda. "Let's see, we got Mountain Dew and we got Coke...I bet you're a Mountain Dew man, aren't you?"

Edward bobbed his head, "Yes, please, I'm so thirsty..."

Daniel cracked the top and gently tipped it to Edward's dry lips. "There you go my man, drink up."

I watched all this from my spot with Daniel's back to me. I always found it twisted when he went through this process. He got off on giving his victims the slightest bit of hope before exposing the monster he was. As we had gotten better and better at this, I had watched my friend wade deeper and deeper into the pools of sadism. It was getting to the point where I had to leave the room, usually toward the second half of his playtime. It didn't bother me; I just didn't need to see it.

"Thank you," Edward exclaimed as Daniel pulled the empty soda can away.

"Better?" Daniel asked.

Edward nodded, the sack slipping down his face. "Yes. Now please, call my father, he'll make you rich. Just…" his words started to bubble. "Please don't hurt me."

Daniel pulled the sack up to the bridge of his nose again and I saw Edward's trembling lips covered with leaking snot. Gross.

Daniel placed a reassuring hand on Edward's leg. "You think we're going to hurt you?"

"Please, please don't," he sputtered through tears.

Daniel tut-tutted and reached back into the plastic bag. "How about a candy bar? You hungry, champ?" Daniel began unwrapping a piece of chocolate and held it to Edward's mouth. "Here you go, get some of your energy back. Open up!"

Edward took a bite, the chocolate mixing with his snot as he chewed, wincing and still crying. "Just let me go, please, please, please," he sobbed, swallowing.

"One more bite, then I'll let you go," Daniel said, waving the chocolate under Edward's nose so he could smell it. Edward nodded pathetically and opened his mouth.

Daniel pulled a hammer out of the plastic bag and smashed it against Edward's teeth. Screams and blood erupted in a storm of pain as Edward's head flew back, chair rocking from the blow. I watched his two front teeth hit the ground in a splatter of blood. I took another swig from my beer and realized I was going to need another.

"Oops!" Daniel laughed. "That's not chocolate, is it?!"

Edward continued howling, his mouth hanging open in numb pain as drool and blood poured from his lips.

Daniel inspected the hammer's head as he waited for the screaming to subside. After a few minutes, Edward fell into a series of agonizing whimpers.

"Sorry, chap," Daniel said, humor in his voice, "sometimes I get a little confused, ya know? Here, let me clean you up a bit." He stood up and went to the workbench, picking up a red two-liter bottle. He came at Edward from behind, tilting his head back with one hand. He pulled the sack back down to cover his mouth and then held his head steady with a strong arm as he tilted the bottle.

"Don't want you getting an infection from that," he said, slowly dumping the bottle of rubbing alcohol over Edward's covered face.

Immediately, Edward shrieked, which only made it worse. The simulated drowning mixed with the stinging pain of the alcohol on his raw, bloody gums. Ouch. I lit a cig and drained the last of my beer, watching the whole thing.

Daniel looked up at me, his muscles bulging as he held his prey still. "Not very smart this one, huh? He should really keep his mouth closed, don't you think?"

I chuckled, blowing smoke. "He probably didn't take that class yet." Daniel threw his head back and laughed, all while continuing to slowly pour out the bottle over Edward's face.

Finally, the bottle was empty and Daniel shoved Edward's head forward. "All right, all done, that definitely killed any infection." He tossed the bottle off to the side and slapped Edward's head, "You doing OK?"

Edward gagged in his sack, crying and gasping. He dry-heaved once, then twice.

"I think he's going to puke," I said, pointing.

"Don't you dare!" Daniel yelled, grabbing the base of the sack and pulling it tight against Edward's face.

"Don't you dare!"

From where I sat, I could see the outline of the kid's face, the sack squeezing his features to form eyes and a mouth. I watched as he sucked the sack into his mouth, then violently vomited. Some of it leaked out the fabric, but most was forced back down his throat which made him vomit again, harder this time.

He couldn't get the puke out of his throat fast enough and I could hear him begin to drown in it. Daniel held the sack tight, a big smile on his face as Edward rocked back and forth, gurgling desperately.

"Swallow it! Swallow it, buddy!" he yelled, bucking with Edward as he fought for breath. "You're going to suffocate!"

"Hey, don't let him die!" I said, sitting up suddenly. "Let him breathe, for chrisssake!"

Reluctantly, Daniel released his grip and a torrent of yellow and brown sludge poured down the front of Edward's chest. He was weeping and gasping for breath, his body cramping from the evacuation.

"You better watch it so I get my turn," I said, irritated.

Daniel rolled his eyes. "He was fine." He went back to his workbench and picked up a pair of bolt cutters. He walked around Edward's shivering body, dragging the sharp metal pincers across his puke-stained chest.

He squatted down in front of him and whispered, "Let's stop screwing around, yeah?" And then he went to work.

I finished my cig, listening to the screams, my head rolled back on the couch. I wondered what my sister was doing. What would she think of this? I smiled inwardly. God, she'd hate me. I stood up eventually, casually watching Daniel fire up a blowtorch, and went to dig out another beer from the fridge. I went to the bottom of the stairs and drank deeply, sitting down and pulling out my phone. I scanned my social media and the sport scores. Ah, man. The Sabres lost. I idly flicked through my phone, ignoring the howls.

The night grew late and I eventually went back upstairs. Daniel had started hinting that he was going to cut off the kid's dick and I took that as my cue to leave for a bit. I wandered around the empty building and then went outside, cocking my head to look at the moon. It stared at me, a giant white glow of indifference. The screams echoing up from the basement told me the kid had probably just lost his manhood. I shook my head. Too far, man. Gross.

Next I heard Daniel's furious screams followed by thud after thud. I knew he had reached the part where bloodlust and rage had taken over his senses. He would get venomously angry at the victim and the true brutality began. I sighed and waited, passing the time by counting the stars.

Finally, I heard movement behind me and Daniel emerged from the shadows. He was panting hard, covered in sweat and blood. He pulled out his pack of smokes and lit one up, exhaling heavily.

"All yours," he said. He sounded tired.

"All done?" I asked, turning toward him.

He nodded around a mouthful of smoke, "Yeah. Fucking asshole has some fight in him. I wish I could put him back together so I could do it all over again." He growled, his eyes absorbing the moonlight. A black haze surrounded his persona, a wet blanket of blood and fury. He was gritting his teeth and staring into the woods, his face twisted in hatred.

He glanced at me and saw me watching him. "What?"

I shrugged. "I dunno man, you just seem to get so worked-up these past few times. This is supposed to be fun. I don't know why you get so angry."

He spat. "'Cause fuck them, that's why. I fucking hate all of them so much. I wish I could make them suffer even more. I wish I could make it last for days."

I began to feel uncomfortable. I had never heard him talk like this. Usually he was bursting with energy and joy after working over a victim. But tonight he just seemed tired and dangerous. I eyed him again, then patted his shoulder.

"All right, my turn. You good?"

He nodded silently, not looking at me.

I slowly walked back into the warehouse, letting the anticipation cradle me. It was my turn. This is what I had been waiting for. My footsteps echoed all the way down the stairs, my excitement building the closer I got to the bottom.

There was poor Edward. He was missing a leg, cut off at the knee, and I saw two of his own fingers had been brutally shoved up his nose. The top of the sack was burned away, revealing a shining charcoaled head, bald and cracked. Blood coated him, dripping down the chair and resting in puddles on the floor. He was slowly swaying back and forth, a low guttural sound escaping his mouth.

"Looks like Daniel really did a number on you," I said, making my way to the workbench. Edward said nothing, just continued to moan, barely conscious.

I picked up my knife from the pile of tools. I'd killed quite a few people with this blade. It was ten inches long with a polished wooden handle. The steel gleamed in the light and I grinned. I walked back to Edward and pulled the strip of fabric off his face. He looked up at me, blinking slowly.

I took a deep breath and closed my eyes. Yes. This was it.

"P...P-please," Edward croaked, the sound hardly recognizable.

I opened my eyes and plunged the knife deep into his chest. His eyes bugged open, a sharp gasp escaping his lips. He looked up at me and I stared back, feeling his blood drip over my hand.

I held his gaze in silence until he died.

"God I love that," I muttered to myself.

———————

It was a week later and I had just gotten home from work. I was tired but didn't want to stay in. Work was so boring that I usually felt the need to go out afterward. My small apartment was depressing and lonely. Plus it didn't really hold a conversation very well.

I changed into a pair of jeans and a long-sleeve shirt, hoping either Kate or Daniel were free tonight. I tried Kate first. She answered and after we chatted for a bit she told me she was meeting up with one of her girlfriends tonight. Disappointed, I told her it was fine, that I was just bored. She invited me to hang out with them, but I declined. I told her I had plans with Daniel anyway; I just wanted to see if she was free first. We said our goodbyes and hung up.

Daniel answered on the fourth ring. I asked him the same question and he told me to come over. He seemed out of it, like something was on his mind, but I paid no attention. I was just glad I was going somewhere.

It was a short drive to his apartment, just a couple miles down the street. I parked my car and he buzzed me in.

I collapsed on his couch, taking the beer he offered me and throwing half of it back in one long pull. I wiped my mouth and scanned his apartment. It was small like mine, and he lived alone. I had been here many times over the past couple years, but never had I seen it so filthy. Trash was everywhere, half-eaten food scattered every surface, and the air was thick with a sickly sweet smell.

"Forgot to call the maid?" I asked, dangling my foot over the arm of the couch.

He took a seat across from me in an overstuffed armchair. "What's the point? It only gets dirty again." He opened a beer for himself and drank deeply.

"This place reeks, man," I said, still taking in all the garbage.

He gestured to the window. "So crack a breeze if it bothers you. Geez, you come over here just to complain about my place?"

I pretended I was puking. "It's just…so…filthy…"

He picked up the TV remote from the arm of the chair and

hurled it at my face, "Hey, fuck you man!" he yelled, suddenly pissed.

I ducked under the remote and threw my hands up. "Whoa dude, chill out! What's toasting your titties? Bad day?"

He ran a hand through his hair, shaking his head. "I don't know…I've just been so pissed lately."

I spread my hands. "Again, I ask why? We just had a kill; that usually carries your mood for at least a couple weeks."

He stared out the windows. "It wasn't a good one."

"What do you mean?"

"It just wasn't. He didn't scream the way I wanted him to. He bucked back and forth too much. He had a stupid face. I don't know, man; it just wasn't good!"

I traced a finger around the lip of my beer. "What would you do different?" This was strange, I had never seen Daniel pout like this about a killing. His mood seemed distracted, irritated, like something was buzzing in his ear but he couldn't figure out what or why.

Daniel gritted his teeth, one hand gripping the arm of the chair, "I'd do it slower. I'd make them think about every cut. I'd make them beg, plead with me right before I hurt them. And then I'd destroy them slowly. I'd dig into their minds and find out what they feared most…and then I'd do that, over and over again until they couldn't scream anymore." His voice had turned to a growl and a hardness lined his eyes.

I sat in silence, waiting for him to continue, but he didn't. He just stared out the window looking angry.

After a few moments, I pressed him. "Is this fun for you anymore?"

He looked up at me. "Of course it is." He paused, looking down. "But there's more to it than that."

I sat upright. "Look, man, the whole point of this is to have fun. We both like what we do. But I gotta tell you, the past couple kills, I've seen you get furious halfway through. You didn't used to do that. I remember when we'd stay up until sunrise, burning the bodies out back and burying the bones, recounting all the things we did to them. We'd laugh and drink, toasting each other to another success. But lately, man..." I paused. He was looking at me again. "Lately man, there doesn't seem to be any joy in what you're doing. To me, you just seem miserable by the end. Screaming and pounding on them like they did something to you. And then when we're done, you just drag the body away and burn them while I dig a hole. I miss the fun we had doing this. I miss the excitement we shared afterward." I stopped talking and saw that he was nodding.

"I know, man," he said. "I know you miss it. We're different, though. Our tastes are different. I wouldn't ever expect you to understand. It's just," he trailed off waving a hand in the air, "it's just I can't help but get mad at them. I don't know why...I just see their stupid screaming bodies thrashing around and...goddamn, it just pisses me off. The more I hurt them, the more they scream, the angrier it makes me. I can't explain it. I know it probably doesn't make sense to you, but I just feel this furnace in my chest, this fire in my gut. It makes me want to rip them apart. They just look so pathetic. So helpless. I control everything they feel, how much they feel, when they feel it. And that makes me want to...fuck, it makes me want to take them to the limits of agony."

I didn't know what to say. I knew he enjoyed torture, that it was his thing, but what he was describing was something else.

"Are...you starting to get bored of this?" I asked cautiously. "Is it not enough anymore?"

He shrugged, "I don't know. I'm not bored of it, that's for sure. But...I don't know. Fuck." He shifted in his chair, "I feel like there are ways to hurt them that they're not telling me."

"The people we kill?"

"Yeah. I feel like each person has a method of torture that when used on them, it causes so much fear and pain that they lose their mind and become insane. I want to find that. I want to be able to pluck that from a person, flash it in their face, and then do it to them."

I took a sip of my now-warm beer. "And you haven't been able to do that? That's why you get so pissed?"

He looked at me and nodded. "Yeah, basically."

"Shit, man...I don't know what to say."

"Of course you don't; all you like to do it prick 'em with that knife," he laughed suddenly. "One of these days I'll get you to join me in the fun."

I waved him away. "Keep trying, keep trying. You know I don't care for that."

"Oh, I know. Don't think I don't see you leaving when the going gets good. Can't handle it? Does it bother you? Getting squeamish?" he teased.

I rolled my eyes. "No. I just don't really care to watch some of the shit you do. Especially when you start getting mad. Does it offend you when I leave?"

He chuckled. "Not really. Most the time I'm so into it I don't realize you're gone until later. Still, I think you're growing a soft spot."

I grabbed my crotch. "This is the only soft spot I have for you, you bastard."

We both laughed and he went to grab us more beer. As he passed me one and sat back down, he licked his lips and spoke, suddenly serious.

"Look, dude. I want to get another one."

I coughed up a mouthful of beer. "Jesus, already?!" I sputtered. "It's only been a week, man; why don't we let things settle a bit? Have you seen the news? That kid's dad was a big deal! Everyone and their mother is looking for dear ol' Edward right now!"

He waved a hand dismissively. "They'll never find him. They never find any of them. Look," he said, scooting forward in his chair, "I already scouted out someone. I'll grab them tomorrow, bring them to the warehouse, and no one will know. You can meet me there after work."

"It's too soon," I said, shaking my head. "No fucking way."?

Daniel formed two fists, his voice dropping. "Come on, dude, it'll be fine."

"We need things to cool down!" I argued, throwing my hands up.

Daniel stood up suddenly, his whole body trembling. "I need this. You don't understand. I fucking need this right now, OK? I'll be at the warehouse with a new friend. Can I count on you to be there?"

I sighed, looking at my friend towering above me. "All right, man…all right. Just settle down."

A dark smile split his face. "Wonderful."

"What's this poor sap's name?" I asked.

"Andrew."

I raised my beer. "Enjoy your last night, Andrew, wherever you are."

2. ANDREW

I turned my car off, the night air cool as I stepped out into the chirping darkness. A breeze shook the trees and their branches reached out and stroked the warehouse. Daniel's car was already here. I checked my phone as I walked inside and saw it was almost midnight. I fished out a small flashlight from my pocket and clicked it on.

I made my way through the empty iron graveyard, listening to the wind howl through the building. It created noises that made me look over my shoulder. I saw light coming from the bottom of the stairs and I made my way down.

Daniel was sitting on the couch, playing with his phone. His face lit up when he saw me.

"There you are! I was starting to worry!" He hopped up and waved his hand to the middle of the room. "May I present our guest for the evening...Andrew."

A bag was over the man's head, but I could tell from his body type and grunts that Andrew was probably in his forties, slightly overweight, and poor. He wore a cheap button-up shirt and dirty khakis, with worn loafers on his feet. Hearing Daniel speak, he began to struggle against the ropes that held him to the chair.

"You gag this one, too?" I asked, crossing my arms and assessing the soon-to-be corpse.

"Yeah, he's got a set of lungs on him. Figured I'd shut him up until you got here."

I walked over to the man and pulled the bag off his head. Andrew was balding and his bright blue eyes blazed up at me with sharp terror. He was confused, scared, and desperate to get away. I patted him on the head.

"Settle down, big boy."

I went and took my familiar seat on the couch, watching Daniel. He was over at his workbench scrounging through his tools. He eventually settled on the baseball bat resting against the side. He tucked it under his armpit and took a stance behind Andrew, resting his hands on the man's shoulders.

"You're trembling," he noted. He reached around and pulled out the gag. Andrew coughed and ran his tongue over his cracked lips.

"You don't have to do this," he said, his voice higher than I expected. "Whatever it is you think you need to do, you don't. We can talk this out. Whatever you want, I'll get it for you."

Daniel rubbed the man's shoulders, working out the knots. "Oh, calm down. You don't even know why you're here, do you?"

Andrew shook his head, staring at me, shrugging away from Daniel's hands.

Daniel gave him one last squeeze, then went and stood in front of him. He put his hands in his pockets, the baseball bat poking out from his armpit.

"You're scared, aren't you?" He asked. Andrew nodded, his eyes widening at the sight of the Louisville Slugger.

Daniel looked down at it, then back at Andrew. "Does this scare you?"

Another nod.

"Do you think I'm going to beat you with it? Is that why it scares you?"

Andrew said nothing.

Daniel took the bat in his hands and pressed the end of it into Andrew's chest. "I asked you a fucking question."

Andrew licked his lips. "Yes. Please...what's this about? Why are you doing this? I have a son, a little boy, he's going to wonder where I am."

Daniel squatted down, never breaking eye contact. "You love him? Your son?"

"Yes, of course, he's everything to me. I need to get back to him, he's going to be scared without me, he needs his father!" Andrew cried, his voice shaking. I couldn't blame him. I'd be shitting my pants if I were in his place.

"I could go get him," Daniel said casually. "Bring him here. Would you like that?"

Andrew's eyes went wide. "No! No, leave him alone!"

Daniel looked down, nodding. "Have it your way. I need to ask you something. If I think you're lying, I'm going to hit you as hard as I can with this bat," he said, tapping it. "But if I think you're telling the truth, I'm going to let you go. How's that sound?"

Andrew was visibly sweating now, his breath shallow and fast. "Whatever you want."

Daniel stood up, looming over his prey. "What scares you the most?"

The man was quivering and I saw a wet patch spread across his groin.

"He pissed himself," I remarked, crossing my legs in front of me.

Daniel glanced at it and groaned. "Already? Jesus Christ." He flexed the fingers, gripping the bat. "Why are you pissing yourself? I just asked you a question. I haven't done anything to you. Now take a deep breath and tell me…what scares you the most?"

"I-I don't know!" Andrew cried, his voice cracking. He paused and saw the fire in Daniel's eyes. He swallowed hard and mumbled, tears spilling onto his chest. "My son. Losing my son."

Daniel froze and from behind, it looked like he had turned to stone. The light cast long shadows of his figure that ran across the man tied to the chair. He said nothing. Then, ever so slowly, I saw his hands begin to shake with fury.

"Well, your son isn't here, so what else scares you?" Daniel spat.

"That's it!" Andrew cried, tears beginning to run down his face. "That's what scares me the most! I'm telling the truth, you have to believe me!"

"That's not the truth I wanted to hear! I can't do anything with that!" Daniel yelled, his whole body tensing.

"I did what you asked, now let me go! I beg you!" Andrew sobbed, shrinking away from the pillar of rage that stood before him.

"Not a fucking chance," Daniel growled.

He gripped the bat with both hands and swung it with incredible power. It struck the man on the shoulder, producing a meaty *thunk!* Andrew howled, almost falling over from the force, his head cocked back in pain. Daniel moved to the other side and batted another home run to the opposite shoulder.

"What a fucking waste you are," Daniel snarled, spinning the bat in his hands. "There's got to be something else, anything!" He let another one rip, blasting the man in the shin so hard I heard bone crack.

"What do you love more than your son!?" Daniel screamed. "It's yourself, isn't it?! Your image, your status, your body! Right?!" He cracked the man's other shin, bringing fresh screams. "In the end, we all only care about ourselves! That's just the way people work! That's how we survive!"

Through tears, Andrew looked up at Daniel. "You don't get it..." Deep breath, labored breath. "Once you have a child, you'd give your life for them..." Another breath, raw and ragged. "Your own life is meaningless! I answered your question, I swear, I answered it honestly, now please stop!"

Oh you stupid bastard, I thought. *That is not what he wanted to hear.* I knew Daniel was trying to prod some fear of the flesh from this man, prying him for something he could bring physical pain upon. This man cared more about his son than anything else. And we weren't about to go and kill a kid. That left Daniel frustrated and murderously angry.

"You want me to stop?" Daniel whispered, grabbing the man's sweating face. "You want me to stop? I'll stop when I break this bat over your body."

I lit a cig, watching as Daniel went at him. He didn't hit his torso or head, knowing that could potentially end Andrew's life, but instead worked over his legs and arms. I lost count of how many times he hit him. The screams seemed endless, my ears ringing by the time the bat eventually broke.

Daniel was leaning against the wall, sweating and breathing hard. Andrew was sobbing, rocking back and forth, his broken bones throbbing. He looked like he was going to pass out, so I stood up and slapped him around a bit. When his eyes focused, I nodded and gave him a thumbs-up. If he passed out I was going to have to wait longer for my turn. And with Daniel's current mood, I wanted to get to it as quickly as possible.

"Cut his pants off," Daniel said from behind me.

I turned, "What? No, you do it. This is your show, man."

"Just fucking do it, please?" he said, wiping sweat from his forehead. "Give me a second to catch my breath?"

Groaning, I went and got my knife. I grabbed the man's legs and straightened them, causing Andrew to howl as his broken bones shifted. I ignored him, slicing through the fabric at mid-thigh. It took less than a minute. I stood up and inspected my work.

"Thanks," Daniel said, going to the workbench and putting the bat down. He picked up a crowbar and a hatchet, weighed them in his hands, then took both. He pulled up a chair and sat down across from Andrew, placing the two tools down on each of his thighs.

He snapped his fingers in front of Andrew's face and then pointed at the crowbar and hatchet. "Do you want me to break both your kneecaps or cut off a foot?"

Andrew collapsed his head onto his chest, weeping, big wet tears rolling down his face. "Please...let me go...please!"

Daniel slapped him across the face, leaving a red mark. "I

asked you what you preferred. If you don't answer me in five seconds, I'm going to do both."

Andrew was rattling out big wet hoarse sobs, snot pouring from his nose. "The foot…just do the foot…please…just let me go home…" he trailed off.

Daniel stood and threw the hatchet off his lap. He gripped the crowbar with both hands and brought it down with all his might across Andrew's kneecap.

I winced, turning away as Andrew's knee shattered, his leg kicking out in a spasm of excruciating agony. It was the loudest I heard him scream that night. After a few seconds, his howls faded and he blacked out.

"Goddamn it," Daniel growled. He grabbed Andrew by the hair and shook his head violently. "Hey, wake the fuck up!" No response. "You piece of shit, you goddamn fucking worthless fuck," Daniel yelled, storming around to the fridge and pulling a beer out. He smashed the glass neck over the side of the workbench and dumped the brew over Andrew's face. Andrew stirred and slowly opened his eyes.

"Don't you pass out on me again! If you do, I swear to God I'll find your son, drag his ass here, and rape him in front of you. Do you FUCKING UNDERSTAND ME?!" Daniel screamed, his whole body shaking.

I sat up on the couch. This wasn't good…he was losing it. For the first time ever, I felt a slight tingle of fear tickle my spine. I needed to calm him down, get him back under control.

"Hey, it's going to happen from time to time," I said, shrugging.

Daniel slowly turned his head to me, his eyes wide. "What did you just say to me?"

I swallowed. "Nothing, man, but he's going to pass out if you hit him like that. That's just the human body."

Daniel pointed the crowbar at me. "Sit back and shut the fuck up before I break a brick across your fucking face."

I did as he said. I realized that my heart was racing. He had never talked to me like that before. Never in all our years of friendship had he ever threatened me. It pissed me off. And it also scared me. I had seen what he was capable of, what he did to people. Best if I just sit back and keep my mouth closed until he was finished.

Howling with frustration, Daniel broke the man's other kneecap. Andrew didn't even scream this time; his head just slumped onto his chest as a sharp *pop!* announced his new broken bone.

"God DAMN it!" Daniel yelled, throwing the crowbar onto the workbench. It collided with the other tools and a few of them loudly clattered to the ground.

"Wake UP you...piece...of...SHIT!" Daniel continued yelling, every word punctuated by a fist to the face. Andrew's flesh absorbed the blows in silence, fresh cuts forming on his cheeks.

Daniel suddenly kicked the chair over, howling, shaking, his eyes wild. He kicked Andrew's motionless face once, twice, three times. Then, still screaming with rage, he crawled on top of him and balled his fists together, bringing them down over Andrew's nose.

"You fucking trash! You fucking piece of trash! Wake up so

you can watch me kill you!" His voice was ragged, his hair hanging down over his eyes in sweaty clumps.

I stood up, heart thundering. "Jesus, man, you're going to kill him, lay off!"

Daniel snapped his eyes over to mine, a crazed, lost look dancing in them. "Isn't that the point?" He stood up, his knuckles bloody and raw. "Isn't that what we do down here?" He took a step toward me. "Or are you afraid you won't get your turn?" He cocked his head at me, a sick smile growing across his lips. "Well, go ahead…kill him."

My heart fluttered. I was hit with nausea deep in my gut. "Just…" I stammered, "just go ahead and do it."

Daniel took another step toward me, the madness in his eyes growing as he got closer. "What the fuck did you just say? You want me to do it?"

I nodded, licking my lips. "Yeah, man, go for it. Just not feeling it tonight. I think you need it more than I do right now."

Daniel stood there for a moment, sweating and breathing heavily. Finally he turned away, shaking his head. "How disappointing. You really are going soft."

"I'm just not cool with you losing your shit!" I yelled suddenly. "This is exactly what I was talking about!"

Daniel turned back to me, his eyes cold as winter ice. He spit onto the floor, then turned back to the workbench. Andrew groaned from the floor. *Bad time to wake up,* I thought, watching Daniel cautiously.

I heard the rev of a chainsaw.

Grinning without humor, Daniel turned around, his arms shaking from the idling machine. He revved the blade a few times and watched as Andrew closed his eyes and began to sob again. He knew what was about to happen.

Daniel walked over to him and placed a foot on his throat.

"Open your fucking mouth," he growled.

Christ, I thought, turning away.

Daniel applied more pressure to Andrew's throat. "I said open your fucking mouth."

Andrew's face began to turn blue, refusing to do as he was told, trembling with terror.

"Motherfucker," Daniel spat.

He drove the chainsaw down into Andrew's face, across his eyes. Skull fragments and wet meat erupted in volcanic fashion, spraying Daniel as he smiled, his white teeth shining through the red.

And he did it slowly.

I counted to fifteen before Andrew stopped screaming. I turned and saw Daniel kick the top half of his skull across the floor at me.

"Here's your cut," he said, switching off the chainsaw. He wiped blood from his face and pulled out a cig. He walked over to the couch and collapsed into it, lighting up. I didn't move. I looked at the body, blood gushing from the halved head.

"Are you happy now?" I said, trying to keep the anger from my voice. I knew it was stupid to get into an argument with him, but I was pissed off.

He looked up at me, blowing smoke. "It's not my fault you wimped out, so don't go throwing your sarcasm at me, fucker."

"You're losing control of yourself," I said, turning to go. I didn't want to be around him right now. I was too angry and confused, the dissatisfaction from the whole night crumbling in around me.

From behind me, Daniel yelled, "You sure it's not you who's losing it? Can't even stab someone anymore? Are you done? Going to walk away from all this now? Go ahead, piss off! Piss off, you weak motherfucker!"

I said nothing, climbing the stairs as his voice bounced off the walls toward me. He was in a crazed state right now and I didn't want to deal with it. He was becoming unpredictable and increasingly angry.

As I reached the top, I heard Daniel below me start screaming and throwing things. I shook my head, walking away from the destruction below. Christ, what a night.

———

A few days passed, my life returning to the normal drone of a non-killer. The day-to-day that the mass population endured, pressing forward toward the weekend. I got a few texts from Daniel apologizing for his outburst. I sent a couple back, stressing that I was just worried about him. Another day passed and we continued to text, our friendship rebuilding. Guys have a talent for that. We shrug off the bullshit we do to each other and laugh it off over name-calling and high-fives.

He called me on Thursday night and asked if I wanted to hang out on Friday. I told him I was hanging out with Kate but that he could join us. We were just going to drink and chill at her new place. Daniel and Kate had a good friendship, with me as their medium. They never hung out with each other without me, but when I brought him along he was always welcomed.

Daniel was charming in his own way and he usually brought life and energy to a conversation that my sister found amusing. After hanging up, I dialed my sister and told her he was coming. She enthusiastically approved and I felt like things were finally settling down. Even though I hadn't killed Andrew, the relief of getting my friend back overshadowed the whole episode.

Friday came and after a dull day at the grocery store, I went home, changed, and drove over to Kate's.

Kate met me at the door and gave me a big hug. I told her it was good to see her, and she invited me in. I was impressed with the modern look of her new apartment. It was clean and sparse in that hip way successful adults like their living space. Black leather, bright white tile, and cool soothing light filled the space.

"This is awesome," I said, taking it all in. I went to the kitchen and opened the stainless steel fridge. "Oh, even had the foresight to buy some beers."

Kate walked in behind me dressed in a tight black T-shirt and jeans. "Well, I knew my alcoholic brother and friend were coming over, so yeah."

I chuckled. "Bitch. How was the party last weekend? That was last weekend, right? I remember getting a text from you, but I forgot to respond."

She joined me by the fridge and grabbed two beers. "It was good. I think everyone was super-impressed by what a responsible adult I've become."

"If only they knew the truth," I smiled, taking one of the beers from her.

"If only," she said, opening her beer.

I propped myself up on a barstool and we chatted idly, both of us recapping the time in between seeing one other and all that entailed. Well. I left out the torture bit.

After a little while we heard a knock at the door. Kate went to answer and I heard Daniel from the entranceway give my sister a hearty hello. They walked into the kitchen together and I stood up and gave my friend a hug.

"You look good, man, it's been a while," I said, smiling. And he did look good. His long hair was pulled back from his face, smelling clean, and his face was freshly shaven and glowed with life. In his hand he held an assortment of flowers.

"Those better be for me," I said.

"If only you were prettier," he laughed, handing them across the counter to Kate, who was digging out another beer for him. Kate rolled her eyes and they exchanged beer for flowers.

"You're wasting your money on me, but it's sweet of you. Thanks," Kate said, searching through the cupboards for a vase.

"I wish you'd stop hitting on my sister all the time," I said, sucking beer down.

Daniel laughed. "I'll get that date one day. The key is to keep trying. You have to wear them down."

"Speaking of dates," Kate said, finding a vase and filling it with water, "have you gone on any lately, little bro? Have you found the apple of your eye yet?"

I stared dead-eyed at her. "Yeah, she was a real Golden Delicious. Baked her into a pie then made sweet sweet love to it."

Kate laughed. "Gross...just gross." She fluffed the flowers and nodded approvingly. "Thanks again, Daniel, that was really sweet."

He winked at her. "All this and more could be yours. If only you would give me the chance."

This was an old game, Daniel flirting with her and Kate rejecting him with fluttering eyelashes. It made me uncomfortable at times, but I knew my sister wouldn't even dream of entertaining the idea. But she liked the flattery and attention, and so she let it continue.

"You guys wanna play cards or something?" I asked, breaking into their flirty banter.

"Let's do it!" Daniel cried, pumping his fist into the air.

"Hope you losers are ready to get slaughtered!" Kate said smugly.

Daniel threw me a wink that only I saw. I grinned.

The night grew late, the conversation light and playful. We played cards, drank heavily, laughed and joked, all of us enjoying each other's company. It was a good night, free from the stress of life, away from all our problems and worries. Daniel was in high spirits, his quick wit and flirty personality birthing smiles from my sister and I. Time seemed to freeze for us, that whole evening wrapped in a bubble of happiness and contentment.

Eventually, as the beer began to run out and eyelids started to droop, we decided to call it a night. I went to the bathroom and splashed water on my face, slapping sobriety into my cheeks. I blinked at myself in the mirror a few times, then nodded and went to leave.

Kate begged us to call a taxi, but we both waved her off,

assuring her we were fine. We hugged her, thanking her for a good night, and left after she made us promise we'd do this again soon.

It was cold as I made my way to my car. Daniel walked beside me, hands in his pockets.

"That was great, man," I said, laughing as my mind replayed some of his antics.

He smiled and nodded. "Yeah, dude, that was fun. I'm glad I came."

"I'll see you around, dude," I said, offering a fist for him to bump.

He bumped my fist and then pulled me in for a hug. "Take care, buddy."

We detached from one another and got in our cars. As I pulled away, throwing a peace sign at Daniel, I felt more content than I could remember feeling in recent memory.

Then my phone buzzed.

I hit the brake and pulled up the text from Daniel.

"I need it again. Soon."

I looked across the parking lot and saw him sitting in his car, his white face smiling at me from his window.

"Fuck," I said out loud.

At this point, it was just a waiting game. I knew sometime in the next week I would get a call from him, telling me he had taken someone. He was always the one who took them ever since this bizarre partnership started. In the beginning, it had seemed fair. After all, he spent the most time with the victims, torturing them, and I would step in at the end and finish them off.

At first I thought he chose and kidnapped the victims because he felt like he got the most out of it. That his prolonged sessions with the poor souls were somehow more meaningful than mine. That he owed me the work and effort of going out and retrieving them. He didn't understand that when I plunged my knife into their hearts, that was all I needed. The feeling of the blade sinking into their chest, the way they always gasped, the shape and dilation of their eyes. That was all I needed. I didn't need them to suffer, didn't need them to scream. I didn't take pleasure in those things.

Now, though, I had begun to understand why Daniel was the one who chose who to kill. It was because he enjoyed watching them, staking them out. He enjoyed seeing them live their life before exposing them to his tools and fire. He wanted to know exactly what it was he was stripping them of. And he wanted to beat misery and despair into his victims before allowing me to kill them. He wanted to replace all the happiness he saw them live out with horror and pain. He wanted to take every smile away from them, tooth by bloody tooth.

He watched them so he could learn how to hate them.

My phone rang in my pocket and before I even checked the number, I knew it was him. It had been five days since our get-together. I had just finished dinner, a lovely meal of hot dogs and ramen. I turned off the TV, took a deep breath, and answered my cell.

"Hey, Daniel."

"You up for a little something different tonight?" he asked, his voice raspy.

I shifted the phone to my other ear. "What do you mean?"

He was breathing heavily as he spoke. "Come to our spot. Make sure you're not followed."? I began to feel uneasy. Something was off. I could hear it in Daniel's voice. Memories of how he had been last time came flooding back. The way he had lost control, the way he had threatened me. I was hoping all of that had been repaired, that all of that was in the past, washed away by a good night of drinking and laughter. It was stupid of me to think that.

I could hear how dangerous he was through the phone. I could hear the volcano of rage waiting to erupt, boiling just under the surface of his words.

"Can you tell me what's going on?" I finally said.

He was frustrated. "Just get your ass to our spot. And could you bring your axe and a hammer? I can't find mine."

I steadied myself, "Yeah…OK, man. No problem. But…you have to give me some kind of clue about what's going on."

I heard him breathing into the phone, then finally, "I have two of them. And…they're sisters. You better get over here."

"Daniel, wait!" I started. The line was dead. I threw my phone down onto the couch, frustrated. Two? We had never done two before. This was spinning out of control. We were going to get caught, someone was going to notice something. The rate at which we were killing was worrisome. It made my stomach churn just thinking about it. We had to slow down. We needed to let things cool off.

And he took two girls. Sisters. I gritted my teeth, shaking my head. He knew I didn't like killing girls. He knew I felt the slightest twang of empathy for them, the same as I would a cute little kitten.

I sighed. Maybe this was what I needed. Maybe a good kill would help settle my mind. Push away the worry, push away the stress, and clear the air. Fucking girls, though...why did it have to be girls?

"A kill is a kill," I reminded myself. I went to the closet and dug out a hammer and axe from the bag I kept there.

Throwing on my jacket, I turned off the lights to my place and stuffed my leather gloves into my back pocket. Time to go kill. I heard thunder rumble across the sky as I left.

3. THE SISTERS

It was pouring as I pulled up to the warehouse. The rain was coming down in sheets of blustering, cold waves, soaking me as soon as I got out of my car. I pulled my jacket up tight around my neck, making a break for the warehouse. I stumbled inside, shaking the wet off of me, listening to the drum of rain on metal sheeting. It was loud, almost sounding like an audience applauding. If only they knew what lie below.

I trotted down the stairs, already hearing Daniel's voice. As I reached the bottom, I saw he had adjusted the kill floor. Both girls were stripped down to their bras and underwear, dirty bags covering their heads. One of them was tied to the familiar metal chair, hands bound behind her.

The other was bent over Daniel's workbench, now empty of tools and dragged into the middle of the room. She was bound in a semi-standing position, her arms stretched out and tied to the legs of the table opposite her. Her ankles were secured to the other set of metal legs where she was folded over. I could see goosebumps where her bare torso met the surface of the workbench.

They were both gagged and from the muted sounds they made it sounded like Daniel had done an extra good job stuffing their mouths. I heard small whimpers come from both of them as they twisted hopelessly in their restraints.

"About fucking time," Daniel said, acknowledging me.

"The storm slowed me down," I muttered. "It's pouring out there."

Daniel looked like hell. He was naked from the waist up and his hair hung down in greasy strands. He looked pale and sick, dark puffy bags clinging to his eyes.

"Did you bring the hammer and axe?" he asked.

"Shit, I left them in the car," I said.

He waved me off. "Forget it. I feel like getting creative tonight."

He was quiet, but I could hear the darkness behind it. His tone was black ice, his movements fluid and deliberate like he had a plan. He went over to the pile of tools on the floor and began picking through them.

Cautiously, I sat down on the couch, watching the two girls. They looked like they were in college, but I couldn't be sure because of the sacks that covered their faces. They were fit, both of them sporting tight bodies that looked taken care of. I could hear the one bent over the table weeping into her gag.

Picked the wrong night to go out, I thought to myself, *should have just stayed in and studied.*

Daniel turned from his pile of tools and walked back to the girls. He crouched down in front of the one tied to the chair, placing a hand on her thigh.

He said nothing, just stayed in that position, staring up at her covered face with unblinking eyes. His hand gently ran over her leg, back and forth, fingers tracing patterns on her skin. ? Finally, he reached under the hood and pulled the gag out, letting the sack fall back over her face. The girl sucked in air, whimpering, but wisely remained silent.

Daniel continued to stare up her, his fingers in constant motion on her thigh.

Then, his voice like cold fire, "Do you want me to rape you tonight?"

My breath caught in my lungs, heart skipping a beat. Fuck…

The girl shook her head back and forth. "N-no…please…" She was trying her best to be brave, not letting him show how terrified she was.

Daniel's fingers traced up her thigh. "Don't you types…like to get fucked, though?"

"I'm so scared, just please, let us go…" she sobbed, sniffling.

Daniel stood, the light reflecting off his bare chest. "I think I'm going to rape one of you tonight. I'm not sure which one, though."

He strolled over to the girl who was bent over the bench and grabbed her ass that stuck out because of the way she was bound. She immediately shrieked into her gag, rolling her head around in her sack, trying to get it off, trying to get away from this clawing menace.

"Maybe I'll do you both," he said darkly, his eyes two black holes in his head.

I was terrified at this point. I could see that over the past week Daniel had transformed into the demon I knew he was becoming. This wasn't about having fun anymore, this wasn't about the things we could get away with. This wasn't about the rush anymore.

This was about something deeper, something darker. This beast that had spread its black wings over my friend wasn't leaving anytime soon. It grew by the day, its fury increasing, ripping the strings of humanity away from him.

This wasn't fun. This wasn't something I wanted to be a part of.

"Daniel," I called, my voice weak.

He took his hand off the girl's ass and turned to me, shadows spilling across his body like dark coffins.

I licked my suddenly dry lips. "Dude...I don't want to do this. Can we just kill them? Really do something different for a change? I'll take this one in the chair, you take that one. What do you say?" I just wanted to get out of here, get away from whatever it was that was about to happen. Get away from Daniel.

He said nothing at first, just stared at me with empty eyes. Then he slowly made his way to where I was sitting and placed a foot on the lip of the couch, leaning forward.

His voice rasped. "You're going to sit here and watch everything tonight. Do you understand me?"

I shrank into the cushions, heart thumping in my chest. "Look, man, I know things have been kinda rocky the last couple of times…" I trailed off miserably. He was shaking his head, back and forth, his mouth a thin line.

"Shut up. Sit there. And watch." He turned to the girls but paused, instead turning back to me. He lowered his face to mine, inches apart.

"If you get up and leave before I'm done, I'm not going to be pleased," he said quietly, his breath smelling like a dead animal.

I said nothing, gulping and feeling the first trace of sweat form on my brow. He turned away from me and back to the girls.

Wordlessly, he began beating the one in the chair. She screamed as his fists rained down on her, pummeling her body and face. I felt sick just sitting there and watching it happen. He was hitting her hard, his blows coming fast and frequent. With the sack covering her face, she had no way of knowing where the next one was coming from, and I could see her body rock with each strike.

Finally, Daniel stopped. He ripped the bag off her head and grabbed her face. She was beautiful, probably early twenties, maybe a senior in college. Her light-brown eyes were filled with tears and her honey-colored hair spilled out over her face and mixed with the blood that poured from her nose.

She met Daniel's eyes, wincing from his grip on her face.

"Do you want to leave?" he asked, his voice like frozen iron.

She nodded, face contorted in pain and fear. She didn't know why she was here, didn't know why this animal was beating her, didn't know what she had done to deserve this.

Daniel leaned in and kissed her forehead, using his thumbs to wipe away her tears. "Don't cry. I just get angry sometimes and snap. It's not your fault. You want to go? I'll let you go. I'm sorry about all this. I really am."

He reached into his back pocket and pulled out a small knife. He leaned over the girl and cut her wrists free, then stepped back.

"Be careful on your way out. It's a little dark once you get to the top of the stairs," Daniel said, turning away from her.

I couldn't believe it. My heart was pounding in my chest, every ounce of me screaming for the girl to get out. I didn't care if she went to the police, didn't care if she led them back here. I would be long gone and maybe that would force Daniel to go into hiding for a while and get his head on straight.

The girl stood, her legs wobbling beneath her. She rubbed her face, staring at Daniel with eyes full of fear and mistrust. She looked at me, then back at him, then to her sister on the table.

She pointed, her voice weak. "Please, let her go, too…"

Daniel turned away from his tools to her. His expression was death made flesh.

"Get the fuck out of here," he said, walking to her. "You're free to go."

The girl, her bottom lip trembling, looked at both of us again, then her sister. Then she bolted for the stairs.

Daniel's leg shot out and tripped her before she had taken two steps. She fell, her momentum bouncing her off the hard ground leaving splashes of blood as her nose crunched into the cement. She screamed and clutched her face, rolling.

Daniel roared with laughter, clutching his sides and doubling over. He gasped for breath as tears of amusement rolled down his face.

"Oh man, you crashed and BURNED!" he howled, pointing at her.

She looked up at him, face a bloody mess, and realized she was never getting away from this nightmare. In a last-ditch effort, she summoned what little strength she had and began crawling toward the stairs.

Daniel watched her, suddenly silent, all traces of laughter gone. He bit his lip and grabbed his crotch as she pulled herself away.

"Seeing that does something to me," he said, glancing at me. "I mean, damn, doesn't she look good?" He licked his lips, suddenly yelling after her, "You're turning me into a horn dog, girl! Well, bark bark, here I come!"

He suddenly dropped to all fours, sniffing the air and crawling toward her like a dog. She looked over her shoulder and screamed, horror pushing every other emotion away.

Daniel began barking and let his tongue roll out of his mouth. His eyes never left hers. He made his way in front of her, blocking the way to the stairs.

"Maybe go a little faster next time," he grinned. He then started to growl, still on all fours, only a few feet away from her.

Terrified, she began backing away, crying and looking at me pleadingly. My eyes met hers and I felt my stomach turn. There was nothing I could do. Daniel was out of control and I risked him turning his tools on me if I interrupted. I looked away.

Daniel bounded forward and hopped in a semicircle around her, loudly barking and lashing out like he was a rabid dog trying to bite her. She curled into herself, covering her head with her hands and screamed.

Daniel quieted suddenly and began pawing closer to her, sniffing her. She shrunk away, her body shaking. He nuzzled his nose against her shoulder, then stuck his tongue out and licked a drop of blood from her skin.

"Fuck, you taste good," he said quietly, taking another lick. "Do you really not want me to fuck you?"

She shook her head violently. "Please, stop it, I don't want this! Let me go, please!"

Daniel sighed dejectedly, then stood up suddenly, brushing off his naked chest. "Fine, fine. I won't fuck you. But I need you to go and sit in your chair while I introduce myself to your sister, OK?"

The girl said nothing. She just stared at him with wide, sad eyes.

Daniel reached down and grabbed a handful of her hair, hauling her up. "Go! Do what I say or I'm going to make you suck off a chainsaw, you understand?!"

Crying and clutching her head, she obediently went and sat down, pulling her legs up and hiding her face between her knees.

Daniel pulled out a cig from his back pocket and lit it up. He blew smoke and looked at me. "I always knew it wasn't going to be her. She's got the body, but the attitude is all wrong."

I remained silent, just watching him from the couch. My mouth was dry and my palms were sweaty. I didn't know who this was standing in front of me. I didn't recognize his face, his voice, anything. This monster was a complete stranger, an evil shade of the devil's shadow.

"You don't like the show tonight?" Daniel said, ashing his cigarette on the floor.

I took a breath. "You know how I feel about this. Just get it over with, would you?"

He took another drag. "You better watch how you talk to me. My patience for your sympathetic streak is growing increasingly thin."

"I don't even know what you are anymore," I said softly. I knew I was pressing my luck.

He threw the cig down on the ground, stomping it with a boot. "Let me show you then."

He went over to his tools and picked up a baseball bat. It looked like he had replaced the one he had broken on his last victim. I watched as it twirled in his hands, his fingers running over the polished wood. He walked to the girl folded over the workbench.

He stood behind her, his crotch pressed against her ass, and ran his hand along her bare back. With her face pressed against the cold surface and hands bound to the far corners, she could only sob into the sack covering her face.

"Oh yes," Daniel said quietly, almost to himself. "I think I want you." His fingers ran under the band of her underwear and let them snap against her skin.

He took a step back and assessed her position. "You seem to be in a prime position already…why let it go to waste?" He paused. "There's only one thing…you see, I know you girls like them big…and I'm afraid I'm of quite average size." He grabbed his crotch. "Surely not enough to please you. But I want to…and so I guess we'll have to make do, yeah?"

Horrified, I watched as he placed the tip of the bat to her ass and gently prodded her underwear. He looked at me and saw me watching. He smiled and I saw the Devil in his eyes. I saw every nightmare I ever had. I saw death.

The girl screamed into her gag, feeling the intrusion prod and test her body. She squirmed and banged her head against the bench, knowing what was going to happen.

Daniel pulled the bat away and pulled her underwear down. He licked his lips and smiled. "Perfect. Though I don't think I can go in dry…I'm not an animal after all. I'm not going to force it in without some help. Excuse me, I'll be right back." He went to his pile of tools and began digging through them to find a lubricant.

I was shaking, unable to believe what was about to happen. I couldn't let it happen. I didn't want to be a part of this. We had never done anything like this before. When we had killed the one girl before, Daniel hadn't acted like this, hadn't sexually humiliated them. He had barely even tortured her.

Stop this, I thought. *You can't just sit here. If you let him do this, you're never going to be able to forgive yourself.*

As I was about to stand, Daniel turned back. I froze, body halfway rising from the couch. He stared at me, his eyes bitter, cold darkness. I lowered myself while his gaze bore holes into my skull.

And then I saw what he was holding.

He had wrapped the baseball ball in barbed wire.

I immediately felt sick as the anticipation of what was about to happen slugged me in the gut. I had seen him perform all manner of horrors on our victims before, but not like this. This was hatred. This was sadistic, brutal humiliation.

My heart hammered in my chest, breath coming in sharp pulls as I watched him. I steeled myself. I didn't want to have to listen to the screams, the high-pitched, heartbreaking shriek that only a female could produce.

Daniel placed the batting end of the bat against her bare ass, the barbed wire pricking her skin, letting her feel what was to come. She started thrashing, screaming into her gag, frantically trying to free herself. Daniel wasn't smiling. He looked like the angel of death, a dark haze rising from his body as the shadows painted him black.

"This isn't going to work," he said, his voice rumbling like the gates of hell opening.

He pointed to the girl in the chair. "Get over here."

Shaking, she looked up at him, fresh tears rolling down her battered face. She couldn't move, her body paralyzed in crippling fear.

"I'm not going to ask again," Daniel snarled. She stood, hands wrapped around herself, and timidly walked forward.

Daniel grabbed her by the back of the neck and shoved her to her knees. "Get the fuck down." He shifted the bat in his hands and held it out to her, the end still pressed against the other girl's ass.

"Hold it," he instructed. She took the grip in her trembling hands and held it there, eyes cast down, sobbing.

Daniel went to the tools and picked up a sledgehammer.

He hefted it in his hand and went back to stand in front of the girls.

"Don't you fucking move," he instructed both of them.

Time seemed to slow down as I watched Daniel raise the sledgehammer and swing it with terrifying power. It connected with the bat and drove it like a stake into the girl bent over the table.

I turned away as her screams erupted, tearing into my soul. My mind shook and my vision swam, cracks forming along the edges of my sanity. I felt vomit and bile crawl up my throat and I clenched my fists, feeling like I might pass out.

I looked back at them.

The girl on her knees had let go, crawling away backwards, screaming and crying. The one bent over the table had thrown up in her sack, the contents seeping through the fabric in thick, brown splotches. The baseball bat had been driven inside of her a couple of inches and just hung there, dripping blood, the barbed wire cutting into her flesh and gripping it for support.

Daniel raised the hammer again and brought it down, driving the bat deeper. The sickening sound as it sliced and shredded her made me grit my teeth, my jaw popping. Her body jerked and spasmed, her vomit now mixed with blood as it pooled under the sack onto the table.

Daniel brought the hammer down again, slamming the barbed wrapped wood deeper into her. The girl convulsed violently and her howls ceased. She flopped around, her body slapping against the bench and then mercifully…she was still.

Blood ran down the handle of the bat, now visible by only a few inches. Daniel stood motionless, his bare chest heaving as he stared at the scene, watching the gore leak out of her. He had a hard-on as he dropped the hammer, letting it fall carelessly at his side.

He closed his eyes and gripped his crotch, head rolled back. He was smiling.

Slowly, he rolled his head over so that he was looking at me. "I did it. I found the excitement again. I fucking did it." He sighed and closed his eyes again, taking in every moment, every sound, every smell, sucking it all up into his memory.

The remaining girl was screaming, hands covering her face. She had backed herself against the far wall where she sat shaking and cowering in horror.

Daniel looked at her like he had forgotten she existed. He looked at me. "You want to kill her? I think I'm done for the night." His voice was soft and a smile danced on his lips.

"No," I croaked, voice coming out like a pulled splinter.

He shrugged. "All right."

He walked over to her and picked her up by the hair. Without a word he twisted her neck back until it shattered like dry wood. Her body slumped to the floor, dead.

The silence screamed at me. I sat glued to the couch, the unimaginable nightmare I had just witnessed howling through my skull. I swallowed back a mouthful of vomit and shut my eyes against it. I watched the darkness swirl behind my eyelids and prayed that when I opened them I'd be away from this, out of this basement, away from Daniel.

"Aw, shit."

My eyes snapped open.

Daniel was looking at me, shaking his head, a frown on his face.

"W-what?" I managed to get out.

He sighed. "There's something I forgot to tell you."

I didn't move, my whole body feeling like dead weight. "What is it?"

He licked his lips and ran a hand through his long hair, "I might have twisted the truth a little bit when I spoke to you earlier."

"What the fuck are you talking about?" I asked.

He looked at me with eyes that held no light, "They weren't sisters."

A dawning, creeping terror began to squeeze my throat. "What do you mean? Who the hell are they, then?"

He smiled sadly at me, "Just two coworkers. In fact, that one over there whose neck I just snapped wasn't even supposed to be a part of this. She was just in the wrong place at the wrong time."

My mind was screaming, my heart trying to tear itself from my chest. I felt dizzy and tears began to form as I opened my mouth.

"Daniel, who is that?" I asked, pointing to the girl on the table.

He smiled apologetically, "You know who that is."

I ripped myself from the couch and bounded over to the workbench. I placed a sweaty hand on the vomit-soaked sack. I couldn't breathe. I couldn't think. I pulled the sack off her head.

It was Kate.

I fell to the floor, eyes bugging out of their sockets, a wave of darkness threatening to take me away. Her dead eyes slammed into mine, their gaze empty and glazed. *No...No, no, no, God please no, not her, not her please, Jesus, no, NO!*

I screamed. I screamed until my throat went raw. I clawed

at my face, trying to pull the sight from my eyes. My entire body shook as the horror blasted every fiber of my being like a shock wave. I vomited onto myself, my body trying to evacuate the twisted reality before me.

Daniel leaned down and patted my head. "There, there. I know this is hard. I'm sorry it had to be her. I really am."

Shaking, vision blurry, my mouth tasting like bile, I looked up at him with tear-filled eyes, "W-why did you do this?"

He sighed. "Because I liked her. I've never tortured someone I liked."

I looked at my sister, her dead, mangled body lying slumped against the bench. Tears ran down my face and I felt something *click* inside me.

I *saw* every cut, every drop of blood. I saw every scrape, every bruise. My eyes traced up her body, forcing myself to take in every bit of gore, every detail of her mutilated flesh. And I *felt* her pain. I *felt* her suffering. I heard her screams, suddenly real and meaningful. That had been my sister screaming in agony. There was a person behind all that. There was a life behind all that.

My eyes widened and it all came crashing down on me like a crumbling mountain. These were *people*. Every time we killed a person…there was someone out there who felt like I did right now. There was someone who felt like their entire world had been ripped away. There was a hole that we tore in their life that could never be filled.

And we had done this for…*fun*?!

"Are you OK?" Daniel asked, breaking into my thoughts. "I know this must be rough, but I'm back, man. I'm fucking back. I feel SO much better. I feel like myself again. Me and you, man, we're back! It's going to be how it used to be, I promise."

I stood slowly. My body shook as I looked him in the eye.

"You did it...because you *liked* her?" I said, taking long deep breaths. "You killed my sister because you wanted to *feel* better?" Tears ran down my face as I took a step toward him, my voice rising. "You took my sister away from me and brutalized her because you needed to FEEL BETTER?!"

He raised his hands to me. "I'm sorry! I thought you'd understand! I thought you wanted to get things back to the way they were!"

I pointed at my sister's body, hot tears dripping from my cheeks. "Not like this, you heartless motherfucker."

He took a step back. "You don't need her! I'm you're family! What we have together runs so much deeper, runs so much truer! We have these desires in us that no one understands! Me and you, we're bound in blood!"

I wiped my face, feeling my body grow cold, "I'll show you blood."

I rocketed toward him, my body smashing into his. I came out on top, snarling, growling, feeling myself become lost in anger and hopeless fury. His head hit the hard ground and his eyes lost focus as I brought my fist down into his face.

"How could you DO THIS?" I howled, raining blow after blow down upon him. I couldn't grasp it, couldn't allow my mind to comprehend what he had done. I knew then that I would never truly understand Daniel, what drove him, what part of his soul had been burned to charred remains.

I stopped punching him, realizing that he was unconscious, his blood-smeared face empty of expression. I sat up on him, wiping my knuckles on his shirt. I sucked in mouthfuls of air, my head splitting, feeling like I was miles underwater.

I stood, hands gripping my temples, lost and confused. What the fuck was going on? What had happened? Daniel lay motionless below me, my sister dead on the table.

I covered my face with my hands, feeling panic bring a new wave of tears. "Fuck, fuck, fuck," I cried.

I cried and then I began to scream.

———————

I placed my sister in the back seat of my car, the dark clouds overhead emptying themselves onto me, a thick wall of rain washing the blood from my arms.

I had removed the bat, weeping the whole time how sorry I was. How sorry I had let this happen. How sorry I was for *what* I was. If I wasn't such a monster, if I wasn't born with this desire to kill, she'd still be alive. And that burned me up until I thought my eyes would shoot flame from their sockets.

I took off my coat and draped it over her, hands shaking. Thunder boomed as I leaned down and kissed her on the forehead. My tears dripped into her dead eyes as I closed them, turning away, sobbing.

I don't know how long I sat in my car, listening to the frantic drum of rain on the roof. I gripped the steering wheel and forced myself to stop weeping. I gritted my teeth and drew in long, labored breaths, slowing my heart rate.

I had bound Daniel to the workbench, laying him out on his back on top of it, tying his limbs to the four corners. Why did he do this to me? How could he do this? As I sat there, watching the night through a rain-blurred windshield, I realized something.

Daniel didn't give a shit about anyone but himself. Whatever he felt, he did. I had just followed along, happy that someone understood me, that someone accepted me. I had misinterpreted our activities as friendship, excited by the fact that he provided people for me to kill.

"Tonight is the last time," I said out loud as a bolt of lightning lit the sky.

I sat in silence then, my heart thumping in my chest. I closed my eyes, listening to the rain. I listened to the way it rolled and tapped against my car. I listened to the thunder crack the sky open. I saw the lightning behind my eyelids. I listened to the way the trees screamed against the wind. I listened to them bend and crack like dry bone.

I listened to the violence in the storm.

My eyes popped open, a black, hateful calm draping itself over my tired shoulders. The world spun for a moment and then righted itself. I looked in the back seat at my sister.

I looked at myself in the mirror.

"I fucking hate you," I whispered.

I grabbed the axe and hammer from the front seat, tools meant to be used on my sister, and got out of my car.

The wind tried to rip the skin from my face, the rain beat itself against my body, and thunder rang in my ears. I cocked my head back and shut my eyes, feeling the energy and brutality of it all.

"Here I come," I whispered into the night.

I opened my eyes and became the storm.

4. DANIEL

I slapped Daniel hard across the face, stirring him from the depths of his nightmares. He blinked a few times, then recognition dawned in his eyes. He licked his lips lazily, trying to clear the haze from his mind.

"What the hell is this?" he asked, finding himself bound.

I said nothing, a vicious, resentful poison filling my head at the sound of his voice. My black leather gloves cracked as I gripped the axe I was holding.

Daniel looked at me, the last bit of fog leaving his eyes. "Hey, what the hell is going on? Why am I tied up?"

Still silent, I walked over to his pile of tools. My eyes appraised them, noting the filth and dry blood that stained them. How many people had we killed now? How many screams had I heard? How many hours had I sat and watched him dance about our victims, slicing a little here, cutting a little there?

"Stop fucking around!" Daniel yelled from behind me, struggling against the ropes. "I thought you'd understand, I thought you wanted me to be how I used to! I did this for us! I did this so things could go back to how they were!"

"Nothing's changed," I said darkly, my back to him.

"But they have!" Daniel said, voice getting higher. "Whatever it was, it's gone! The anger, the frustration, the confusion, it's all gone! I'm me again!"

"It just had to be her, didn't it?" I asked, my voice void of emotion. "You had to take her away from me, didn't you?"

"That wasn't why!" he cried, pounding his fists against the workbench. "I just needed something new, something fresh, something I had never experienced before!"

I turned to him, my eyes two black slits of ice. "You wanted to fuck with me, didn't you? You thought I was growing soft and that pissed you off. You thought I was having second thoughts about our murder sprees, didn't you? You thought I was losing the taste for it." My voice shook, a boiling volcano of searing venom rising in my throat. "Well, let me show you how wrong you were."

I walked over to him in three quick steps, spinning the axe blade-side up. I raised it over my head, staring down at him, my bloodshot eyes bulging with violence.

"I'm going to fucking *destroy* you, Daniel."

I brought the blunt side of the axe down onto his mouth, the metal clinking against his teeth and shattering through them. Blood spewed from his lips and mouth as his breath left him in a howl. He fought against the ropes, body thrashing in overwhelming pain.

I lowered the axe and watched his face contort in agony, watched the blood leak from his mouth, watched the way his eyes rolled in his head. I waited for him to calm down, waited for his breathing to steady.

I placed a hand on his shoulder, his eyes meeting mine, terrified and bloodshot.

"Get comfortable," I whispered.

I reached into my back pocket and pulled out a screwdriver

I had taken from the pile. I held it up so he could see it, twisting it in the white light.

"I'm going to use this to rip out every single one of your teeth," I said. My mind and body were surging with hateful energy, my heart raced in my chest, and I could feel demons in my blood.

"Don't do this to me," Daniel cried through broken teeth.

I leaned down. "I'm not. You are." I placed my mouth to his ear and whispered, "Let me show you what Daniel is like."

And then I began digging into his gums, blood squirting over my hands as I worked. It took almost an hour to get them all out. But I was diligent and I was patient. I didn't even register his screams as I went about my task, the screwdriver prodding and pulling with unflinching precision.

When I was done, I stepped back and wiped the sweat off my face. Daniel had passed out as I ripped the last molar out. I tilted his head to the side and let the blood empty from his mouth, not wanting him to drown in it. That would be too easy.

I went to the pile as I waited for him to wake. My hands searched through the assortment of horrors, looking for just the right one.

I picked up a pair of needle-nose pliers. When he woke, I pulled off all his fingernails and then spent another twenty minutes breaking all his fingers.

And I did it slowly, bending them back one by one, listening for the steady crack as the bone began to splinter. Oh, how he screamed. He begged me to stop, apologized over and over for what he had done, slobbering over himself in excruciating pain.

I didn't stop. I didn't even hear him. I wasn't me anymore. I was something else. Something dark and vengeful, something that needed him to scream, needed him to cry. I was a shadow of sanity, the bloody crack of a fractured soul. I was pain and torment with ebony eyes.

I took the sack my sister had worn and soaked it with gasoline. Then I pulled it over Daniel's face and lit it on fire. I sang "Happy Birthday" to myself and then beat his face until the flames went out.

I twisted his toes off with a vise grip.

I cut his nose off with a hacksaw.

I bent his knees up until they snapped.

I broke his shins with a hammer.

I pulled his ears off with my bare hands.

I flayed the skin from his arms.

I made him eat lit cigarettes.

I shattered his elbows with the sledgehammer.

I heated nails with my lighter and drove them into his thighs.

I made that monster *suffer*.

Daniel was barely recognizable. His body lay in a stinking bloody heap on the table, his chest feebly rising and falling with short, shallow breaths. I didn't think he knew where he was anymore. I didn't know if he could feel anything anymore. But he was still alive. And so I wasn't finished.

My clothes were splattered with his blood, my eyes stung with it, and my hands cracked under layers that had dried over my knuckles. I smelled horrible, a rotten, coppery odor clinging to my skin. Sweat carved trails in blood down my face.

"Almost done," I said, leaning over the table and looking at Daniel. His charred, nose-less face slowly rocked back and forth, the raw muscle in his cheeks quivering.

I held up the barbed-wire baseball bat. "Look familiar? This is what you used to kill Kate and this is what I'm going to use to kill you."

He moaned, his voice weak and dry. He was wheezing, his burned lips curling back to reveal bloody, toothless gums.

I gripped the bat and tilted his head up so that his neck arched toward the ceiling. I gripped his face and growled, "Now don't fucking move."

With one quick jab, I crammed the bat into his mouth, the barbed wire tearing through his cheeks and down his throat. His eyes widened and his body began to thrash as a long, drawn-out scream tried to escape. Tears pooled in his eyes as the intense anguish erupted in his nerves.

I let go of the bat and it stayed in its place, the sharp pricks clinging to his bleeding gums. I bent down and picked up the sledgehammer.

"I'm going to pound this down your fucking throat," I snarled, my eyes meeting his.

"Goodbye, Daniel."

I swung the hammer and it connected squarely with the end of the bat. Blood exploded from his neck as the skin popped and tore from the inside, the barbs poking from his throat like bloody ants. I grit my teeth and swung again. And again. And again. I didn't stop until the bat disappeared.

Blood dripped off the table in little streams as I leaned

onto the sledgehammer for support, gasping for air. My blood thundered in my ears and my eyes stung with sweat. My mouth was dry and my fingers numb. I felt dizzy and sick, the smells and exhaustion I felt sinking deep into my stomach. I looked at the work bench.

Daniel was dead.

———————

I sit here, telling you all this, so you know what we've done. So you know the kind of people we were. I've lost my taste for killing. I've lost my desire for everything. There's nothing left anymore. I am broken and empty and I deserve it.

I am no longer human. I am a soulless shell of broken sanity. If hell exists, I know I will burn forever for what I've done.

And I am sorry. I'm sorry to each and every person my actions have affected. I am sorry for the sorrow I've caused. I am sorry for the misery I've created in your lives. I'm sorry for killing your loved ones. I am sorry for what I am and what I've put you through.

I hope someone finds this. I hope someone out there can forgive me.

After I finish writing, I'm going to take my knife, the one I've used to kill so many, and plunge it deep into my heart. It's the only solace I can give you, knowing that I am dead.

Daniel and I, what we did, was unspeakable, and I hope you find comfort knowing we won't hurt anyone else. We won't cause any more suffering.

I don't have any excuses for what we did. I don't have any words to help you make sense of it all.

Daniel and me…we were the worst kind of monsters.

About the Author

Elias started writing when he was fifteen and hasn't stopped since. As he experimented with different genres, he felt himself pulled to the darker side of fiction. He lives in New England, alone, and spends entirely too much time muttering over his keyboard and nervously looking over his shoulder. He thinks horror deserves some fresh ideas and is doing his best to breathe new life into the genre. Bloody, foul, filthy life.

Thought Catalog, it's a website.
www.thoughtcatalog.com

Social

facebook.com/thoughtcatalog
twitter.com/thoughtcatalog
tumblr.com/thoughtcatalog
instagram.com/thoughtcatalog

Corporate

www.thought.is